THE TESLA FORMULA

Nicolas Kublicki

Published by Rellihan Satterlee LLC
4701 SW Admiral Way #269
Seattle, WA 98116

The Tesla Formula. Copyright © 2011 by Nicolas M. Kublicki.

Published December 2012

ISBN 978-0-9849352-2-2

Cover and map Design: Yoyostring Creative
Interior Design: Stephanie Martindale

To my wife Molly and our daughters Ava and Juliette,
with love, admiration, and hope.

In memory of Nikola Tesla (1856-1943) and Cary Grant (1904-1986)

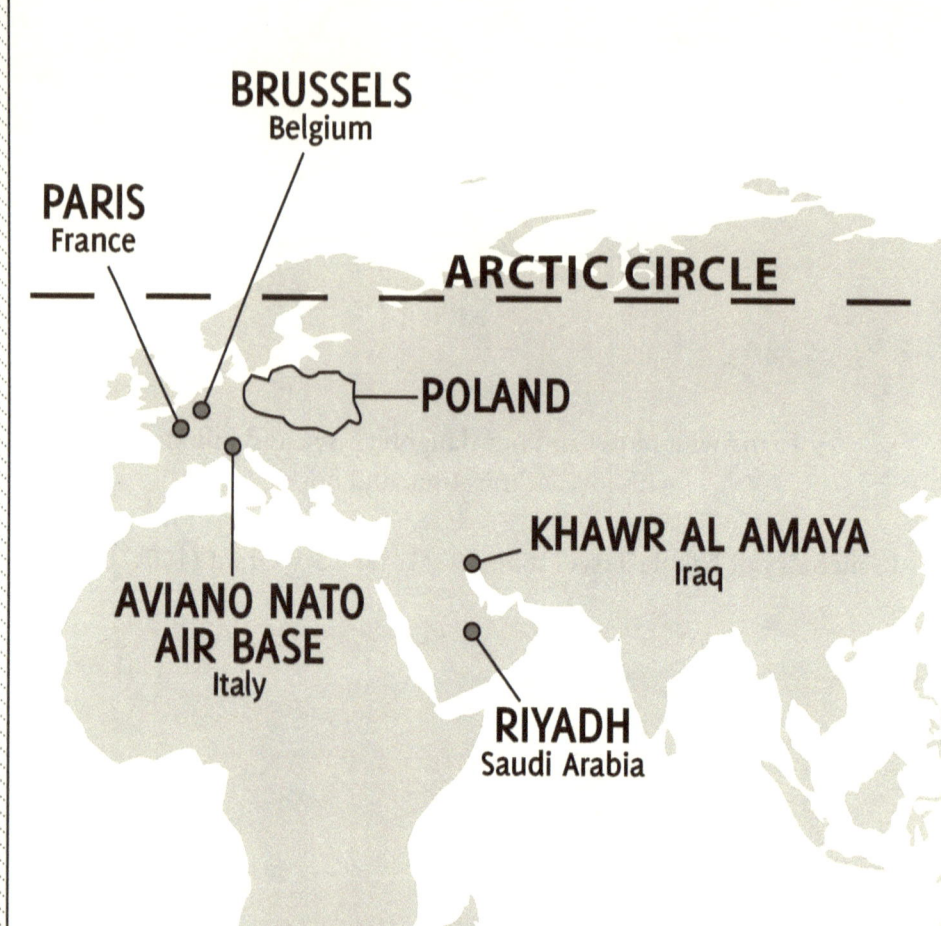

BRUSSELS
Belgium

PARIS
France

ARCTIC CIRCLE

POLAND

KHAWR AL AMAYA
Iraq

AVIANO NATO
AIR BASE
Italy

RIYADH
Saudi Arabia

WORLD MAP

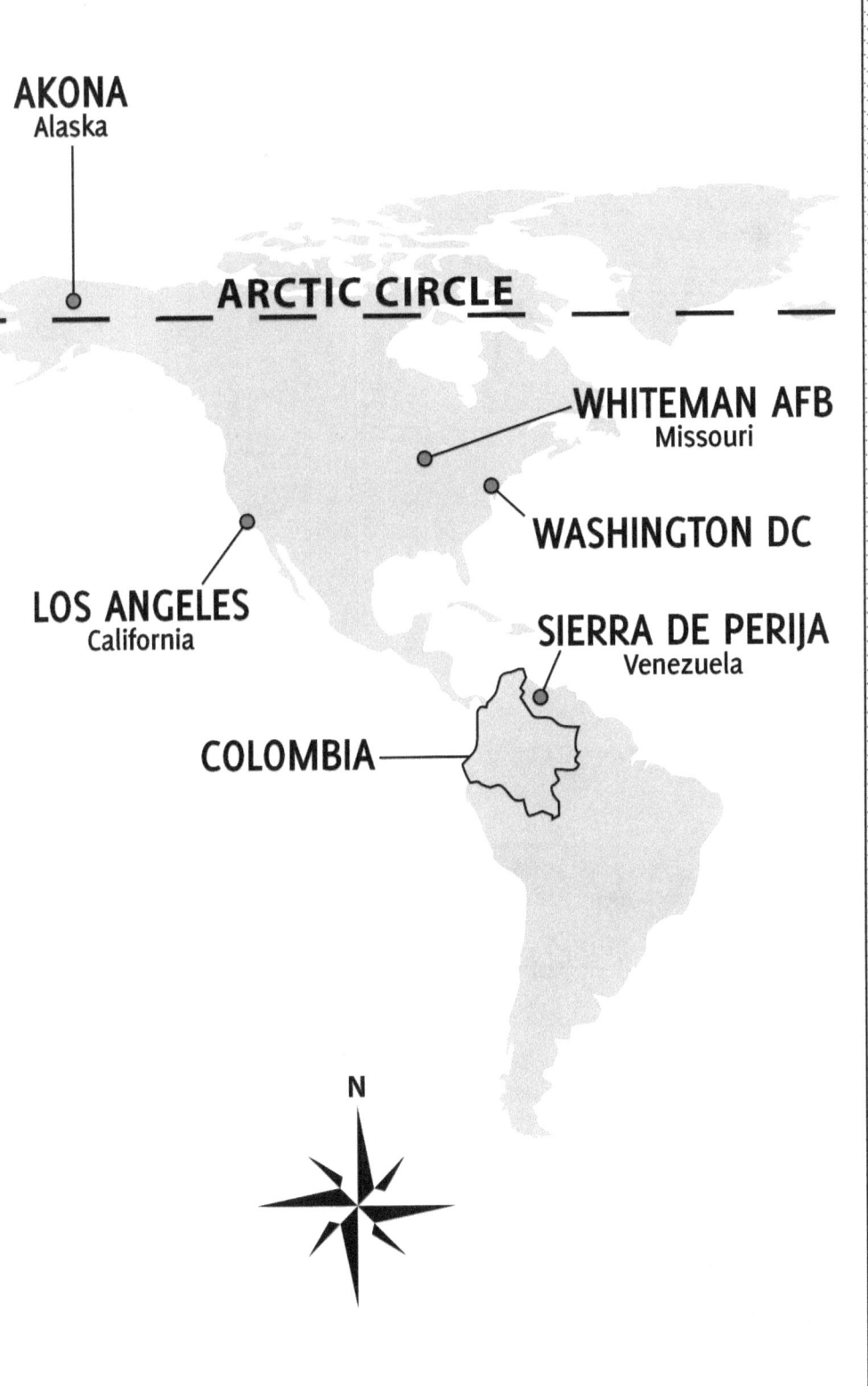

N

CASTEL
MACLEAN

LOMA VISTA

SUNSET STRIP

COCK N'
BULL*

BEVERLY HILLS
HOTEL*

BEVERLY
HILLS

CAÑON DRIVE

15 miles
to Malibu

WESTWOOD

UCLA

SUNSET BLVD

BEVERLY
THEATRE*

LOS ANGELES
FBI FIELD
OFFICE

SANTA MONICA BLVD

SANTA
MONICA

WILSHIRE BLVD

ST. JOHN'S
HOSPITAL

PACIFIC COAST HWY

PACIFIC
OCEAN

5 miles to LAX

*in 1942

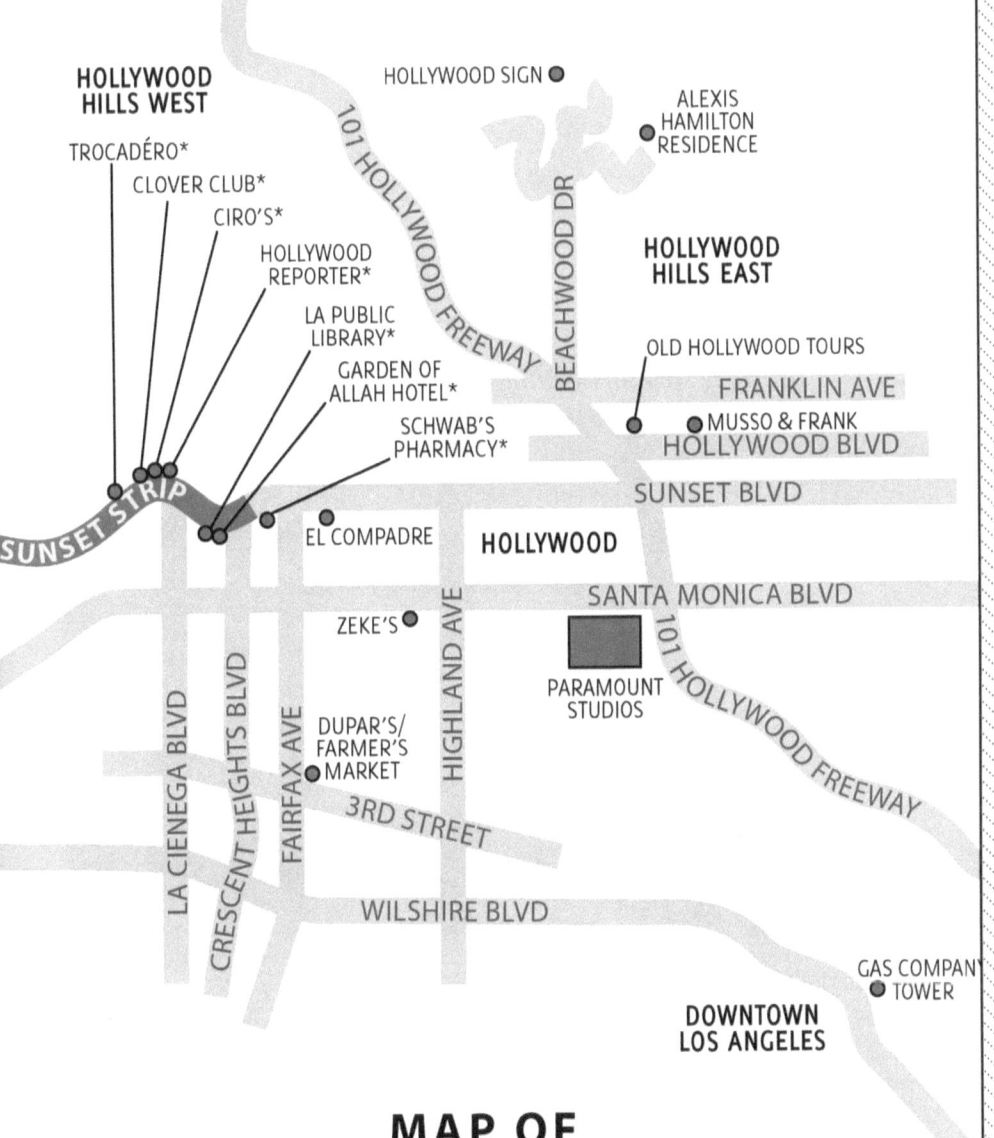

HOLLYWOOD SIGN

HOLLYWOOD
HILLS WEST

ALEXIS
HAMILTON
RESIDENCE

TROCADÉRO*

CLOVER CLUB*

CIRO'S*

HOLLYWOOD
REPORTER*

LA PUBLIC
LIBRARY*

GARDEN OF
ALLAH HOTEL*

SCHWAB'S
PHARMACY*

HOLLYWOOD
HILLS EAST

OLD HOLLYWOOD TOURS

FRANKLIN AVE

MUSSO & FRANK
HOLLYWOOD BLVD

SUNSET BLVD

EL COMPADRE

HOLLYWOOD

SANTA MONICA BLVD

ZEKE'S

PARAMOUNT
STUDIOS

DUPAR'S/
FARMER'S
MARKET

3RD STREET

WILSHIRE BLVD

GAS COMPANY
TOWER

DOWNTOWN
LOS ANGELES

101 HOLLYWOOD FREEWAY

BEACHWOOD DR

SUNSET STRIP

LA CIENEGA BLVD

CRESCENT HEIGHTS BLVD

FAIRFAX AVE

HIGHLAND AVE

101 HOLLYWOOD FREEWAY

MAP OF
LOS ANGELES
(WESTSIDE)

1 mile

100 miles to Big Bear ➡
107 miles to Palm Springs

The three steps of lightning are:
electrical charge, lightning stroke, and thunder.

INTRODUCTION

On the night of January 7, 1943, the visionary Serbian-American inventor Nikola Tesla quietly passed away in room 3327 of the Hotel New Yorker as snow fell on the city below. The holder of 272 patents in 25 countries, acclaimed for his invention of revolutionary electric marvels such as the alternating current (AC) now used worldwide, Tesla had become increasingly eccentric, devoting his last years to researching wild theories that the scientific establishment derided. Once hailed as the patron saint of modern electricity, he died ridiculed, penniless, nearly forgotten.

Upon entering Tesla's hotel room the following morning, his nephew Sava Kosanovic noticed that some of the inventor's documents were missing, including a black notebook marked 'Government'. Kosanovic was shocked to find a door open to a secret room packed with scientific papers in disarray. He immediately contacted the Federal Bureau of Investigation.

Government agents stormed the hotel room, carted away its contents in two large trucks, and placed them under top secret seal.

With the United States in the throes of World War II, the government was desperate for any new technology that Tesla may have invented to help turn the tide against the Axis, no matter how far-fetched. The FBI ordered Special Agent in Charge P.E. Foxworth to review Tesla's papers. Working feverishly around the clock, the agent pored through thousands of pages of documents.

And discovered something.

Something so extraordinary that Foxworth decided to reveal it only to the man in the wheelchair who occupied the White House. One problem: Franklin D. Roosevelt was in Casablanca meeting with Winston Churchill and Charles de Gaulle. Despite the legion dangers looming in the wartime skies, Foxworth was undeterred, considering his discovery too important to wait until the president's return or to reveal it to J. Edgar Hoover. He boarded a military transport aircraft for Morocco.

It exploded over the Atlantic Ocean.

There were no survivors.

These facts are true.

Despite nearly 70 years of effort, the United States government never learned what the FBI agent found.

Until a clue was recently discovered.

Nicolas Kublicki
Los Angeles, California

PART ONE - CHARGE

"Whoever wishes to get a true appreciation of the greatness of our age should study the history of electrical development. There he will find a story more wonderful than any tale from the Arabian Nights....The impossible has happened, the wildest dreams have been surpassed and the astounded world is asking: What is coming next?"

Nikola Tesla
September 9, 1915

"We choose to go to the moon in this decade and do the other things, *not because they are easy, but because they are hard, because that goal will serve to organize and measure the best of our energies and skills, because that challenge is one that we are willing to accept, one we are unwilling to postpone, and one which we intend to win,* and the others, too."

President John F. Kennedy
(emphasis added)
Rice University, Houston, Texas
September 12, 1962

"Our one source of energy
Electricity
All we need to live today
A gift for man to throw away
The chance to change has nearly gone
The alternative is only one
The final source of energy
Solar electricity"

Orchestral Manoeuvres in the Dark
Electricity

1 STAR

December 30, 1942
Beverly Theatre
Beverly Hills, California
7:03 PM

Montgomery Grant did not know that he was about to die.

As a rule, movie stars do not escape from their own movie premieres. Grant did.

As soon as the lights dimmed and the silver screen glowed to life, Grant rose from his private balcony seat. Careful to make sure that no one noticed him, he walked down the utility staircase to the ground floor exit. The movie stars, studio executives, film critics, and adoring fans in the audience were watching Grant's latest film, *Infamous*, but it was Montgomery Grant that they had come to see. America could not get enough of the talented actor with the dimpled chin, sly smile, athletic build, New England meets Old England accent, and impeccable sartorial grace.

Grant glanced at his watch. *Infamous* was one hour and twenty minutes long. Just enough time to drive to his meeting and return to the theatre before the movie credits started to roll.

Although exhausted from his urgent Boeing Stratoliner flights to and from New York, adrenaline coursed through his veins. Grant cracked the exit door open. Two police officers were walking down the alley behind the theatre. He waited for them to turn the corner, then pulled down his black fedora and stepped across the alley to the Bekins Storage parking lot, trailing the scent of Acqua di Parma cologne.

On such crisp and clear winter nights, Grant preferred to drive his white Packard roadster. Tonight, he had left it at home. He could not risk anyone noticing him until he was back inside the crenellated walls and under the white onion dome of the theatre inspired by the Arabian Nights. He opened the driver's door of his glossy black 1939 Cadillac Series 90 limousine, slid into the dark red leather seat behind the wheel, replaced his fedora with a chauffeur's cap, started the massive V-16 engine with a push of the firestarter.

It's just like a movie role, he repeated to himself, as he had done many times before.

Grant accelerated North on Cañon Drive. Resisting the urge to speed as fast as the powerful car would go, he obeyed the speed limit to avoid attracting attention. He rolled down his window and lit a Chesterfield cigarette as he drove through the leafy residential neighborhood to the 'Pink Palace' Beverly Hills Hotel, then turned right on Sunset Boulevard, heading East toward Hollywood. He checked the clock in the varnished wood dashboard, took a deep drag from his cigarette. He was on schedule, but knew from experience that he would not relax until after returning to the theatre. He exhaled a plume of blue smoke into the cold night air, clicked on the radio. After a short announcement extolling the virtues of Lux soap, the enchanting melody of Glenn Miller's *Sunrise Serenade* wafted through the dashboard speaker. It soothed his anxiety, yet he remained on edge.

Grant had worked long and hard to rise from misery to international stardom and wealth - not an easy feat during the Great Depression. He could easily have avoided military duty, yet he could not forget that he owed every bit of his fame and fortune to his beloved adoptive country. Like the hundreds of thousands of young American GIs fighting and dying in faraway lands to defeat the scourge of fascism, he would do his duty.

Despite his resolve, tonight's mission felt different from the others. More dangerous. Grant felt the enemy lurking in the urban shadows, watching, tracking, waiting. Perhaps it was the nature of the documents he carried that made tonight's mission feel so perilous. When the scientist had entrusted them to him in New York less than 72 hours ago, he had told Grant that they would change the course of history.

Grant stubbed out his cigarette, reached inside his Carroll & Company tuxedo jacket. His fingers touched the envelope. Still there. He took deep breaths of the chill air as he drove past the Cock N' Bull English pub, crossed Doheny Drive, and arrived at the brightly illuminated Sunset Strip. Fashionably dressed couples and a few uniformed soldiers on leave animated the liveliest destination in town. The winding avenue was thick with traffic. Grant slowed the ponderous car to a crawl, slid past the Trocadéro restaurant, the Clover Club mob gambling joint, and the offices of the Hollywood Reporter.

The Cadillac crept by Ciro's supper club. Giant klieg lights were stationed in front of the hotspot in anticipation of the *Infamous* movie premiere party that would grace its sumptuous interior in less than two hours.

Suddenly, a black Ford Deluxe coupe parked in front of Ciro's made a daring U-turn, arcing across the crowded boulevard amid honks of protest, ending up directly behind Grant's Cadillac. He was about to dismiss the maneuver as the antic of an overworked valet parking attendant when he realized that there was not one but two men inside the car, now positioned inches behind his gleaming chrome bumper. Grant's neck muscles tightened.

Maybe his imagination was playing tricks on him. He had been exceedingly careful in leaving the theatre. Grant was certain that no one had seen him leave. If the enemy had followed him from the theatre, they would not have had to make a U-turn across Sunset to catch up with him.

He clicked off the radio and glanced at himself in the rear view mirror. From behind the wheel of the limousine, with his cap instead of his fedora, Grant looked like a chauffeur. More handsome, perhaps, but unrecognizable from the other Hollywood chauffeurs at the helm of their wards' steel and chrome yachts. How could they have recognized him from across the boulevard?

Grant figured it out when he saw a knockout blonde cross the road and stare at the glossy Cadillac with undisguised admiration. He cursed under his breath. The enemy knew that he had arrived at the Beverly Theatre in his Cadillac. It was the car they had recognized, not him. They had not followed him from the theatre, they had been lying in wait for him.

He wanted to gun the massive engine, but the stoplight at the intersection of Crescent Heights turned red. As he slowed, then stopped, Grant saw the Ford abruptly change lanes, pull up beside him on his left. He turned his face away from the men inside, anxious for the light to change, praying that he was wrong. As soon as the light turned green, he pushed hard on the accelerator. The Cadillac's sixteen cylinders roared to life and shot him through the intersection. The weaker Ford strained to follow. Grant's glee at his superior horsepower disappeared as soon as he noticed a bottleneck up ahead. He would soon be trapped. He had to get out. Now.

Grant jerked the wheel to the right, pulled into the Schwab's Pharmacy parking lot, screeched to a halt. Leaving the Cadillac in the middle of the parking lot, he leaped out and raced into the pharmacy that doubled as an actors' hangout, resisting the urge to look behind him. A squeal of tires and the sound of rapid footsteps told him all he needed to know.

They were following him.

Grant dashed past Ronald Reagan and other fellow actors seated at the counter, stepped into the men's room, locked the door. He felt his heart pumping in his chest. Before thinking of his own escape, he had to destroy the documents. Whatever the cost, Grant could not allow the documents to fall into the enemy's hands. He did not have much time. He removed the envelope from his jacket pocket, tore it open, unfolded the five pages inside, and began to set each of them on fire with his solid gold Zippo lighter. A loud knock sounded on the door.

"We got to speak with you, Mr. Grant," a hard voice announced, without a trace of an accent. "It's urgent."

Grant blew on the sheets to fan the flames. The first one was almost completely burned. It sizzled as he dropped it into the toilet bowl. "Who are you?" He asked.

"The man in New York sent us."

"Who?" He torched the second sheet.

"Please, Mr. Grant. Don't crack wise. Just let us speak to you. He just wants you to deliver another message is all."

Grant placed the second incinerated sheet into the bowl, lit the third. If the scientist had wanted Grant to deliver another message, he would have contacted him in the prearranged manner. He would not have sent two unidentified thugs to follow him.

Grant dropped the carbonized piece of paper in the toilet, lit the last two sheets. The black smoke accumulating in the confines of the small bathroom made him cough. He looked at the small window above. It was latched.

"I see. Just give me a second. I'm on the can, for crying out loud."

"We don't have time, Mr. Grant."

Grant let the remains of the last two sheets fall into the toilet bowl, stood on the rim, unlatched the window. He pushed it.

It did not budge.

He shoved it a second time, harder.

It swung outward. The narrow opening would have presented a daunting challenge to most persons, but Grant had begun his career as a circus acrobat. In a fluid series of movements learned through years of training, he flushed the toilet, pushed himself up, contorted his lithe body through the window. Hoping that the flush would mask the sound of his escape, Grant reached up and pushed the window back into place before jumping to the pavement below. He landed on his feet. His first thought was to run along Sunset Boulevard, but that would present an easy target for the men following him. Instead, Grant sprinted through the buzzing traffic across Crescent Heights Boulevard.

The lazy residential area that greeted him on the other side was a godsend. Dark shadows of dense vegetation embraced him as he ran through a grove of trees, through the lush oasis of the Garden of Allah Hotel, and through the tidy green backyards of small homes. It was a perfect cover for his escape.

Too perfect to last.

Several homes farther, Grant ran out of backyards and into a chain link fence. He leaned against it and gripped it with his manicured hands. Panting, he turned to look behind him, listened.

No one.

His heart raced. He took deep breaths, forced himself to calm down. He had nearly caught his breath when branches cracked behind him.

The enemy had followed him through the gardens.

Grant crouched low behind a short nearby hedge, his pulse accelerating. He wiped the sweat from his face.

The men were thugs, he reflected, but they were well-trained thugs. They would soon find him. He could not remain where he was. Sunset Boulevard was only a dozen yards away, but it might have been

100 miles away, blocked as it was by a high wall. Grant turned to the fence, peered into the darkness beyond. From the dim glow of the streetlights, he spotted a sign erected near a tractor. It read *'Los Angeles Public Library - Sunset Branch - Opening February 1943'.*

He smiled, his hope renewed.

There were a myriad places to hide in a construction site. Grant started to climb the fence. Despite his well-practiced acrobatics, it rattled loudly as he ascended. He landed on his feet on the other side and darted into a large building under construction, not daring to look back.

The unfinished library was a collection of unplastered walls, rickety wood floors, and roof beams without a ceiling. It was pitch dark inside. Grant groped his way forward, touching the walls, stopping every few feet to listen for his pursuers. At first he heard only the sound of rushing traffic on Sunset Boulevard. Then of footsteps echoing through the empty building. Nearly paralyzed with fear, Grant forced himself to push deeper into the darkness. He hesitated, wondering whether he should flick on his lighter to illuminate his path, decided against it. The flame would give away his position. He would lose his only advantage.

He continued onward, walking in short, halting steps on the tips of his toes. The thin sheets of wood flooring flexed and creaked. He grimaced in anticipation of each next step. Several steps farther, there was no creak. Instead, Grant stepped into thin air and fell six feet before landing hard on a cement floor. His right ankle buckled under the force of the impact. He suppressed a yelp, but the sound of his fall echoed through the half-finished building.

Grant sat on the cold floor, wincing at the sharp pain, clutching his throbbing ankle. It was already swelling. He pricked up his ears. The footsteps had stopped. Grant was about to exhale a sigh of relief when an engine coughed to life far away. A lightbulb flickered on overhead. The thugs had found the electric generator. His hope evaporated. Even if he managed to extirpate himself from the basement, his twisted ankle would prevent him from escaping to safety. It was already swollen to the size of a grapefruit. He had destroyed the documents, but it was not enough. He patted down his tuxedo jacket, felt his Parker fountain pen and the outline of the *Infamous* movie premiere program. He removed them from his inside pocket.

The footsteps grew louder.

He was running out of time.

Grant paused to think, then scribbled on the program, stuck it between two wood beams in the basement's low ceiling.

The footsteps stopped. Directly above him.

He looked up. Two faces glared down at him. The larger of the two men bent over the opening.

"We just wanted to speak with you is all, Mr. Grant. You didn't have to up and run away," he announced. It was the same voice that he had heard outside the bathroom door. Low, filled with malice.

"Speak, then," Grant replied, sitting on the floor, massaging his aching ankle.

"We just want you to give us what the man in New York gave you."

"He gave me nothing," Grant replied.

"Mr. Grant, please stop cracking wise. We don't have much time." He removed a black Colt .38 Special revolver from a shoulder holster.

"Give me the papers," the larger man said, holding out a meaty hand.

"I don't have any papers," Grant continued, adamant.

"Come on, Mr. Gra-"

"Listen, you Nazi vermin. I don't have them," Grant shouted, still unable to stand. "I had them. I had them and burned them and flushed them down the toilet. If you're going to shoot me, do it, because that's the only answer you're going to get. I don't have them."

The larger man turned to his partner slowly, then peered down at Grant. He sighed. "Then you don't have any time left."

Three gunshots roared through the half-completed library, felling Grant. He slumped to the cement floor, bleeding, his breath ragged. Darkness closed in.

The larger man dangled over the side of the opening to the basement floor, patted down Grant's clothes, sifted through his pockets. He removed his wallet, gold Zippo, and cigarette case, pocketed them. Finding no documents, he pulled himself up with his partner's help. Both men disappeared down the hall without a further glance at the bleeding movie star.

For Montgomery Grant, there would be no more movie premieres. No more Cadillac limousines or Packard convertibles. No more *Sunrise Serenades*. As his life ebbed away at the apex of his career, Grant peered up at the basement ceiling and hoped that the right people would find his note.

2 PROGRAM

Patrick Carlton sat in the rear of the tour van, watching the vestiges of old Hollywood through tinted windows as it pulled into a parking lot and stopped. Dressed in worn jeans, black cowboy boots, and a dark blue baseball cap with 'Navy' stenciled in yellow letters, he waited for his fellow passengers to file out before joining them in the scorching summer heat. Squinting against the brilliant sunshine, he pulled down the bill of his cap, leaned against a hot concrete wall, listened to the tour guide.

Her enthusiasm made it appear as though it was her first tour. This was the spot, she explained, where silent film star Alla Nazimova had turned her Spanish Colonial Revival mansion into the Garden of Allah Hotel in 1925. Sadly, developers had razed the elegant structure in 1959 to erect a bank, leaving behind only the Joni Mitchell lyrics 'they paved paradise and put up a parking lot'.

A woman rushed up to the group in a panic, interrupting the guide.

"Have you seen him?" She darted her head left and right, eyes wide with fear.

Carlton recognized her as a fellow member of the tour. "Seen whom, ma'am?" He asked, pushing himself off the wall.

"Spencer. I can't find him. I've looked everywhere."

Carlton saw her teeter on the edge of sorrow and terror. She was trembling. He remembered the little boy with her. "Spencer is your son?" He asked, leaning close, looking straight into her eyes.

She gave a frightened nod. "He must have run off while I was talking. I checked the van, the parking lot, all over. I can't find him anywhere. He's only four. I should never have-"

"We'll find him," replied Carlton in his most reassuring voice. "He can't be far away."

While the other members of the tour group scoured the parking lot and retail shops for the boy, Carlton looked around, then ran down Sunset Boulevard. Fifty yards away, he arrived at a construction site blocked off by a chain link fence. A dust-covered sign proudly announced 'Your Tax Dollars at Work: Los Angeles Municipal Public Library - Sunset Branch Reconstruction Project.' He walked through the entrance gate into the noisy project area. Trucks, tractors, and construction workers were busy digging up, tearing down, and rebuilding different portions of the old Spanish Mission style library. Despite work crews watering down the project, the frenzied activity still managed to send clouds of dust billowing into the hot, dry air. Carlton stopped, scanned the site.

No sign of the boy.

He hurried to the entrance of the building, dodging a spray of water and a bright yellow tractor carrying construction debris in its raised front bin. One by one, he searched possible hiding places: behind a short brick wall, inside deep trenches, amid piles of broken tiles.

The child was nowhere to be found.

Carlton stopped next to a stack of old bricks, wiped sweat and dust from his forehead. Maybe he was wrong. Maybe the boy had not come here at all.

His gaze focused on a lumber pile in the entrance courtyard. A pair of eyes peeked out from behind it, below a bowl-cut mop of hair.

"Spencer!" He shouted, running toward the boy. The playful child was not finished with the man in cowboy boots who wanted to play hide-and-go-seek. He giggled with delight, running around the woodpile. Carlton rushed after him. The kid was quick.

He was only ten feet away when Spencer bolted away from the stacked wood beams. Instead of moving toward Carlton, he tore across the front of the library building, ducked under a loose portion of the fence, squirmed inside.

Carlton stared in horror at a sign hanging above.

Danger - Demolition.

Carlton halted at the fence, rattled it hard. "Spencer, stop!"

The boy stopped and turned, grinned, waved, then darted into a portion of the building pockmarked with advanced signs of approaching demolition. Plaster was torn from the wall in several areas, exposing tired red brick and crumbling gray mortar.

The bottom part of the fence was too narrow for Carlton's bulky six-foot frame. He searched for an alternative entrance and abruptly stopped at the sound of a bone-jarring crash.

He swiveled.

Amid a haze of dust, a black iron wrecking ball the size of a truck tire dangled from a crane at the end of a thick steel cable. The monstrous orb swung back from a gaping hole that seconds before had been a brick wall. Debris tumbled into the building not more than ten feet from where Spencer had entered, sending a cloud of dust into the air. With a portion of its support destroyed, the roof began to sag, accompanied by ominous creaks.

No time to find an entrance through the fence. Carlton grabbed the upper part of its chain links, kicked himself off the ground, used the tips of his boots to climb to the top. He twisted his body, jumped off, fell to the ground on the other side just as the wrecking ball slammed into the library anew, transforming yet another section of the wall into rubble and dust, a mere five feet from where Spencer had entered. Wood beams detached from the weakened roof and crashed to the ground.

Carlton jumped up and down, gesticulating wildly to capture the attention of the ball operator. He was about to run to the person at the controls, but stopped. The operator was perched one hundred feet above the ground behind protective metal mesh. To make matters worse, he wore goggles and sound-suppressing earmuffs. Carlton would never be able to reach him in time. Two or three more blows and the roof would cave in on top of the boy.

Carlton positioned himself in the crane operator's line of sight and continued jumping, shouting, waving his arms. The operator did not notice him, directing his attention to the wrecking ball swinging away from the building, making sure it did not hit anything as it increased its destructive momentum. When it had completed its backward arc, the crane arm reversed course. The wrecking ball followed with startling speed, directly at the wall - and Carlton. He dove to the ground an instant before the massive sphere plowed through another section of the wall.

He coughed, spat out a glob of dirt. For a second, he thought that the crane operator had seen him. He realized that he was mistaken as soon as he saw the crane arm accelerating backward. This was not working. He had to change tactics.

He studied the area in front of the building. A large yellow tractor was parked near the fence a dozen feet away.

The idea was crazy, but he was desperate. If he did not stop the demolition immediately, tons of debris would rain down, crushing the child. Crazy was all he had. Crazy would have to do.

He ran to the tractor, hoisted himself up its mud-caked side, scrambled into the driver's seat. Thank God I was raised on a farm, he thought, locating the ignition key. He twisted it, pressed the firestarter. As the monster engine roared to life amid a belch of oily black smoke, he started shoving gears in hopes of finding the right one. The tractor lurched backwards. Carlton hit other levers, finally causing the five-ton beast to roll forward on its giant wheels. He waited until the wrecking ball swung back from its latest devastating impact, then lurched the tractor toward its next target. Carlton stopped a few seconds later, leaped off, sprang back up, ran inside the building. He stood inside the nearest doorframe, gripping both sides to protect himself in case the roof gave way.

He had barely stopped moving when the wrecking ball slammed into the tractor with an agonizing screech of twisting metal. Carlton saw the tractor rise up on its side tires, then fall to the ground in a cloud of dust. A klaxon blared.

He felt a momentary sense of relief. Someone had triggered the alarm.

Agitated construction workers swarmed around the tractor's mangled remains, speaking with animated gestures. A barrel-chested man wearing a hard hat and a look of authority spotted Carlton running toward him, glared.

"Are you the idiot who-"

Carlton shot his hand out. "A little kid ran in here," he shouted back. "I couldn't reach the crane operator in time."

The man's anger shifted to panic. "I'll get help," he replied, dashing off.

Carlton could not wait for help to arrive. The repeated blows of the wrecking ball had severely weakened the old roof. It sagged and groaned. Wood planks fell to the floor with increasing frequency, accompanied by a steady rain of roof tiles and dust. Only moments remained before the roof collapsed.

Carlton raced inside.

A few minutes later, he burst out of the building cradling Spencer in his arms, dashing to safety. He was barely ten feet out of the creaking structure when he tripped and fell to the ground, losing his hold on Spencer. Quickly checking that the boy was all right, he scrambled to his feet when he heard the din of splintering wood and crumbling brick behind him. He crouched and shielded Spencer as wood beams, tiles, plaster, and bricks crashed down, sending a cloud of dust rushing out through the demolished front wall directly toward them. Choking dust and debris engulfed the pair.

Then there was silence. Coughing, blinking, and shaking off a crust of dust, Carlton muttered a prayer of thanks, looked at Spencer. The boy wailed uncontrollably, but appeared unharmed. Both looked as though they had been dipped in milk chocolate.

Arms plucked the boy from him. Carlton peered up to see Spencer's mother squeezing her son tight. Tears of joy streamed down her face. His sobs subsided.

"I don't know how I can ever thank you."

"You just did," he replied, standing. He grinned while ruffling Spencer's brown hair, dirt falling away from both in sheets.

"I think you just made a new best friend," she replied, watching her son finally smile. "How did you know he would be here?"

Carlton shrugged. "This is where I would have gone at his age. Construction sites and monster trucks are magnets for four year old boys."

Carlton noticed Spencer clutching a folded piece of paper in his tiny balled fist.

"What do you have there, big guy?" He asked, peering at the paper.

Thinking that Carlton was playing a game, Spencer giggled and yanked his hand away.

"Spencer, give it to the nice man," his mother instructed. She turned to Carlton, rolling her eyes. "He's always picking things up."

The boy complied, offered the find to his newest friend.

"Thanks, buddy," replied Carlton, taking the paper. Like them, it was caked with dust. He shook and blew it off, unfolded the page. It was a faded premiere program for a movie entitled *Infamous*, printed on heavy paper stock measuring about five by six inches. Yellowed and brittle with age, it proudly displayed a black and white frame of the dapper Montgomery Grant in the lead role, with its title scrolled above. Below the photo and movie credits read:

December 30, 1942
7:00 PM
Beverly Theatre, Beverly Hills
Reception at Ciro's following the screening

Carlton peered closer. A handwritten address was scrawled diagonally in the top left corner, barely legible in faded ink. He squinted. It looked like '2232 Watt Heights Road', followed by the letters 'BR'. He reluctantly handed the paper to Spencer's mother.

She shook her head. "You keep it," she replied. "As a memento. I insist."

Spencer did not object.

Carlton grinned, tickled the boy. "Thanks."

He was still staring at the piece of Hollywood memorabilia when a reporter and cameraman materialized.

"Tina Delgado, LA News," she announced, shoving a microphone in his face, firing a barrage of questions. "Are you the one who rescued the boy? Is this him? Is this his mother? What's your name? How did it happen? What do you have in your hand?"

A modest man, Carlton was about to utter 'no comment' and walk away when Spencer's mother foreclosed on the possibility.

"This man is a hero," she announced, pointing to Carlton.

He was about to disagree, but realized that giving him credit would help the woman forgive her momentary inattention to her son. He relented, dutifully answering the reporter's questions, showing her the old movie premiere program, noticing with a supressed grin that Spencer was enjoying the interview far more than he as the boy reached out and grabbed the reporter's microphone.

Carlton was searching for a way to disentangle himself from the reporter's clutches when he spotted the tour guide. Before the reporter could ask yet another question, he raised his hand.

"Please excuse me. I have something to attend to." He turned and walked to the tour guide in brisk strides, more dust falling away from him with each step.

"That was amazing. Just like in the movies, except they use stunt men. That took a lot of guts," she announced, removing her cap, releasing a cascade of blonde hair styled in a peek-a-boo cut reminiscent of Veronica Lake. Long wavy strands partly hid her left eye.

Carlton shrugged. "I just guessed where Spencer was."

She leaned forward, incredulous. "You ran into a crumbling building."

"Actually, I ran *out* of a crumbling building, which is a lot easier," he precised, smiling. "Anyone else would have done the same."

The look on her face made it clear that she did not agree.

He extended his hand. "Patrick Carlton."

"Alexis Hamilton." She grimaced at his strong grip.

"I think you would be interested in this, Ms. Hamilton. Spencer found it inside the library. It's a movie premiere program for *Infamous* with Montgomery Grant." He carefully wiped the faded paper on his dust-caked jeans, handed it to her.

Alexis's eyes opened wide. She took the yellowed paper from him, handling it with reverence, as though it was a museum piece.

Carlton studied her while she read with rapt interest. Her pale angular face, straight pointed nose, and large mahogany eyes would have given her a cold, patrician air if not for her full red lips, which seemed to smile even when at rest. Though her tour guide uniform was far from flattering, it failed to mask the graceful bearing of her five foot five frame, slim but not starved.

She looked up at him, astonished. "Did you know that this was the building where Grant was murdered?"

It was Carlton's turn to be stunned. He only knew that Grant had died at an early age. "Murdered?"

"His body was found in the library in 1942. *Infamous* was his last movie. He disappeared from the movie premiere and was found dead in this building the next morning." She brought the paper program closer, squinting. "Looks like someone wrote in the corner."

"An address, I think," replied Carlton. "Since Grant's body was found here, do you think that maybe this was his program?"

"Probably. It would be too much of a coincidence otherwise."

Carlton gazed at the writing on the program. "If it was his movie program, chances are that he made the notation." He looked back up at Alexis. "Who killed him?"

"The Nazis," she replied, reluctantly handing the program back.

Carlton noticed the reporter making a beeline toward them, waving her microphone. "I've had enough of the press for today. Give them an inch, they want the whole nine yards. Thanks for the tour." He smiled. "Except for the last part, I really enjoyed it."

Without giving the reporter an opening, Carlton walked across the street to a prewar luxury condominium building, jumped into the blue cab waiting out front.

Heck of a way to start a vacation.

* * *

In truth, a vacation was the last thing Carlton desired. What the U.S. Department of Justice (DOJ) prosecutor really wanted was to lock terrorists plotting against America in metal cages.

Ironically, that was why he was on vacation to begin with, he reflected, rubbing his temples.

Deputy Assistant Attorney General Frederic Edison had sought an experienced DOJ hand to help organize his newly-created anti-terror National Security Division. Touching forty, Carlton had a distinguished history of prosecution victories below his belt - many originally deemed unwinnable by the DOJ aristocracy. Distinguished enough to keep him swimming in litigation partnership profits at any number of white shoe law firms. Yet Carlton had left the world of mega law firms behind years ago, never looking back. Money was not his quest. Edison knew it, luring him by promising a hefty anti-terror caseload once the new DOJ division got off the ground.

With his memories of Iraq painfully fresh, Carlton had not thought twice about leaving behind his hard-earned position in DOJ's Antitrust Division, with its more impressive title, higher pay, and larger office with a better view. Yet a year after joining Edison's division, Carlton was still buried waist-deep in administrative work, rarely seeing the inside of a courtroom. His meager cases were dog bites compared to the lion attacks that Edison assigned to the legal stars Carlton himself had recruited to staff the man's National Security Division.

He began to consider moving to another DOJ division when the FBI arrested Abu Hassan, the Saudi-born leader of 100 radicalized Americans and Europeans hours before they could launch an attack against the painfully obsolete U.S. electric grid and plunge the nation into darkness, chaos, and ruin. It was clear that Hassan had a handler, but he refused to divulge his identity. Extracting it through harsh interrogation was no longer a legal option - or a practical one after a major New York newspaper had refused to keep the critical FBI investigation confidential, giving it - and Abu Hassan - instant worldwide attention. Edison assigned Hassan's prosecution to Carlton, finally giving him his first meaningful anti-terror case. Carlton could not wait to tear into it - and the terrorist.

That was before FBI Counterterrorism Special Agent in Charge Faraday, in charge of the Hassan investigation, somehow convinced Edison to reassign the case to the U.S. Attorney in Houston. Carlton had no idea how the agent had pulled it off, but he knew why. Faraday bore a deep grudge against Carlton over a past incident. Unwilling to admit succumbing to Faraday's pressure, Edison cited jurisdiction as the reason for reassigning the case. Valuing loyalty and honesty above all else, Carlton received Edison's weasel lie as a personal insult - and a punch in the gut. He confronted his boss, receiving only a question in reply. It still rang in his ears.

Are you so gung-ho about putting Hassan behind bars because he is a threat to the United States or so you can expiate your guilt over what happened in Iraq?

It was the wrong question.

Carlton's anger exploded. The ensuing shouting match swiftly earned him the choice between suspension for insubordination or a forced vacation. Faced with a career-ending blot on his exemplary DOJ record and hoping to survive another day at DOJ to prosecute terrorists, Carlton had little choice.

He took a deep breath in the rear of the cab, unclenched his fists. He forced his anger aside, gazing at the ornate French Normandy and Spanish Colonial Revival prewar buildings lining Crescent Heights Boulevard, focusing instead on what had just transpired.

He soon found himself wondering why the Nazis had murdered Montgomery Grant.

3   FBI

Castel McLean
Beverly Hills, California
8:30 AM

Crow's feet on the edges of his blue eyes greeted Carlton as he shaved the next morning. A decade in the DOJ trenches had transformed his once carefree smile into an impassive mask, his bronzed Southern California glow into a pasty-white complexion. The events in Iraq and his ensuing romantic breakup had aged him, both inside and out. His current state of limbo at DOJ certainly was no source of rejuvenation. A daily jog with weights kept him in shape, but they could only delay evidence of aging, not age itself. His weaknesses for barbeque, coffee, cigars and gins and tonic were no help. At least his black hair was still as thick as during law school.

Almost twenty years ago. It was only when he took time off that he noticed how quickly time was passing. Maybe that was why he rarely took vacations. The current one had been thrust upon him, but at least it had given him the opportunity to visit his old friend Max McLean.

As a rule, few people have friends who are billionaires and billionaires have few real friends. Carlton and McLean were exceptions. Carlton had met McLean during a case several years ago, alerting the billionaire to looming danger. In return, McLean had saved Carlton's life. Although many at DOJ frowned upon his friendship with a man with such a dark family history, Carlton considered McLean a brother. The bond was mutual.

McLean insisted that Carlton stay at his home whenever he visited Los Angeles. Carlton was happy to oblige. Designed by noted LA architect Gerhard Heusch and interior decorator Suzy Lehman, *Castel* McLean was a breathtaking hilltop aerie of vast glass walls, brushed steel, and polished exotic hardwoods overlooking Beverly Hills. Carlton's guest bungalow alone was larger than his modest house in Northern Virginia.

His cell phone rang as he scraped the last dollop of shaving cream from his face. He considered ignoring the annoying trill - forced or free, a vacation was a vacation - but found the habit difficult to break. At least he was not tied to the office with a Blackberry electronic umbilical cord, he reflected, reaching for the device.

"Good morning, Mr. Carlton. FBI Special Agent Javier Echeverria, Counterintelligence Division. I hope I'm not calling too early."

"Not at all," replied Carlton, elated by the possibility that the FBI had finally seen through agent Faraday's personal vendetta and decided to let Edison reassign him to the *Hassan* case.

"Good. I was wondering if you would be available to answer a few questions."

Carlton's hope evaporated. The agent was merely calling about an existing case. "Ordinarily, I would. But I'm out of town on vacation. If you give me the name of the case, I can direct you to the attorney responsible for-"

"I'm sorry, Mr. Carlton. I did not make myself clear. This is not about a DOJ case. This concerns the movie premiere program you found yesterday. Your name was in an *LA Times* article this morning as the person who found it. You are that Patrick Carlton, are you not?"

"Yes," Carlton replied, confused. "I'm not sure what-"

"Good. Could you come down to the LA office?"

Faraday had far from endeared the FBI to Carlton, yet he considered it unfair to impute his ill-feelings toward Faraday's Counter*terrorism* Division to Echeverria's Counter*intelligence* Division. Echeverria was a fellow federal warrior. Carlton decided to be helpful.

"Sure. How is tomorrow morning?"

"I'm afraid this cannot wait. Can you come in right away? I'm in the Federal Building in Westwood."

On a Sunday? Carlton sighed. "I'll be there in a half hour."

"Good. Be sure to bring the movie program with you."

* * *

Carlton's annoyance bled away as he folded down the convertible top and slid behind the wheel of McLean's latest addition to his large automotive stable: a rare 1942 lavender-on-black Series 62 Cadillac, its body professionally restored down to the last bolt. The engine had not been rebuilt, but McLean informed him that it ran well. Despite his love of vintage Cadillacs, Carlton's government salary enabled him to own and maintain only one: a 1958 Eldorado Biarritz convertible whose rakish tailfins had caused him to nickname it the 'Shark'.

Carlton proceeded West on Sunset Boulevard, Sinatra crooning from the single dashboard speaker about feeling youthful. Fifteen minutes later, he pulled into the Federal Building's parking lot near the sprawling UCLA campus. A fierce police contingent protected the seventeen story white building, which doubled as the site of choice for political demonstrations of all stripes. After showing his identification and walking through a metal detector, Carlton rode an elevator to the first of the FBI's eight top floors.

The doors opened to a world operating at a far more frenetic pace than the one outside. Even on a Sunday morning, the no-frills, utilitarian government office was abuzz with activity. Men and women with regulation haircuts strode up and down corridors, in and out of offices, many wearing Glock 23 handguns in belt holsters.

Despite his beef with the Bureau, Carlton felt at home. Except for the guns, the office reminded him of Main Justice back in Washington, down to the meat locker air conditioning. He walked past a wall displaying a large seal of the Federal Bureau of Investigation, with its motto of *Fidelity-Bravery-Integrity*, between a photograph of President John Douglass and another of FBI Director Pete Riebling. He announced his presence to a harried receptionist, who made a call. Moments later, she pointed to a man walking down the long linoleum hallway.

Even on a Sunday, the Special Agent followed Bureau regulations to a tee, dressing in a navy blue suit, a crisp white shirt - *de rigeur* since the days of J. Edgar Hoover - a bright blue tie, and shined lace-up oxfords. He wore his jet black hair closely cropped. Carlton noticed that the agent had put on his suit jacket to greet him, a sign of respect. In his late thirties, he walked with long, confident strides, his lantern jaw a perfect match for his square frame. Carlton wondered if the agent's squinting dark brown eyes belied professional stress or simple nearsightedness. His crooked nose seemed oddly out of place with the rest of his handsome Latin features, reminiscent of a Picasso portrait. Given a nose job, if

Echeverria had not opted for government service, Carlton surmised that the tan Latino agent could have become a movie star.

"Special Agent Echeverria," the agent announced, still squinting, extending his hand.

"Patrick Carlton." Carlton distrusted weak handshakes and approved of the agent's strong grip.

Echeverria flashed a perfunctory smile. "Thank you for coming down. This should only take a few minutes." Echeverria turned on his heel and led Carlton into a windowless conference room decorated in 1970s Federal Government style, complete with white linoleum flooring, scuffed white walls, and a drop-tile acoustic ceiling. A plain pine table sat in the middle of the rectangular room, scratched from years of use, just short of being scarred.

"Have a seat," offered Echeverria, closing the door. "Coffee?"

"No thanks," Carlton replied, sitting in one of the wood and cloth chairs. A purist, he knew of few brews worse than government joe.

Echeverria sat across from him, held up a small recorder. "Do you mind?" He asked.

Carlton smiled. "I don't know. Do I need a lawyer?"

"You can have one present if you wish," replied Echeverria, dead serious.

"That was a joke. No, I don't mind." Apparently, even in LA the FBI had no sense of humor, reflected Carlton.

"I see," said Echeverria, still without a trace of a smile. He leaned forward in his chair. "Did you bring the movie program?"

Carlton reached into his jacket pocket, removed the yellowed *Infamous* movie premiere program. He unfolded it, slid it across the table.

Echeverria reached for the paper greedily, like a hungry child. He examined it carefully in silence, turning it around several times, making certain that there was nothing on the reverse side.

He placed the document on the table, pressed the 'record' switch on the device in his hand, recited names, date, time, and place. "Mr. Carlton, please describe the events leading up to your discovery of the program."

Carlton left nothing out.

Echeverria listened intently, then cocked his head. "Would you be able to show me where you discovered the program?"

"The boy discovered it," Carlton corrected. "I could show you, but you would not find anything."

Echeverria cocked his head in the opposite direction. "Why is that?"

Carlton had already told him. "As I said, the entire building collapsed shortly after I got out."

"Could you explain exactly where the boy found the program?"

He had already told him that, too. "As I said, I can't explain where because I was too busy trying to avoid becoming a human pancake. My guess is that he found it in the basement area that he fell into."

Echeverria nodded impassively, neither accepting nor rejecting Carlton's explanation. "Why did you keep the program?"

Carlton was starting to get annoyed. He was used to working with the FBI and knew how the Bureau's interrogations worked. The questions began with generalities, then focused on specifics, repeated endlessly in an effort to highlight discrepancies to a point where the person could no longer keep their story straight and confessed or at least gave up vital information. But that was the technique for interrogating *suspects*. Carlton had simply found an old movie premiere program. And he was a federal prosecutor to boot. Why the heat?

"I'm an old Hollywood buff and the program is a great piece of memorabilia."

"I'd like to keep it," said Echeverria, reaching for the program.

Carlton beat him to it, slid the paper toward him. "So would I. I'd be happy to give you a copy." The FBI had shut him out of the *Hassan* prosecution. He was not going to let it swipe his trophy.

Echeverria again cocked his head. "Why not the original?"

Carlton let out an exasperated sigh. "As I told you, I'm an old Hollywood buff. You'll pardon me for saying so, but as a DOJ prosecutor, I know that if I give the Bureau the original, I'll be collecting Social Security before I get it back. I'm happy to help you, but I keep the original. I'm going to frame it."

Echeverria stared at Carlton for a moment, then nodded. "Fair enough." He clicked off the recorder. "Give me a couple of minutes to make a copy."

Carlton was pleased that the room was heavily air-conditioned. Despite his familiarity with the FBI, he found himself sweating. Echeverria's form of questioning made him angry. And uneasy. There was something that the Special Agent was not disclosing. Ordinarily, Carlton would have let it slide and gone on his merry way. Yet after cooperating with Echeverria, Carlton considered a simple explanation not just a matter of inter-agency cooperation, but of principle.

Echeverria returned and handed Carlton the original program, which he replaced in his jacket pocket. The agent slid a pad and pen toward him. "I'd like to get your local address and telephone number in case the Bureau needs to get in touch with you while you are in town."

Carlton complied.

"Thank you for coming. The Bureau appreciates your help," said the agent, managing the cliché with sincerity, handing Carlton his business card. "If you remember anything else, please call me." He stood and opened the door for Carlton.

Carlton stopped inside the doorway, turned to face Echeverria still inside the room. "Before I leave, I'm curious about something. Why is the FBI interested in a 65 year-old movie premiere program just hours after it was discovered? And what does it have to do with counterintelligence?"

Echeverria grimaced, clearly not accustomed to the role reversal. "I'm afraid I cannot discuss ongoing investigations, Mr. Carlton. You're with Justice. I'm sure you understand."

The FBI was now officially teeing him off. "I'm not asking for confidential information. I'm just curious why it's so important. I told you everything I remember, but knowing what you are looking for might help me remember something I overlooked," he explained. "You're with the Bureau. I'm sure you understand," he added.

Echeverria paused for a bit longer than was comfortable, then reached behind Carlton and closed the door.

"Montgomery Grant's murder was never solved," he announced in a low voice.

It was Carlton's turn to be surprised. "I thought that the Nazis killed him."

"That's the official explanation and the cult buzz, but it was never proven. Grant was a high-profile personality, even compared to other stars. As you know, the Bureau pursued Nazi spies in the U.S. during the war. Since Grant was murdered during wartime and the Nazis were suspected, the LA Counterintelligence Division handled the case - it was called the Security Division back then. Once a particular office has a case, it never really goes away until it's solved."

"You think Grant's program will help you solve his murder. Is that what the handwritten address leads to?"

Echeverria stood straight. "Mr. Carlton, I have to order you not to investigate this matter," he announced, sidestepping the question.

Carlton squinted. His jaw tightened. Now the FBI was ordering him around. Carlton had given Echeverria all of his information. Instead of reciprocity, all he got was a stone wall. Like with Faraday. His anger blossomed.

"I'm not investigating anything," Carlton snapped back. "I'm asking a simple question based on what I already know. I'm a DOJ prosecutor, for crying out loud. We're the ones who prosecuted those Nazi spies you guys hunted down during the war. We're on the same side. I'm not asking for the names of the aliens at Area 51. All I'm asking for is-"

"I cannot divulge any further information," interrupted Echeverria, hands raised, palms out. "The facts of this investigation are code-word classified. It would be much easier for me to talk about Area 51 than about the Grant investigation. Now please enjoy your vacation and let the Bureau do its job."

Carlton wanted to shout back, instead forced himself to take a deep breath. He did not have the government ladder needed to scale this wall. "Very well," was the only response he could manage, delivered through clenched teeth.

* * *

As he rode the elevator down to the lobby, Carlton reflected that Echeverria had divulged nothing more than what he could have learned by reading a detailed biography of Montgomery Grant.

Yet he knew that after 9-11, the FBI had enlisted nearly every available agent among its 12,500-strong force into counterterrorism. Grant's murder may never have been solved, but the FBI had far more important things to do than solve 65 year-old murder investigations, even those of Hollywood icons. There was a reason for the FBI's urgent interest in Grant's movie premiere program, but Grant's unsolved murder was not it. Echeverria was keeping him out of the loop. LA was beginning to feel a lot like DC.

Then he realized that Echeverria *had* divulged something. In a simple comment. Despite what many Hollywood screenwriters thought, classified cases were as common in government as bad coffee. Classification simply restricted material to people with a certain level of security clearance. The halls of government were crawling with people who had 'secret' clearances. Carlton's own clearance was even higher. *Code-word* classification was in an entirely different league. 'Code-word classified' restricted material to a specific list of *individuals*, regardless of others' level of clearance. Names of agents inside terrorist organizations, advanced weapons technology, special ops deployments, submarine positions - those were code-word classified, not 65 year-old murder investigations. Because 'code-word classified' did not mean important, confidential, or privileged.

It meant national security.

4 BUNGALOW

Castel McLean
8:33 PM

Returning to *Castel* McLean after a long drive past favorite LA haunts and Mass at his old college church, Carlton wound his way through the estate's manicured gardens, trailing fragrant cigar smoke. Despite McLean's constant temptation with a humidor stocked full of the best Cuban *habanos*, Carlton stuck with his daily Dominican Romeo y Julieta Bullys.

Far from the madhouse of Main Justice in DC, Carlton felt his tension ebb. He soaked in the peaceful summer night filled with the song of crickets, gazed at the tall parasol pines swaying in the warm breeze, casting shadows in the bright glow of the crescent moon. He stepped into his Polynesian Tiki-themed bungalow, turned on the lights.

And immediately sensed that something had changed.

Carlton remained immobile, observing the thick woven reed mats on the varnished teak floors, the bamboo walls, the polished mahogany beams along the angled ceiling. Large Tiki masks stared back at him with wild expressions. Brightly colored fish swam lazily among pink coral reefs and orange sea anemones in the wall-length saltwater aquarium, oblivious to any danger. Other than crickets, the only sound was the rustling of palm fronds and banana leaves outside. Despite his nagging feeling, nothing appeared out of place.

Perhaps his mind was dealing with the loss of the *Hassan* case by imagining things. He shook off the notion. He had long ago learned to trust his instinct. Right now, it was sounding an alarm.

Carlton walked to the rosewood armoire, removed his aluminum gun case, tumbled its combination lock, clicked it open. He pulled out his Glock 23 handgun, pulled back the slide and let it snap forward, chambering a .40 caliber Smith & Wesson round.

Gun in hand, he searched the kitchenette's black lava counters and stainless steel appliances, then the bedroom adorned with a canopy bed and swirling ceiling fan. His ebook reader and the pale green silk pillows strewn on the carved wood bed seemed to be in the same positions as he had left them, but he could not be certain. He opened the closets, even searched under the bed as he had as a child, looking for monsters.

Nothing.

He stepped into the bathroom. A multicolored airline poster extolling the tropical delights of 1950s Hawaii kept a nacreous seashell sink company next to his shaving kit and a carved coral stone shower. All exactly as he had left them.

After a fruitless search, Carlton determined that his bungalow was free of intruders and that nothing was out of place. Sleep. He needed sleep. And a drink. He poured himself his favorite libation, a Bombay Sapphire gin and tonic with lots of ice and plenty of lime, then replaced the Glock in its case.

Before closing it, he peeked into the side pocket.

And froze.

The movie premiere program was gone.

Carlton grabbed the telephone, called McLean.

His host arrived a minute later with Hans Davos, his head of security, in tow.

Carlton pulled out a copy he had made of the movie program, showed it to McLean and Davos, explaining how he had found it and detailing his FBI questioning session.

His friend nodded. "I read about your *Raiders of the Lost Ark* heroics and the program in the *LA Times.*"

Both remained silent while Davos went to work, first examining the bungalow's doors and windows.

In contrast to Carlton's jeans and dusty boots, McLean was resplendent in a pinstripe navy Kiton suit, pale blue Loro Piana cotton shirt, and black suede Gucci moccasins worn without socks. His only jewelry was a simple gold wedding band and a Vacheron-Constantin Jubilee watch. With his pronounced aquiline nose, brown hair neatly combed back, perpetual tan, and the little cloud of Acqua di Parma cologne that trailed him everywhere, McLean could easily have passed for an old-time Hollywood star. Not for the first time, Carlton noticed that his friend bore a striking resemblance to Montgomery Grant.

Now in his fifth decade, McLean had entered the world as the only son of mafia *don* Giancarlo Innocenti. Sensing the winds of federal law enforcement blowing through the *cosa nostra* empire in the 1950s, his father had gone legit. He divided his share of illegal activities among the other *famiglie* - families - and raised his only son as far away as possible from the ugly world of his former criminal activities. He gave Max a new family name - pronounced 'Mac-Lane', an international education, training in the manners of cultured society, charity work, and world travels before starting Max in business with his own restaurant, a present shortly before Innocenti's death from natural causes.

Respecting his father's wishes, McLean had remained squeaky clean, steering clear of illegal activities and communication with his father's former associates, all the while using his innate business acumen to expand his single restaurant into a global food and hospitality empire. Unlike other billionaires, McLean devoted little time seeking greater wealth, influence, and status. His life was a celebration of beauty in both form and concept, spanning gastronomy and wines, a collection of art and architectural homes, fortunes donated to charity, right down to his regal sartorial appearance. Bitten by the classic car bug after driving Carlton's 'Shark', his latest passions were collecting automobiles and alternative fuels research to make cars run clean. Although he possessed global social and business connections that diplomats and CEOs could only dream of, McLean devoted the bulk of his time to his esthetic passions and his beloved wife Claire, two decades his junior.

Both watched as McLean's impish head of security with a long mustache and a scowl to match it scoured the rooms for any evidence of the trespasser, grunting now and then to make a point that only he understood. Finding nothing, he walked outside and circled the bungalow with a flashlight.

The commission of a burglary in his bungalow on his friend's property made Carlton far angrier than the loss of Grant's movie program. Yet judging by the FBI's immediate interest in the program - and now its theft from the bungalow, the program was clearly very valuable to someone. But to whom and why? He thought of calling Special Agent Echeverria, dismissed it as a waste of time.

"We can eliminate your staff," said Carlton. "They have access to millions of dollars of jewelry, cars, and art 24-7. The program is only worth a few hundred dollars at most in a memorabilia shop."

"The FBI?" Asked McLean.

Carlton shook his head. "I know the FBI," he replied. Only too well, he did not add. "If they wanted the original, they would have insisted on it."

"I can't see how anyone got in or out," announced Davos, baffled, running a hand through his bushy gray hair. "Mr. McLean has not spared any expense to ensure the safety of the estate and its occupants. Even some large banks and museums do not possess our level of security. Guards, dogs, infrared, pressure and sound sensors, laser beams, low current electric fences. Spiderman couldn't get through without us knowing."

Carlton flashed a wry smile. "Then we can eliminate Spiderman from our list of suspects. That does not change the fact that someone did get through."

"Who could possibly get through this level of security undetected?" Asked McLean.

"I don't know," replied Carlton, recalling his unanswered questions to Echeverria. "But as sure as God made little green apples, I'm going to find out."

Once McLean and Davos had departed, Carlton sat and finished his drink. For the first time since his arrival in LA, he wished he was back on his turf in DC. He despised the town's bureaucratic politics, but at least in Washington he had close access to DOJ's National Security Division staff and contacts in multiple federal agencies. The City of Angels had been his turf long ago, but it reinvented itself into a totally new town each time he visited. Despite his familiarity with the city, his attachment to its old haunts, and his friendship with McLean, he now felt like an outsider.

Carlton relit his Bully, clicked his Zippo shut. The battered aluminum lighter had been with him since the very day of his lateral move from a soul-sucking mega law firm to DOJ. It had become his talisman. He gazed at the DOJ seal affixed to it: an eagle atop a shield, clutching arrows and an olive branch in its talons. The Department of Justice's motto was scrolled under it.

Qui Pro Domina Justitia Sequitur.

The unknown origins of the seal and the uncertain meaning of the motto were a subject of great debate at DOJ. Carlton had his own interpretation, based on his parochial school Latin.

He who seeks to rule must follow justice.

Carlton was wondering what sort of justice was done in Montgomery Grant's case if the FBI was still looking for clues 65 years after his murder, when his cell phone rang.

What now?

"Hi, Mr. Carlton? This is Alexis Hamilton, your tour guide from yesterday?"

"Hi," replied Carlton, pleased at the caller's identity. He smiled at the typically Southern California way in which she turned her statements into questions. "Any buildings cave in on your tour today?"

"No. But who knows, maybe the Chinese Theatre will implode tomorrow."

Carlton chuckled. He liked women with a sense of humor. Many of those he met in Washington seemed to have had theirs surgically removed. "What can I do for you?"

"I'm sorry to bother you. I got your number from the tour group list. I was wondering if you could read me the handwritten address on the movie premiere program you found."

Carlton's smile disappeared. *Not her too.* "In fact, I know it by heart. It's 2232 Watt Heights Road BR, whatever that last part means."

"I thought maybe I had written it down wrong," she replied, audibly unhappy with the result.

Carlton remained silent, wondering what he should tell her. Not only was the program part of a national security case, but within twenty-four hours, it had resulted in an urgent FBI interrogation and a high-tech burglary. Carlton wanted to protect Hamilton from danger. He reasoned that she would have a better chance of avoiding it if she knew enough to stay away.

"I have to warn you about something," he announced sternly.

"Warn me? About what?"

Carlton recounted the events since his departure from the tour, pleased that he had sufficiently embellished the story to stop her from investigating.

Her reply was the opposite of what he planned.

"Can we meet? There is something I have to tell you."

5 PRINCE

Sharia Palace
Outside Riyadh
Al 'Arabiyah As Sa'udiya (Kingdom of Saudi Arabia)
10:33 AM

Saudi Interior Minister Prince Hakim ibn Khaled Suleiman al Najd bore a scowl of outraged moral superiority as he paced the soundproofed room like a caged lion. His *dishdasha* robe billowed behind his tall frame as it struggled to keep up. Swept for electronic listening devices every hour, the small, bare, windowless room was a sharp contrast to the prince's ornate *Sharia* palace that housed it, named after the body of strict Qu'ranic law. Standing patient and immobile nearby, Sayyid Yassin noted that today, his master's burning black eyes and chiseled features above a neatly trimmed beard revealed an additional expression he was not used to seeing.

Fear.

Both expressions were in stark contrast to those of Prince Hakim in his youth. Growing up with vast funds and near boundless authority instead of attention and discipline from his distant father, Hakim had acted as a spoiled brat - an 'unholy terror' as his palace minders had secretly labeled him. Despite his high rank in the royal family, he ignored his royal duties, religion, studies, and future subjects, treating those around him with impunity. He rode his Harley Davidson 'hog' through the royal palace. He set his closest servants up for theft. He instigated fights between lower ranked family members. Riddled with jealousy over the belief that his father had sidelined him in favor of his twenty brothers, Hakim spiraled downward as he aged, graduating to private yacht cruises awash in gluttony, booze, drugs, and sex. This last addiction was not a surprise, given Hakim's almost preternatural beauty, with his svelte physique and light cocoa complexion that seemed to meld all races into one. Many women and men threw themselves at him. His only physical flaw was a gnarled index finger; its flesh, skin, and nail seared off during a drunken bout of freebasing.

As his brothers ascended the rungs of royal responsibility with honor, Hakim's rage burned hotter, the void inside grew more hollow. Rather than make a U-turn, he supercharged his hedonistic lifestyle. His parties became orgies, punctuated with multiple accidents, not a few fatal. All were silenced with torrents of cash and physical threats rather than harsh parental punishment. During one particularly debauched gathering with teenage slaves purchased from the Russian *mafiya*, the victim was Hakim himself. His drunken, drug-addled fall over an atrium railing onto a marble floor thirty feet below resulted in broken arms, legs, ribs, and severe skull fractures. During his painful, immobilized recovery, during a bout of agonized shrieks from alcohol and drug withdrawal, Mohammad Khalifiya Abdul al Shayk had paid him a visit. The Wahhabi Sunni cleric was so fundamentalist that he had once prevented the escape of girls from a burning school because they lacked veils. All the girls perished, but al Shayk's reputation for fundamentalism grew, increasing his stature among other Wahhabi clerics.

Hakim's minders anticipated an explosive conflagration.

Quite the opposite occurred. Instead of berating the spoiled prince for his violations of Islam as other clerics had dared in the past, to their demise, al Shayk announced that it was the Americans who had secretly ordered his father to sideline him. They were the ones responsible for his emotional torment - and his now very physical one as well. Yet the emptiness, hopelessness, sadness Hakim felt were none other than a call from the Great One, announced al Shayk. A call to lead the righteous in crushing the enemies of Islam and return the Saudi Kingdom to its holy duty as the keeper of the pure faith and holiest sites. Lost and enraged, in pain, craving validation, direction, and meaning, Hakim soaked it up like a parched sponge. He set his life on a new course with a ruthlessness he had until now applied only to his sybaritic lifestyle.

Al Shayk became Hakim's mentor, an adjunct father. The wizened cleric spent hours teaching him the *usouliyya*, the basic principles of the *kalam*, the Islamic theology. He showed Hakim how many non-Wahhabi Muslims had corrupted Islam from its golden years, the *ummah* of the seventh century. How they had twisted Islam with their music, their idolatrous veneration of the Prophet, their mysticism, and their desire for peaceful coexistence with the infidel Christians and Zionist devils. How the belief in free will that had caused Hakim so much pain was the root of all evil, seducing the weak, destroying their souls, including members of his own royal family. How politics and religion were one and the same, inseparable. How the Qu'ran could not be interpreted through reason but only understood by its fundamentalist Wahhabi reading.

Al Shayk's tutelage bore fruit more quickly than even the cleric had hoped. Prince Hakim turned away from the *jahiliyyah*, the barbarism that is forever the enemy of the faith, toward *tawhid*, the fundamentalist Wahhabi strain of Sunni Islam. He adhered unwaveringly to the *rukn*, the five pillars of Islam. Not for show, like so many of his princely blood relatives. He believed every word without question, lived them in public and private, even alone. After all, it was his destiny. No more yacht cruises in the South of France, orgies in the South of Spain. No more boozing, gambling, whoring, and snorting.

Yet deep within, Hakim still craved his former pleasures. Fearful of giving in to the temptations of his flesh, he banned all women from his presence, now considering them fit for nothing more than child bearing - as well as suicide bombers and human shields - and kept his other former desires at bay by prohibiting them absolutely, for everyone. Instead of being defined by what he loved, Hakim became defined by what he hated: anyone different than his new self. It prompted him to begin funding al Shayk's twisted interpretation of *jihad* - holy war against America, the Crusading Idol of the Age, its Zionist adjunct Israel, and their allies throughout the world, including those inside the Saudi Kingdom itself.

As al Shayk guided Hakim to his holy destiny, he introduced Sayyid Yassin. The British-trained former banker had found himself unsatisfied with his job, wife, and children, despairing that there was nothing more in life, yearning for the glory of a greater cause. Al Shayk had radicalized him too, convincing Yassin to quit his job, abandon his family, change his name, use his training in the great *jihad* for the faith. Wildly intelligent and assiduous, Yassin proved himself quickly, becoming a trusted confidant to Hakim who could get things done quietly, away from the prying eyes and ears of their many enemies. Meanwhile, al Shayk's hardline allies in the royal family caused Hakim's appointment to increasingly influential government posts, culminating with the Interior Ministry he now controlled.

Hakim accelerated his pace inside the small room, increasingly looking like a sandstorm to the calm Yassin. "As crown prince, King Fahim showed great restraint against the reforms the Americans demanded after the attacks of 9-11," he told him. "But ever since becoming king, his majesty has become more accommodating. Too accommodating. He increased the Kingdom's collaboration with the American crusade against our *jihad* to force our misguided Muslim brothers back to the pure faith. He diluted the power of the *mutawaeen* religious secret police and our holy clerics. Instead of using the trillion dollar windfall that the Kingdom amassed during the oil price spike to promote the pure faith, Fahim is using it to diversify the economy like that Western whore Dubai, to create a middle class that keeps demanding more freedoms, more permissiveness. Immoral movies. Alcohol. A free press. A free internet. Government transparency." Hakim snorted. "Women are demanding the right to unveil themselves in public, to drive, even to consort with who they choose!"

"As if the right to go to school and to work was not enough for them," replied Yassin. He had heard Prince Hakim's diatribes before. Yassin wholeheartedly agreed, but was more pragmatic, often playing devil's advocate. "Diversifying our economy is critical to maintaining domestic stability, especially now that oil production levels have dropped below the break-even point, despite the new price spike," he proposed, referring to the price point below which Saudi oil revenue was less than the Kingdom's vast welfare payments to its underemployed domestic population. "His majesty may have realized that if Iraq could become a fledgling democracy, it would only be a matter of time before his subjects demanded the same." He was about to mention the popular Arab Spring uprisings in Tunisia, Egypt, Libya, Algeria, Syria, and Bahrain, fueled by a desire for freedom and sparked by economic despair, but decided it would only send Hakim even further off the edge. "His majesty is probably trying to maintain both stability and power, minister."

Yassin waited for his master to burst into outrage anyway.

Instead, the prince nodded calmly. "That is what I thought. Especially after the king's vast increase in social welfare and the absolution of debt to calm the people after the uprisings in the Middle East and North Africa. And any reform could be abolished by a simple royal decree," he replied, continuing his rapid gait. "As long as the strictly interpreted Qu'ran remains the only source of law in the Kingdom, the righteous control the laws. But history teaches us that once a king gives up even a little power, the whole system explodes and the king ends up losing all his power - or even his head. Just ask Louis XVI.

"To diversify and develop the Saudi economy, the king must attract foreign capital, as he has done by opening the *Tadawul* to foreign investors," Hakim continued, referring to the Saudi stock exchange. "But to attract foreign capital, the Kingdom must have laws that provide certainty and transparency. To do that requires more than a few reformist decrees as window dressing. It requires a fundamental change to the system. One in which the Qu'ran is no longer the ultimate source of law in the Kingdom and the king and clerics no longer its only interpreters." Hakim stopped abruptly, turned to Yassin, his coal black eyes aglow with terror. "The king is about to announce a constitution."

Yassin blinked in shock. Despite his many contacts inside the royal family and al Shayk's clerical circle, he had not heard anything about it. The king must be very serious if he was keeping his plan so secret.

Hakim could not control his trembling arm. "Unlike the current *majlis al shura* that can be dissolved by royal decree, his majesty's constitution will bind even himself and the clerics; create a separation of powers. It will establish a permanent legislature with authority to pass everything from criminal to commercial laws, directly elected by all Saudi subjects, even women," he sneered, the volume of his voice rising. "In time, subjects will be able to decide whatever they want, even if it is against the faith." His eyes glowered. "It is bad enough that the simple-minded will be given such freedom. Far worse is the transparency that the legislature will impose over the ministries to assert its new powers. Including mine."

Yassin cringed. He knew exactly why Hakim feared this last item. All Saudi laws were based upon the al Shayk clerics' Wahhabi interpretation of the Qu'ran and *Sharia* law. Replacing them with a civil constitution as the supreme source of law enraged Hakim, but it was government transparency that the prince truly feared. Once the new Saudi parliament opened a window into the inner workings of government ministries, first the Saudi people, then the entire world would discover how Hakim had cooked the Interior Ministry's books, skimming and moving vast sums to the numbered banks accounts of so-called charitable foundations to fund everything from *madrassas* brainwashing the young with the radical Wahhabi version of *jihad*, to weapons purchases and training camps for Al Qaeda, Taliban, Hamas, Islamic Jihad, and scores of other groups, even the Shiite Hezbollah.

Hakim wagged his mangled index finger. "This is all the doing of the Americans, with their blasphemies of free will and the separation of religion and state. Their president is responsible for this. I am informed that he demanded that Fahim enact the constitution in exchange for a guarantee of Saudi security against Iran. Now that the Satanic Iranian Shiites are about to possess nuclear weapons and will threaten the Sunni world with them, the president backed the king into a corner." He resumed his frenzied pacing. "The only way to stop Fahim's constitution is to stop the American pressure."

"We have intensified our efforts against the Americans, minister," Yassin replied, feeling the same growing prickle of fear as his master. "Funding a new insurgency in Iraq and-"

Hakim stopped in his tracks. "Enough with Iraq and Afghanistan!" He roared. "I am sick and tired of hearing about those lost causes. I will remind you that the Americans have already won in Iraq. Not only by vanquishing the insurgents despite the pockets that remain, but by instituting elections and keeping their promise to withdraw all but a few thousand troops, to the entire Arab world's amazement. Afghanistan is a different story, but continuous American drone strikes there and against safe havens in Pakistan ensure that we will not be able to use them as staging areas for large scale attacks. We can keep fleeing to other countries like Yemen and Sudan, but sooner or later they will chase us there too." The prince lowered his voice, clenched his teeth. "Like it or not, the Americans are the strongest tribe."

Yassin was incensed by the admission, but forced himself to remain calm, swallowing dryly. "We have not limited ourselves to Iraq and Afghanistan, minister."

"The plots against America have all failed miserably as a result of their increased vigilance after 9-11."

"Other attacks are planned."

Hakim shook his head, stroked his beard. "You and the others still have not learned the lesson, Yassin," he announced, in a tone generally used with a young child. "Main Street is not the Arab Street. If 9-11, Iraq, and Afghanistan have shown us anything, it is that killing people and destroying buildings will never stop the Americans. We cannot defeat them with guns and bombs. I said it before the attacks, but our people did not listen." He lifted his mangled finger. "Only one type of attack can stop America from fighting us around the globe, bring the demon to its knees. An attack against the one thing that makes America the strongest tribe. The idol that Americans worship the most."

"Money," said Yassin.

Hakim nodded. "To defeat America, we must decimate her economy."

"They have almost done the job themselves with their real estate bubble, banking implosion, national debt, and debasement of the dollar," Yassin commented, smiling.

"Precisely. Their economy is more vulnerable than ever. One big push and it will plunge into the abyss."

Yassin saw where Hakim was headed. "Stop the flow of oil?" It was not a novel idea. In 1973, the late Saudi King Faisal had embargoed OPEC oil exports to America to protest U.S. support for Israel after Soviet-backed Egypt and Syria surprise-attacked the Jewish state in what became called the Yom Kippur War. "His majesty would never allow it."

Hakim shook his head. "Nor should he. If oil production were still high, we could afford it. But it has dropped below the level we need to keep the Kingdom economically and politically stable despite the rising price of oil, as you pointed out. Shutting off our oil taps would devastate our economy and ignite riots across the Kingdom as soon as welfare payments ceased. It would also bring swift American intervention to protect a key source of Western oil. You saw how a single American aircraft carrier decimated half the Iranian navy hours after the *ayatollahs* recently blocked the Strait of Hormuz. The Americans have *twelve* of them. And that is just their navy. If we shut off our oil taps, the Chinese and Indians would join them in taking over our oil fields to feed their economies."

Yassin was baffled. "Then how? Oil is the only weapon we possess."

"And it is oil that we will use," replied Hakim. "But not by shutting off the taps. I have another plan. Unfortunately, it involves an alliance with another Western power and one of their oil companies, but that cannot be avoided. We will use our leverage to right that wrong in due time," he added, before outlining his strategy in detail.

Yassin's eyes grew wide. He had grossly underestimated his master. "It is brilliant," he whispered, stunned by the magnitude - and simplicity - of Prince Hakim's plan. No. It was too brilliant for Hakim to have devised it. He sensed al Shayk's masterful crafting. No matter. The important thing was that it would work.

"And the surplus that the Kingdom accumulated during the oil price spike? It is fast eroding from increased welfare payments to keep the population calm, but it is still high."

Hakim flashed a wicked smile. "I have a plan for that, too," he replied, before explaining. "In the meantime, most of the royal family has either joined King Fahim on his reformist adventure or been exposed and removed from power. We must use the few allies we still have. That is where you come in. Here is what I want you to do," he said, before issuing his orders.

One hour after Hakim had delivered his instructions, Yassin was on a flight to Paris under a diplomatic passport bearing one of his many different identities.

He had little time.

6 RUMOR

El Compadre
Sunset Boulevard, Hollywood
9:53 PM

El Compadre was proof that some of the best restaurants are found in holes in the wall. Carlton had little difficulty finding the restaurant Alexis Hamilton selected as their meeting place, located in a improving area of Hollywood where crime had receded but seedy motels still rented rooms by the hour. He was anxious to discover why she wanted to meet him so urgently.

The smell of Mexican food enveloped him as soon as he stepped inside. How he missed that smell in DC. Simple and dark, El Compadre was a study in LA Mexican kitsch. Dark red vinyl booths rested under fake sloping tiled roofs reminiscent of an outdoor hacienda. Wrought iron grilles and bad moonlight seascapes completed the décor.

Carlton scanned the crowded tables for Hamilton, did not see her, sidled up to the dark bar.

"A Bombay Sapphire and tonic with plenty of ice and lots of limes." He gave the man a good tip, knowing that bartenders survived on them. These days, every bit helped. He sipped his cocktail and sat, hooking his boot heels into the barstool's legs, taking stock of his surroundings.

A Beltway commentator once remarked that people in DC were the same as in LA, only smarter. A Hollywood personality retorted that people in LA were the same as in DC, only better looking. Hip, trim, and fashionably pale, the young entertainment industry crowd presented a marked contrast to Washington's bar cattle, most of all because they smiled. Carlton admired Hollywood's remarkable creativity but had a tough time swallowing its dysfunctional denizens' conspiracy theories and penchant for portraying America as the source of the world's woes rather than as the exceptional country he considered it to be, despite its past sins and current problems.

"Mr. Carlton?" The woman's voice snapped him out of his mental meanderings. Carlton turned and looked directly into Alexis Hamilton's eyes, one partly hidden by the familiar fall of blond hair that gave her a slightly mischievous look. She smelled of lemons.

He smiled. "Mr. Carlton is my father. I'm just plain old Carlton," he said, extending his hand. This time, she anticipated his grip, squeezed his hand hard.

"Alexis."

He followed her and the hostess to a table. Her jeans and white blouse were sexy but not risqué. Although she turned men's heads, Alexis resembled the pretty girl next door rather than the hordes of LA starlets that plastic surgeons turned out as though on assembly lines, sculpted to clinical perfection. Carlton observed that hers was a natural face, complete with the small imperfections such as a pointed nose and a slightly crooked front tooth that made a woman unique rather than perfect, charming rather than cold, genuine rather than fabricated like a mannequin.

Alexis ordered the house special Flaming Margarita with a lemon instead of a lime wedge from the waiter who set down a basket of chips and a bowl of salsa.

"Thanks for meeting me on such short notice. I'm sure you've got a busy schedule visiting LA," she said, crowding her words. She seemed tense and uncomfortable rather than shy. Carlton's curiosity swelled.

"Busy doing nothing," he joked, smiling to put her at ease.

Alexis gave him a confused look.

"I live in Washington, D.C., but I'm originally from Southern California. In DC, I'm a Justice Department prosecutor," he explained, noticing a flicker of apprehension cross her face. He was accustomed to the reaction. "Here, I'm on vacation. I took your tour because I love old Hollywood. I fell in love with it when I was in college in LA. I won't tell you how long ago that was, but back then dinosaurs roamed the Earth."

She chuckled, their mutual love of old Hollywood placing her more at ease. "USC?"

"Sorry. UCLA."

"Well, no one is perfect," she replied, flashing a wicked grin.

Carlton laughed heartily, from his gut. It felt good. It had been a long time since he had engaged in the famous Trojan-Bruin interschool rivalry. He dug into the chips and salsa with gusto.

"This is going to sound like a bad line, but I've taken a lot of Hollywood tours. Yours was the most interesting."

Despite the dim lighting, Carton noticed her blush.

"You're right. It is a bad line."

"In this case, it's the truth."

Alexis blew out the flame atop her margarita, removed the lemon wedge and sucked on it. "Thanks. I appreciate that. Although I try to have a cave-in at least once a week. Keeps the tourists on their toes."

Carlton grinned. "How did you become a tour guide?"

"My father was Jack Hamilton. He was an old-time Hollywood director."

Carlton nodded, impressed, rattling off several of Hamilton's famous titles.

"I'm glad not everyone has forgotten him. I grew up surrounded by his memories of old Hollywood. I knew the old haunts so well that I worked as a tour guide during college one summer. After graduation, I opened Old Hollywood Tours. I've been doing it for about six years."

Carlton performed a quick mental calculation. Alexis was in her late twenties. He surprised himself by comparing his age to hers in the way one analyzes a possible relationship, the first time since his breakup. He quickly dismissed the thought. *You're in LA to disconnect, Carlton. Not to hook up.*

"I thought about going to grad school, but my father died a few years ago," she continued, a shadow of sadness obscuring her face. "Suddenly, of a heart attack."

Carlton grimaced. "I'm sorry to hear that."

"Walking around old Hollywood lets me commune with his spirit. My friends tell me that I live in the past, but the past is often more appealing to me than the present."

He nodded. "I share that sentiment. I drive a '58 Cadillac, listen to Frank Sinatra, and have photos of the old stars on my walls. My grandfather used to tell me stories about when he came to Hollywood on leave during World War II. I feel the same way about him when

I'm in Hollywood," he said, realizing that he had never revealed it to anyone. "Your father must have known a lot of the old time actors."

"Almost all of them. Hollywood was a small place back then."

"Including Montgomery Grant?" Carlton prodded, guiding the conversation back on track.

Alexis nodded, removed the lemon wedge from her mouth. "Grant gave my father his first big break, threatening to quit a movie if my father didn't get to direct it. Grant died shortly thereafter. My father never got a chance to thank him," she explained sadly.

The waiter came to take their order. They chose without looking at the plastified menu. "And a plate of lemon wedges, please," Alexis added.

Carlton smiled at her request as the waiter scribbled on his pad before hurrying off.

* * *

Mitch Savitch walked straight past Carlton and Alexis, resisting the urge to look at them. There would be plenty of time for that. Tables were available in the front section, but Savitch insisted on the one in back.

"Here you go. The Guns N' Roses table," said the hostess, motioning to the wide corner nook. Local lore was that the rock band used it whenever it had frequented the restaurant.

Savitch sat. He was a lawyer, but his talent for dirty tricks far outweighed his legal abilities. After a long and fruitless search, only one man had offered him a law job. In turn, Savitch had given him his loyalty. The job quickly turned to the type of work at which Savitch excelled. The more unsavory his appointed task, the more he relished it.

Savitch had hand-picked his team members from the large group of angry young law school graduates who craved the life, influence, and riches of big time lawyers but who were unable to make the cut, marinating in a seething pool of greed and jealousy, pining for money, power, and revenge. Trained in disciplines more useful in covert operations than legal work, they constituted a formidable force.

Savitch had a clear view of Carlton and Alexis, but the din of patrons drowned out their conversation. He hid in the dim light behind his menu, sneering. He had researched his quarry. He loathed honest, successful lawyers who advanced purely on merit. He reserved particular hatred for those who gave up large salaries in mega law firms to serve the public in government or nonprofits. He had a name for them: altar boy lawyers. Carlton was one of them. And he was in the company of an attractive young woman to boot.

Savitch was about to signal the waiter when he stopped in mid-chew, chip in hand. He stared at the couple, turning his attention away only long enough to send his employer a text message.

* * *

"I made you a copy." Carlton removed a color photocopy of the movie premiere program from his pocket, slid it across the paper tablecloth toward Alexis.

"Thanks." She turned it around, peered closely at the handwritten address, selecting another lemon wedge from her plate.

Carlton's curiosity about the reason for which she had requested the meeting continued to swell, yet he sensed a certain reticence in her. It was not shyness, he thought, unable to place his finger on it. He sidestepped the issue, instead pointing to the plate. "I'm sorry, but I have to ask. What's with the lemons?"

Alexis turned to him, lost in thought, then smiled a dazzling grin, brushing her long strands of hair away from her face. "It's just one of my things. My father took me to Capri when I was sixteen. The island's fascination with lemons rubbed off on me."

"At least you'll never die of scurvy," joked Carlton. He could no longer contain his curiosity. "So why did you ask me to meet you? Other than my irresistible charm and dashing good looks."

She flashed another quick smile, then became intensely serious, remaining silent for a long moment, as if deciding whether to continue.

She finally leaned closer. "You're going to think I'm crazy, but I think Grant was involved in something much bigger than his movie premiere on the night he was killed. And I think your discovery of his program resurrected it."

Far from making him question her sanity, Carlton reflected that it was the most prescient observation he had heard about the day's events. "I don't think you're crazy. But what makes you think that?"

She pointed to the address scribbled on the program. "I checked this address. There was no Watt Heights Road in 1942, either in Los Angeles or anywhere else in the United States."

"That *is* strange."

The waiter arrived with their order. Carlton attacked his tacos while Alexis picked at her tostada with little intent, leaning closer to Carlton.

"After you showed me Grant's program, I reread portions of my father's diary and did some research of my own," she explained. "Grant was photographed entering the Beverly Theatre before the premiere, which started at 7:00PM, but no less than Ronald Reagan reported seeing him rush into Schwab's Pharmacy at around 7:30PM. Which means that Grant was not killed after the *Infamous* movie premiere, but during the screening."

"Why would a star leave his own premiere?"

She nodded. "Mystery number one. Mystery number two is that no one knows who killed Grant. Reagan and other eyewitnesses told the police that they saw two suspicious men follow him, but they were never identified. The persistent rumor is that the Nazis killed him, but it was never proven. There were no arrests."

"That's what the FBI agent told me, but police files are filled with unsolved murders, especially in the 1940s, before modern forensics."

"Except that Grant was a huge star. The investigation into his murder would have been a priority," she countered, spearing a tomato with her fork. "The FBI's involvement is also strange."

"If the Nazis were suspected, that would have been enough for J. Edgar to claim jurisdiction over the investigation and send in his G-men."

"Which brings us to mystery number three. Why would the Nazis kill Grant?"

"Another good question."

"One that I may have found an answer to." Alexis leaned toward him again, her voice hushed. Her quick breaths smelled of lemons. "In 1942, my father wrote that he had overheard a drunken officer at the Hollywood Canteen say that Grant was working as an undercover military courier."

Carlton recalled Echeverria's information about the case's code-word classification. Military courier. *National security.* "You think Grant was carrying something for the military on the night he was murdered?"

"It would explain why he left his own movie premiere. The screening would have been a perfect cover. No one would have suspected him of leaving until the movie ended."

"And it would explain why the Nazis would want to kill him," added Carlton, feeling the familiar rush of solving an initial mystery in an investigation. He took a quick sip of water. "Maybe the FBI was trying to retrieve what Grant was carrying that night," he proposed.

Alexis shook her head. "His killers would probably have taken whatever he was carrying."

Carlton went rigid. "Unless he was not carrying anything at all."

Alexis squinted. "I don't follow."

"Whatever Grant was carrying must have never been found. If it had been, the FBI would not be interested in the program more than half a century later. And no one would have stolen it from my bungalow." He paused. "I think Grant hid what he was carrying before his killers could get to it and left the address as a clue."

Alexis shook off a shiver. "I just got chills. It's creepy. As if time stopped when Grant died 65 years ago and started up again as soon as you found the program."

"The question is: what was Grant carrying and who other than the FBI is looking for it?"

"Not to mention what the address means." She took a deep breath. "It sounds like there are a lot more questions than answers."

Luckily, Carlton knew someone who might help answer them.

* * *

Savitch waited until Carlton and the woman paid their bill, then followed them out the back door into the dim parking lot behind the restaurant, trailing them at a distance of a half dozen yards. He resisted the urge to place his hand on the grip of the Beretta M9 handgun protruding from the shoulder holster under his jacket, instead watched them approach the woman's immaculate candy apple red 1956 Ford Thunderbird. His boss's coded text reply had been clear. He was here to steal, not kill.

What was it with these two and vintage cars, he wondered, appreciating that the situation could not be better. The small lot was packed with cars, devoid of people. He would accost the two near the car, take the program, escape into the dark alley. The pair stopped next to the Ford. Savitch coiled his body for the maneuver, began to close the distance.

Bright headlights shined in his eyes as a white van pulled into the parking lot directly in front of him, blocking the two from view.

Savitch stopped cold, muttered a curse, altered course to loop around the van, blinking away the spots of light still flashing in his vision.

When he cleared the van, the T-Bird was pulling away in the alley. And Carlton was nowhere in sight.

7 AGENCJA

Embassy of the Republic of Poland
Hotel de Monaco
Paris, France
3:13 PM

Set on the busy Rue St. Dominique in Paris's well-to-do seventh *arrondissement*, the Hotel de Monaco was built circa 1776 for a member of that principality's ruling Grimaldi family. Since 1937, it had housed the Polish embassy.

Behind its front Doric columns and friezes lay a rococo interior decorated much like the palace of Versailles, crammed with frescoed ceilings, florid moldings gleaming in gold leaf, carved cherubs atop cornices, and polished inlaid wood parquet floors, all glowing in the light of glittering crystal chandeliers. Certain rooms were so magnificent that its occupants sometimes imagined that they had been transported from the daily toil of international diplomacy to an aristocratic 18th-century fantasy.

Some, but not Major Tadeusz Sobieski. *Ta-day-oosh*. Dressed in a navy blue suit instead of his official military uniform to avoid attracting attention, Sobieski was a special attaché from the *Agencja Wywiadu*, the Polish Foreign Intelligence Agency. *Ah-gen-see-ah Viviah-doo*. A descendant of a Polish royal line dating back to King Jan Sobieski III, who had turned back the horde of Ottoman Turks from Europe at the decisive Battle of Vienna in 1683, Sobieski was in his mid-forties, basketball-player tall, with a bald scalp as shiny as a billiard ball, eager to do his family duty for a Poland only recently unshackled from 40 years of Soviet communist domination.

He was married, but not to a woman. His spouse was his job. Not out of a ladder-climbing desire for career advancement, but because he knew from a string of failed relationships that until he achieved a major intelligence coup, he would always place his mission first. Possibly thereafter as well, he feared. Sobieski refused to place a wife and children in a position where they had to compete with his duty to country; a competition that they would consistently lose.

Based in Paris, the Polish agent was tasked with obtaining intelligence in France and Belgium, whose capital of Brussels doubled as the administrative capital of the European Union. Foreign intelligence provided information on a myriad issues, yet at present, Sobieski was focused on only one: Saudi terrorists.

He glanced at his watch, waiting for his field operative to return. He sat up in his chair, hunted for his pack of Marlboros through the geologic strata of papers on his utilitarian desk, a sharp contrast to his ornate surroundings. He slipped one of the few remaining cigarettes from the battered pack, lit the crooked smoke with a disposable Bic lighter. Sobieski had collected a panoply of expensive lighters over time, but preferred the colorful plastic lighters. They were simple, reliable, and cheap. Everything that his present case was not.

Sobieski took a deep drag, opened a file folder stamped *Scisle Tajne* - Top Secret - and reread the case summary. The convoluted facts made for dense reading, yet they were the impetus for his operative's latest mission.

In 2007, Sunni insurgents in Iraq had launched attacks of unprecedented violence in Samarra, part of the deadly 'Sunni Triangle', slaughtering 50 Iraqi civilians working on a water project and fifteen Polish soldiers de-mining a schoolyard. The following day, the beheaded bodies of ten Polish engineers working on an electrical reconstruction project were discovered hanging from a nearby bridge over the Tigris River. Enraged, troops of the *Wojska Specjalne Rzeczypospolitej Polskiej* - Polish Special Forces - hunted down every lead. They learned that the organizer was a Saudi named Mohammed Adawal, by then nowhere to be found. Warsaw made finding him the *Agencja's* top priority.

At a U.S.-European Union counterterrorism conference, Sobieski learned of a Cyprus bank account used to channel funds to the *Harakat al-Muqāwama al-Islāmiyya* - Hamas - in the West Bank shortly before the elected terrorist group launched a series of suicide bombings against the new Israeli government in Tel Aviv. Knowing of Hamas's Saudi links, on a hunch Sobieski called in a favor with an Interpol contact working on money laundering. He searched Brussels' Society for Worldwide

Interbank Financial Telecommunication - SWIFT - payments system serving 8,000 banks for any common transactions between Adawal's Iraqi account and Hamas's Cyprus account.

His hunch turned into a lead.

Although separated by multiple wire transfers spread among several banks with the information on each transfer 'stripped' to prevent the next bank from learning the true source of funds, the accounts ultimately shared a common upstream account in Venezuela. This did not surprise Sobieski, as such countries had supplanted Switzerland after it increased its banking transparency to counter terror funding. What stunned him was that this was not just any Venezuelan bank account, but the same one the FBI had identified as feeding Abu Hassan's operational accounts in his efforts to decimate the U.S. electrical grid.

Sobieski studied the chart he had created.

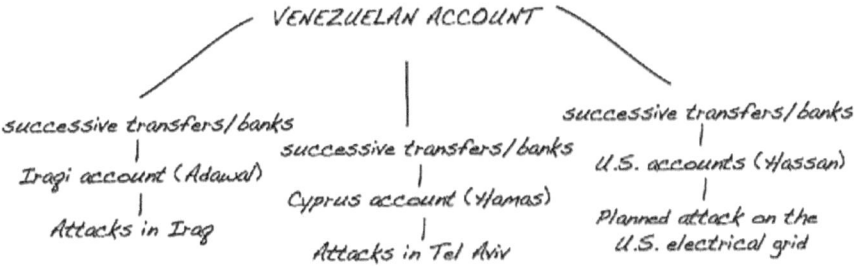

Despite repeated requests from Washington and Warsaw, Venezuelan authorities refused to divulge the account's owner, arguing there was no evidence of *direct* terror funding. No surprise there, given Venezuelan dictator Hugo Chavez's virulent anti-Americanism.

Sobieski changed tack, contacted the Iraqi and Cyprus banking authorities. Offering a warmer reception to his terror concerns, they revealed that an Abdul Rallah had opened the accounts on behalf of Christian and Jewish charities, but had no photo of him. The charities' supposed Judeo-Christian identities did not fool Sobieski. Islamic charities now presented such a red flag for authorities that terror groups had begun to hide behind the names of fictitious Christian and Jewish charities - some revealing how little radical Islamists knew of their perceived enemies. His personal favorite was the 'Rabbi Benedict XVII Fund'.

The information enabled him to add detail to his chart.

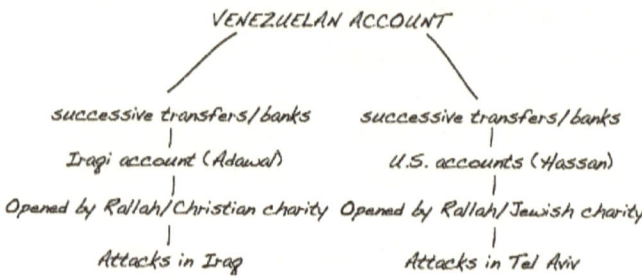

Rallah was clearly a terrorist conduit, but Sobieski could not uncover his link to Adawal.

That changed a week ago, when Sobieski's sharp-eyed operative Zuzanna 'Zuza' Kwiatkowska - officially the Polish embassy's Assistant Press Attaché - distinguished a man darting into the dim background of an internationally televised press conference in Riyadh, Saudi Arabia. Saudi Interior Minister Prince Hakim had called the press conference to decry the attempted attack against the American electrical grid and pledged to track down any members of Abu Hassan's network who might be present inside the Kingdom. Sensing the man's reticence to appear on camera and the fleeting look of anxiety on his face when he realized that he had, Zuza fed his image into the shared U.S.-E.U. terror database.

It had no record of him.

Undeterred, she obtained the conference attendance list through a series of press contacts and eliminated all those known to them, except one: Sayyid Yassin, who appeared to have neither official title nor government affiliation.

There was nothing special about the information, but as it involved Saudi, on another hunch Sobieski sent Yassin's photograph to the Polish Special Forces' commanding officer in Samarra, Iraq. The soldiers showed it to former Sunni insurgents who had since laid down their weapons and allied themselves with the Coalition following the U.S. troop surge. They identified the man in the photo as Mohammed Adawal, who had engineered deadly 2007 attacks.

The twin conclusions were inescapable. One, the terrorist Adawal and Yassin were the same person. Two, he was linked to Saudi Prince Hakim or at least to his Interior Ministry.

Sobieski immediately circulated Adawal/Yassin's photograph through the *Agencja*, to the E.U. counterterrorism task force, and Interpol. Although Adawal/Yassin bore no known relation to Abu Hassan, based on their mutual Venezuelan bank account, he shot the photo over to Jack Thundercloud, his FBI contact at the U.S. embassy in Paris.

Yesterday, Thundercloud alerted Sobieski that a man matching Adawal/Yassin's photograph had entered France under a Saudi diplomatic passport bearing the name Abdul Rallah. Sobieski still did not know the true identity of the Venezuelan account owner, but was finally able to tie the information into a neat bow: the operative Adawal, the funder Rallah, and the Saudi close to the Interior Ministry, Yassin, were the same person.

His chart was nearly complete.

Sobieski immediately contacted the French Foreign Ministry, commonly known as the Quai d'Orsay - *Kay Dor-Seh* - by its geographic location along the Seine river in Paris, requesting that Rallah be detained. The Quai replied that Rallah was a common Arabic name and that his bank transfers were so far removed from the terror accounts as to be coincidental at best. In any case, the man enjoyed Saudi diplomatic immunity. They promised to investigate, but for now, "our hands are tied," they replied.

Infuriated and with no other legal option available, Sobieski tasked Zuza to track down and follow Adawal/Rallah/Yassin.

He was crushing his cigarette into an ashtray forested with upright butts when a knock sounded on his door, shaking him from his thoughts. "Come in," he replied, closing the file, swiveling his chair toward the green damask-covered door.

A thirtyish woman with raven hair dressed in black slacks and a white blouse entered. She stood at attention, saluted. "*Panie majorze.*" Major.

Sobieski stood to his impressive height and returned Zuza's salute. "Good afternoon, *pani poruczniku.*" Lieutenant. He pointed to the simple wood chair in front of his desk and remained standing, gazing at the chameleon before him. He was lucky to have such a dedicated field operative under his command, he reflected. Dedicated and talented. Capable of transforming from inconspicuously homely to cover girl stunning in less time than most people took to brush their teeth. "What did you learn?"

She sat. "Yassin met with none other than Prince Qhibli, the Saudi ambassador to the United States. Prince Qhibli arrived in Paris yesterday. From what I could learn, he was on his way to his annual summer vacation at his villa in the Cap d'Antibes," she explained, referring to the elite sunny enclave in the South of France. "After the meeting, Yassin drove back to Roissy," Zuza added, using the common name for Charles de Gaulle airport outside Paris. "My contact in customs said a Saudi diplomat named Rallah left the country an hour later."

Sobieski massaged his jaw. "So Yassin took the risk to fly into France just to meet the Saudi ambassador to the United States. Makes sense, actually. After the failed attack on the U.S. electrical grid, all Saudi nationals in America are under suspicion, especially in Washington. Yassin would have shined bright on their radar if he met Qhibli in Washington."

Zuza edged to the front of her seat. "There is more. I checked with a contact at Roissy. Prince Qhibli took off an hour later, not to the Cap d'Antibes, but back to Washington." She shrugged. "Of course, it could be a coincidence."

Sobieski furrowed his brow, shook his head. "*Nie.*" Knee-eh. No. "Yassin is not one of the 7,000 Saudi princes or even an official government employee. He would not casually meet with a high-ranking prince like Qhibli. And Qhibli would not cancel his beloved Cap d'Antibes vacation unless he absolutely had to. There is something important going on here." He paced the small office. "*Skurwysyn*," he muttered. *Skoor-vee-sin.* Son of a bitch.

Zuza frowned. "Something else is strange. Given Qhibli's stature, I thought the two would have met at an out of the way location. Oddly enough, they met at Fouquet's," she explained, referring to the expensive restaurant on the Champs Elysées, where stars, politicians and wealthy businessmen enjoyed seeing each other and being seen, often with high-priced escorts.

Sobieski ran a hand over his bald pate. "There is safety in the obvious, lieutenant. Yassin is unknown to the public, but as you implied, the Saudi ambassador to Washington is noticed everywhere by those in the know. If they are going to meet, they may as well meet in a place so visible that it will not arouse suspicion."

Zuza shrugged. "They could have met at the Saudi embassy," she suggested.

"*Tak.*" *Tahk.* Yes. Sobieski raised his index finger. "Unless they wanted to hide their meeting from people at the Saudi embassy, who might have listened to them at the embassy or found it strange that they would meet in an out of the way location. The problem isn't that they met in an obvious place, but that they met, at considerable risk. And that Prince Qhibli immediately returned to Washington, Yassin to Riyadh. Yassin appears to be serving as a conduit between the Saudi ambassador to Washington and the Saudi Interior Minister outside regular government channels. We must find out why."

"What do you suggest, *panie majorze*?" Asked Zuza.

"If Yassin is back in Riyadh, we cannot touch him there."

"*Nie.*"

Sobieski gazed down at his desk, reflected on his possible courses of action. He was tasked with gathering intelligence only in France and Belgium, not in the United States. Yet the Saudi ambassador to the United States had entered his sights while he was in Paris - an important technicality.

He looked back up at his field operative through squinted gunmetal gray eyes.

"Here is what I want you to do."

8 BLACK

Impatient for results of his inquiry, yet unable to do anything but wait, Carlton drove to the venerable Farmers' Market for breakfast. He wound his way through grocery stalls fragrant with ripe fruit and freshly-baked pastries before stepping into the newly refurbished 1938 Dupar's diner. A hostess in a black and white apron wearing her hair in a beehive hairdo to compensate for her diminutive stature ushered him past a row of cakes under glass bells to a red vinyl booth.

He was rarely hungry in the morning, ordered only a cup of coffee - black, no sugar. The waitress arrived with it at the same time his cell phone vibrated. He answered it quickly, hungry for answers.

"Good morning, Mr. Carlton. My name is Brendan Wallace. I'm with the Department of Energy."

It was not the call he had expected. But DOE suggested a link to the *Abu Hassan* case. His hope soared. "Good morning. What can I do for you?"

"Hopefully, quite a bit." Wallace paused. "Is this a good time?"

If it was about the *Hassan* case, any time was good. "Sure."

"Good." Wallace cleared his throat. "As you know, attacks against DOE facilities have increased dramatically since 9-11, everything from espionage to cyberattacks to physical terror plots. DOE has always relied on Justice to prosecute the perpetrators. But now, after Abu Hassan's attempted attacks on the electric grid, DOE has decided to create a National Security Unit to prosecute the cases ourselves."

Carlton was crestfallen. This was not about the *Hassan* case. Still, it involved prosecuting terrorists. And he was far more interested in bringing them to justice than in preserving Justice Department fiefdoms.

"I'm glad to hear it," he replied sincerely. "It should free up DOJ resources and speed up prosecutions." And royally tee off his boss Edison, he did not mention, whose National Security Division at DOJ currently handled such cases. Keeping them in-house at DOE would decrease Edison's jurisdiction and authority. After caving to FBI pressure, reassigning the *Hassan* case away from Carlton, lying to him about it, then questioning his motives, Edison deserved it, yet Carlton found no pleasure in the notion. He wanted to put terrorists behind bars, not seek bureaucratic revenge against his own.

"That was our thinking also," said Wallace.

Maybe it was because the caffeine had not hit yet, but something did not make sense to Carlton. "But I'm at DOJ. I'm not sure how I can help."

Wallace paused. "We would like you to head DOE's new National Security Unit."

Carlton was stunned. It took him a few moments to recover. "I'm... flattered. I don't know what to say."

"You can say yes."

He was on the verge of doing just that, yet he had been at DOJ for a long time. Unlike other government agents who hopped from agency to agency in search of the slighest promotion or other advantage, Carlton's loyalty ran deep. This was not a decision he could take lightly. "What I mean is why me? Surely there are plenty-"

"-of DOE lawyers who want the job," continued Wallace, finishing Carlton's sentence. "Yes. But they are not seasoned prosecutors like you and we cannot afford on-the-job training. We need someone who will start prosecuting terrorists on day one. You will forgive me for saying so, but it's not exactly a secret that DOJ has failed to use your talents efficiently as of late. The *Hassan* case, for one. At DOE you would have full prosecutorial authority and an initial staff of five lawyers. If you feel strongly about some of your people at Justice, you could bring them along. I know that you are not in government service for the money, but the position is two pay grades above your current level."

"When do you need an answer?"

"Very soon, I'm afraid."

"How soon?"

"The end of today. I apologize for the urgency, but DOE heads are cranking up the heat to elevate someone in-house. I'm already taking enormous flak for even considering someone outside the agency."

Carlton was far too familiar with agency politics. The federal government was not a monolith as much as a group of fiefdoms, each intent on maintaining its power and amassing more, often with powerful staff mounting veritable internal insurgencies against the political appointees who were technically in charge. "I understand, but that doesn't give me much time."

"I realize that. And I sympathize," replied Wallace, lilting in apology. "If it were up to me, I would give you until the end of your vacation, but believe me when I tell you that it is beyond my control."

"Very well, Mr. Wallace."

"Brendan."

"Very well, Brendan. I'll let you know by the end of the day."

"Thank you. If you have any questions, please call me." Wallace read off his number.

Carlton hung up. He reclined in his seat, stunned and elated, drained his cup. Washington was a global power capital, yet also a tiny village. For once, he was pleased that its secrets did not remain secret long. *DOJ has not used your talents efficiently as of late.* Smooth. Although Wallace had the decency not to state it outright, it was clear he had learned not only of Edison reassigning the *Hassan* case away from Carlton, but likely of Carlton's falling out with his boss. Wallace had seen the opportunity, struck fast. When one door closes, another opens, he reflected.

The short time fuse on the job offer was not as unnerving as the choice he had to make. Carlton had only risen through the DOJ ranks after years in its prosecution trenches. He had great loyalty to DOJ, if not to Edison, and felt that moving to DOE would betray it. Was his falling out with Edison over the *Hassan* case a sufficient justification for leaving DOJ behind? He was not sure. Yet even before his row with with Edison, it was clear that he was not making any prosecutorial headway in DOJ's National Security Division. The fact that his career was not advancing in the NSD was far less important than the fact that he was not making a difference in NSD. And making a difference by putting the enemies of America in jail was why he had left lucrative private practice and joined DOJ in the first place. And loyalty was a two way street, he reflected. If DOJ was not being loyal to him by assigning him red meat cases in exchange for his financial sacrifice, why should he remain loyal to DOJ? After all, it was not as though he would be abandoning DOJ's prosecution ranks to defend criminals in private practice. He would be going from one prosecution outfit to another. And at DOE, he would head the prosecution unit. He would finally have the authority to prosecute terrorists that he never had at DOJ.

The hop up two pay grades was not a major motivating factor, as Wallace knew, but it certainly added points in the plus side of Carlton's decision ledger. It would allow him to make some repairs to his house, sock away a few more dollars towards retirement, maybe allow him to buy a vintage garage companion for his 'Shark'.

It only took a few minutes for Carlton to realize that the decision was in fact a no-brainer. Yet his grandfather had taught him long ago not to make critical decisions on the fly if given time to decide. He did not have much time, but he would use the time he had to think about it.

As the waitress refilled his cup, he decided to let his subconscious work on the problem by focusing on another. He speed-dialed Henri Monet.

"Hi Henri. Find anything yet?" Carlton pronounced the man's name in the French manner. *On-ree*. He imagined the incorrigible French-American chain-smoking illegally in his cramped office in the labyrinthine maze of tunnels that ran under Main Justice in Washington.

"How is *la Californie*?" Monet asked in a gravelly smoker's voice laced with a heavy French accent. *Ow ees*. "Not like this *bouillabaisse* we have here, I am sure," he said, referring to the French fish soup.

"Better than Club Med," Carlton replied, clicking his battered DOJ Zippo lighter open and shut out of habit.

"*Impossible*. I am jealous. And you should not work. You are on vacation," he reprimanded.

"It's not work. It's a personal matter." Carlton lowered his voice. "For an attractive blonde," he added, knowing Monet's incurable romanticism.

"Ah. That's different. Now I understand."

Henri Monet was one of the National Security Division's computer researchers. In Carlton's estimation, the best. Monet's vast computer skills caused DOJ to turn a blind eye to his long list of eccentricities beyond smoking in his office, hours spent on Facebook and Twitter, and refusal to use anything but Apple hardware. They included his daily breaches of office dress policy, his proclivity for lectures on French history and culture, and his insistence on six-week Club Med vacations and two-hour restaurant lunches with wine, all of which he considered essential parts of Gallic *savoir vivre*.

Monet often bent the rules to fit his purposes and was known to be uncooperative with those on his *liste noire* - his black list - regardless of their rank. Luckily, Carlton did not fall into that category. Monet was unswervingly loyal to him ever since Carlton had gone to bat for him with the DOJ aristocracy a few years ago, even moving with him to the National Security Division.

Although Monet had been born in the United States, many at Justice considered the French-American out of place because of his cultural chauvinism and heavy French accent, results of his education in France through high school. Carlton had even assigned him a ringtone on his cell phone: *La Marseillaise*, the French national anthem. Yet Monet's loyalty to the Stars and Stripes was unswerving. And despite his long vacations and lunches, Monet was an incorrigible workaholic, pulling so many all-nighters that he had installed a military cot in his basement office. Carlton's only beefs with him were Monet's predilection for speaking in riddles and his fetid Gitanes cigarettes. Not to mention his constant requests to perform undercover fieldwork, despite Carlton's repeated disclaimers of his lack of authority in the matter.

Carlton was becoming impatient. "So did you find anything?"

"I found something by not finding anything."

Carlton grimaced. Another trademark Monet riddle. "Which one is it?"

"I pulled the government files on Montgomery Grant, but there was no information."

"Strange."

"*Oui.* But not for the reason you think."

Carlton grunted. "Henri, you just said that you didn't find any information."

"But I did not tell you why."

Carlton sighed, forcing himself into patience, knowing that Monet always came through in the end. "Fine. I'll bite. Why not?"

"Because his files are black."

Carlton's frustration morphed into surprise. "What do you mean, black?"

"Blacked out. Redacted. Censored. All of them. One hundred twenty two pages of government files. Except for the words 'and' and 'the', nearly all the text has been blacked out."

Despite the summer heat, Carlton got goose bumps. He knew why Monet's search results had turned up black. Echeverria had told him: Grant's files were code-word classified. But why *all* of them?

Carlton thought of something. "What agencies did Grant's files come from?"

"One was DOD, which at the time was called the War Department. They had his information, although Grant was not listed as being in the service. The others were the FBI and the Federal Power Commission."

"The Federal Power Commission?" The name made him suspicious. "I've never heard of it."

"*Moi non plus.* Me neither. I looked into it. The FPC was formed in 1920 to regulate power throughout the U.S. It was reorganized and renamed the Federal Energy Regulatory Commission in 1977, the organization that allegedly allowed Enron to bilk *grandmères* out of their life savings. It's an adjunct of the Department of Energy. In fact, I got Grant's Power Commission file from the DOE database."

Carlton felt as though a ball of ice had formed in his gut.

DOE?

He did not believe in coincidences. A job offer on the heels of a major case reassignment and a falling out with his boss he could accept as natural in the Washington bureaucratic sandbox. But a job offer from DOE when he was investigating the handwritten deathbed note of a possible secret government courier who had a DOE file - a *blacked out* DOE file - was too implausible for mere coincidence. Particularly after such swift interest from the FBI and his bungalow's burglary. The two had to be linked. But how?

"Henri, can you look up a guy named Brendan Wallace at DOE? I'll wait."

"*Bien sur.*" Of course. Carlton heard tapping. "Brendan Wallace. Director of New Technology at DOE. Political appointee. Portfolio includes all alternative energy research. Has been in the position for two years. Before that he was a partner at the law firm of Farnsworth Tate in DC. Does not say what practice area."

"I would guess energy, technology or venture capital." Law firms and government were separated by no more than a revolving door, he knew from personal experience, although for Carlton it had been a one way trip. "Thanks, Henri. Please keep digging."

"*Oui.*"

The call from Wallace at DOE had appeared to come out of the blue sky. For all the heralded employment postings and resume submissions, Carlton knew that jobs in government were more often obtained through the same source as in law firms: personal contacts. But Carlton had never had any contact with Brendan Wallace or even DOE.

DOE must have known that he was investigating Grant's program. But how? Echeverria could have told Wallace, but as far as the FBI agent knew, Carlton was not investigating. Why DOE wanted him so urgently was as puzzling as how a Hollywood movie star with blacked out files was connected to an obscure part of the same agency 65 years ago.

Monet had said that Grant had not been in the service, but that he had a DOD file. That would give credence to what Alexis had reported from her father's diary, that Grant had been a covert military courier. The only link to DOE Carlton could think of in Grant's case was that the star's role as a wartime military courier might have involved something related to energy. Could Wallace also be looking into it? If so, why call Carlton with a job offer? DOE had an investigative arm. Why not have it ask him what he knew, just as Echeverria at the FBI had done? If Wallace wanted information, making Carlton a job offer seemed a strange and inefficient was of obtaining it.

He suddenly thought of something else. Could DOE have broken into his bungalow, stolen Grant's program, and now want Carlton to back off? Perhaps, but if so, why the job offer?

Carlton thought about turning the tables and asking Wallace directly. He decided against it. According to Echeverria, Grant's case was highly classified. If he was going to ask Wallace questions, he needed to know more. It was time to go outside regular channels.

He drained his second cup, dialed Alexis's cell phone.

"Yeah?" She barked.

"Good morning to you too," he replied, taken aback. "It's Carlton."

"Oh, hi," she whispered, quickly changing her tone. "I'm sorry. I can't talk. I'm on a tour."

"Just a quick question. Does your father's diary mention a link between Grant and anything involving energy?"

She paused. "Not off the top of my head, but I'll look as soon as my tour is over. Do you want to meet later?"

Carlton surprised himself by smiling at the prospect. "How about Musso and Frank at eight?" He proposed, referring to the oldest restaurant in Hollywood, a venue Alexis was sure to enjoy.

"I love Musso. I'll see you there."

9 WOLF

Lex (U.S. Registry yacht)
Chesapeake Bay, Maryland
12:33 PM

Grover Wolf grimaced behind his shipboard desk, balancing his weak chin between sweaty palms. As a senior partner at one of the oldest, most powerful law firms in the nation's capital, Wolf was used to stress. He thrived on it. What Wolf felt this afternoon was not stress, but the cold fist of anxiety gripping his psyche. As though his rope might snap while rock climbing up a sheer cliff.

He glanced at his watch, an outrageously expensive, oversize model that made the septuagenarian's bony, mottled wrist appear much older. His prized client would arrive any time now. How would he tell him?

Wolf walked to the port side window, gazed at the muddy brown water of the Chesapeake, felt his stomach churn. On another man, Wolf's slender physique, long nose, and straight white teeth might have imparted professional charm. Yet Wolf's personal demons had sucked the energy from his soul, morphed his physical appearance into a lawyer's version of Dorian Gray's portrait. His eyes had grown suspicious, his nose beaklike, his smile sickly. Together with his slight frame, gaunt face, balding cranium, perpetually hunched shoulders, and black suit, they made him look like a hungry undertaker.

After learning legal theory at Yale Law School, Wolf had been confronted with the harsh legal reality of modern private law practice at the 150 year old Washington law firm of Farnsworth Tate: solid legal work and long hours were insufficient for equity partnership and its attendant profits. To reach the law firm apex, Wolf had to obtain either a great many clients or a single Holy Grail client, a whale: one with countless legal matters and a bottomless pit of funds to pay legal fees.

A quick study, Wolf had soon set his sights on a client with all the right attributes. Powerful. Wealthy. In trouble.

The Kingdom of Saudi Arabia.

After years of careful plotting, brown-nosing, and creating problems out of thin air only to fix them as if by magic, Wolf had become indispensable to the Saudi ambassador.

The Saudi Kingdom did not exist in a vacuum. Wolf began to collect a vast retinue of clients who sought to curry favor and contracts with the oil-rich desert power, further solidifying Wolf's partnership.

In turn, Wolf had become indispensable to Farnsworth Tate. His greedy partners were so afraid to lose the Kingdom to crosstown rivals, so pleased at the massive influx of fees it generated, that they indulged his every whim. They agreed to his multimillion dollar annual base salary plus a large percentage of the Kingdom's fees. They leased the sleek 150-foot yacht *Lex* - Latin for law - with its state of the art equipment and lavish accommodations to entertain the Saudi ambassador and those seeking his favors. They opened a Brussels office to handle the emerging practice of European Union law, one of Wolf's pet practice areas. They even funded his obscure Special Transactions Team, which worked only on his matters.

Wolf had achieved his goal, but soon found that keeping a whale was more of a full time job than harpooning it in the first place.

What he soon had to tell the Saudi ambassador was a perfect example. The prince did not suffer bad news gladly. This news was worse than bad. And he would have to deliver it on the occasion of the prince's birthday, in honor of which he had hastily organized the afternoon cruise once he had learned of his return from France.

Wolf heard a distant thumping, glanced up at the pale blue sky. His stomach churned anew. The outline of a Dauphin Eurocopter came into view. He hurried back to his desk, popped a couple of antacid tablets - the fifth pair that day - then headed topside, nerves atwitter.

* * *

His Excellency Prince Quibli Abdulaziz ibn Yousef Hamad al Najd, Ambassador of the Kingdom of Saudi Arabia to the United States of America, peered at the gleaming white yacht floating placidly below.

He had enjoyed his Washington posting, but knew it would soon end. He had cast his lot with the fundamentalist hard-liners in his royal family, believing they were the most likely to advance his position. He had miscalculated.

Instead of continuing the failed appeasement of violent fundamentalists in exchange for promises of peace inside the Kingdom, King Fahim had changed course after the attacks on the Khobar Towers near the Saudi national oil company headquarters in 1996, more so after 9-11, and most dramatically after the popular 2011 'Arab Spring' uprisings in the Middle East and North Africa, whittling down their like-minded allies within the Saudi government, religious police, and diplomatic corps. Despite his high position in the royal family pecking order, Quibli's present ambassadorship and future leadership role in the Saudi government were precarious at best. Yet changing course and tossing in his lot with the reformists now would alienate him from both camps. Believing that the fundamentalists would win in the end, he had double-downed, allying himself with Interior Minister Prince Hakim through the intermediary of Sayyid Yassin, who Qhibli had originally met when the man was a banker, stashing revenues undeclared to the rest of the royal family for him in obscure accounts across the globe.

It was all political maneuvering, for Qhibli's Wahhabi religious fervor did not run deep. The main reason that he relished his job was its distance from the stifling moral restrictions in Saudi Arabia. Justifying his voracious appetite for the good life, Qhibli had officially adopted the Islamic concept of *al-taqiyya* - dissimulation - which allowed him to lie and disregard tenets of his faith in public to further the faith and the Kingdom's diplomatic interests. Diplomatic insiders referred to him as an 'airport Wahhabi': one who espoused the strict tenets of Wahhabism only when he arrived at Riyadh's King Khared International airport, casting them back off as soon as he was wheels-up.

He had been wise to double-down with Hakim, thought Qhibli. He would miss the dissolute life he led in America, but would gain far more. For he now knew that Hakim was about to strike.

Qhibli emerged from the helicopter shortly after the aircraft kissed the *Lex's* aft helipad. He smiled broadly despite the sweltering heat and humidity. Instead of traditional white *dishdasha* and black *bisht* robes and red and white checkered *khaffiyeh* headgear held by *agal* goat wool rings worn by the noble ranks of his countrymen, the chameleon diplomat wrapped his considerable girth in a dark gray Savile Row suit, a French cuffed white Charvet shirt that contrasted with his cocoa complexion and dyed black goatee, black handmade John Lobb lace-up shoes, and his trademark dark green Lanvin tie that matched the color of the Saudi flag. Although Qhibli enjoyed his own State Department Diplomatic Security Service protection detail - a privilege accorded to no other ambassador in Washington - today he had wisely dismissed his government minders.

It looked as though Wolf's thin frame would be blown overboard under the helicopter's rotor wash had he not been grasping one of the yacht's chrome railings tight in his bony hand. He extended the other to his client. "Welcome, excellency. Happy birthday."

The portly ambassador pulled him into a bear hug, making the disproportional pair resemble a weird version of Laurel and Hardy. Both felt the rumble of the *Lex*'s engines through their feet as the yacht immediately began its cruise up the Chesapeake, past its picturesque inlets.

"If I may have a minute of your time before you greet your guests, excellency," said Wolf, forcing himself to utter the words.

Qhibli nodded, followed his lawyer unsteadily to his office below deck, waited for him to close the door.

"You look as though you are about to deliver bad news, Wolf."

Wolf swallowed hard. He could not delay any longer.

"Someone discovered a document belonging to Montgomery Grant, believed to be from the night of his death. Not just anyone, but a Justice Department prosecutor on vacation. He appears very interested. As you know, I gave strict orders that anything discovered concerning Grant be sealed in secrecy. The investigation should have remained in-house at DOE, but somehow the FBI was alerted." Wolf did not mention that the man responsible for the task had lazily given the job of monitoring anything concerning Grant to a staffer, who had diligently informed the FBI.

Quibli arched his bushy eyebrows. "What have they discovered?"

"As of now, nothing."

"That might change."

"I have taken steps to ensure it will not, excellency."

Qhibli muttered something in Arabic. "You're my lawyer, Wolf. I pay you to fix problems, not to tell me about them." He pointed at Wolf menacingly with a thick finger. "Fix this before he discovers anything."

"I have the matter under control."

"You had better. Not just because of what is at stake, but because it might jeopardize another urgent matter we must dicuss." He got to his feet with a groan. "Be at the embassy tomorrow morning."

"What is it, excellency?" Asked Wolf, unable to hide his hungry curiosity. A summons to the embassy generally signified a lucrative assignment.

Qhibli fixed him with glowing black eyes. "Our future. Now I must greet my guests."

He led the way into the *Lex*'s main salon, grabbed a scotch on the rocks from a waiter, fired up a Cohiba Siglo IV *habano* cigar. After several minutes of small talk with a select contingent of Beltway insiders, including the Secretary of Energy and the chairmen and ranking members of the House and Senate Energy Committees, Qhibli's gaze fell on a tall woman. Like a child, she had large, long-lashed eyes and pouty bee-stung lips, yet her figure was all woman. The combination ignited a flash of lust in his blood. He turned to her.

"I am Prince Qhibli," he announced, smiling, kissing her hand, making her giggle as his goatee tickled her pale skin.

"Good evening, your highness," she replied, bowing deferentially.

She wore a pink Chanel suit, a white silk blouse opened far enough to reveal an ample clue of what it concealed, and pink Louboutin high heel shoes. The Cartier Baignoire diamond watch on her slender wrist, river of diamonds around her graceful neck, and sapphire and ruby ring on her finger would have turned each of Prince Qhibli's eleven wives green with envy. Wolf had outdone himself, he reflected.

"What is your name, child?"

"Violet, your highness," she replied, playfully biting the tip of a long French-manicured nail.

"And more beautiful than the flower. I would consider it an honor if you would be my guest at dinner."

She beamed, turning to hide her blushing face. "Thank you, your highness."

Prince Qhibli made short shrift of the other guests to focus all of his attention on Violet. He found her knowledge severely limited, which made him feel even more clever than usual. Yet he knew that everyone was good at something. He was determined to discover what secret talents Violet possessed - other than feeding him from her fingertips. After a painfully long banquet, Qhibli thanked his host and guests, then excused himself amid their postprandial libations. He could not wait any longer.

Violet followed him as he squeezed his portly frame through the polished wood doors of his ornate private stateroom below deck. He collapsed on a leather armchair that creaked in protest, wiped the sweat from his forehead with a silk handkerchief.

Violet closed the door, locked it. Qhibli's heart pumped wildly as she slipped an iPod from her Louis Vuitton purse, placed it on a dock, and removed her pink top. Her breasts strained hard against her thin silk blouse as she gyrated to the music. She kept the heels on and uncovered her long, shapely legs that ended in a bulbous backside. Violet slowly unbuttoned her blouse, leaned toward Qhibli, jutting her breasts a hair's distance from his face as she continued writhing to the music.

She reached into the refrigerator and poured the chilled contents from a bottle of Bollinger RD Champagne over her chest, causing her nipples to stand erect as the effervescent golden liquid traveled down into Qhibli's hungry mouth below. She ran her long fingers over her flat stomach and played with her diamond stud belly button ring. Every so often, she purred in his ear, then taunted each of his nerve endings with a lascivious smile or wink. Qhibli felt his blood throb as Violet finally removed her nearly invisible G-string.

Her striptease was the first in a series of birthday pleasures that Quibli could handle for only a half hour before passing out on the oversize bed, spent and snoring.

Much later, when all the guests save the escorts had departed, Violet got up from her feigned sleep and tiptoed into the gilded private bathroom. She studied herself in the mirror and shuddered. The things she did for Poland never ceased to amaze her, forcing her to assume so many aliases and personalities that she sometimes forgot where they ended and she began. The only time she truly knew was with her boyfriend. Thank goodness she had never told him what she really did at the embassy - and had kept everyone at the *Agencja* out of the loop about their relationship. Yet she was fervent in her cause.

Stripped of its independence by the Austro-Hungarian empire for a century until the end of World War I in 1918, invaded and partitioned by *both* the Nazis and Soviets at the inception of World War II, slaughtered and turned to rubble, then lorded over by the Soviets until 1990, Poland had 150 years of absence from the world stage to make up.

Zuza dressed quickly, suppressing her sadness at having to return her designer clothes and jewelry - all on loan from her contacts in the French luxury world. She decided to keep the gaudy diamond and emerald encrusted Piaget watch that Prince Qhibli had given her from his wrist, jokingly nicknaming it her new 'Sheiko'.

Hurrying to complete the last phase of her assignment before a launch returned her and her fellow escorts to shore, Zuza removed a small plastic pillbox from her purse, dumped a dozen miniature devices resembling flies onto the counter, then blew them into the air. The microflies immediately registered motion and engaged their tiny gossamer wings, sending them buzzing erratically, following a computer-generated random pattern. As soon as Zuza opened the bathroom door, the microflies swarmed toward the drunken mass of Prince Qhibli's snoring body, then took up positions in various parts of the stateroom.

Minutes later, Zuza stood on the prow of the launch in the muggy night air of the Chesapeake Bay, reflecting on the devices she had just activated. An agent of the *Direction Générale de la Sécurité Exterieure* (DGSE), the French foreign intelligence directorate, had stolen the experimental devices from their inventor and developer, the American Defense Advanced Research Projects Agency (DARPA). A Colonel Hulot, if she recalled correctly. Zuza could only imagine Hulot's surprise when he had discovered that the *Agencja* had stolen the technology right from under his upturned nose. If the enemy of an enemy is a friend, then one who steals from a thief is not a thief, she legitimated.

The microscopic devices that she had hidden in Prince Qhibli's food and fed to him had adhered to his esophagus. Homing in on their signal, the microflies would follow the ambassador everywhere, continuously recording, encrypting, then transmitting to a receiver in the Polish embassy. Their batteries' lifetime was four days.

Long enough for their transmissions to shake Washington to its foundations.

10 SALE

Thick plaster walls insulated Alexis from the summer sun pounding the exterior of her Hollywood Hills home.

In addition to a lifetime of old Hollywood anecdotes and a classic automobile, Alexis's late father had bequeathed her the 1926 John DeLario Spanish Colonial Revival architectural masterpiece. The two-story white plaster and red tile roof house sat on a choice promontory in the hills above Beachwood Canyon, its twin turrets offering a spectacular view of Los Angeles stretched out like an ocean for miles below. The iconic 'Hollywood' sign stood proudly on Mount Lee less than a mile away, its original suffix 'land' having crumbled long ago and never replaced. Alexis had lived in what she considered her hilltop castle since childhood, in the same placid neighborhood that Humphrey Bogart, Bela Lugosi, and Doris Day had once also called home.

Yet the coolness of the heavy wood ceiling beams, forged iron hand railings, and glazed terracotta floors gave Alexis little respite. At Carlton's request, she had searched for a link between Montgomery Grant and energy since returning from her early morning tour. Without avail.

She looked up from the stacks of open books on the carved wood table, exhaled loudly amid the background melody of Glenn Miller's *American Patrol*.

I need a break.

She walked down her front steps to narrow Rockcliff Road. The winding street was still. All her neighbors were away at work. The unrelenting sun had diluted the sky into a pale cloudless blue, blanketing the hillside in silent lethargy. Not even the many birds that inhabited the hills made a sound, as though they too were avoiding the midday heat with a *siesta*. She proceeded down the steep slope, inhaling the inebriating scents of dry earth and native scrub brush.

Initially reflecting on her fruitless research, Alexis soon found her thoughts straying to Carlton. She was still amazed not only by how he had risked his life to rescue the boy, but by how he had not considered it heroic, believing that anyone else would have done the same. *Not in this town.*

Unlike most men she met, Carlton did not talk incessantly about himself. In fact, he had revealed little, confident enough to laugh at himself and listen to her instead. He was older, mature, unlike her flaky former boyfriend and the LA *poseurs* with only one thing in mind. He even shared her passion for old Hollywood. Most of the men she encountered lived only for the present and had little appreciation for the past. Carlton was not quite handsome in the LA sense, but attractive in a serious, wise, experienced kind of way. Her father had taught her the word for it in Latin: *gravitas.*

Yet she sensed something else in him. An intensity in his gaze, a confidence in his manner, a hunger that set him apart from other men. Not simply because he was probably ten to fifteen years her senior. It was something else, intriguing enough for her to notice that he did not wear a wedding band, although these days, many married men had roving eyes and did not wear one. Or worse - removed them.

Despite his attributes, Carlton had one major flaw: he was a federal prosecutor. Not that she had broken any laws. She simply did not trust federal government types, for a good reason.

Before realizing it, Alexis reached the intersection of Ledgewood Drive. She turned on her heel and began the arduous hike back up to her house. As she rounded a corner, a white Chevy Suburban SUV rushed down the narrow street at breakneck speed, heading directly for her.

Without time or room to run, she pressed her body flat against a high stone wall, screwed her eyes shut, held her breath. She felt a rush of air as the behemoth roared past her without so much as braking, then a hard slap as its sideview mirror hit her right arm.

"Watch where you're going!" she shouted, startled, breathless. She blinked away spots in her vision, caught her breath, massaged her forearm. The SUV's mirror would have broken it had the device not folded under the impact. Close calls were common among the curved canyon roads, but it was no excuse for driving like a madman and not stopping to apologize. Where were those prosecutors when you needed them?

Alexis continued home, bleeding off her anger with quick steps up the steep hill. Back inside, she hummed to Glenn Miller's *String of Pearls*, cut a lemon into small slices before resuming her research into Grant's possible connection with energy. As she sat at her desk, she noticed that her biography of Grant was open and that her pen had fallen to the tile floor. She stared at it before picking it up. She always lodged her pens in her books before closing them to keep her place. How could the book be open and the pen be resting on the floor? She had not felt an earthquake.

Alexis was still thinking about it when her 1940s vintage telephone rang, raising more suspicion. She mostly used her cell phone. Almost no one called her on her unlisted land line. She thought it might be Carlton, but remembered that she had not given him her home number.

She shrugged off the thought and answered.

* * *

Carlton sat at a booth in Zeke's Smokehouse, his favorite LA barbeque joint next to the 1930s-era Formosa Café, enjoying the smoky aroma. One could hardly go wrong with a waiter nicknamed Elvis who wore bowling shirts and a long beard half-dyed purple, he mused.

He began digging into his plate of mouth-watering Memphis ribs when his cell phone rang. He wiped his sticky hands, answered.

"You're not going to believe this, but some guy just offered me five hundred bucks just for a copy of the program," Alexis delivered in rapid fire.

Carlton froze. The FBI had a copy of the program. Whoever had broken into his bungalow had the original, possibly DOE. Now someone else wanted a copy. "Who?"

"His name is Jaime Drake." Alexis outlined her telephone conversation.

"You didn't agree to sell it to him, did you?"

"Of course I did."

"Are you out of your mind?" Carlton shot back. "Do you realize how-"

"Don't shout at me," she snapped. "He knew I had the program, Carlton. What was I supposed to tell him? I'd rather sell the copy than have it stolen by burglars."

Carlton took a deep breath. Grant was dead, but his movie premiere program seemed to have brought the Hollywood star back to life. How did this Drake even know that she had a copy of the program? Carlton was the one whose name had been in the paper, not Alexis. He had given her a copy only last night and Alexis told him that she had not informed anyone.

Alexis's interest in the program lay in its mystery, Carlton knew. A mystery steeped in the past glory of old Hollywood that enabled her to commune with her late father and the star who had given him his first big break. Carlton understood its romantic appeal, but sensed danger behind the mystery. He knew the wickedness of which the human psyche was capable. And he knew that evil was present, even if she did not.

"I'd like to sell him the program personally," he proposed calmly. "Alone."

"I'm perfectly capable of selling it to him myself," Alexis fired back indignantly. "I'm not a child."

Carlton bit his lip. *Good going, Carlton.*

"That's not what I meant. This does not pass the smell test, Alexis. The less involved you are in this, the better."

"Too late. I'm already involved. Whoever Drake is, he already knows that I have a copy of the program. What makes you so special?"

"I'm a Justice Department prosecutor, Alexis. It's my job. Trust me."

Silence.

"Alexis?"

"I heard you."

"Please trust me, Alexis." Why was she refusing? She was the one who had called him, after all.

"I want to."

"I promise that I'll give you the money."

"It's not about the money," she replied angrily.

Great, Carlton. You managed to insult her twice in a single conversation. He kept quiet, waiting for her response.

Finally, she took a deep breath. "I'll let you do it, but only if I come with you."

Carlton did not have much of a choice. "Fine. Where and when are you meeting him?"

"Two. At my office. I left the program there." She gave him the address.

Carlton barely had time to return to his bungalow. He still had no idea what Grant had been carrying on the night of his murder, if anything, but there were far too many coincidences for comfort. The twin links to DOE chief among them. And he could not shake feeling naked in LA, outside his official government turf. He opened his gun case, strapped on his Galco leather shoulder holster, verified that a round was chambered in his Glock 23 handgun.

As he drove McLean's vintage Caddy East on Sunset Boulevard toward Hollywood, Carlton called Monet using the mandatory LA bluetooth screwed into his ear, asked him to dig up information on Jaime Drake. When he hung up, he realized that his itinerary was likely the same one Grant had followed on the night of his death. It made him shiver, as though Grant's ghost was sitting beside him.

Help me out, Monty.

Carlton calmed himself by imagining the way the Sunset Strip would have looked 65 years ago, when Grant had taken his fateful drive down the fabled boulevard. The old Hollywood haunts had succumbed to the inexorable redevelopment that defined LA's ever-changing face. Yet the Strip remained as vibrant as ever. He gazed at the cars, hillside homes, outdoor restaurants, fashions, and attitudes, always amazed by how glaring ostentation passed for style in the City of Angels. It was a far cry from DC, where influence was the coveted luxury. Observing the LA Westside, he thought, one would never know the country was suffering through the worst economic crisis since the Great Depression.

Blessed with uncanny parking karma, Carlton found a spot for the Caddy in front of the refurbished Art Déco Hollywood First National Building, noticed the car was leaking oil. He would have to tell McLean about that.

As he walked to the lobby, he came across a man curled up on the sidewalk in the beating sun. He had a filthy beard and wore a tattered olive green Army jacket. A cardboard sign next to a plate read '*Homeless and hungry. I protected your freedom. Please help me.*'

The sight of a homeless vet in a city where homes sold for multiple millions in an economic crisis wrenched his gut. He didn't have a dollar bill, so he put in a five instead, muttered a silent prayer, forcing away painful images of Iraq.

Alexis's Old Hollywood Tours office was on the sixth floor behind a blond wood door marked with the company's logo in the shape of the Hollywood sign. The small office was clean, neat, and simple, emanating a smell of old documents that reminded him of Grant's premiere program. Its walls were decorated with posters of Hollywood classics, including his favorite, *Casablanca*. A well-watered ficus had a prime view out of a large window. A receptionist unsuccessfully attempting to mask her age with makeup sat at the front counter.

"Good afternoon. My name is Patrick Carlton. I'm here to meet Alexis Hamilton."

She appraised Carlton from head to toe and gave him a flirty smile. "Well hi there, *shugah*. Her car broke down. I keep telling her to get a new one, maybe one of those nifty new hybrids, but she insists on driving her late daddy's dinosaur. She's at the mechanic, asked me to give you this," she said, sliding the copy of the movie premiere across the counter.

"Thanks." Carlton stared at the copy of Grant's movie program. "What have you started?" He mumbled.

"What's that, *shugah*?"

Carlton looked up at her. "I was wondering if you had an envelope."

The receptionist was happy to oblige. He placed the single page in the proffered envelope, sealed it, then sat in a gray cloth chair in the little lobby, waited for Jaime Drake.

He did not have to wait long. At precisely 2:00PM, a man dressed in a navy suit and shiny matching silk tie walked into the office. He flashed a toothy smile as genuine as a game show host's and approached the receptionist with long strides.

"Jaime Drake. I have an appointment with Miss Hamilton."

"That gentleman right there will help you, *shugah*," the receptionist replied, pointing to Carlton.

Carlton thought that Drake looked familiar, a feeling that grew when he noticed the look of surprise in the man's eyes - feral eyes that appeared to have witnessed much pain, Carlton knew from his experience in the Middle East. Probably much of it inflicted by the man himself, he presumed. Perhaps Drake recognized him from the photograph in the paper. His powerful build and nervous agitation radiated trapped energy straining for a way out. Carlton felt Drake appraise him, as if searching for weakness before pouncing. Noticing a familiar bulge under his jacket, he was glad that he had brought along his Glock. He stood, turning slightly to give Drake a glimpse of the holster under his own jacket.

"Alexis Hamilton asked me to give you this envelope," he said, waving it. "She said I was supposed to get five hundred dollars from you."

"That's right." Drake paused, still staring at Carlton with undisguised interest before flashing his sharklike smile. He pulled out a black leather billfold, counted out ten fifty-dollar bills, handed them to Carlton.

Carlton's religious beliefs did not prevent him from feeling a superstitious sense of dread. His grandfather had loved to play the ponies and once told Carlton that racehorse tracks never gave fifty-dollar bills to gamblers because they were considered cursed. He shrugged off the bad omen and accepted the bills, handed Drake the envelope.

Drake tore it open, removed the page inside, scanned it carefully, unable to disguise his interest in the handwritten address in the upper corner. Carlton mentally kicked himself for not whiting out the address and recopying the program before Drake arrived.

"Great," said Drake, smiling once more, this time sincerely. He darted from the office without another word.

"Have a nice day, *shugah*," said the receptionist.

This guy was anything but *shugah*, thought Carlton. More like acid.

He cracked the door open. Once Drake stepped into the elevator, Carlton ran to the stairwell. The clang of his boots on the metal stairs reverberated through the old stairwell as he rushed down the six stories to the lobby. He watched Drake exit the elevator, walk through the ornate carved wood lobby, exit through its polished brass framed glass doors.

Carlton walked onto the sidewalk and spotted Drake getting into a white Chevy Suburban. He commited its license plate to memory as it sped away.

Who was he and why was he so interested in the program?

There was only one way to find out. He screwed in his bluetooth, hit the speed dial on his cell phone as he peeled out of his parking spot, leaving behind a large puddle of oil.

"Henri. I need you to run a California license plate for me." He recited its numbers and letters. "I'll wait."

"While I check, I looked into Drake. Almost all of the Jaime Drakes alive in the U.S. are women. Only three are men."

"Aces. Give 'em to me."

"One is a retired welder in Laramie, Wyoming. The second is a farmer in Merced, California. The third is a ten year-old in Atumwa, Iowa."

Unless the welder or farmer was a rabid Montgomery Grant fan who kept up with local LA news or the ten year old was a child prodigy on growth hormones, the man to whom Carlton had just sold a copy of Grant's program was not Jaime Drake.

Whoever Drake was, Carlton knew that he was hiding far more than his identity.

Carlton remained on the line, swerving around cars to keep up with Drake's SUV heading North on Vine past Hollywood & Highland's Renaissance Hotel.

"OK. The license plate. White Chevrolet Suburban?"

"That's it."

"It's registered to a California limited liability company." He provided the name.

"Doesn't ring a bell," Carlton responded, disappointed. Membership interests in an LLC could be owned by other entities, themselves owned by others, on and on, obscuring who held the reins.

"Let me try something," said Monet. Carlton heard tapping. "There are several corporate buffers," he continued a minute later, "but if you go upstream far enough, the LLC is owned by Farnsworth Tate LLP. *Eh*, isn't that the DOE official's former law firm?"

"Sure is. Thanks Henri." The ball of ice rematerialized in Carlton's gut. It looked as though his DOE job offeror Brendan Wallace had bought a copy of Grant's premiere through his old law firm. Why not have DOE do it? Stranger and stranger. He did not want to make the next call, but his gut told him to.

Special Agent Echeverria answered on the first ring as Carlton swerved around a bus to continue following Drake's monster SUV.

"I take it you remembered something, Mr. Carlton?"

"Someone broke into my bungalow last night and stole the original movie premiere." He gave him the details. "No traces of entry or how they got in or out. Now I need some information."

Echeverria sighed. "I appreciate your informing me of the theft, but I still cannot tell you about the case."

"I'm not calling for information about the case. It's more along the lines of career advice." Given Echeverria's explicit directive, he was not about to inform the FBI agent that he had sold Drake a copy of Grant's program. He slowed as Drake's SUV stopped at a red light.

"I beg your pardon?"

"I received a job offer this morning. Out of the blue. From the Department of Energy. A man named Brendan Wallace. I have never worked with anyone at DOE and the offer came shortly after our meeting. I thought there might be a connection."

"Why would there be a connection between a movie premiere program and the Department of Energy?"

"You tell me."

Silence.

Carlton thought his call had been dropped - a frequent occurrence in LA. "Hello?"

"I'm in no position to offer you career advice, Mr. Carlton. But I would be very careful."

"Careful? Why?"

"I'm afraid there is nothing more I can tell you."

"Thanks anyway."

He hung up, keeping his eyes on the white SUV heading North on Cahuenga, past the Hollywood Bowl complex on the left, staying close behind it while leaving a few cars between them as buffer. The Caddy was nothing if not conspicuous.

So there was a connection, he concluded. Echeverria could have said that he had never heard of Brendan Wallace or that he had no idea of any connection between the case and DOE. Instead, he had urged extreme caution - not exactly a comment that comes to mind with a job hop between agencies. The agent's response made it clear he knew who Wallace was. Echeverria was telling him something without saying anything. Just as he had when mentioning the code-word classification of the Grant case. But careful of what?

Carlton's initial suspicion had been that Wallace's job offer came at too perfect a time for mere coincidence. Then that Wallace was connected to the Grant case through DOE. His calls to Monet and Echeverria made Carlton's theory evolve a step further. *Time to test it.* He glanced at the dashboard clock. It was past 5:00PM in Washington.

He dialed the stored number that Brendan Wallace had used while maintaining his focus on the speeding SUV up ahead.

"Mr. Wallace. Patrick Carlton."

"Good afternoon. Great to hear from you."

"I've done some thinking," Carlton announced, laying the groundwork. "I'm inclined to accept your offer."

"I am thrilled to hear it." Wallace sounded more relieved than pleased.

"I will be available to begin at DOE in two weeks, after my vacation."

A long pause followed. "As I mentioned, Mr. Carlton, we need you urgently, right away. I'm afraid that two weeks is too long." Wallace's words came quickly, his voice tinged with alarm.

"Actually, that is not what you said. What you said was that because of political issues at DOE, I had to *decide* right away. Now that I have accepted, you can announce it to those clamoring for the job at DOE and put the matter to rest."

Another pause. If not for the loud Caddy engine and the speeding traffic along the busy highway, Carlton was convinced that he could have heard the gears grinding in Wallace's mind. It validated his theory more than anything else Wallace could have said.

"I apologize, Mr. Carlton. I must have misspoken. What I meant was that you were *needed* right away."

It was Carlton's turn to pause before floating his theory directly. "If I did not know better, I would say that you are trying to make me leave LA."

"LA? I didn't even know that you were in LA. Only that you were on vacation. Our intent is not to destroy your vacation, I assure you. But DOE does need someone of your caliber and experience right away," Wallace responded.

The words came too quickly, the man was trying too hard. Carlton decided to prod further. "About that. Surely you could find someone else with more experience than I, perhaps at your former firm of Farnsworth Tate?" He jabbed, watching the SUV owned by Wallace's ex-law firm speeding up ahead, pressing down on the accelerator to keep up.

Wallace's pause was again too long. "I don't see what Farnsworth Tate has to do with this, but you're the one we want. Think of the opportunity to have full prosecutorial authority, authority that Edison has denied you so unfairly for so long."

"I must say it is hugely attractive, but I fail to see how a two week delay would change anything. The *Hassan* case is already out of your new unit's hands at the Houston's U.S. Attorney's Office and I have not heard of any recently uncovered planned or attempted attacks on DOE facilities that would require immediate prosecution." As the number two person in DOJ's National Security Division, Carlton received daily reports on such matters and Wallace would know it.

"As I explained, it's not about handling cases immediately, but quenching the political firestorm over hiring someone from outside the agency."

"And as I said, announcing the hire would quench those flames whether I'm in DC or LA." Wallace was now going around in circles, out of ammunition. Satisfied that his theory about Wallace wanting him out of LA held water, he changed tack. "As you probably know, I rarely take vacations. I am especially enjoying this one. I found a great piece of Hollywood memorabilia yesterday and I have tickets to a Montgomery Grant retrospective that begins tonight."

Another pause, this one menacing.

"My offer is real. You would be well advised to accept it and stop your investigation." Wallace announced, all amity and pretension gone.

"That's what the FBI told me."

"Wise advice."

"Then I must decline. But I do have one more question: why did DOE black out Montgomery Grant's files?"

"You have no idea who or what you are dealing with."

"I intend to find out."

He hung up just as Drake's SUV turned onto the on ramp of the 101 freeway, speeding East. Wallace had basically confirmed that he was linked to Grant's case. But it did not answer the question about Drake's identity or how he was involved.

Carlton merged onto the freeway, gave the Caddy more gas, and followed, determined to find out.

11 EMBASSY

Embassy of the Kingdom of Saudi Arabia
Washington, D.C.
5:23 PM

Wolf's chauffeur-driven Rolls Royce Phantom pulled up to the Saudi embassy's main gate. Quibli's male assistant had rescheduled their meeting from the morning, explaining that the ambassador was indisposed. Wolf knew why. Between the booze and the escort, he was amazed that Qhibli would make the meeting at all.

The imposing white embassy complex's location between the Watergate Hotel and the John F. Kennedy Center for the Performing Arts was fitting. The people inside represented a Kingdom as corrupt as the incident for which Watergate was most famous and deceived the American public as convincingly as the actors on the capital's most illustrious stage.

Wolf slid down his window. He had visited the embassy so many times that he recognized the guards, but they always acted as though they had never seen him.

"Name, identification, and purpose of meeting." A statement, not a question.

He answered, handing his ID through the open window, infuriated.

The guard checked his list, nodded to his colleague who raised the gate arm. The Phantom purred up the main entrance.

Wolf's fury quickly abated. He generally looked forward to an invitation to the embassy, particularly when new business was to be discussed. Today, Prince Qhibli's urgent summons filled him with anxiety. He had yet more bad news to deliver to his prized client.

Contrary to the nauseating gaudiness with which many wealthy Saudis were not unfairly criticized, the Saudi embassy's public areas were simple and understated. Qhibli's assistant ushered Wolf past the lobby and reception hall into a private elevator, then directly up to the ambassador's office on the top floor.

"Welcome, Wolf," exclaimed the prince, immaculate in another Savile Row suit, this one as dark as his coal-black eyes. He hoisted his portly frame partly up from behind a gilded Louis XVI desk, encased his guest's bony hand in a meaty grip while waving off an errant fly with the other. His leonine head betrayed no trace of a hangover. Excedrin, Wolf surmised. Or something less legal. The gaunt lawyer wrinkled his nose. The office reeked of his client's trademark Cohiba *habanos*.

Considerably more ornate that the embassy's public areas, Quibli's lair boasted walls of dark green marble, a molded white ceiling, and a gilded chandelier of Austrian crystal that bathed the large office in bright white light. A mandatory DC 'power wall' was adorned with countless photographs of Qhibli with current and past U.S. presidents and key members of Congress, foreign heads of state, energy secretaries, oil industry heavy-hitters, Saudi King Fahim. Qhibli's eleven wives and thirty children adorned an adjacent wall, above an elaborate prayer rug positioned so the ambassador could face Mecca in prayer. Wolf had never seen him use it, doubted that he ever did.

"Please sit," urged Qhibli, gesturing to two matching red velvet chairs across from his desk. "May I offer you some coffee and pastries?" He inquired, obeying the Islamic and Arab dictate of warm hospitality. "It's the least I can do after the wonderful birthday celebration you gave me last night. I'm still recovering," he added, winking.

"I'm glad you enjoyed it," replied Wolf, sitting uncomfortably. His stomach was churning, yet he knew better than to refuse the ambassador's hospitality. For a second, he thought about asking for Rolaids or Tums. "Coffee would be wonderful, thank you, excellency."

Qhibli punched the intercom button, placed the order. He offered his guest an open box of Cohiba Siglo IV *habanos*, which Wolf politely declined as his stomach somersaulted. He detested the things.

Wolf suppressed his rising nausea as the ambassador clipped one of the fat cigars, lit it with a long cedar match.

"Where are we with the Grant matter?" Demanded Qhibli, blowing a pillar of smoke toward the glittering chandelier, all diplomatic smiles gone from his jowled face.

Wolf fidgeted. "Unfortunately, we still have not been able to obtain a copy of Grant's document, excellency. The FBI refuses to give it to

DOE, citing the classified nature of the case. And it appears that the Justice Department prosecutor - Carlton - has teamed up with a female Hollywood tour guide."

Qhibli snorted and stared at him, as if trying to decide if this was for real.

"They have not discovered anything."

"Yet." The pause and frown that followed sent Wolf's blood pressure soaring. "You said that you had the matter under control, Wolf."

Wolf clenched his teeth, averted his client's accusatory gaze. "I thought I had."

Quibli puffed hard on his cigar, making its tip glow bright. "The lawyer must be guiding that partnership. I'm sure our many friends in the government would not mind steering him clear of the program."

"The FBI ordered him to cease investigating, but he ignored it."

"An order from higher up, then."

Wolf shook his head. "Forgive me, excellency, but that approach won't work with Carlton. I had my people look into him. He's in the National Security Division. Served two years in Iraq as a Navy Reserve lieutenant commander. Purple Heart for injuries in battle. Obeys in the battlefield but acts like a cowboy at Justice, right down to the boots he wears. Carlton does not take 'no' for an answer, not without a good explanation at least. He almost got fired for confronting his boss and now disobeyed a direct FBI order not to investigate."

"How much can a Justice Department lawyer make?" Asked Qhibli, careful not to use the word 'bribe' even in the privacy of his office despite its twice daily electronic sweeps.

Wolf shook his head again. He was not getting through. "Carlton is more interested in prosecuting than in a fat salary. He jumped ship from a lucrative law firm to prosecute at Justice for a fraction of the salary. He may be a cowboy with superiors but he's as straight an arrow as they come. Apparently he even reimburses DOJ for personal photocopies and postage. He won't smoke Cuban cigars because they are illegal to purchase." Wolf caught himself, quickly adding: "in the United States, that is." He paused. "Offering Carlton a bribe would be like pouring gasoline on a fire, excellency." Unlike his client, Wolf knew there still existed people like Carlton who could not be bought. They frustrated

Wolf to no end, particularly because he was not one of them. He knew that he had sold out to the devil long ago.

Qhibli grew frustrated, shifting in his seat, the tip of his cigar burning an angry red. "A job, then. A legitimate government job."

"Wallace offered him a dream prosecution job at DOE. I just spoke to him. Carlton turned it down," replied Wolf, without detailing that Wallace had managed to stoke Carlton's suspicions in the process. Just like the monitoring of any new evidence on Grant, Wolf should have known better than to leave the matter to that lazy former partner of his, but it was too late. The opportunity had been missed, the damage done.

"You will recall what he did to the diamond monopoly a few years ago after being ordered not to investigate," Wolf added to drive his point home.

Prince Qhibli's eyebrows arched high. "That was him?"

Wolf nodded.

Qhibli's eyes bored into Wolf's brain. He pointed at him with an index finger as thick as the cigar clenched between his perfectly straight teeth. "Then you must solve this problem."

"Wallace will shut down the FBI's investigation. We will have a copy of Grant's premiere program soon. And we will follow Carlton and the woman. If they find something before we do, we'll know it."

"You are not hearing me, Wolf. You must *solve* the *problem.*" Qhibli paused, blowing a plume of smoke across his table at Wolf, enveloping the lawyer's sunken face, causing him to turn green. "Finding Grant's papers ourselves has become a secondary priority."

Wolf was astounded. The papers had been Quibli's main preoccupation and top priority since he had divulged their existence to Wolf years ago. For good reason.

"As I hinted yesterday, I just received instructions from Riyadh. There is a major new transaction in the works. More important than anything attempted in the past. If anyone discovers the papers, especially a cowboy federal prosecutor who does not bend to pressure, it would devastate Riyadh's plans. Preventing that from happening is now the top priority. Carlton's snooping is a dire problem. You must bring that problem to a final solution."

The last two words, shrouded in the ghastly horrors of history, finally made Wolf understand what Qhibli was demanding. He winced, his heart racing.

Like the world of every lawyer, Wolf's was composed of paper. With his morals long ago dissolved by greed and social climbing, Wolf had no qualms about diplomatic backstabbing, unethical practices or even illegal acts. He charged handsomely for them. Wolf was willing to do wrong, but only up to a point. Qhibli was not asking him to commit his usual white-collar crimes, but murder. That was a line even Wolf dared not cross.

"Is that not, ah, extreme, excellency?" Wolf asked as diplomatically as he could, feeling sweat plaster his shirt to his back.

"So are your legal fees," Qhibli shot back, waving away the annoying fly. "All I am asking is for you to provide legal services. Isn't that what your Special Transactions Team is for?"

"Legal services?" Wolf repeated, not knowing what else to say. Qhibli was not instructing him to backdate contracts. He was ordering him to murder two innocent people. His head swam. Was the ambassador being sarcastic or had Wolf failed to notice that his client was a psychopath?

"Legal services of a...specialized nature, shall we say," Qhibli amended, carefully severing the white gray ash of his Cuban cigar in a crystal ashtray the size of a small pond.

What had sprouted as anxiety blossomed into outright terror. Wolf was close to hyperventilation. He stared at Qhibli, his vision blurry, his throat parched and speechless while his mind scrambled to find a way to refuse.

"I did not ask you to come to discuss Carlton and the woman, Wolf," Qhibli continued, "but rather Riyadh's plans."

Wolf shifted in his seat, relieved by the change of topic. His breathing slowed.

"The Interior Minister, Prince Hakim, has tasked me with making a proposal to the European Union and Euroil," he announced, referring to the European energy giant. "The proposal is highly confidential and extremely urgent. But ever since the Abu Hassan incident, the State Department has been following me and my entire embassy staff very carefully, maybe even on your yacht last night. I cannot take the risk of delivering the proposal to the Europeans myself. That is why I returned from France."

Qhibli examined the tip of his cigar before looking back up at Wolf. "I want you to do it."

Wolf was stunned. Never before had Qhibli asked him to perform legal work for the Saudi Kingdom outside the United States.

"You acted with great foresight by forcing Farnsworth Tate to open an office in Brussels. Prince Hakim's plan will provide enormous benefits to that office, and therefore to you. You will of course have *carte blanche* in making any expenditures you deem fit to ensure that the E.U. and Euroil accept his proposal. If you can get them to agree to Prince Hakim's terms, you will receive a substantial bonus." He scribbled a number on a piece of paper and held it up so Wolf could see its many zeros. The sum was staggering.

Wolf's greed erupted, eclipsing his fear.

"Since Wallace will close the FBI investigation into Grant's program, Carlton and the girl are the only impediments to Prince Hakim's proposal. I hope that you will solve those impediments. If you fail, I will have no choice but to seek outside counsel with greater powers of persuasion."

Another jolt of terror coursed through Wolf's body. He had known it but until now never quite realized it: in making himself indispensable to the Saudi ambassador, Wolf had made the Saudi ambassador indispensable to his career.

Like the mafia godfathers of the *cosa nostra*, the desert *don* sitting before him would not ask a second time if Wolf refused his first request. Wolf would lose his most important client. All of his other clients put together did not amount to the legal fees that the Saudi Kingdom generated. And the overwhelming majority of those were his clients only because of his access to the Kingdom.

He would never be able to replace the Kingdom with a client who would generate as many fees, especially in the current economic crisis. His enormous income would evaporate. Wolf's jealous law partners would turn on him like jackals, banishing him from the firm. Without clients, he could not hope to obtain a lucrative partnership at another firm. His trophy wife would find greener pastures. Maybe even his spoiled children, whom he barely knew but enjoyed as puppets, would disown him. What he had worked so hard to achieve would topple like a house of cards.

Wolf could not allow it. *Would* not allow it. He had a responsibility to his partners, his wife, his children. Was it his fault that Carlton and the tour guide had stuck their noses in the wrong place? That Carlton had refused to obey the FBI's order to stop investigating? It was not as though he himself would be pulling the trigger. Wolf would merely be following a client's orders. As for fear of being discovered, Wolf should have none, he reasoned. Unlike the bumbling Wallace, his accomplice was exceedingly competent. And Wolf would leave no record, setting his man up as the fall guy who had acted on his own, misinterpreting Wolf's orders.

Wolf straightened in his chair with a renewed sense of purpose. Even Qhibli's fetid cigar no longer affected him. "They will not remain an impediment for long, excellency."

Qhibli's cigar and black eyes glowed. His mouth creased into a brilliant white smile above his goatee, giving him the look of a fat Mephistopheles. He placed the cigar in the ashtray, reached for a file folder on his desk, tossed it on Wolf's bony lap.

"Memorize it. Then I will burn it."

Wolf opened the folder, began to read Qhibli's handwritten notes. Blood drained from his face. The plan was as simple as it was monstrous. Unlike terrorist acts to date, there would be no violence, but the results would be far more severe.

Wolf had no reservations about the plan, legitimizing it as he had so many lesser ones before it. He was the lawyer, not the client. He had abandoned all vestiges of patriotism to greed long ago. He worked for Qhibli and the Saudi Kingdom, not the U.S. government. And although the effects of this plan would be disastrous to the United States, it was completely legal. Who was he to prevent his client from acting to his advantage within the bounds of U.S. law? After making a mental note to move all of his money out of the U.S., Wolf cleared his throat, handing the file back.

"When am I supposed-"

"The E.U. foreign secretary and the CEO of Euroil are expecting you in Brussels tomorrow, 8PM local time."

12 TRAIL

101 Freeway
Hollywood, California
2:33 PM

Carlton raced along the highway, careful to stay several car lengths behind Drake's Chevy Suburban. The SUV was good news and bad. Good because the hulking vehicle was easy to track. Bad because Carlton had not expected to give chase to an automobile. If he had, he would have borrowed one of McLean's newer cars instead of a 65 year-old relic leaking oil.

He glanced at the Cadillac's temperature gauge. Combined with the summer heat, the strain on the engine caused the needle to creep up steadily, barely remaining within the normal range. The oil gauge was even more worrisome, indicating a steady drop in pressure due to the leak.

He was relieved when the SUV shot down an off-ramp at the sprawling LA Live complex in downtown LA. The stoplight at the end turned red as the two cars approached. The Suburban accelerated, rushed across the street instants before traffic filled the intersection. Carlton muttered a curse, pumped the soft drum brakes, screeched to a halt.

Had Drake noticed him?

He waited for the traffic to clear before looking left, right, then gunned the Caddy through the red light. He prayed that there was no police around. He could flash his DOJ badge and explain the situation, but by the time he continued the chase, Drake's trail would have grown cold.

Carlton noticed that the needle now touched the red part of the temperature gauge. Without air blowing in, the old engine was beginning to overheat, burning even more of the scant oil that remained. He pressed on, hoping Drake's destination was near.

He caught up to the Suburban on Figueroa Avenue as it drove past the mirrored cylindrical Bonaventure Hotel towers, then up a steep side ramp on the right. The Caddy followed it up the hard slope, shuddering in complaint as it climbed, losing speed and oil pressure fast. Wisps of steam began to trail out from under the hood. He could smell burning oil.

The engine was losing power. The car crawled forward, sluggish and unresponsive.

"Come on!" Carlton shouted, hunched over the steering wheel, goading the limping Caddy onward as it neared the top.

Ten more feet. Five.

It finally crested the hill. He peered down the leeward side, saw the Suburban five hundred feet away, turning right on Olive Avenue across from the massive Superior Court complex.

It disappeared from sight.

Carlton allowed the Cadillac to coast down the slope. The heavy car accelerated to over fifty as he approached Olive. He hit the brakes before turning the wheel, but the car was moving too fast. Tires shrieking, the Caddy fishtailed wildly, nearly hitting a cement truck before straightening out, earning a terrified honk and shouted Spanish expletive in protest.

He scanned ahead. The Suburban was still five hundred feet ahead of him, then darted down a ramp to the right and disappeared anew.

Carlton pressed down hard on the accelerator. The vintage hunk of steel crept forward at an anemic pace, then began to shake, steam billowing from under the engine cowling, the temperature needle deep in the red, oil pressure nonexistent.

He was a dozen feet away from the edge of the ramp when the engine finally seized up.

The Caddy was still rolling. Carlton jumped out amid swerving cars, pushed hard against the hot concrete with his boots, imparting enough momentum to keep the wheels turning. As soon as its front whitewall tires angled down on the slope, he slid back in, let the car coast to the bottom. This time he pumped the brakes far before approaching a parking garage entrance under the glass-sheathed Gas Company skyscraper on Bunker Hill. Still, the massive car continued to roll under its own weight, coming to a stop only once the automatic gate arm closed in front of him, scraping the glossy hood with a painful nails-on-blackboard screech.

Carlton leaped out, ran into the dark garage. He heard the Chevy's tires squeal in the distance.

He ran up to the next floor, sweating in the trapped heat, looked all around, searching for the glow of brake lights, pricking up his ears.

Nothing. The SUV had disappeared.

Carlton walked out of the parking structure, panting. He pushed the dead Caddy away from the entrance, cringing at the deep gouge in the flawless lavender paint. He found a rag in the trunk, wrapped it around his hand, popped open the hood, propped it up with its metal rod. The wash of heat from the engine nearly seared his face off.

Hot engine, cold trail. He leaned against the front left fender and called Monet, waiting for the engine to cool, hoping it would start again.

"What is Farnsworth Tate's address in LA?"

Monet soon read off the address of the parking garage into which Drake's SUV had just disappeared.

The ball of ice reappeared in his gut. Farnsworth Tate was one of the oldest, largest, most elite law firms in Washington, DC, with offices around the globe. Now it was involved in trying to protect a 65 year old national security secret tied to energy. Law firms did not act on their own, he knew, but on behalf of clients. Farnsworth Tate represented multinational corporations, pension and hedge funds, banks, universities, foreign governments, and high-ranking U.S. government officials, including former presidents. Had Wallace used his former law firm to get Grant's program or was Farnsworth Tate using Wallace's position at DOE to obtain it, he wondered.

"I don't know if you can get the following information, Henri, but-"

"Try me. What do you need?"

"A list of Farnsworth Tate's energy clients."

"I'm on-"

A gunshot exploded, immediately followed by a resonating ping against the Caddy's raised hood. Carlton instinctively ducked below the fender, stared at a deep dent in the underside of the hood's thick curved sheetmetal skin. The car's 1940s American craftsmanship had saved his life.

Another shot rang out, this time followed by shattering glass as the unlaminated windshield blew apart. A third gunshot drilled a hole in the left fender inches away from Carlton's face, followed by a fourth hitting the oil case, igniting what little remained of the superheated oil inside.

Carlton wanted to run, but waited for the shooter to stop firing before bolting from the car. Two shots rang out as he ran, the bullets chipping the asphalt to his left and to his right before he leaped for cover behind an aged pale blue van, falling hard against the rough asphalt. He scrambled to his feet, stood with his back against the vehicle, unholstered his Glock, chambered a round. He waited, caught his breath, turned around, chest pushed hard up against the van.

Carlton was about to peer around its side when Jaime Drake appeared on a balcony railing two stories above the garage entrance, aiming a handgun. He ducked just as it fired, bullet pinging against the roof.

The parking entrance around him was devoid of people, but he was not sure about the railing above where Drake stood. He wanted to fire back but feared hitting an innocent bystander. Besides, Drake was too far for an accurate shot. Instead, he waited behind the van, gripping his Glock with sweaty hands, heart racing. Not hearing any additional shots, Carlton waited some more, then peeked up at the balcony over the van's roofline.

Drake was gone.

Carlton ran back to the injured Caddy. Flames engulfed its engine. He slid under the trunk, disconnected the fuel line to prevent the gasoline in the tank from igniting. Still, the engine continued to burn, sending billows of oily black smoke into the air.

It would not take long before the police and fire department arrived. The last thing Carlton wanted to do was answer questions. There was no time to mourn the fatally wounded Caddy that had saved his life. He reluctantly sprinted away from the scene.

"Max is going to kill me."

* * *

High up in the Gas Company building, Savitch dialed the DC office.

"The good news is that I have a copy of the program, with the inscription on it."

"And the bad news?"

"The inscription is a faded handwritten address. I did a quick search and will continue, but for now it does not match any known address." He paused, lowering his voice in embarrassment. "Carlton was the one who showed up at the meeting. Armed. There were too many people around to do anything there. I almost got to him afterwards, but he escaped," Savitch explained, omitting that he had allowed Carlton to follow him and had aimed from too far away.

"So now he knows what you look like," howled Wolf. "This is a disaster."

Savitch blushed in shame. "I know how to get Carlton."

"I'm listening."

"I'm going to get the tour guide and let Carlton come to me."

13 INTEL

Polish Embassy
Paris, France
12:33 AM

Zuza had done a superb job yet again, reflected Sobieski, striding down the embassy hallway. At this time of night, it was deserted. He clutched the first transcript of conversations from Zuza's microflies. It had just arrived by diplomatic courier from the Polish embassy in Washington. He could have obtained it faster and more cheaply via encrypted email, but certain powers, including his host country of France, had ramped up electronic espionage to such a degree that he felt more secure using an old school person-to-person transfer, complete with handcuffed attaché case.

Even that precaution had not been sufficient for Sobieski. A person reading the pages now in his hands would obtain no information. The receiver at the Polish embassy in Washington had automatically encrypted the transmitted data and only Sobieski possessed the decryption algorithm.

He walked into his office, closed the door, fed the pages into his scanner, engaged the decryption program on his computer. The scanner whirred as it pulled in each page. Fishing a Marlboro from the crumpled pack in his shirt pocket, Sobieski lit it with his disposable plastic lighter while waiting for the program to run. He only had time to take a couple of deep drags before the laser printer spit out a legible version. He sat down to read.

He immediately forgot the cigarette, which soon burned down to his fingers.

"*Skurwysyn*," he whispered, not more than halfway through. Son of a bitch.

Prince Hakim was not only involved, as Sobieski suspected. He was giving orders to Saudi ambassador Qhibli in Washington using the terrorist Yassin as a conduit. In turn, Qhibli was tasking his lawyer

Wolf - perfect name, he thought - with the dirty work. What had Quibli said? *Final solution.* Sobieski shuddered, knowing exactly what those words meant. The Nazis' 'final solution' had exterminated nearly all of Poland's Jews and many others in concentration camps during World War II. Qhibli was ordering the murder of two people, one of them an American Justice Department prosecutor, no less.

He stopped in mid page, rubbing his forehead. He despised this part of his job. He knew that the man and woman were targeted for assassination. They did not. From the transcript, he did not know the woman's name, but it mentioned Carlton's. Sobieski wanted to warn him. Every shred of his humanity was telling him to pick up the phone and call him.

He took a deep breath.

He could not. Warning Carlton, even anonymously, might expose that Qhibli was under surveillance, perhaps even its method. He could not allow such an important source to become silent, especially since the microflies' power source lasted only four days. As an intelligence officer, Sobieski had to weigh the benefit to one man and one woman against the goal of his mission. He squinted, shook his bald head. Uncovering Hakim's plan and network was too important.

He lit another cigarette, allowing his mind to legitimate the decision. According to the transcript, Carlton was a federal prosecutor and a naval officer. He would know how to recognize danger, protect himself and the woman. He might already know that they were in danger, Sobieski hoped. It was a weak argument conjured to quell his conscience, he knew, but it would have to do.

He blew out a cloud of smoke, read on.

"*Co to jest?*" *Tso tow yest.* What's this?

Qhibli had directed Wolf to make a proposal to the European Union Foreign Secretary and to the CEO of Euroil. The transcript did not indicate the nature of the proposal, but it was sensitive enough for Qhibli to destroy the information after Wolf digested it. Whatever it was, if it involved Yassin and came in the same conversation as an assassination order, it could not be good.

He reread the transcript a second time, then a third before walking to a cabinet and opening the door, revealing a wine rack with half the cubby holes occupied. Unlike the Polish stereotype, Sobieski preferred red wine to vodka. He did not drink often, but badly needed one now. The more he needed a drink, the more expensive the bottle. He didn't earn much as an intelligence officer, but this was the Paris embassy, where wine was plentiful. Every once in a while, Sobieski sneaked a bottle from the *cave* in the basement. It was an embassy use, after all, he rationalized. Why should the ambassador have all the fun?

He selected a high priced bottle of Château Margaux, uncorked it with a nervous hand, poured its dark red contents into a dusty decanter atop the cabinet. He reclined while letting the wine breathe, lit a fresh Marlboro with the butt of his previous one.

Why would the Saudi Interior Minister make a secret proposal to an energy giant like Euroil instead of the Oil Minister, he wondered. And why would he task the mission to the Saudi ambassador to America? Even the ambassador was afraid of detection, delegating the task to his lawyer. All Sobieski could conclude was that the Interior Minister was attempting to circumvent the King and Oil Minister. But why?

He had no idea, but his instinct told him that his search to identify those who had planned the killings of Polish Special Forces and civilian engineers had netted a new and completely different operation. Which begged a more immediate question: what to do with the information? Should he pass it along to his superiors? Doing so might expand the *Agencja*'s intelligence on the matter. But it could also impede his investigation, sidetracking it with bureaucratic politics since it involved the E.U. Foreign Minister. He had spent too much time and effort to allow that to happen. The information could only be disseminated on a need-to-know basis, he reasoned. Especially if he was prohibiting himself from warning Carlton. At present, he knew nothing of substance, only that there was a proposal.

He poured a glass of wine, swirled it around, took a small sip, then a bigger one. The velvety claret felt warm going down.

Before anyone else needed to know anything, Sobieski decided, he had to obtain more information. But there was a major impediment. Zuza had bugged Ambassador Qhibli, but Qhibli would not be at the meeting in Brussels, scheduled for tomorrow. Sobieski would not be able to learn anything that was discussed. He had to bug one of the people attending the meeting, but Zuza only had enough microflies left for a single person.

He swallowed the full contents of his wine glass, replaced it on the cabinet.

Who should Zuza bug?

14 RESCUE

Gas Company Tower
Downtown Los Angeles
3:23 PM

Carlton ran, not understanding why people scattered from him in panic, some screaming, until he realized that he was still clutching his Glock. He holstered the weapon. It took him a few moments longer to recover from his initial shock and realize that he was no longer looking into the Grant case from the sidelines. Whoever Drake worked for had targeted him for far more than simple theft.

Which meant that he was not the only one in danger.

He ran faster, dialing Alexis's number on the fly. Her telephone rang for what seemed like minutes. *Come on.* He was about to hang up and dial again when she answered on the seventh ring.

"Alexis Hamil-"

"Thank God," he blurted out, panting.

"How was your meeting with Drake?"

"He nearly turned me into a human sieve."

"What?"

"Drake tried to kill me. Which means that he's going to try to kill you too. I want you to go to the nearest police station and-"

"My car is in the shop. My friend dropped me off at home."

Carlton had forgotten about her car trouble. "Call the police. Stay inside. Lock your door. Don't answer it. I'm coming over. What is your address?"

He committed it to memory and prayed that he would get there first.

With the Caddy ready for the junkyard, he needed transportation. Taxis were as difficult to find in LA as natural blondes. Los Angeles public transportation was better than most imagined, but it was slow and did not reach into the hills where Alexis lived. He needed a car, fast. There was no time to rent one, but he soon realized that might not be necessary - McLean garaged much of his automobile collection at his corporate headquarters, less than a mile away. He slowed to get his bearings, then changed course and broke into another sprint, dialing once more.

"Mr. McLean is out of town for the day, sir," replied Maxfield, his friend's British-accented valet.

"I need a car, Maxfield." Carlton reflected that he had no idea what the septuagenarian British man's first name was or if he even had one. "It's an emergency." Avoiding any mention of McLean's ruined Cadillac, he explained his situation between gasps for air. *Damn cigars.*

"I will make the necessary arrangements, sir."

True to form, Maxfield did not disappoint. Ten minutes later, Carlton slipped behind the wheel of another gem in McLean's automobile collection: a spanking new red open-top Tesla Roadster Sport. Trying hard to ignore that the sleek American sports car's price tag nearly equalled his annual salary, he studied the simple controls, started its motor with the push of a button. Unlike conventional automobiles that gained torque as their engine speed increased, the full power of the Tesla's all-electrical motor was available at a standstill with the simple push of a pedal. Unprepared for its acceleration, Carlton literally flew out of the parking garage, landing in a hail of sparks on the street.

Even in car-blasé Los Angeles, other drivers yielded the right of way without cavil to the rare, futuristic automobile. Twenty minutes later, Carlton rocketed North on Beachwood Drive in the East Hollywood Hills, still amazed that an electric car with only a single moving motor part, two gears, and no clutch, belts, spark plugs, cylinders, motor oil, or exhaust could move so fast - with no more than a high-pitched whine.

Following the navigation system's prompts, Carlton raced up the winding canyon roads, slowing only once he had reached the 6100 block of Rockcliff Road. He identified Alexis's house, unholstered his Glock, parked, looked up and down the street before stepping out of the low-slung sports car.

No one. At least not in sight.

He dialed Alexis's cell number.

"It's Carlton. I'm outside."

He walked toward the house, again searching for any sign of danger. The stately home was spectacular, with painted shutters and doorways framed with vibrant yellow and dark blue ceramic tiles. Forged iron grillwork lined a tall balcony groaning under the weight of blooming purple bougainvillea.

The heavy carved wood door creaked open from inside.

Carlton's heart skipped a beat as his gaze fell on Alexis. She was dressed in a black satin dress cut just above the knees and black high heels with straps, looking like a beauty queen from the 1940s. She wore only a hint of makeup, except on her lips, painted a shade of red that inspired emotions in him as untamed as the Tesla. Her glossy hair shimmered in the sunset. Carlton again detected the scent of lemons.

"Do you always pick up your dates like this?" She asked, forcing him out of his stare.

The events had made him forget all about their dinner date.

"Only when people are trying to kill me. I'm afraid that Musso and Frank will have to wait." He grabbed her by the arm, led her down the narrow path to the curb, pointing the Glock in front of them.

"Mind telling we where you're kidnapping me to?" She asked, shutting her door, easing into the leather bucket seat.

Carlton zapped the electric motor to life, turned to her. "Malibu."

* * *

The nimble Tesla raced down the hill, its wishbone suspension hugging the pavement in hairpin curves. They soon barreled past the Beachwood Market and Café at the bottom, shooting past twin stone pillars demarcating the original Hollywoodland entrance. The turns ceased once they emerged onto Beachwood Canyon, straight as a razor. Cars parked on both sides at the edge of manicured lawns made the avenue narrower than it appeared. He relaxed, slowed. They were now three miles from Alexis's house.

His calm was short lived.

A white Chevy Suburban sped up Beachwood Canyon in the opposite direction.

"Aw, hell."

Alexis pointed to the oncoming SUV. "That truck almost ran me over this morning!"

Carlton knew the truck well. "Drake's truck."

"That's why my pen was on the floor! Drake must have searched my house for the program," she exclaimed.

Without asking for an explanation or moving his gaze from the road, Carlton removed the Glock from his shoulder holster, handed it to Alexis, butt-first. He was afraid that she might shy away from the fearsome weapon. Instead, she grabbed the black polymer handgun, expertly verified that a round was chambered, lowered her window.

She smirked at the look of surprise on his face. "Male chauvinist."

The Suburban blurred past them. Carlton glanced at the rearview mirror, saw the monster SUV brake. It screeched into a U-turn and lay chase.

"Hold on," said Carlton, pressing down on the accelerator, rocketing the bonded extruded aluminum vehicle through the intersection of Glen Alder at close to 80 miles an hour.

Despite being out-horsepowered, the Suburban took advantage of its mass and Beachwood Canyon's straight downward slope. It soon matched the Tesla's speed.

Alexis pushed deep into her seat and cringed as they blew through the stop sign intersection with Gower Street. The Tesla had many horses to spare, but if Carlton increased his speed among the legion potholes and lumpy patches that passed for streets these days in LA, he was sure to lose control.

The Suburban similarly ignored the stop sign, crept up on the Tesla, now only twenty yards back. A gunman in the SUV's passenger seat stuck his head out of the window and let loose a volley of machinegun fire. The Tesla was too low-slung, the gunman's firing angle too steep to hit the rear tires, but the fact was of little comfort to Carlton and Alexis as bullets shattered the rear window and pierced the trunk's skin, narrowly missing the lithium-ion battery.

"That tears it," said Alexis. She lowered her window, found the opening too small. Undeterred, she looked up, unlocked two latches, and pushed upward with both hands, lifting the removable targa top into the fast moving air, hurtling toward the SUV. The truck jerked aside to avoid the flying piece of reinforced plastic, falling back a few feet before regaining its original position behind the Tesla. Alexis swiveled in her seat, kneeling on it facing backwards, fired two shots.

One went wide. The other found its target on the SUV's front grille. It ricocheted harmlessly, but granted them another small respite as the surprised driver backed off by a few yards.

"Nice shooting," exclaimed Carlton, fast approaching Franklin Avenue at the bottom of Beachwood Canyon.

Unlike the sparse traffic on Beachwood, Carlton knew that Franklin would be jammed with cars. No matter how powerful the Tesla's motor, crossing the intersection at high speed would be suicide. On the other hand, the SUV gunman would make short shrift of them long before they could squeeze into traffic. Carlton racked his brain for a solution and whizzed past another stop sign, missing a vintage VW Bug by mere inches in the intersection of Graciosa Drive. The Suburban did the same, quickly getting back on track, closing the gap.

The gunman had recovered from Alexis's fire. A staccato of shots quickly followed, exploding Carlton's side mirror.

Alexis squeezed off two more rounds at the Suburban's windshield, scrunching back down upon realizing it was armored.

Carlton continued to scour his mind for a solution as Franklin Avenue loomed ahead. Their only option was a U-turn, a sprint back up into the Hollywood Hills, and an attempt to lose the Suburban in the maze of narrow winding streets.

"How well do you know the side streets?"

"Like the back of my hand," Alexis replied, snapping her belt shut.

Carlton glanced at the rearview mirror, miraculously still in one piece. The Suburban was only a dozen feet behind. If he attempted a U-turn now, he would first have to slow down, causing the behemoth to mash into the light Tesla, turning them into crash test dummies. He had to increase his distance. He punched the accelerator. Instantly applied to the rear wheels, the massive electrical field hurled the automobile near 100 miles per hour down the straightaway.

The jolt of acceleration was no match for the Suburban. It began to recede just as the gunman loosed another volley from his machinegun, splintering the Tesla's front windshield into a spiderweb of broken glass.

Carlton cursed, braked reflexively. "I can't see a thing."

Alexis paused for a second, then slipped off her shoes, placed the floor mat against the windshield. She kicked once, twice, three times, then let the mat fall away, revealing a ragged hole amid the broken safety glass, large enough to navigate through.

"My cell phone was on the dash. I think you kicked it through the window."

"Sorry. You can use mine."

Carlton had a lot more to worry about than his cell phone as they barreled through the last intersection before Franklin Avenue, now a mere block away. It was time.

He took a deep breath. "Hold on."

Carlton checked the rearview mirror one last time, braced himself for the desperate maneuver.

It was not to be.

A gray Toyota Prius pulled out of Scenic Drive just as the Suburban rushed after the Tesla through the intersection, colliding with the Suburban's right quarter panel.

The feather-light car was no match for the titanic SUV careening down Beachwood. Its entire front end was torn off like so much *papier maché*, the impact pushing the Suburban only a foot off course.

Without even glancing back at the mangled automobile, the Suburban's driver readjusted his heading, but swerved too sharply given his high speed. As he turned the steering wheel to correct the maneuver, he overcompensated, causing the SUV's heavy back end to fishtail. By the time he twisted the steering wheel once again, it was too late. The SUV's rear quarter panel plowed into a row of parked cars at over 80 miles an hour, immediately pulling in the rest of the vehicle, slamming it against the wall of stationary cars.

Carlton heard a deafening crash of twisting metal, shattering glass, and car alarm klaxons as the Suburban mashed the parked cars aside like so many miniature toys. He glanced at the rearview mirror to see body panels ripping away from the SUV, hoping no one was inside the cars. The Suburban's front wheel assembly tore away next. Its engine-heavy front end fell hard against the pavement, scraping against it in a shriek of metal against concrete, showering sparks on the open side of the street like the jet of a magical street washer before the SUV finally crumpled into the last car nearly head-on, turning it into an accordion.

"They're not going anywhere," exclaimed Carlton as he stood on the brake pedal.

The electrical field disengaged as soon as he stepped off the accelerator, replaced by the stutter of the antilock braking system as they continued rushing toward the packed traffic on Franklin Avenue, now only forty yards ahead.

He pumped the brake pedal.

Twenty yards. Ten. Five.

The Tesla came to a standstill a mere two feet from the bumper to bumper traffic on Franklin.

Carlton took a few deep breaths before ungluing his hands from the leather steering wheel. His heart was pumping wildly, his shirt clinging to his back with sweat.

"That was close," he whispered hoarsely, breathing hard, blinking away the thick traffic on Franklin Avenue seared into his vision. It was the second time today that one of McLean's cars had saved his life, he reflected. He would have to spend the rest of his life reimbursing his friend, but they were still alive.

He turned to Alexis, managed a lopsided grin. "Department of Justice. Never a dull moment. Where did you learn to handle a gun like that?" He asked, recovering his Glock before punching out the rest of the windshield, cutting his hand.

Alexis stared at him, paler than a ghost. "My father taught me," she stammered, dabbing his cut with a Kleenex from her purse.

"He taught you well. I hope you don't have to do it again," he said, slowly merging onto Franklin Avenue.

His instinct told him otherwise.

15 TESLA

Malibu, California
5:43 PM

Despite its missing windshield, exploded sideview mirror, shattered rear window and bullet-peppered body, the Tesla remained driveable, if with a worrisome buzzing sound emanating from the rear. Carlton's hard driving had severely depleted its batteries, yet the vehicle's range of 220 miles allowed them to reach Malibu 40 miles away.

The setting sun was dipping toward the horizon as they drove into the quiet elite enclave, painting the ocean and sky a vibrant orange. They turned off Pacific Coast Highway, pulled up to the Malibu Colony guardhouse under the watchful gaze of Pepperdine University's bell tower high in the hills above.

Carlton slid down his window, gave his name to the shocked security guard. The man tried hard not to ogle the mangled Tesla or Alexis dressed to the nines in the passenger seat. Luckily, they were expected. Thinking ahead, Carlton had called Maxfield for permission to use McLean's beach house on the way to Alexis's house, warning him and Davos not to allow their employer anywhere near it. He would explain later, cringing at the thought of telling McLean about the cars he had mutilated.

The guard handed Carlton a set of keys, raised the gate arm, waved him into the exclusive beachside compound favored by Hollywood stars and moguls. Carlton parked the wreck in the garage of a spectacular white mid-century style beach house, immediately closing the door behind them.

"Welcome to *Villa Acqua.*"

"Water villa," Alexis translated. "Appropriate name for a beach house."

"It's not Capri, but maybe we can find you some lemons," he joked, ushering her inside.

Dressed in her black satin dress, hair wild from the topless ride up the coast, Alexis walked barefoot on the polished concrete floor, heels dangling from her hands. She looked right at home in the multimillion dollar house already illuminated by timer-controlled lights. A giant plate glass window provided a dramatic view of the foamy surf rushing up on the sandy beach a few yards away. She craned her neck to admire a giant canvas of orange and red squares hanging on the vast white wall of the soaring two-story living room.

She whistled. "Rothko?"

Carlton nodded, once again impressed. He could not have identified the famous artist's work from that of a five year old's if Max had not told him. "The McLeans have a thing for abstract expressionists."

"Beverly Hills bungalow, Tesla sports car, Malibu Colony house, multimillion dollar painting. For a government prosecutor, you have some rich friends."

"They get by," he replied, smiling, inhaling the home's scent, a combination of sea air, fresh sheets, and aromatic candles. All of McLean's homes smelled like a modern luxury boutique.

Alexis sat on the bottom stair of the teak and brushed aluminum staircase. Carlton sensed that events were catching up with her, as they were with him. His adrenaline was ebbing, leaving his body exhausted, his emotions raw, bound in tight knots of anxiety. Despite the accumulated heat inside the shuttered house, Alexis held herself tight around the shoulders to keep from shivering. He sat next to her.

"I guess you were right about the meeting," said Alexis, an embarrassed expression spreading over her face. "I'm sorry I doubted you. It's just that-" She stopped, looked down, smoothed her dress.

Carlton remained silent, giving her time to choose her words.

"I don't trust the federal government," she finally said, still looking at the floor.

Carlton was about to reply that he didn't either but did not want to appear flip. Her explanation had been long in coming, deeply personal. She turned to him.

"The House Un-American Activities Committee dragged my father in for questioning during McCarthy's 1947 witch hunt," she explained. "He was an ardent anti-communist, but they subpoenaed him anyway based on someone's false accusation, said they would disregard the accusations if he named names. My father refused to inform on others, so they blacklisted him, barred him from working on movies." She paused. "He loved making movies so much. It destroyed him. It took him nearly twenty years to get his next job. The only time I ever saw him cry was when he told me that story. I've distrusted the government ever since."

She gazed at Carlton, tears welling in her mahogany eyes, the emotions of her father's pain and of their narrow escape blending. "When you told me that you were a Justice Department prosecutor, I just- You seemed different, but I wasn't sure. Now I know. Drake would have killed me. You saved my life." She wiped her tears away, sniffing, streaking her mascara.

Carlton nodded, not having the heart to tell her that despite McCarthy's deplorable tactics, 1940s Hollywood *had* been rife with communists seeking to overthrow the government. "I understand. I'm sorry about your father, Alexis, but things have changed."

"Have they? I want to believe that, but I keep hearing about civil liberties being eroded, government authority growing virtually unchecked. I don't want an all-powerful government."

Carlton shared some of her concerns, yet as a DOJ prosecutor and Iraq War veteran on the front line against terror, he had a different take on federal anti-terror laws and methods. Out of respect for Alexis and her deceased father, he did not press the matter.

"Neither do I," he simply replied. "And speaking of Drake, that isn't his real name. Which reminds me: I owe you some money."

He pulled out the sheaf of fifty dollar bills, handed them to Alexis. It was still too early to tell whether they had brought him good luck or bad.

She pushed his hand back. "You're going to need every dime to repair the Tesla. Who do you think Drake is?"

Carlton summarized Monet's information and the possible connection with Farnsworth Tate while looking through the plate glass window at the deepening sunset casting flecks of silver on the Pacific. "Until we get more information, I'm afraid we're more in the dark than we were yesterday."

"Maybe not," Alexis suggested.

Carlton cocked his head.

"You asked me to look into connections between Grant and energy, remember?"

He arched his eyebrows. "You found something?"

"Grant was friends with the namesake of your friend's car."

Carlton sat up. "Nikola Tesla? He invented the alternating electrical current."

"I'm impressed. I had to look him up."

"Tesla was one of the greatest inventors of the twentieth century. He also invented neon tube lighting and remote controlled vessels. Some of his inventions were so advanced that scientists didn't even realize Tesla held certain patents until they tried to patent the same inventions 50 years later, like the digital logic gate used in computers. He was obsessed with finding a way to transmit electricity through the air, like with his Tesla coil, but on a much bigger scale."

"The device that causes electricity to arc through the air from a charged ball to a magnetized cage around it. They have one at the Griffith Observatory."

Carlton nodded. "It's amazing that he and Grant were friends. They were so different. Grant was a dapper star, Tesla a tragic figure. He was more interested in helping mankind than making money. He was horrified that his inventions might be used for war. Tesla once tore up his shares in an electric company to keep it afloat, only to have the company refuse to pay him millions in royalties. He invented most of the radio, but Marconi got the credit even though the Supreme Court later ruled in Tesla's favor. Thomas Edison once promised Tesla a huge sum if he could fix a piece of electric machinery, then reneged when Tesla succeeded, saying it was a joke." It reminded him of another reneging Edison, this one at DOJ.

Alexis whistled. "You would clean up on *Jeopardy*."

Carlton shrugged. "I was a science geek in college. Unfortunately, I'm terrible at math, hence law school. What else did you find?"

"Let's see." She counted off on her fingers. "Tesla suffered from what today would be called obsessive-compulsive disorder, was fixated on the numbers 3 and 18 and on pigeons, had a photographic memory, was terrified of germs, and claimed that images of completed inventions flashed into his mind. Many considered him crazy. Despite winning more than 200 patents that changed the way we live, Tesla died broke, defrauded, and ridiculed. Even his identity could not rest in peace. He was culturally and religiously Serb, yet geographically Croat. He should have been a uniting figure for the two. Instead, both camps have bitterly fought over him since his death, even though Tesla considered himself equally Serb and Croat and treasured his American citizenship papers more than any other honor he received during his life. And he-"

Carlton held up his palm. "What I mean is: what did you find out about Grant and Tesla?"

"Right. Well, as the story goes, the two were avid boxing fans. In 1939, Grant learned that Tesla could not afford tickets to a boxing match in New York. He invited Tesla to sit in his box to watch the match. They remained good friends until Grant's death."

Carlton was crestfallen. He had expected more. "Interesting, but not much to go on."

"It gets better. Grant met Tesla at a boxing match in New York's Madison Square Garden the day before the *Infamous* movie premiere, only a few days before Tesla died."

Carlton squinted with renewed interest. "Maybe Grant was carrying something that Tesla gave him."

Alexis sat up. "Maybe. From what I read, at the end of his life, Tesla was working on a system that he said would provide an endless supply of free electricity. He started developing the system by building a tower on Long Island, but the men who made astronomical profits from his inventions thought he was crazy. They refused to give him more money. Tesla was forced to abandon the project."

Carlton felt a twinge of danger. *An endless supply of free electricity.*

He thought of Hassan's attempted assault on the U.S. electric grid. At a time when life had so little value to so many, Carlton did not want to imagine how many people someone would kill to obtain such a prize.

"What are we going to do now?" Alexis asked in a low voice.

"For the moment, we hide," answered Carlton, trying hard to sound reassuring. "Whoever Drake is, he doesn't know that we're here. We're in a guarded, gated community."

"We should call the police."

Carlton shook his head. "If the FBI can't get a handle on this, whoever Drake and Farnsworth Tate are working for is way beyond the LAPD's reach. I'd call Echeverria, but I'd just hit another wall." He winced, feeling a pang of guilt. "I should have listened to the FBI and stopped investigating." He gazed at her. "I'm sorry I got you into this mess, Alexis."

Alexis shook her head. "I'm the one who asked to meet you, remember? And I called you about Drake." She paused. "But sooner or later, he is going to track us down. What then?"

It was a good question, Carlton admitted.

Alexis did not cease to impress him. He had assumed that she would unravel as soon as she understood the naked truth of her romantic idea of an old Hollywood mystery: a life and death struggle. Instead, she was proving surprisingly resilient, yet without losing an ounce of her feminine charm. It made her even more attractive.

Carlton felt the urge to put his arms around her. He shook off the thought. This was neither the place nor the time. Besides, he doubted that she shared any of his growing feelings.

"We'll cross that bridge when we come to it. Until then, let's focus on something else."

"Such as?"

He smiled. "I don't know about you, but there is dinner in my immediate future," he replied, walking to the state-of-the-art kitchen that Maxfield kept fully stocked. "What do you fancy?"

* * *

Savitch sat with three members of his Special Transactions Team in the chilled rear compartment of a black Hummer H2. He had a penchant for using gas-guzzling SUVs during operations, particularly when the Saudis were footing the bill.

Savitch had finally managed to obtain Grant's program, with little to show for it. Neither he nor his team could make heads or tails out of the handwritten address. Based on Wolf's latest instructions, he had shifted his focus on Carlton, but the altar boy lawyer was proving surprisingly slippery. And dangerous. Two members of his team had been killed chasing Carlton and Hamilton in the Hollywood Hills. Worse, Carlton's trail had grown cold.

The altar boy lawyer was no fool. Knowing he was followed - and targeted - he would go deep. How would they find him? Savitch rubbed his eyes, searching for a solution. He sat up in his seat a minute later.

"The Tesla has to belong to McLean," he announced. "If we track it down, we can find Carlton."

His second in command turned to him. "Sir, the team reported that the car had no plates."

"We don't need plates," replied Savitch, grinning, typing a search command on his smartphone.

"But sir, how can we track it down if-"

"It's rare and expensive. It must have an anti-theft locator system."

She understood. "If we can get its VIN number, we can track its GPS or activate its locator system and find Carlton. But how do we get its VIN?"

Savitch held out the face of his smartphone. "There is only one Tesla dealership in LA. Let's pay them a visit."

* * *

Alexis looked at Carlton in surprise. "You cook?"

"Female chauvinist," he jabbed back. She laughed, thankful for the lighthearted break. "Doesn't your boyfriend cook for you?"

"I don't have a boyfriend," she replied, turning from him to gaze at the rushing surf beyond the window. The outdoor flood lights lit up the white ocean foam like bath bubbles in a giant bathtub.

"What a tragedy," he commented melodramatically, surprised and pleased. The warmth inside him felt good, he reflected, rummaging through the extensive wine rack. Lighter than a Cabernet, heavier than a Merlot. He selected and uncorked a bottle of Stag's Leap Pinot Noir, decanted it.

Alexis stood, feeling the cool stone floor against her bare feet. "The last one had a roving eye and liked to stray, so one day I told him to keep walking." She walked to the Caesarstone kitchen counter near Carlton. "What about you? Does anyone cook for you back in DC?" She asked, perching herself on a kitchen stool, playing with a strand of hair.

"Monet does sometimes. He's a genius around the kitchen. A master of the omelet," he joked, kissing his fingertips before going to work on a Cornish game hen.

Alexis laughed. "You know what I mean."

Carlton dropped his mask of humor. "I had someone," he said wistfully. "But law is a jealous mistress. She always demands center stage."

"You chose law over love," Alexis concluded, disappointed.

"No. My girlfriend did."

The comment took her by surprise. "I'm sorry to hear that," she said softly.

For the first time, the recollection did not possess its familiar sting. And had he detected a faint smile on her face before she looked away? Maybe she...

"You're not like any of the lawyers I've met. What made you chose law? Other than not being good at math."

She certainly was a good listener, reflected Carlton. "Like most lawyers: money," he replied frankly, dousing the hen in olive oil, lemon, and herbs before placing it in the oven.

Her expression made it clear that she had anticipated a more noble motive.

"You expected me to say that I became a laywer to defend the little guy, put criminals and terrorists behind bars, defend America?"

"Something like that."

"That came later." He filled two bulb glasses with wine, handed one to Alexis. "Cheers."

They clinked glasses before taking deep swallows.

"I grew up in a modest family in El Centro, near the Mexican border. My parents are farmers."

She pointed at his feet, smiled. "Hence your boots."

"You can take the man away from the farm..." He joked, before becoming serious again. "We never wanted for anything, but we didn't have much. I was the first person in my family to go to college. After seeing how some people lived in LA, working my way through college and law school, I wanted to make the big bucks, turned my back on my family's sense of faith and humility. Got a job in a huge DC law firm, bought a Porsche, wore Italian suits, lived the high life."

"Sounds like the American dream," said Alexis, observing him while playing with the rim of her glass.

"At first. After a while, I knew I had made the wrong choice. The hours were grinding, I found the work meaningless, and I disliked many of the clients and most of the law partners. The money was not enough. I christened the firm the 'Merchants of Pain' and went through an existential crisis."

Alexis took a sip. "I went through one when my father passed away. Is there nothing more? Why am I here? What am I meant to do with my life?"

Carlton nodded. "I spent a couple of years soul searching, reconnected with my faith."

"You don't wear it on your sleeve."

"I dislike those who do. Preachiness just highlights one's own faults. And I've got too many of those." He smiled. "Besides, actions speak louder than words."

Her expression made it clear that she shared his view. "I was raised strictly secular. Sometimes I wish I had faith, but then I see what the extremists do. What made you reconnect?"

"A story about a church in Europe, bombed during World War II. A statue of Jesus had lost its arms and legs. The parishioners wondered how they would restore it. The priest told them they should not, that the statue's mutilation represented Christ's death. From now on, it was they who had to be Christ's arms and legs. It made me consider that God did not put me here to serve me, but for me to serve others and make the *world* a better place. Before the golden handcuffs got too tight at the Merchants of Pain, I hopped to DOJ."

"To do good instead of doing well," commented Alexis, resting her head in her hands, watching him. Her large mahogany eyes warmed him more every day.

"Exactly." Carlton was struck by her comment. She understood perfectly. He was so used to having to explain his career decisions, even to his DOJ colleagues. "To protect the good from the bad." It sounded cliché, he reflected, but it was true.

He explained his turf battle with Faraday at the FBI while steaming vegetables, but stopped short of discussing his grim tour of duty in Iraq. Too raw, too painful. "And now this."

"Look on the bright side," said Alexis, finishing her wine, flashing a sly smile. "You met me."

Carlton felt more warmth spread through his chest. He was thinking up a clever reply when Alexis's cell phone rang.

She answered it, handed it to Carlton. "For you."

"Carlton. It's Henri."

Carlton had called to give him Alexis's cell phone number since losing his along Beachwood Canyon. "You always know when to call, Henri. I need some more information."

"Great minds think similar."

"Alike," Carlton corrected. "Whatever you did to get Grant's government files, I need you to do the same with Nikola Tesla."

"The inventor?"

"*Oui.*"

"Did you know that he spoke fluent French?"

"I did not," replied Carlton, ever amazed by Monet's knowledge of all things French. "Your turn."

"Farnsworth Tate represents many energy companies, everything from oil companies to alternative energy startups, but none as lead counsel, which is strange considering their size and reputation."

Carlton did not want to know how Monet had managed to learn that last bit of information, but mulled it over. He recalled Echeverria's warning about Wallace. Farnsworth Tate was in deep with DOE and the Grant case. Maybe also with the FBI. Too deep to be doing the work for a minor client.

"Thanks, Henri. Keep looking."

Alexis turned in immediately after dinner, drained. Carlton plucked a Tatuaje cigar from *Villa Acqua*'s humidor, smoked it in the darkness while walking through the vast beach house, making sure that all doors and windows were locked and the alarm system was activated.

They would not remain safe for long.

He went to bed wearing his shoulder holster.

16 CHOCOLAT

Charlemagne Building
Rue de la Loi
Brussels, Belgium
10:23 AM

Zuza sat in the rear seat of the Mercedes taxi, peering at the sterile glass and steel buildings lining the *Rue de la Loi* - Law Street - in Brussels' European Union Zone. She was on her way to interview the E.U. foreign minister for the *Gazeta Wyborcza*, Poland's major daily newspaper. At least that was her cover.

Following World War II's devastation, French statesmen Jean Monnet and Maurice Schuman boldly set out to end Europe's long history of bloody wars through a framework of economic and political alliances once proposed by Benjamin Franklin while he served as envoy to France during the American Revolutionary War. Sixty years after World War II, the E.U. boasted 27 member nations covering over 1.7 million square miles, a single economic market roughly equal to the United States', a standardized passport for its nearly 500 million inhabitants, and the euro as a single currency among a growing number of its members. Although the E.U. had no unified military force, barely perceptible military funding, and suffered from a host of severe undemocratic structural defects, some of its leaders wanted it not only to provide a counterbalance to the U.S., but to replace it as the world's sole superpower - a bit optimistically considering the E.U's debt and currency woes.

The cab dropped Zuza off in front of the ultramodern Charlemagne building, named after the Frankish emperor who had forged the first European union in the 8th century. Even though it was a muggy summer day, the giant curved slab of glass and steel made her feel cold. Perhaps it was due to the dark gray overcast blotting out the sun, but it reminded her of the drab buildings of communist-era Warsaw when she was a little girl.

An armed entrance guard compared the color photograph on her *Gazeta Wyborcza* press card with the raven-haired woman standing before him. She wore her hair pulled back tight in a bun, scant makeup, thin wire-rimmed eyeglasses that failed to hide the carefully applied dark circles of article deadlines under her eyes, a severe black Max Mara suit over a white blouse buttoned up to her neck, sensible flats, and a simple watch and wedding band as her only jewelry. Every inch the serious reporter.

Nodding his approval, he ran her scuffed reporter's briefcase and gift-wrapped package through an X-ray machine before allowing her to enter one of the silent elevators, which she rode to the twentieth floor. Whether in Warsaw, Paris, or Rome, nowhere was summer in Europe so pronounced as in the bureaucracy, she reflected, encountering not a single person as she walked down the padded, soulless hallway.

Past another armed guard seated at a desk in front of a wide glass door etched with the E.U. circle of stars symbol, a dour middle-aged woman greeted her with a humorless expression, ushered her through an empty lobby into a spacious office that evidenced its occupant's taste for the modern. The only items providing a view to the past were brightly illuminated paintings sandwiched between portraits of de Ville's ancestors.

"*Dzien dobry, pani* Korbonska," announced François de Ville in her native Polish with a pronounced French accent, clasping her hand for a moment too long. *Gene dough-bray*. Good morning.

"*Monsieur le ministre.*" Mister minister. De Ville's official title was High Representative for Foreign and Security Policy but he was generally referred to as the E.U.'s foreign minister. He gestured to a couch.

"*Merci*," she replied, observing the man.

François de Ville was tall and svelte, handsome in the manner of senior European diplomats that made many women swoon. With his gray hair combed straight back, dressed in an impeccable navy suit and yellow Hermes tie, he looked more like a wealthy corporate executive than the coordinator of Europe's foreign affairs and common security. He smiled with a wide grin and slightly squinted brown eyes with crow's feet at their edges.

Zuza may not have been a real journalist, but she played the part expertly, assiduously preparing for the interview by researching the subject matter - and de Ville. A member of an aristocratic French family dating back to the 1600s whose ancestor had supported the terror and bloodbath *Révolution* of 1789 to maintain their vast land holdings and avoid the *guillotine's* blade, his full name was François Jean-Marie Hubert de Ville-Chambord, Comte de Floraine. Although his ancestors had renounced the title of count, de Ville used it liberally whenever useful. His keen intellect had been sharpened at the *Ecole Nationale d'Administration* (ENA), which groomed France's elite into high mandarins and corporate executives. His gift for speech and *Enarque* connections greatly facilitated his rise to French foreign minister before the current socialist French president lobbied hard to get him appointed to his present post - mostly to ship the loose cannon out of Paris. Although charming, well-mannered, and supremely cultured, de Ville tended to see everything through the prism of his monarchist-born French nationalism and virulent anti-Americanism.

For all her research, Zuza had failed to uncover any skeletons in his closet. His family fortune rendered him immune to financial bribery. Married with children, he maintained mistresses in both Paris and Brussels - no great scandal in Europe these days. Yet Zuza had uncovered one extremely important fact. It was seemingly innocuous, but would permit an opening.

She sat on an equally beautiful and uncomfortable leather and chrome couch near a floor-to-ceiling plate glass window offering a wide view on the busy *Rond Point Schuman* below. First removing her note pad and recorder from her bag, she handed the white gift-wrapped box adorned with the simple label 'Mary' to her host with a flourish.

"*Pour vous*," Zuza announced with a smile. For you.

"You know that I cannot accept gifts, *mademoiselle*," de Ville replied, eyeing the box with desire, toying with his gold family crest pinky ring. He knew what was inside. Mary was one of the oldest and best *chocolatiers* in Brussels.

"Then I suggest we eat the evidence," suggested Zuza conspiratorially, unwrapping the box. She selected a chocolate truffle and popped it into her mouth, crinkling her eyes, smiling with delight. "My mother has a saying. Why dirty your mouth for only a single chocolate?"

De Ville laughed. "A wise woman," he agreed, gormandizing a series of truffles before leaning back into his armchair. "*Alors. Commençons.*" So. Let us begin.

Zuza posed all the questions a reporter for the *Gazeta* would ask the E.U. foreign minister, pressing him, but not too hard, throwing a few softballs for good measure and ego-stroking. The economic crisis. Relations between the old and new member states. Membership for increasingly Islamist Turkey. The issues of Kosovo and Macedonia. Disputes with Russia over gas supplies and U.S. missile defense. The role of NATO. Western European protectionism against Polish workers.

An hour into the interview, Zuza excused herself to use the *toilettes*. De Ville ushered her to his private bathroom. Once inside the room tiled entirely with small strips of mirror, she locked the door, carefully placed a half dozen microflies from her makeup case onto the cement and steel sink. She blew them into the air with a puff. They immediately began buzzing, searching for the homing devices she had hidden in the truffles, now lodged in de Ville's esophagus. To prevent his suspicion, Zuza allowed only one of the microflies to escape with her through the door.

After concluding the interview, Zuza thanked de Ville, who beamed with confidence over his charming press performance. He escorted her to the hallway.

On his way back to his office, de Ville heard a buzz in his ear. He slapped his hand against the back of his neck, crushing the fly.

"*Sale bête,*" he muttered. Dirty beast.

17 CLAIRE

Villa Acqua
Malibu
7:33 AM

The doorbell jolted Carlton out of bed. Flush with adrenaline, he stumbled into Alexis's bedroom, shook her awake.

"Hide," he whispered hoarsely before hurrying down the hallway. The doorbell rang again.

Still wearing his shoulder holster, Carlton removed the Glock, rushed down the stairs barefoot. He tiptoed to the front door, peeked through the peephole. He immediately relaxed, holstered the weapon, opened the door, careful to remain hidden inside.

"You scared the living daylights out of me. What are you doing here? Didn't Maxfield and Davos tell you not to come?" He asked Max and Claire McLean in rapid fire.

McLean hoisted a Louis Vuitton weekend bag, shot Carlton a reproachful look. "Good morning to you too. We wanted to spend a few days at our beach house - if that's OK with you. I had no idea you were here. I thought Maxfield was. And I haven't talked to Maxfield or Davos since yesterday morning. What is-"

"I'm sorry. I'll explain as soon as you get inside," interrupted Carlton, peering cautiously past the McLeans at Malibu Colony Road beyond. No one. The only parked car was the beige 1936 Packard 120 convertible from McLean's collection in which the couple had arrived.

Forcing aside McLean's likely reaction to his incinerated Caddy and violated Tesla, Carlton opened the door wide, stood aside to let his friends enter, pecking Claire on the cheek. He reflected that Max's age difference with the young French-American marine biologist was far greater than between himself and Alexis.

McLean's bright white smile disappeared as soon as he entered, noticing Carlton's gun and shoulder holster. "What's going on, Carlton?"

"I apologize. I thought you were someone else," he said, closing and locking the door.

"I gathered that," replied McLean, walking into the airy living room, trailing his trademark scent of Acqua di Parma cologne. He was dressed in a white linen Dolce Gabbana suit, pale pink Sea Island cotton Charvet shirt, and suede Gucci loafers, without socks as usual. Claire wore a simple periwinkle summer dress and gold sandals.

"A lot has happened since the burglary, Max," said Carlton. "Let's sit down and I'll fill you in."

As they did, Alexis padded down the staircase barefoot wearing low cut jeans, a tiny white T-shirt, and a serious case of bed head. "Thank God that was a false alarm."

McLean and Claire swiveled in unison. Claire turned back to Carlton, flashed him a sly smile. McLean took several more seconds to admire Alexis.

"It's...not what you think," stammered Carlton, trying to explain, feeling himself turn as red as the mangled Tesla in the garage.

"You don't have to explain yourself," replied McLean, arching his eyebrows and nodding in approval.

Carlton sighed, knowing there was no way for him to prove his innocence.

"Alexis, these are my friends Max and Claire McLean, the owners of this house and the Tesla."

McLean turned to him. "The Tesla? I thought you were driving the Cadillac."

Carlton went livid. He pretended not to hear. "Max and Claire, this is Alexis Hamilton, the tour guide from my visit to the library in Hollywood," he continued, finding himself admiring Alexis' flat stomach.

"As the saying goes, any friend of Carlton's is a friend of ours," Max announced, kissing Alexis's hand in his traditional European manner.

She blushed and turned to Claire, shook her hand. "We left in a rush. I borrowed some of your clothes in the closet. I hope you don't mind."

Claire observed her clothes on the younger woman. "Not at all. I hate to admit it, but they fit you better than me."

Alexis beamed.

"What's all this about us not coming here?" Asked Max, ensconcing himself in the white leather couch.

"Yesterday, I -" Carlton stopped as something caught his attention in his peripheral vision. He turned to the window.

"Get down!" He shouted, pushing Alexis to the floor as a spray of machine gun fire shattered the giant plate glass window, raining shards throughout the living room. Carlton recognized the compact black weapon as a Heckler & Koch MP5K submachine gun. Deadly.

He leaped to the floor toward McLean, yanked him off the far sofa with one arm, reached for his Glock. He fired three rounds at the two attackers standing on the wide balcony before ducking behind the sofa as one crumpled to the floor. Pushing hard on one end of the heavy mahogany coffee table, grunting, he tipped it on its side. He was moving it between them and the sofa just as the other gunman loosed a sustained full-automatic burst, sending rounds tearing through the sofa, drilling into the thick wood table where they came to rest. Carlton crawled to Claire, huddled near the edge of the table, pulled her in closer.

His mind raced. How could they have gotten in, he wondered, firing blindly above the sofa before adjusting his position, realizing that the Malibu Colony was completely gated off from Pacific Coast Highway, but not from the beach.

The gunman stopped firing. Carlton waited a few seconds, his ears ringing, was about to shoot blindly when he saw something bounce on the sofa and land on the rug a few feet away.

Grenade.

He slid toward the oblong device, snatched it. In his flat position on the floor, he did not have enough room to pull back his arm very far, but had no time to stand. Instead, he lobbed the heavy metal ball as far as he could. It barely cleared the ruined sofa.

That saved them.

The grenade exploded just beyond the sofa, which absorbed the brunt of the explosion along with the thick wood table, shielding Carlton and the others from the burning shrapnel. The rest of the metal shards blew out the rest of the window, turned two walls into lace, tearing the Rothko masterpiece to shreds.

His hearing obliterated by the explosion, Carlton could not tell what was occurring past his field of vision, now blurred with dust and debris. He lifted his arm above the smoking remains of the sofa and fired blindly before slowly raising his head. One gunman was still down, face contorted in agony, clutching his torso. No sight of the other.

Carlton scrambled to the jagged edges of the window and ran onto the balcony, ignoring the slivers of glass strewn on the floor, bloodying his feet. He kicked the weapon out of the fallen gunman's hand, leaned over the railing.

His partner must have escaped before the grenade exploded. Unharmed, he was sprinting like the devil up the beach toward an all-terrain vehicle with fat tires. Carlton aimed and fired. Puffs of sand sprayed up from the ground, nipping the man's heels. The last round hit the man in the right arm, causing him to lose balance and fall. Carlton aimed to fire at the now stationary target, but he had emptied his clip. The man struggled up, resumed his dash.

Carlton ejected his spent clip, removed a fresh one from his holster strap, slammed it into the gun's grip, pulled back the slide, resumed firing. By then, the gunman was astride the ATV, sending twin plumes of sand flying into the air as he sped away.

Carlton crouched, checked the fallen gunman. One of his rounds had hit the man in the chest. The shrapnel from the grenade had sliced into most of the rest of his body. He lay sprawled on the balcony, apparently unconscious, bleeding profusely. Carlton headed back into the living room. Claire was lying on the floor, Max and Alexis bent over her. He approached with increasing trepidation.

My God.

Claire's dress was soaked in blood. She took ragged breaths while Max clenched her hand tight.

"Claire. Claire! Can you hear me?" Asked Max, frantic, his voice trembling, the words only minimally making it past Carlton's still buzzing ears. "Stay with me, Claire!"

Her eyes glazed over as she mumbled something unintelligible. Her body went slack.

Carlton grabbed the nearest telephone, dialed 9-1-1. He retrieved his wallet, then walked back to Alexis, wrapped his arms around her as she stared at Claire in shock.

The Malibu fire station was located a hundred yards from the Malibu Colony gate. A paramedic unit arrived two minutes later, preceded by a black and white California Highway Patrol cruiser and a Malibu Colony Patrol car. Two CHP officers in tan uniforms darted into the house, guns drawn.

"Highway Patrol! Everybody down!"

McLean lay down on the floor near Alexis. Carlton had already laid his gun aside, now threw up his arms, clutching his badge in one hand. "U.S. Department of Just-"

"On the floor! Now!" The officer repeated, pointing his service pistol at Carlton with one hand under its grip.

Carlton did as he was told. Under cover from his partner, the CHP officer walked toward him, plucked the badge and ID from his hand, examined them.

"Sorry, sir. You can get up. What the blazes happened?" He asked, gazing at the scene of destruction before holstering his weapon and motioning for the paramedics to enter. One kneeled down next to Claire and began assessing her injuries, pushing McLean back firmly. "Please let us work, sir."

The second paramedic walked onto the balcony, pronouncing the injured gunman dead a few moments later, then called for an ambulance.

Still in shock, Carlton took deep breaths before giving the lead CHP officer a quick summary of the attack, identifying his three friends. "They are cooperating in a federal investigation. There cannot be any mention of their identity. And Claire McLean will need protection at the hospital."

The officer was well acquainted with the type of people who owned homes in the Colony and too smart to mess with a DOJ prosecutor.

"Understood, sir. I'll arrange a protective detail. Until we're told otherwise, her name is Jane Doe, but the detective will want statements."

Carlton did not want to involve the FBI, but he no longer had a choice. "The FBI Special Agent handling the case is Javier Echeverria at the Federal Building. Your detective should speak with him first."

Carlton stepped aside as the ambulance workers placed Claire on a gurney and rolled her outside with McLean in tow.

Carlton turned to one of the paramedics. "How is she?"

She did not answer directly, but the grimace on the woman's face gave Carlton little hope. He and Alexis followed McLean as he stumbled into the rear compartment of the ambulance, deep in shock. One of the ambulance workers stopped Carlton and Alexis from climbing in after him.

"Sorry. Family only."

Carlton flashed his badge. "I'm her Uncle Sam. This is my other niece," he replied, climbing in with Alexis. "Let's move it."

18 PROPOSAL

Zaventem Airport (BRU)
Brussels, Belgium
7:03 PM

Prince Qhibli's luxurious Boeing Business Jet landed in Brussels with a slight jolt before taxiing to the general aviation terminal. Wolf had made judicious use of the customized Boeing 737's circular bed and marble shower with solid gold fixtures to limit his jet lag. Well rested, he proceeded through customs and stepped into the waiting glossy black Farnsworth Tate Mercedes S600 for his meeting.

A half hour later, the Mercedes pulled up in front of the Charlemagne Building and disgorged its rail-thin passenger clutching a similarly wafer-thin attaché case. The case was more show than substance. The only physical evidence of Prince Qhibli's proposal was a heap of ash in the ambassador's incinerator.

The E.U. foreign minister's dour assistant met Wolf in front of the imposing building, ushering him past the guards to her boss's top floor private office, immediately closing the heavy door behind him. Wolf wondered why European politicians were so taken with modern architecture when their U.S. counterparts clung to centuries-old styles. Perhaps Europe needed the new because it was so old and the U.S. needed the old because it was so young, he ruminated. Not that he cared either way. As long as there was money behind it, style was of no moment to Wolf.

"Good evening, Mr. Wolf," de Ville greeted him with a diplomatic smile. He shook Wolf's hand with both of his before waving off an errant fly. "This is Monsieur Metz, CEO of Euroil."

"*Bonsoir*," said Wolf, shaking Metz's hand. It was as cold as the man's stony gaze.

Short and stocky, Metz looked like a corporate version of Napoléon Bonaparte, complete with a taciturn demeanor and a look of perpetual suspicion. He seemed aggressive even while immobile and silent.

Dressed in a slightly rumpled black suit, his sunken eyes and pallid face betrayed the fact that he had avoided his country's mandatory six weeks of vacation by planning corporate strategy in shadowy boardrooms. His lack of even the slightest smile was a sharp contrast to de Ville' gregarious manner.

Wolf had reviewed Savitch's research on both men during his flight. De Ville's story was not atypical of French high mandarins. Metz's bio revealed why he was a perfect recipient for Prince Qhibli's proposal - and not simply because he was the CEO of the European energy giant. His ambitious, overbearing French-German parents had rushed him into school two years early, rode him relentlessly. Metz had remained socially awkward, less emotionally developed than his peers, yet always an overachiever, always one step ahead, always in a hurry, never able to enjoy the present unless it involved planning for a conquering future. Unmarried and romantically unattached, it was reported that the closest Metz came to genuine passion was when he expanded the Euroil empire's reach and gobbled up competitors - something that he had achieved with frightening speed and diligence since becoming CEO only a few years ago.

"I take it we are private?" Asked Wolf.

De Ville nodded. "The office was swept an hour ago, the door is soundproof, and my staff is gone, including my personal assistant."

Wolf had assumed that de Ville had taken such measures based on Qhibli's request, but he had to be certain. "Very well," he replied. "Before we begin, gentlemen, and at the risk of repeating the terms of the confidentiality agreements you have signed, what I am about to propose on behalf of the Kingdom cannot be disclosed to anyone, no matter how secretly, including to anyone in the Saudi or E.U. governments or at Euroil. I am sad to say that the Kingdom's enemies are legion and quite well infiltrated."

De Ville and Metz nodded silently, with the E.U. foreign minister doing a far better job of concealing his impatience than the diminutive CEO of the European energy conglomerate, who tapped his fingers with nervous curiosity.

"As you know, Saudi Arabia sits on the world's largest oil deposits and is the world's largest oil producer. Yet its present oil fields are quickly running dry, including Ghawar and Safaniya," he explained, referring to the world's largest conventional and offshore oil fields. "Although they have enjoyed a reprieve due to decreased oil demand during the global economic crisis, demand is increasing anew. The reprieve will soon evaporate."

Metz flashed Wolf a look of naked disbelief.

Wolf produced a pained smile. "I can see that the Kingdom's effort to keep this information secret has been successful. Most believe that Ghawar and Safaniya have another 20 years of production. In fact, at current production levels, they have at most five years. A long time if there were other Saudi fields to replace it."

"But there are none," interrupted Metz, shifting impatiently in his seat. "Are there?"

Wolf paused, shook his head. "No. To replace them within five years, the Kingdom must immediately develop its known untapped oil fields and discover new ones. Despite a rise in the oil price, it is now below the Kingdom's break-even point due to the massive increase in welfare payments necessary to keep the Kingdom stable after the Arab Spring uprisings. The Kingdom is fast using up the surplus it accumulated during the last oil price spike to make up the difference. It does not have the funds necessary to develop new fields, much less discover new ones.

"Money is the first problem. The other is expertise. As you know, Saudi Aramco produces 97 percent of the Kingdom's oil, mostly through American petroleum engineers and oil companies," continued Wolf, referring to the Saudi Arabian Oil Company, once wholly owned by U.S. oil companies, then progressively nationalized by the Kingdom.

"Before 9-11, but especially since, the presence of American engineers has exacerbated relations between the royal family and the Saudi population, which increasingly opposes their presence as they did that of the American military during the first Gulf War. Attacks against the royal family and American workers are up. Yet without foreign engineers and companies, Saudi oil production and exploration would stop within a matter of weeks and send the Kingdom into ruin."

Wolf paused dramatically, allowing the men's anticipation to build. He turned to Metz.

"The Kingdom proposes a simple solution to both problems," he announced, before presenting Hakim's plan.

It did not take long. When he had concluded, Metz and de Ville stared back at him in mute shock, with the E.U. foreign minister nervously twisting his family crest ring.

Pleased at their reaction, Wolf continued.

"Not that you require it after such a proposal, but as a further incentive, the Kingdom will ensure that there will be no terror attacks by Al Qaeda or its affiliates on any E.U. members or diplomatic missions," Wolf announced, before turning to Metz, "or against any Euroil facilities." He watched the short CEO scowl and bear his teeth. There had been no Al Qaeda attacks against any Euroil facilities. Stating that there would not be any was nothing less than a direct threat of attack. His expression shifted to puzzlement. The threat was credible coming from someone sent by Saudi Arabia, although strange coming from a Saudi government representative. The Saudi government had screwed down tight against terror groups.

Wolf raised his hand, cutting off any questions. "I am not at liberty to reveal how this can be accomplished, but it will soon become clear to you," he announced, his gaze fixed on Metz. "The Kindgom will also ensure that the American Tesla electrical system does not come on line."

De Ville gave Wolf a confused look before turning to Metz for an explanation.

The CEO was ghostly pale as he gave de Ville a thumbnail sketch of the still-theoretical energy system. Through French DGSE moles inside DOE, Euroil had sought to learn as much as possible about the yet untested system. For good reason: if it ever came on line, it would render most of Euroil's products and services obsolete and infeasible, spiraling the giant energy company into bankruptcy.

"I did not know that the Tesla system was anywhere near to coming on line," croaked Metz, still in shock.

"Not yet, but there has been a major recent discovery," explained Wolf. "Of course, what has been uncovered can be covered back up."

Prince Hakim had chosen the two recipients of his proposal wisely, reflected Wolf, gazing at them. He knew exactly what they were thinking.

Metz was ruthless in executing Euroil's buy-them-or-destroy-them strategy against competitors. He did not care with whom Euroil did business as long as it increased the company's bottom line. To critics who assailed his policies of signing lucrative contracts with the world's most ruthless dictatorships, Metz preached the standard pabulum that trade rather than sanctions would bring about human rights and regime change, despite the lack of evidence.

Combined with his lust for gobbling competitors, it made Metz the perfect recipient for Hakim's proposal. In a single stroke, the deal would transform Euroil into the world's largest energy company, dwarfing its American, British, Dutch, and French brethren and, by extension, make Metz the most important private oil player in the world.

As for de Ville, his interests were political rather than economic, yet parallel to those of Metz in this matter. Officially, as E.U. foreign minister, de Ville headed the 8,000 member E.U. diplomatic service, oversaw its $12 billion foreign aid budget, and was responsible for speaking with other countries on behalf of the E.U. On a personal level, de Ville would do almost anything for France to regain its global prominence of old, which would ensure his election to the presidential Elysée Palace. A fact evidenced by the paintings of Charlemagne, Napoléon, De Gaulle and de Ville's aristocratic ancestors hanging on the wall.

De Ville knew the plan would wreak havoc on the U.S. economy. The more the better, the Gaullist politician reflected bitterly, knowing yet unable to realize or care that it would have the same effect on the European economies. He considered it high time for the enlightened, tolerant, secular European Union led by France and Germany to replace the arrogant American *hyperpuissance* - hyperpower. The recent change in White House occupancy, tone, and foreign policy would never assuage men like de Ville, whose bugaboo was not American policy but American exceptionalism. In his opinion, America had an overexaggerated sense of destiny, naïve policies, childish religionism, Puritan attitudes to work and sex, and lowbrow pop culture, which had made the country outgrow its once-noble birth midwifed by France. Since the E.U.'s congealed socialist welfare economies could not compete with the freer, more innovative American market on their own despite increased U.S. regulation and taxes, de Ville saw the Saudi proposal as a powerful boost to the E.U. economy that might allow it to eclipse the America leviathan. And for the euro to shine brightest among the firmament of currencies.

Neither man was disturbed by the fact that the Saudi proposal would severely destabilize the Middle East after its remarkable yet still tentative steps toward freedom emerging from the overthrow of the butcher Hussein in Iraq and the Arab Spring uprisings against many of the remaining autocrats. Provided that the proposal benefited the E.U. and France and increased Euroil's dominance, neither de Ville nor Metz had any qualms about allowing the cradle of civilization to become its coffin.

Wolf was far too skilled a negotiator to expect either of the two men to accept or reject Hakim's proposal on the spot. He would let them discuss it among themselves and allow Metz to perform the hardest negotiations for him, putting the screws to de Ville to convince the E.U. to accept the Kingdom's conditions. Yet Wolf knew it would not be enough. De Ville had power and influence, but even the E.U. foreign minister could not single-handedly approve all the conditions the Kingdom demanded. De Ville would have to convince both the European Council and the Council of the European Union. Hakim had exhibited great foresight in planning for that also.

"To show my good faith, I would like to share an investment tip," added Wolf, describing an investment fund out of Zurich. He did not have to explain a mechanism that men like Metz and de Ville instinctively understood: they could guide E.U. officials whose support they needed to the fund, in which they could make token investments and receive huge returns, amounting to legal bribes.

"The Kingdom's proposal will remain open for exactly three days. After that, the Kingdom will be forced to look elsewhere. I remind you that Euroil is not the only energy giant in Europe. I am certain that British Petroleum, Royal Dutch Shell, Total, and Statoil would be interested in hearing the proposal, to name a few." He knew that these would never countenance Hakim's proposal or remain silent, yet smiled at the bluff. "Thank you for your time, gentlemen. I look forward to hearing from you soon. *Bonsoir*."

De Ville and Metz were so stunned that they remained screwed to their seats, not even standing as Wolf grabbed his attaché case and departed the office.

Even the errant fly buzzing around de Ville's head no longer annoyed him.

19 FAMIGLIE

St. John's Health Center
Santa Monica, California
10:43 AM

Strobes flashing and siren blaring, the speeding California Highway Patrol cruiser parted traffic and led the ambulance to the nearest emergency room, at St. John's Health Center in Santa Monica. Alerted to their impending arrival, a medical team immediately prepped and rushed Claire McLean into the operating room. After making sure that a CHP officer stood guard in the hallway, Carlton joined McLean and Alexis outside the operating suite. He detested the sterile antiseptic smell of hospitals, recalling the one in which he had recovered after the bloodbath in Iraq, blinking back nightmarish memories.

They waited together for news of Claire's surgery; numb, silent, in shock. McLean was hunched over, face in his hands. Carlton prayed in silence, gripping a new bead of the frayed rosary he kept in his pocket after each prayer while Alexis rested her head on his shoulder.

Davos and one of his guards soon arrived, enraged by the attack, positioning themselves with a view of the entire hallway. Carlton could tell by the glare on Davos's face that the man blamed him for the attack. He felt the same.

Three long hours passed before the surgeon appeared, ruts of exhaustion on her pallid face. McLean stood, grim with worry. Carlton watched his friend steel himself for the worst, as did he.

"The bullet hit your wife in the stomach," she explained, looking up at McLean. "It's never a good situation when that happens, but we were able to get in quickly enough and fix the damage. The bullet didn't rupture any other major organs. It will take some time, but her stomach should heal."

McLean exhaled a long breath. "Thank God," he whispered, wiping budding tears from his eyes before placing his hands on the shorter woman's shoulders. "Thank you, doctor."

The surgeon grimaced. "I'm afraid that isn't all." She paused. "Your wife has slipped into a coma."

McLean's eyes opened wide. "A coma? But I thought you said-"

"The coma was not induced by the gunshot wound. From what we could tell, your wife received a blunt trauma to the head."

McLean squeezed his eyes shut, thinking back to the attack. "She may have hit her head against a coffee table after being shot."

The surgeon nodded. "That could have caused it."

McLean remained silent, nearly paralyzed by the pronouncement to come.

"Comas come in different forms. Hers is relatively deep, eight on the GCS scale from three to fifteen, with three being the worst."

"When will you know if..." His voice cracked before it trailed off.

"There is no way to know at the moment. Comas generally last from several days to several weeks. We will monitor her around the clock. For now, all we can do is wait."

Carlton stood immobile as he listened to the doctor's prognosis. A maelstrom of emotions roiled through his heart and mind. Fear. Anger. Sadness. Strongest of all, the same emotion he had felt in Iraq on that fateful day and every day since: guilt.

He had tried to warn the McLeans not to come to Malibu, but the notion provided him little comfort. He felt acutely responsible for Claire's injury. Drake's associates had most likely fired the bullet that ripped through her, but they would never have gone so far had Carlton refrained from investigating a matter that was none of his business to begin with, particularly after the FBI had expressly ordered him to stop. Now she was in a coma.

He had patronized Alexis earlier, concluding that she was only interested in Grant's movie premiere program because of its old Hollywood mystery. Yet she had a reason to investigate. It made her feel closer to her late father and she had not broken any rules in the process. What was his reason? Why had he, a seasoned federal prosecutor, broken the rules and taken the law into his own hands?

Carlton didn't need a shrink to figure it out. He had a beef with the FBI and had used the investigation to get even. In retrospect, it made no sense since Faraday and Echeverria were different agents in different offices and different departments, but acting on emotion rarely did. He should have obeyed the FBI and refrained from investigating Grant's program.

It was no use chewing himself up by looking back, he knew from recent experience. He could not change the past. But he could change what happened from now on. It was time to stop his investigation. It had achieved nothing other than putting Claire into a coma and almost getting himself and Alexis killed. For what? Revenge against the FBI? Expiation of his guilt over Iraq as Edison had suggested? Ego? Whatever the reason, he would have to lock it away deep, accept Faraday's short-circuit of his drive to put Abu Hassan and his thugs behind bars, turn over what he knew to Echeverria, and follow the rules - even if it meant placing himself out of the game.

He looked down, sighed. The decision should have relieved him of his guilt, made him feel better. It did not. He knew the reason for that, too. The only way for Carlton to quiet the storm raging in his soul was to ask for forgiveness. He had already asked God, but that was not enough. God forgave all who repented. People were far less forgiving. Carlton had to ask McLean. It would not be easy, but if he wanted to live with a clear conscience and retain the friendship he treasured most, it had to be done.

He stepped to McLean. His friend's jade eyes were puffy with sorrow, bright with anger.

"I'm so sorry, Max," Carlton muttered painfully. "It's my fault. I should never have gone to your beach house or investigated this damn program to begin with. It was none of my business." His windpipe constricted. "Please forgive me."

McLean shook his head gravely. "There is nothing to forgive, Patrick. It's not your fault. You tried to warn us."

"I should have done a better job."

"My home was burglarized. You were trying to discover who committed the crime. You tried to warn us not to come to Malibu, even if I did not get the message. If you hadn't returned fire and tossed the grenade back, we would all be dead. There is nothing else you could have done." McLean paused, took a deep breath. "The coma is devastating, but Claire is still alive. She is a fighter like me, but also a much better person. God will help her. We must pray that she recovers."

Moved by his friend's resilience and faith, Carlton felt tears well up. "Max, I-"

"But prayers are not enough." The anger in McLean's eyes intensified. "I want to know who did this. And I want them punished."

"So do I, Max."

"You misunderstand me."

Carlton's alarm bells rang. He dreaded what he knew was coming, steeled himself. His warning had failed once. He was not going to fail again. He placed a hand on McLean's shoulder. "You didn't get my earlier warning, Max, so please listen now."

He told McLean everything that had occurred since the burglary, including what he had discovered about Grant, Tesla, Drake, DOE, and Farnsworth Tate.

"We've known each other for a long time, Max. Please trust me. This can only get worse if you get involved. Let the FBI take charge of finding those responsible. Don't make the same mistake I did," said Carlton, feeling a pang of hypocrisy as he heard his words.

McLean opened his mouth to speak, then closed it and led Carlton out of earshot from the CHP officer standing guard. He glanced at Davos, pointed to Alexis, directing him to watch over her.

"You know who I am, Patrick," he began in a low tone, more severe than Carlton had ever heard. He never used Carlton's first name. "You know that I cannot simply let this go, let some agency handle it. I may be renamed McLean, but I am still my father's son. His blood runs in my veins. I cannot let this go unpunished. Those animals tried to kill my wife, Patrick. They put her in a coma. My wife!" He shouted, before taking a deep breath, regaining his composure.

"Whoever did this thing, they would never have done it to my father. All his life he shielded me from the world of crime and killing and *vendetti* and family wars. I was a good son. I obeyed. I never stepped back into the world he left behind. And for what? So that animals can violate my home, put my wife in a coma, and nearly kill my friends?" McLean's eyes grew feral, ablaze with the thirst for revenge.

Carlton was moved to compassion for his friend, but had to defuse the explosion he knew was coming. "Your father shielded you from his criminal roots for a reason, Max. He lived in that world. He knew it was no good. He knew that a law-abiding life carries risks, but after living in the world of crime, he chose the world of law for himself and for you. Nothing good can come from taking the law into your own hands. Look what happened when I did."

"What good is a law-abiding life if I cannot protect my own wife? What kind of man am I? These animals have to be found and punished, Carlton. From what you told me, the FBI is neither able nor willing to do it. If the FBI cannot do it, neither can the police." He took a deep breath and paused. "My father's people are the only ones who can. The other families. The *famiglie.*"

Carlton winced. His friend had always taken great pains to stay away from his father's former associates unless they had a mutual legal interest. This was neither a mutual interest nor a legal one. McLean was about to ask his father's former associates to do him a favor from which he could never escape, incur a debt he could never repay. Carlton had done significant harm by breaking the rules and taking the law into his own hands. He could not allow his friend to travel down an even darker path.

"You once saved my life, Max. Please let me return the favor. Honor your father by accepting his wish for you. Don't make the mistake of thinking of his former associates as allies. They may find out who shot Claire. They may fit them with concrete shoes or put them to the *garrote*, but they will own you afterwards."

"They already owe my father for giving them his share of the syndicate. It will simply be a payback."

Carlton shook his head. "Don't deceive yourself, Max. You're thinking with your anger. Think with your head. You're a legitimate billionaire businessman. They need you."

McLean grunted. "The *famiglie* have more money than I do. They don't need me."

"They don't need your money. They need your legitimacy. Their money is tainted. It can only buy them so much. Your name is beyond reproach. Imagine what you could do for them with your reputation and clean businesses. If you ask them for this favor, they will never let you go. You will remain in their debt forever, a servant taking orders, just like your father's famous singer friend with Lucky Luciano," warned Carlton.

"The police will identify the gunman's body. They will identify Drake through the security camera tapes from Alexis's building." He had already tasked Monet with it. "I'll give the FBI the rest of the facts. Based on what just happened, they will have no choice but to investigate. They will catch the people behind this. Just give them some time. Trust them to do what they do best," said Carlton, unsure whether he was trying to convince his friend or himself.

McLean gently took Carlton's face in his hands and leaned into him. Carlton had never witnessed such a chilling stare. He felt McLean's green eyes bore through his skull. "I can't even protect my *wife*. What good is this litany of holiness if I can't even do that? Being indebted to my father's former associates is a risk I am willing to take for my family honor."

Carlton shook his head within McLean's hands. "Don't do it, Max," he pleaded.

"Give me one good reason. *Una*."

Carlton's mind scrambled to find one. How could he prevent his friend from making the terrible mistake of calling in the *mafia*? Not the American *mafia*, once powerful but now weakened by incompetence, relentless FBI-DOJ prosecution, and foreign competition into unorganized petty thuggery, but the real *mafia*, the Sicilian *cosa nostra*, the Black Hand that had never really disappeared and was once again resurgent.

Carlton knew how, of course. The answer was obvious, taunting him after the decision he had just made. The only way he could prevent his friend from calling in the *cosa nostra* was to sink deeper into the deadly quicksand of his failed investigation. It would require him to continue breaking the rules and taking the law into his own hands, much further than before. It was an invitation to disaster. Yet if he did not do it, Carlton's loyal friend who had saved his life would destroy his own, become a slave to the very people he and his father had sworn off. And far more important laws than federal agency jurisdiction would be violated, with far more dire consequences.

The situation he himself had created left Carlton no viable alternative.

"I will give you a reason," he said solemnly. He gulped a lungful of air. "You will not call in the *cosa nostra* because *I* will find out who did this."

McLean's eyes betrayed his relief. He pulled Carlton's head toward his until their foreheads touched, continuing to fix him with his chilling gaze. "You are my brother, Patrick. *Mio fratello*. I trust you with my life and my wife's life. I will give you whatever you need." He paused. "And three days. After that, I call in the *famiglie*."

20 HIDEOUT

Safehouse
11:03 PM Local Time

Sayyid Yassin was alone. The cramped room was pitch dark, deep underground. He had kept its existence and location secret from all but a select few with paranoid diligence. Even those who knew about it did not know everything about it.

Kneeling on the floor, using only his sense of touch, he felt for the correct place among the floorboards. Slowly, quietly, he pulled one up by its slightly ragged edge. He placed his hand in the hole, tumbled the knob from memory, pulled, and removed a book the size of a paperback from the cylindrical floor safe before replacing the floor board.

He stood, placed the book in his pocket. Moving to a nearby camp desk with his arms outstretched, he felt for a metal folding chair, then sat before clicking on a battered lamp. He wiped the sweat from his face. The soupy air and sticky heat permeated everything, fed the green slime that constituted the unpainted concrete walls' only decoration. He removed the book from his pocket, grabbed the telephone. Cameras were so small these days that it was impossible to make sure that none were present. Anyone watching would see him remove the book from his pocket at the table and not suspect the floor safe.

One by one, he contacted over fifty bankers in as many banks. All were men - Yassin did not voluntarily converse with women, who the Wahhabist considered beneath men and untrustworthy. He had dealt with these bankers many times. In addition to extreme competence, they possessed the added qualities of round-the-clock responsiveness, complete disinterest in his identity, and an unwavering commitment to secrecy. Only one banker had strayed from those paths. His brutal death in what had been ruled a hunting accident had prevented the man from benefitting from the error of his ways. And sent a powerful message to the small elite global banking community.

Yassin knew that even before 9-11, few communications escaped scrutiny from the U.S.-U.K.-Australia-Canada-New Zealand ECHELON mainframe computers that collected signals intelligence from satellite transmissions, publicly-switched telephone networks, microwave links, and more. The key was not to escape detection by the National Security Agency at Fort Meade, Maryland and other signatory countries' eavesdropping agencies - no one could truly do so - but to prohibit ECHELON from pinpointing the exact origin of his communication. So Yassin's telephone was connected neither to a land line nor to a cell phone tower. Instead, it was linked to an internet connection, which split data into hundreds of separate packets and sent them through a randomly selected list of over 100 foreign cell numbers, changed weekly, each routed through even more cell phone numbers and land lines, making each call nearly impossible to trace in less than four minutes.

He made certain that each of his conversations was even shorter and that they contained nothing remotely illegal or even suspicious.

Each banker required only an account number and a passcode to accept Yassin's instructions. Once he delivered that information, his only questions were: 'What sum can you convert to euros without attracting attention?' and 'How quickly can you effect the trade?'

The bankers knew to multiply all sums discussed for the particular accounts by 1,000, so their answers sounded like normal currency trade discussions rather than the massive currency shifts they entailed. Once satisfied, Yassin instructed each banker to stay at his office and be ready for his call as soon as the funds were received - within the next three days. Given the exorbitant commissions they would earn, allowing each to retire in profligate luxury, the bankers had no compunction against sleeping and eating in their offices to ensure they could carry out his transactions.

Consummate professionals all, each banker provided a similar cautionary statement: 'If you perform such a transaction as quickly as possible, the price of your purchases will become increasingly expensive in a very short time. You may wish to space out your purchases over a longer period.'

Yassin's reply was also identical: "Understood. Do it anyway."

After hanging up for the last time, Yassin reclined in his chair, smiling.

He would enjoy watching the world markets on that day.

21 DEMAND

McLean remained at Claire's bedside in her private hospital suite among a menagerie of soulless beeping electronics. A Santa Monica Police officer had taken over for his CHP colleague posted at the door. Davos and his partner continued to guard the only access to Claire's room, via the hallway.

Drained of emotion, Carlton sat slumped in an adjacent waiting area decorated as a cheery family room. The valiant attempt at homey camouflage fell short of its mark. In a hospital, no room could be cheery. It smelled like a sanitized hotel bathroom. Alexis was stretched out on the flower print sofa, half asleep after a mild sedative. He thought of popping a couple of the pills himself, if only for an artificial break. He craved a cigar, but could not allow himself to leave even for a few minutes.

Her cell phone rang. He peered at the incoming number, answered it, welcoming the interruption.

"You sound like hell," said Monet.

"Better than I feel." Carlton filled him in.

"I went through Tesla's government files. Only three agencies have files on Grant. Twenty seven agencies have files on Tesla. Some I've never even heard of."

"Twenty seven? Was there one from DOE?"

"Yes, but it doesn't explain the link between Tesla and Grant. Each file is black as night, so censored that you would think Tesla found the Holy Grail."

Perhaps the Holy Grail of energy.

"Anything on Farnsworth Tate's possible client?"

"Still working on it," replied Monet, frustrated with himself. "But I was able to obtain the security tapes from Alexis's building."

"Please don't tell me how you-"

"Nothing illegal. I just asked. *Gentillement*. Nicely. They emailed me the video content. The name of the man who visited Alexis's office and called himself Drake is Mitch Savitch. A lawyer."

"Let me guess. Farnsworth Tate?"

"*Oui*. He heads the firm's Special Transactions Team, whatever that means. I'll continue searching through their clients."

Carlton winced. They had a whole *team* of thugs like Drake? "Thanks, Henri. Keep me posted. Watch your back."

Alexis sat up, rubbed the sleep from her eyes, yawning. "What was that all about?" She mumbled.

Carlton summarized Monet's latest information.

"So what do we do now?" She asked, pushing herself up on the florid sofa, groggy.

"We call the FBI," replied Carlton through clenched teeth. He dialed Echeverria's number from the agent's business card. He answered before the second ring.

"I thought I had made myself clear, Carlton. You are ordered to stop investigating this case."

"I'm not calling for permission to investigate."

"The Bureau will not give you any information."

"I'm not calling to get information. I'm calling to *give* information."

"I appreciate that, but the investigation is now closed."

Carlton stood. "Closed? How can the investigation be closed if the-"

"It can because it is."

"Then it is about to be reopened," Carlton shot back.

"I don't think you understand, Car-"

"I'm only going to say this once, Echeverria, so listen carefully. If you want to record this conversation, go ahead. Despite the fact that I'm a DOJ prosecutor and gave you all the information you requested, I never once got a straight answer from you. But here is the additional information I have: I know that DOE is involved. I know that Grant's DOE, DOD, and FBI files are black. I know that Grant was a friend of Nikola Tesla. I know that Tesla's files are also black. Am I getting warmer? Before you answer, there is more.

"After our meeting, the movie program was stolen from my bungalow. Then a man calling himself Jaime Drake asked to buy a copy of the program from Alexis Hamilton, the tour guide. I sold it to him myself and almost had to be shipped back to DC in a body bag. Drake's real name is Mitch Savitch. Savitch is a lawyer with Farnsworth Tate, where he heads the firm's Special Transactions Team. Yesterday, Savitch and his people tried to kill me. Twice. This morning, they tried again. They failed, but managed to shoot Claire McLean, the wife of Max McLean. She's in a coma. I don't have to tell you who he is. I *will* tell you that you do not want to cross swords with him.

"I don't know who in the Bureau closed the investigation or why, but it was a monumental error. Now I am telling you that you have to reopen this case. Not as a private citizen on vacation, but as a DOJ prosecutor in the National Security Division. If you refuse, I will speak with my boss. Not the head of the National Security Division. The Attorney General. Personally." He paused to let the statement sink in, hoping that his bluff was believable. Multiple levels of DOJ aristocracy separated him from an AG who insisted his prosecutors follow the chain of command. "One of the first lessons I learned when I became a lawyer was that an error is not a mistake unless you fail to correct it. I am giving you an opportunity to correct the Bureau's error. Do you want to correct it?"

Echeverria remained silent for a long time. "Where and when do you want to meet?"

"Now. St. John's. Tenth floor. Private wing."

"I'll be there."

"Echeverria?"

"Yes?"

"This isn't personal."

Carlton hung up, dreading his next statement. He turned to Alexis, sitting on the sofa opposite him.

"When he gets here, you have to go into protective custody."

Alexis sat up on the edge of the couch, now fully awake, eyes wide open, incredulous. "What?"

"It will take a while for the FBI to reopen the investigation. Meanwhile, Savitch and his thugs are not going to give up. Sooner or later, they will track you down."

"They'll track you down too," she shot back.

"That risk is part of my job. I'm going back to Washington to make sure that the FBI does its job." He paused. "It's where I belong."

She stood, squinting down at him angrily. "You told McLean you would find the people responsible."

Carlton also stood. "I will. From Washington. That's where the trail leads."

"I don't trust the FBI, Carlton," she shot back, balling her fists. "They never told you about any of this. How can I be safe with people I don't know or trust?"

He did not blame her.

"I admit it started as a curiosity for me, but it's more than that now. I never got a chance to thank my father for everything he did for me. Just like he never got a chance to thank Grant for saving his career. If I can find whatever Grant was hiding, maybe I can accomplish both of those things at the same time. And what's the alternative? Living in fear in FBI custody?"

Carlton was more impressed with Alexis than ever before. She was willing to risk her life, not for fame or fortune, but for her father's memory. He nodded. "You already accomplished that, by helping the FBI reopen the case."

Carlton saw a tear roll down her cheek before she wiped it off in a quick motion, as if ashamed of the emotion that seeped through. "I thought I could trust you." She repressed a sob, angry that she had to. "Now you're throwing me to people even you don't trust just so you can get rid of me and finish the investigation on your own."

The accusation felt like a punch in his gut. "I'm not trying to get rid of you, Alexis." He could not protect her. He could not protect anyone. Sending her into FBI custody against her wishes would guarantee that she would never want to see him again. He hated the thought, but it was the safest thing for her, even if she did not realize it.

"I would much rather have you near me," he blurted out before realizing what he had said.

Alexis flashed him a surprised look. "You would?"

He wished he had chosen his words more carefully, but would not lie to her. "Yes. I would." Meeting Alexis was the only good thing that had happened to him since arriving in LA. And in a long time before that. "But I want you to be safe. And the safest place for you is in FBI protective custody."

She paused, shook her head. "You always think you're right, Carlton. I've figured that out about you. But you're not. FBI custody is not the safest place for me."

"You have to trust me, Alexis. I can't protect you. Not after what happened to Claire. Not after..." His voice trailed off.

Alexis drew nearer, hesitant. "After what?" She paused, not sure how to read him. "What is it?"

He turned away, shutting his eyes tight as graphic images flooded his mind.

She touched his hand. "You can tell me."

He pulled it back, remained immobile. She said nothing, waiting.

After a long moment, he lowered himself into an armchair, head down. She sat near him on the sofa, leaned toward him expectantly, waiting for him to break the silence.

"I was in Iraq. Two years of duty in the Navy Reserve." He paused, finding his words. "I commanded a squadron of PT boats - patrol boats - protecting a place called Khawr al-Amaya, an Iraqi oil terminal on the Persian Gulf. Then as now, oil was the only source of hard currency for the Iraqi government," he explained, the words coming more freely. "Al Qaeda in Iraq and Sunni insurgents regularly targeted the terminal to prevent the fledgling democratic government from getting on its feet. But they were more of an annoyance than a real threat. We had larger numbers, more boats, the best equipment, the best training. And we would spot them long before they could become a threat."

Alexis made to take his hand in hers, but again Carton moved his away. He wanted understanding, not pity. She waited.

"We got cocky. *I* got cocky. I was so used to spotting the terrorists from a distance and defeating their crude methods that I never considered that they might launch a sophisticated attack." He paused. "One day, we spotted their boats again. We got ready to sink them, but instead of firing blindly from far away like before, they sped off. I thought they had given up after so many losses, but a few minutes later, I realized that they had launched a completely different attack. By then it was too late." He shut his eyes as though he could prevent the scene from replaying in his mind as it had had countless times before.

"Before turning back, they launched drones. Little remote-controlled helicopters, the kind you find in toy stores. Except that these were fitted with cameras and rigged with explosives. We had no way of anticipating such an attack, but by the time we figured out what was happening, four of the helicopters dropped onto our boats, blowing them up." He grimaced, running a hand through his hair, grabbing a fistful. "I lost six men. Their bodies were torn apart. Five more were injured, four of them permanently disabled." He lowered his head, placed a hand over his face, rubbed his eyes. There were no tears. He had shed them all earlier, not while recovering at a field hospital, but upon his return to the maddening normalcy of Washington. That was when the nightmares had taken hold. Neighbors heard his screams rending the night for months afterward.

"We found out who the attackers were, but it was too late. They escaped into the desert." He took a deep breath, sat up, his eyes red. "I failed to protect my men. Now they're dead or disabled. If I couldn't protect them in the field with superior numbers, the best equipment and training, and advanced warning, how can I possibly protect you?"

Alexis had never imagined that he had experienced such trauma. He had hidden it well. "I...I had no idea. I'm so sorry."

Carlton was too raw to respond.

Alexis remained silent for a long moment, hesitated, then asked: "Was the oil facility damaged?"

He shook his head. "When the attackers realized what easy targets we were, they focused all the drones on us." His jaw tightened. "The bastards. From that point, on, we installed jammers so remote controlled drones could not come near the facility."

"So you fulfilled your mission."

Carlton's eyes bored into her. "My men were slaughtered!" He shouted before regaining his composure, rubbing his jaw. "I'm sorry. That was out of line."

Alexis remained adamant. "The cost was extreme. But you did fulfill your mission."

Carlton glanced down. "To the facility, not to my men," he muttered.

"You said that you could not have anticipated-"

"I should have."

"I can't imagine what you went through, Carlton. I don't pretend to know the first thing about military tactics." She hesitated anew. "And I am asking this with the deepest respect possible, but are you saying that because you really could have prevented the attack or because you survived and your men died?"

Carlton opened his mouth to speak, closed it. He had often thought about the possibility, but rejected it. He still did not accept it, but hearing it from Alexis, no longer did he fully reject it. He hung his head low. "Honestly, I don't think I'll ever know."

"You fought to protect the facility and you did, just like you've been protecting me and the McLeans all along. Isn't that why you joined DOJ? What was it you told me? 'To protect the good from the bad'?"

Carlton snorted. "Some protection. We got shot at for the past two days and Claire is in a coma."

"You think we simply got lucky in the Hollywood Hills? It wasn't luck. You figured out I was the next victim. You saved me, just like you saved little Spencer. We would have been killed in Malibu if you had not reacted so quickly. Claire is in a coma, but she's alive. So is Max. So am I."

"Tell that to him."

She reached over, took his hand in hers. "I may be younger than you, Carlton, but contrary to what you may think, I'm not naive. After what we've been through, I know what the risks are. Just like your men did. And I also know that the safest place for me is not with the FBI." She paused. "It's with you."

He turned to gaze at her.

This time, he did not let go of her hand.

22. TRANSCRIPT

Polish Embassy
Paris, France
7:33 AM

Sobieski was so curious about the transcript from Brussels that he nearly tore the handcuffed attaché case from the diplomatic courier's wrist. He did not even wait for the scanner to finish decrypting the entire coded transmission, instead reading each page as it slid out of the printer, still warm.

When he finished, his hands were trembling.

"*Boze Swiety*." *Bo-zeh Sh-fieti*. Holy God.

He wiped the sweat from his bald pate, reached for a cigarette, was barely able to light it.

The information on the pages before him was a veritable intelligence coup.

And sheer madness.

Prince Hakim's monstrously simple plan amounted to a devastating attack on the U.S. economy, a fundamentalist Islamic invasion of Europe, an existential isolation of Israel, and a castration of the Vatican. This last point was particularly untenable for Sobieski. Under the leadership of his late compatriot Blessed John Paul the Great, together with Poland's Solidarity movement and the Reagan Administration, the Holy See had been responsible for delivering Sobieski's homeland from the Soviet communist yoke, toppling the first dominoes of the Evil Empire's hegemony - and an evil empire it had truly been, he knew first hand. This one would be worse.

Sobieski was not merely reading an intelligence transcript. He was looking at the beginning of the end of Western civilization.

"*Skurwysyn*." Son of a bitch. How could France and the E.U. go along with such madness?

It wasn't France and the E.U., Sobieski reflected. It was Euroil and de Ville.

Metz would forge Euroil into the world's largest oil company, reaping untold billions, able to swallow its weakened rivals whole, perhaps even becoming a global private energy monopoly. De Ville would be willing to pay any price for the E.U. to replace the U.S. as the world's economic superpower. As de Ville and Euroil were both French, France would sideline reigning Germany as the E.U.'s economic master, able to beat into submission the newly admitted, once resurgent yet now economically teetering Eastern European members. Such as Poland.

"*Cholera!*" *Ho-leh-ra*. Damn it! Sobieski shouted, slamming his open palm against his desk with such force that his lamp clattered to the floor.

Now that he knew what Hakim was planning, he could not keep the information to himself. He steadied himself with a deep breath, grabbed his encrypted telephone, dialed the *Agencja*'s Deputy Director's office in Warsaw.

"I don't care what he is doing. Get him on the telephone right now. *Natychmiast!*" *Nah-teek-meeahst*. Immediately! He shouted to the colonel's secretary, his face beet red with anger.

A few moments later, Sobieski heard the familiar gruff voice of Colonel Witold Peszka. *Vee-told Pesh-kah*. "This had better be good, Sobieski."

"It isn't good, *panie pulkowniku*," he replied. Colonel sir. "It's a nightmare."

"Explain yourself."

"I cannot discuss the particulars over the telephone, colonel. I'm sending you a transcript of the intelligence by courier. You should have it in a few hours."

"We're encrypted."

"Too much of a risk for this, sir."

Peszka sighed. "Very well. I will be waiting."

Three hours and half a pack of Marlboros later, Sobieski answered his telephone.

"It's Peszka. I understand why you didn't want to discuss this over the telephone. This is a disaster."

"I'm pleased that you concur, colonel. We have to give this to the Americans, the Vatican, and Israel."

"Slow down, major. We cannot go to any of them before going through the appropriate channels first, especially not the Americans."

Sobieski felt his stomach sink. "I'm sorry, colonel, but I'm not sure what you mean."

"Poland is no longer a completely independent nation. Like it or not, Poland is now part of the European Union. Before we can go to our counterparts in the CIA, the Vatican Secretariat of State, or the Mossad, we have to go to the E.U. First and foremost, this is a European matter."

Cholera. The E.U.? The E.U. foreign minister was part of the problem, not the solution. This was about international security, not diplomatic politics. Sobieski hated politics, especially diplomatic politics, with its smiling lies and backstabbing pats on the back. What he really wanted to do was get Carlton, fly to Riyadh, and drill a bullet into Prince Hakim's skull in person. Carlton - was he even still alive?

He bit back a curse. "What do you propose, colonel?"

"I will discuss it with Kosinski," Peszka replied, referring to the *Agencja's* Director. "He will pass it on to the prime minister, who will most likely alert Van Der Straat." The Luxembourger Peter Van Der Straat was the first E.U. president since the Lisbon Treaty had changed the post from a six month rotation among E.U. member states to an individual appointed by the 27 E.U. leaders behind closed doors, with no popular vote or input.

"Van Der Straat was the compromise candidate between France and Germany," said Sobieski. "Euroil is a French company and De Ville is a former French foreign minister. If this deal with the devil goes through, Euroil will become the largest energy company in the world. By nationalizing Euroil with a simple legislative vote, France will become the most important national energy player after Saudi Arabia and the undisputed ruler of the E.U. Van Der Straat will do nothing to anger France given those stakes. Even if he agrees to pass this information to other E.U. countries, it may be too late."

"I do not disagree with you, major, but think of Poland's credibility within the E.U. if we go to the U.S. with this information before going to Europe. We are already at crossed swords with France and Germany because of our alliance with the U.S. in Iraq. And in an even worse situation with the thugs in the Kremlin threatening cuts in gas supplies and reasserting Russia's dominance over Eastern Europe, especially now that America has reneged on its missile defense bases after we took the risk to host them. Poland cannot afford to bypass the E.U. on this matter, major. We must go through the appropriate channels first."

Sobieski winced, but the mention of missile defense made him think of another option. "Poland is a member of NATO, colonel. We have an obligation-"

"Major!" Peszka's voice boomed. "NATO is a military alliance. This is not a military matter. We will go through diplomatic E.U. channels first. That is an order. Do I make myself clear?"

Sobieski paused, took a deep breath. "*Tak jest, panie pulkowniku.*" *Tahk yest*. Yes sir, colonel.

"I will be in touch." Peszka paused. "Do not stain your family's pristine name by doing something rash," he warned, before hanging up.

Sobieski slammed the handset down, nearly breaking it, too frustrated for words. The only thing worse than a looming disaster was the inability to do anything about it.

Sobieski stood and uncorked a dusty bottle of Chateau Figeac from the wine cabinet. The Bordeaux was exorbitantly priced, a perfect fit with the rage and frustration that coursed through his veins. Not bothering to decant it, he drank straight from the bottle, feeling the velvet liquid warm his mind and body.

He sat back down. Despite his intense personal feelings, Sobieski reminded himself that he was only a major in the *Agencja*, not its head or even a deputy head. Whether he liked it or not, a major had to obey his colonel's orders.

Until those orders conflicted with his sworn duty to protect Poland.

23 SECRETS

St. John's Health Center
Santa Monica, California
1:43 PM

Carlton watched Echeverria flash Davos his badge before walking down the hospital corridor. Despite their verbal sparring, Carlton felt a sense of comradeship with the FBI agent. He had major issues with Faraday in the Counterterrorism Division, but also great respect for the Bureau's field agents - brick agents, as they were known - dedicated men and women who worked tirelessly to protect the country from attack. Although not widely reported, Carlton knew that FBI agents had suffered so much stress trying to prevent terror attacks after 9-11 that some had committed suicide. Yet their pay was a pittance. Most Americans would have been shocked to learn that some FBI agents serving in high-rent parts of the country technically qualified for food stamps.

A committed, no-nonsense government agent like Echeverria should not be a competitor, he reasoned, but an ally.

Carlton extended his hand to the raven-haired agent. "Thank you for coming, Special Agent Echeverria."

He gave Carlton's hand a firm tug, evaluated him with a piercing look. "My friends call me Eche."

"Mine call me Carlton. Come on in." Carlton ushered him inside the pseudo-living room.

Eche glanced at Davos who had followed him and now stood by the door.

"Please give us some room," said Carlton, closing the door. "As you can see, Max McLean is not taking any chances. Have a seat."

Eche nodded, sat in one of the two armchairs across from the sofa.

Sensing that Eche would divulge less information in Alexis' presence, he had persuaded her to remain in the hallway with Davos. He filled two mugs with mediocre hospital coffee, handed one to Eche before sitting across from him.

The agent nodded his thanks. "I would like to get all of your facts since our meeting." He removed his pocket recorder. "I also want your word that you will stop investigating from now on."

"As to Grant's program, yes. As to the people who tried to kill Alexis and Claire McLean, no."

Eche glared at him.

Carlton shrugged. "I'm simply being honest with you." He leaned forward. "Look, I was wrong to violate your jurisdiction. I've had a beef with the Bureau for some time, but it has nothing to do with you or your Counterintelligence Division. As long as you reopen the investigation, you have my word that I won't step on your turf as far as Grant's program is concerned. But if we're going to mend fences, *you* have to be honest with *me*. Your interest is in Grant's program and what is behind it, not in the people who tried to kill Alexis Hamilton, the McLeans, and me."

"They are one and the same, Carlton. We will find them," replied Eche. His tone carried more apology than will.

"I have no doubt, but you will find them later, after you've solved the matter of Grant's program. Until then, you won't have the manpower to go after the people who tried to kill us."

Eche reluctantly nodded.

"DOJ does. If I find anything that has to do with the program, I will let you know - only you. Is that acceptable?" Carlton asked, avoiding any mention that his division had no jurisdiction whatsoever over the attempted murder of three civilians.

Eche stared at his coffee cup, looked back up at Carlton, nodded anew.

"Aces," said Carlton. "Here is what I know."

"That's a lot of information," announced Eche once Carlton had finished, shutting off his recorder, remaining bent over his cup.

"Way too much for a summer vacation. Now I have some questions."

Eche squinted. "That depends."

Carlton flashed him an exasperated look. "Please don't start with that again. I need answers. For starters, why was the investigation closed?"

Eche remained silent, studying him. Carlton sensed the inner conflict within the agent. Eche was trained not to disclose information, but he was also trained to complete his investigations successfully. Carlton could have returned to DC without giving him any information at all, then stepped on his toes by going to a senior DOJ official. Instead, Carlton had agreed to stop investigating Grant's program and offered Eche vital information. Information that might allow him not only to correct the Bureau's error - or DOE's error - in closing the investigation prematurely, but to avoid a possible career-ending blot on his record at the Bureau, since DOE would likely pin any resulting blame on him. Carlton had also refrained from bargaining with Eche, *quid pro quo*. He had laid out his information freely, no strings attached.

Eche downed the remaining contents of his cup in a single gulp. "I checked your record, Carlton. Impressive. I noticed that some of the information was blacked out, not unlike Grant's files. You don't have code-word clearance on the Grant case, but your clearance is pretty high and as far as I'm concerned, what you've been through and discovered so far places you pretty close to the need-to-know category."

Carlton found himself liking Echeverria more and more. Far from being a blind follower of regulation as he had originally believed, Eche was willing to think and take risks for a worthy goal.

He watched Eche refill his coffee cup, drop a lump of brown sugar into the black liquid, dissolve it with quick stirs of his spoon before sitting back down, this time directly beside Carlton. He leaned over, made sure the recorder was shut off.

"This is strictly confidential, Carlton," he started in a low voice. "Man to man, not agency to agency." He waited until Carlton nodded. "You may not believe it, but I disagreed with the Bureau's closure of the investigation."

"I'm glad. Then why was it closed?"

"The Bureau never called the shots in the investigation."

That surprised Carlton. "Who did?"

"Since 1942, the Bureau has been investigating Grant's case on behalf of a predecessor to the Department of Energy, before DOE was created in 1977. DOE closed the investigation, not the Bureau."

"Brendan Wallace."

Eche nodded.

"The only reason I can think of for his dream job offer was to stop me from investigating." Carlton paused. "Thank you for the warning, by the way."

Another nod.

"And telling me about the code-word classification. You knew I would understand its significance, investigate further. Warning me off the DOE job allowed me to stay in LA and investigate. Tell me when I'm getting warm here." Eche's smile was answer enough. "But why would DOE shut down the investigation?"

"I think DOE wanted to cut the Bureau out and continue the investigation on their own."

Carlton gazed at Eche, confused.

Eche smirked. "I take it you don't deal with DOE much. DOE is riddled with management problems, internal inconsistencies, bureaucratic feuds. It's not a surprise why the government blows billions on unviable alternative energy companies that go bankrupt or why our energy research labs are so porous." He referred to the bewildering security lapses at top-secret labs, so deep and wide that even after 9-11, some were completely unprotected against attack and could not account for computer discs containing top secret nuclear weapons information.

Eche paused, weighing whether he should explain further. "But I don't think jurisdictional competition is the cause here. DOE was the lead agency on the case, but I considered Wallace too...much of a risk to entrust him with Grant's program. I was baffled by why he would cut out the Bureau until you mentioned the lawyer at Farnsworth Tate buying a copy of it from you. Now it makes sense. Wallace cut the Bureau out once he obtained a copy of Grant's program so his old law firm could investigate it alone."

"With no results going to the FBI now that the investigation is closed," added Carlton. "Between the connections to Wallace and Savitch, Farnsworth Tate is far too involved not to be the central player. Law firms work for clients. Any idea who that might be?"

"No, but I hope to find out once I restart the Bureau's investigation." Eche made to stand up. Carlton touched his sleeve.

"One more question. Why are people so interested in Grant's program?"

Eche gazed at Carlton for a long moment, then looked around the makeshift living room. He stood, motioned for Carlton to follow him inside the small bathroom. He closed the door, removed a slim metal box from his jacket the size of a pack of cigarettes, pressed a button on its side.

"Electronic white noise generator," he explained, lowering his voice to a whisper. He leaned close, pausing to choose his words. "Montgomery Grant was an agent for the War Department from October 1935 until his death in December 1942. He and other stars ferreted out over a dozen big name actors and directors collaborating with the Nazis. As you know, Grant became friends with Nikola Tesla. At the time, a Federal Power Commission research lab near LA was working on highly classified energy applications based on some of Tesla's theories."

"I thought the FPC was just a regulatory body," Carlton whispered back, trying to make himself comfortable in the cramped room. He would have felt foolish had he not been riveted by what Eche was at last revealing.

"That's why the War Department used the FPC as a cover. Everyone suspected the War Department, not the FPC. Tesla was too frail to make regular trips between New York and LA. The FPC was about to send one of its agents to Tesla when it discovered that some of their agents were being tracked by foreign spies. Grant's regular trips between LA and New York and his existing friendship with Tesla provided perfect cover, so the War Department enlisted him as a courier. Grant carried information between the two until the night of his death."

"What was he carrying?"

Eche hesitated, deciding how much to reveal. "Tesla was working on several energy applications at the end of his life, but he did not have the necessary technology or funding to complete his research. Before his death, Tesla made a breakthrough, solved a major obstacle to one of those energy applications, which the War Department believed could have military applications. That is one reason why Tesla's files remain black - there are many others. On the night he was murdered, Grant was carrying Tesla's breakthrough formula to the Power Commission scientists in LA. A man named Dalibard. As a Yugoslavian émigré and an opponent of the Nazis, Tesla had many ties to the Royal Yugoslavian

Government in Exile. One of its members was a communist agent. He discovered that Grant was acting as a courier for Tesla's formula and informed the intelligence attaché at the Soviet Embassy in Washington."

"When do the Nazis come into the picture?" Asked Carlton, confused.

"They don't. The Soviets murdered Grant, not the Nazis. The Bureau planted the Nazi story to mislead the Hollywood press and make the Soviets think we did not suspect them. The Bureau already knew that the Soviets were not our friends, but during World War II, they were our allies against the Nazis. News of Soviet espionage inside the U.S. would have caused grave harm to the U.S.-Soviet war effort. Luckily, the Soviets did not obtain the formula Grant was carrying."

"How can you be sure?" Asked Carlton, coughing, his voice hoarse from all the whispering.

Eche grimaced. "If the Soviets had obtained the formula, the entire world would have known."

"If the Soviets didn't get it, why would the FBI still be involved?"

"The Bureau believes that Grant hid the formula before he was shot. We want to make sure we are the only ones who find it."

Carlton crooked his head quizzically. "Why would the FBI care if someone else finds the formula now if the U.S. already obtained it nearly 65 years ago?"

Eche leaned so close that Carlton could smell the coffee on his breath. He fixed Carlton with a cold stare. "The government never obtained Tesla's formula."

Carlton was stunned. *An endless supply of electricity.* Up for grabs. "If Grant died before delivering the formula, why didn't Tesla simply send it to the Power Commission through another courier?"

"That was the plan. But Tesla died before the courier reached him in New York. The Bureau thought it could obtain the formula from Tesla's papers. It removed them from his hotel room the morning of his death, spent day and night reviewing them. The Special Agent in Charge, a man by the name of Foxworth, was reported to have found something of great importance deep in Tesla's papers. His military transport crashed in the Atlantic with Tesla's original papers en route to meet Franklin Roosevelt in Casablanca. He never told anyone what he discovered and we never found any copies."

"But Grant made a copy and hid it somewhere," concluded Carlton.

"That is what we believe. DOE took over the Power Commission's research after the department was created. DOE has its own investigative arm, but the Bureau had been involved from day one, so DOE left the investigation to us. Since Grant's death, several clues to the location of the hidden copy have turned up. We followed up on each, but none led to anything of importance."

"That's why you wanted a copy of Grant's program after you read about it in the paper. So you could see if it contained any clues. And it did, didn't it? The address is the clue," concluded Carlton, feeling vindicated.

Eche nodded. "We confirmed that the handwriting is Grant's, but as you discovered, there was no 2232 Watt Heights Road in the U.S. or anywhere else in 1942. Whoever Farnsworth Tate is working for wants the formula. So do the people who stole the program from your bungalow. I don't know who they are, but now they both have the clue. The Bureau has to decipher it first."

Eche removed a business card from his wallet, turned it over, jotted down additional contact information.

"Your investigation of the program is over, as you agreed," he reiterated, "but if you obtain any additional information you think might help, you can reach me day or night." He handed Carlton the card.

"Agreed, if you do the same in my murder investigation," replied Carlton. He placed the card in his pocket, shook Eche's hand hard. "Thank you for taking me into your confidence." He could have felt used, but did not. He had decided to investigate the program on his own, with no prodding other than the mention of the case's code-word classification. And instead of stopping him, Eche had in fact helped him, subtly.

"Don't be so quick to thank me. Now that you know this information, what you've been through may be just the beginning. *Vaya con Dios*."

He moved toward the door. Carlton held him back. "One final question. What was the energy application that Tesla solved?"

Eche shook his head. "Even I don't know."

"Code-word classified?"

"Even the classification is classified."

24 CASABLANCA

St. John's Health Center
6:03 PM

After Eche's departure, Carlton and Alexis rode the hospital elevator down to the cafeteria and brought dinner back to the makeshift living room. Without a meal since the previous night, they polished off the plastic-tasting hospital food in seconds. Out of government obligation but also for Alexis's safety, Carlton revealed little of what Eche had told him except that Grant had hidden something of great importance to national security. He was relieved when she did not press the matter.

At least they were safe - for the moment. With Eche's revelations still making his head spin, Carlton was in dire need of a mental break. He craved a stogie but St. John's was smoke-free. Instead, he clicked on the television, surfed channels until coming across one of his favorite Hollywood classics, starring Humphrey Bogart, Ingrid Bergman, Sydney Greenstreet, Claude Rains, and Peter Lorre.

"I love *Casablanca*," Alexis announced with delight, similarly pleased at the break. She sat on the couch next to him, pulling her legs underneath her. "It's quite a coincidence, isn't it?"

He shot her a confused glance.

"*Casablanca* was made the year of Grant's death and released when Roosevelt was actually *in* Casablanca meeting with Churchill."

Carlton recalled what Eche had stated about Foxworth's fateful trip to Casablanca. He watched the black and white movie in nervous silence, pleased that Alexis was seated next to him on the couch. *Rick's Café Americain's* neon sign winked off on the screen. The neon tube had been one of Tesla's many inventions, Carlton reflected, when an idea flashed in his mind.

He shot up from the sofa. "That's what it means!"

"What?" Asked Alexis, startled.

"The set," answered Carlton, scrambling to find Eche's home number on the reverse of his business card before grabbing the hospital phone.

"What set?" Asked Alexis, now puzzled. "What are you talking about?"

Hi, this is Eche. I'm not home right now. Leave me a message. Beep.

"It's Carlton. I think I figured it out. Call me as soon as you get this message." He left Alexis's cell phone number and hung up, then left the same message on the agent's cell and work voicemails.

"Are you going to explain or do I have to guess?" Alexis repeated impatiently.

Carlton turned to her. "All this time, we've been thinking about the address on the movie program as a street address, but we know that there was no such address in 1942."

Alexis nodded.

"But if Grant wrote it down, it had to mean something. Grant was an actor. He starred in a whole bunch of movies."

"Forty three," précised Alexis.

Carlton leaned forward. "What if the address on the program is an address in one of Grant's movies?"

Alexis stared back, amazed. "I can't believe I didn't think of it."

Carlton straightened, smiled. "Bruins one, Trojans zip."

Alexis smirked. "Eche is going to have to watch a lot of movies."

They finished watching the rest of *Casablanca*, anxiously waiting for Eche to call back. The local news came on as soon as the movie credits began to roll.

We begin our broadcast with breaking news from Marina Del Rey, where police report that a man has suffered multiple gunshot wounds just moments ago at the hands of an unknown assailant. What you see here is live footage from outside the Mariner's Village apartment complex where the victim was found. Police have not released his identity. The brutal slaying comes one day after the murder of the general manager of a car dealership in Santa Monica. We now go live to-

Carlton stared at the address Eche had jotted down on the back of his business card. "My God."

Mariner's Village Apartments. Marina Del Rey.

He showed it to Alexis before performing a subtle sign of the cross and reciting a silent prayer.

Alexis's face was ashen. "It could be someone else."

Carlton knew it was not, shook his head.

"You still want me to go into FBI protective custody?"

Carlton grimaced. "You were right. I was wrong. Thank God you convinced me. Savitch's people must have killed him. Anything else would be too much of a coincidence."

Putting aside considerable mistrust and institutional jockeying, Carlton and Eche had finally joined forces. Eche had entrusted him with classified information. Both had agreed to share information in their bifurcated investigations. Savitch had not only killed a fellow federal agent. He had killed Carlton's newest partner.

He was going to pay.

Carlton soon came to another realization. "With Eche gone, we won't be safe until we find whatever Grant hid. Until we can figure out its location, we have to get out of Los Angeles."

"And go where?" Asked Alexis, as pale as her white T-shirt.

"Whatever Grant was carrying, chances are that he hid it around LA. We can't stray too far."

"San Diego? San Francisco? Santa Barbara? Palm Springs?"

"Bingo. McLean owns a hotel in Palm Springs."

"We can use Davos's car. Let's go," said Alexis, on her feet and already moving toward the hallway.

"Wait!" Carlton grabbed her by the arm. "Savitch and his thugs have been following us for two days. Your office. Your house. Malibu. If they were able to get to Eche, they may have followed him too, probably from here. We've been here for hours. Savitch probably has thugs at each entrance, waiting for us to leave."

Alexis went slack as the realization hit her. "So what are we-" Her cell phone trilled. She peered at it, saw the 202 area code, handed the device to Carlton.

"I have to call you back, Henri. It's chaos over here."

"It's about to get worse," replied Monet.

The ball of ice reappeared in Carlton's gut. "How can it-" He swallowed dryly. "Tell me."

"I found a link between Farnsworth Tate and energy. Only one, but a giant one. I missed it before because I was focusing only on the firm's private clients, like energy companies."

Carlton remained silent, felt the blood throb in his temples.

"Farnsworth Tate is the main counsel to the Kingdom of Saudi Arabia."

Carlton felt a rush of anger. The insurgents who had killed his men in Iraq were Saudis. But those had been Al Qaeda terrorists. Farnsworth Tate's client was the government of Saudi Arabia, the Saudi royal family, itself an Al Qaeda target for years and a staunch ally of the United States. He then recalled what Tesla had worked on during his final days. *An endless supply of free electricity.* Saudi Arabia was the world's largest exporter of oil. Its economy relied almost entirely on it for revenue. The desert kingdom had the most to lose from such a discovery.

Fear soon supplanted his anger. If the Saudis were behind Farnsworth Tate and Savitch, the enemy had access to far greater resources than he, a DOJ prosecutor in limbo on forced vacation, his only government ally murdered, cut off from headquarters, on the run.

After a quick call to Maxfield, Carlton led Alexis down the hallway, running.

"We can't leave if Savitch's people are surrounding the building," she protested. "You just said so. It's suicide."

"We're going to leave, all right. Just not out the door."

25 DGSE

François de Ville sat at his glass desk, legs crossed, head perched atop his manicured hands. He stared at the night beyond his floor to ceiling window, deep in thought.

The message he had just received was causing him grave concern.

As E.U. foreign minister, the aristocratic *haut fonctionnaire* - high functionary, as the French called them - was charged with conducting foreign relations on behalf of all Europe. In de Ville's reasoning, if France's star shined bright, it would illuminate the rest of Europe's dimmer planets, helping Europe's stature.

The Saudi proposal to Euroil would not only make France shine, but explode with radiance as it had not since perhaps Napoléon or Louis XIV, the Sun King. It was an unprecedented opportunity for France and, by extension, for Europe. Yet the fact that the Polish foreign minister had contacted de Ville's replacement at the Quai d'Orsay in Paris was a cause of great worry. The Pole had merely asked questions, but their nature indicated that the official had far more than a simple suspicion about the Saudi proposal to Euroil. The Polish foreign minister *knew* something.

Which could only mean one thing.

Une fuite. A leak.

Ingrates, he thought, sneering. France and Germany had done Poland a huge favor by condescending to admit it into the E.U. Instead of gratefully following the two European leaders' orders, Poland had allied itself firmly with the U.S., sending Polish troops to Afghanistan and Iraq - not mere trainers who stayed safe in uncontested areas, but special forces, to the most violent areas of conflict. Then Poland again thumbed its nose at France and Germany, agreeing to base a U.S. missile defense shield on Polish soil to defend against the increasingly likely possibility of Iranian nuclear-armed missiles before the new American administration had reversed course.

Now the Polish foreign minister was asking questions about Saudi Arabia and Euroil. It was no coincidence. And it was time to send Poland a clear message in response.

De Ville lifted his telephone handset, dialed a number committed to memory during his days as French foreign minister, waited for the device's encryption status light to switch from red to green. One did not contact a top field agent of the *Direction Générale de la Sécurité Exterieure* (DGSE), the Directorate-General for Exterior Security - France's CIA - without using an encrypted line. Certainly not for the purpose he intended.

"Hulot," a gruff voice answered on the fifth ring, indicating either that its owner had been roused from deep slumber or had been drinking heavily. Knowing the DGSE colonel, probably both, thought de Ville, grimacing. A woman was probably also involved. Perhaps two.

"*C'est moi,*" announced de Ville. It's me.

Hulot immediately understood: no names.

"*Oui,*" replied Hulot, fully alert. In addition to his penchant for *la bonne vie*, the good life, Hulot was dedicated to the French *tricolore* flag mind, body, and soul.

"I have discovered a problem that requires your immediate attention." De Ville paused dramatically. "It is quite...sensitive."

"*Je comprends.*" I understand.

"I have reason to believe the Poles have obtained secret energy information belonging to Euroil. I do not know whether they will use it on their own, give it to an ally, or sell it to the highest bidder, but each of those options would bring severe damage to the company. I do not have to tell you how important Euroil is to France or to the rest of Europe."

He did not. "*Les salauds,*" Hulot hissed. The bastards. Hulot had an axe to grind with his Polish counterparts in the *Agencja*. They were the ones who had swiped the surveillance microdevices that his DGSE team had stolen from America's DARPA less than a year ago.

De Ville was well aware of the tension between the two, which is one of the reasons he had called him. He allowed himself a wry smile.

Hulot had taken the bait. And everything he had told the French spook was true - technically.

"Any leads?" Asked Hulot.

"It could be anyone, but my bet is that the Polish embassy in Paris is heavily involved. It would be very helpful if you would follow its suspected *Agencja* personnel carefully." Foreign intelligence personnel were never labeled as such in their embassy postings. "Just enough to make it clear that we are watching - unless they go too far, of course. In that case, you must do whatever you can to secure Euroil's proprietary information."

De Ville had expected immediate agreement. Instead, Hulot paused.

"Is there a problem?"

"Sir, the DGSE's jurisdiction lies outside of France's borders. Would this not be a job better suited to the DST, especially its Economic Security and Protection of National Assets department?" Asked Hulot, referring to the *Direction de la Surveillance du Territoire*, France's domestic intelligence agency, akin to the FBI.

"I do not have as much confidence in anyone at the DST as I do in you, colonel."

"You flatter me, *monsieur le ministre*, but-"

"And the Polish embassy is sovereign Polish territory," de Ville interrupted, "so your surveillance technically constitutes foreign surveillance. Remember your agency's motto."

Partout ou nécessité fait loi. Everywhere where necessity makes it law.

"I understand."

"*Tres bien.* This is too confidential to go through regular channels. No records, no trail. Report only to me."

26 SUMMERWIND

St. John's Health Center
Santa Monica, California
7:03 PM

Ten floors above the rush of cars on Santa Monica Boulevard, the rooftop of St. John's hospital remained quiet until the thump of helicopter rotors sounded in the distance, growing louder. A minute later, the white fuselage of a Bell 412HP helicopter appeared, a large red cross painted on its side. The windows of the hospital's upper floors vibrated as the heavy-lift Medevac helicopter flared over the rooftop, kissed the helipad with its twin landing skids, sweeping the area clean with its hurricane rotor wash.

The pilot had not yet cut power to the twin Pratt & Whitney Canada engines when the helicopter's side door slid open. Ignoring the deafening engine noise and the rotor downblow whipping their faces, two hospital technicians transferred the bloody, broken body of a teenager struck by a drunk driver onto a gurney, careful not to snag the IV tubes and electronic wires keeping the youngster alive. Seconds later, they rolled the critical patient into the hospital's waiting elevator.

With her patient safely delivered and the helicopter's four-blade rotor now immobile, pilot Molly Gould unfastened her seat harness, removed her helmet, shook her mane of blond hair loose. She opened the cockpit door and stepped out onto the breezy rooftop, walking straight into a man wearing cowboy boots.

"What the- Who are you?" She demanded, startled.

The man held up a silver badge. "Patrick Carlton. Department of Justice. We're your next passengers."

* * *

Immediately upon landing at Los Angeles International Airport, Carlton and Alexis had taken the first flight they could find to throw Savitch and his thugs off their trail, then several others as an added precaution. It had taken all night. As the morning sun rose, they sat in a half-empty

United Express turboprop, finally en route to Palm Springs. Maxfield had proposed his employer's Cessna Citation private jet but Carlton demurred, considering it too easy to track.

Alexis was asleep, shifting in her seat until finding a comfortable spot nuzzling against Carlton despite many available seats. Carlton did not protest. Her head felt good on his shoulder. Awake, Alexis had proven herself a smart, resilient woman. Asleep, she looked like a little girl. Her chest rose and fell slowly, with a calm and peace that belied their perilous situation. He was glad to feel her so close and to leave the City of Angels behind.

He wanted to sleep, but his mind kept focusing on Saudi Arabia.

As part of DOJ's National Security Division, Carlton knew more than most about the homeland of 15 of the 19 9-11 hijackers, the only country in the world named after its royal family. For over 200 years, two clans had shared Saudi power: the royal line, who controlled government, and the clerical line, who controlled religion and culture as descendants of the 18th century fundamentalist Sunni cleric Muhammad ibn Abdul al-Wahhab. Wahhab's hate-spewing diatribes against Jews, Christians, and other Muslims years *before* the United States' founding served as the theo-political basis for modern day Islamist jihadism.

In 1945, Saudi king Ibn Saud had forged an alliance with Franklin Delano Roosevelt. Since then, the royal line relied on U.S. protection and the U.S. on Saudi oil. The mutual dependence grew, inflaming the clerical line, who began to preach and fund jihadi terror, particularly after Islamic fundamentalists stormed the mosque at Mecca in 1979. With the tacit approval of the royal family - and, some alleged, funding as well - the terrorist violence was first directed *outside* the Kingdom, spawning the attacks of 9-11 and providing up to 45 percent of the foreign fighters against the Coalition in Iraq, including those who had killed and maimed his men. After 9-11, the jihadi violence had turned *inside* the Kingdom against foreign and royal family targets cooperating with the U.S. Today, Saudi Arabia was home to only two percent of the world's Muslims, yet financed 90 percent of the world's Islamic institutions, much of their message inseparable from what Al Qaeda preached, except as to who should lead.

Tight links between Saudi and the 9-11 attacks threw the U.S.-Saudi relationship into crisis - for a while. The oil-thirsty U.S. and world markets needed not only Saudi's vast oil reserves, but its unique ability to produce more oil on demand - its 'swing production' - when other oil producing countries pumped at maximum capacity. In turn, the Saudi royal family needed U.S. help to defend against its internal and external enemies, including Iraq under Saddam Hussein, who had planned to invade Saudi Arabia after Kuwait in 1991 - the stationing of U.S. troops on holy Islamic soil during the first Gulf War had inflamed the Islamic fundamentalists long after their departure - and now a soon-to-be nuclear-armed Iran.

So the dance continued, with most of the Saudi ire directed toward the U.S., and not just from the fundamentalist crazies. Whereas radical Saudis considered the U.S. the demon of the age and the royal family its co-conspirators against Wahhabi Islam, moderate and pro-reform Saudis blamed the U.S. for propping up its corrupt, authoritarian monarchy rather than pressing for democratic reforms as it had elsewhere, such as Iraq. It would not take long for things to come to another boil unless the U.S. could defuse the situation by maintaining Saudi security while forcing real reforms in a country that still outlawed demonstrations, political parties, a free press, and not only non-Islamic but any non-Wahhabi religious observance. Carlton had heard rumors that the Saudi king's recent removal of a few religious hardliners from office had occurred just because of such pressure from the new administration, and would culminate in the announcement of a more democratic Saudi constitution, but with Saudi, it was often difficult to separate truth from fiction.

He sighed, gazing at the sandy scenery below, finding little humor in the irony of escaping from the Saudis by fleeing into the scorching desert. Yet Palm Springs itself elicited a wan smile. The desert town was synonymous with the Golden Age of Hollywood. People flocked to the oasis to burn in its year-round sun, sip bottomless poolside martinis, smoke without shame, and commune with the ghosts of Hollywood past, including Carlton's beloved Frank Sinatra and, of course, Montgomery Grant.

Soon after landing, Carlton and Alexis stepped out of the frosty airport terminal into the burning desert sun, gasping. He noticed an outdoor digital thermometer that read '117 F'. The desiccated air sucked every molecule of moisture from their bodies. Despite gusts of kerosene-imbued air, it felt clean, sanitizing.

"Who says there is no global warming?" Commented Alexis, panting.

The heat reminded him of his unbearable summers in Iraq. "This is what Riyadh must feel like on a winter day," replied Carlton, seeing her gaze stray to the curb behind him, eyes opening wide.

He swiveled, watched a bright orange 1965 Rolls Royce Phantom V bearing the Summerwind Hotel logo pull up and stop. "McLean's hotel has a Sinatra theme," he explained. "And-"

"And orange was Sinatra's favorite color," Alexis finished.

"I'm impressed," said Carlton, smiling with approval. "I'm glad McLean sent an inconspicuous car."

She chuckled. "You're forgetting where we are. In Palm Springs, an orange Rolls *is* inconspicuous."

* * *

The Summerwind Hotel was one of the many architectural boutique hotels in McLean's growing portfolio. Restored by McLean's star architect Gerhard Heusch to its original 1950s glory and renamed after Old Blue Eyes' unforgettable song, the five-star hotel rolled the Rat Pack, Jetsons, and Richard Neutra into a stunning midcentury package.

Carlton and Alexis walked into the soft orange-hued lobby. The Voice singing about something under his skin wafted through the citrus-scented air among brightly colored retro paintings by Shag and local artist Cherry Capri. Hotel manager Richard Bernhardt welcomed them with a dazzling smile of perfectly bleached white teeth. Highly efficient, with a penchant for gold jewelry and a severely bad toupee, Bernhardt resembled a cross between Liberace and a senior banker. He personally escorted them to one of the hotel's private villas, opening the door by punching in an access code, then departed with a curt bow.

Alexis whistled, admiring the mid-century décor and ubiquitous electronics. "Frank Sinatra meets James Bond."

Carlton opened a large package, removed the note inside.

> *Enclosed is what you requested. CM still in a coma.*
> *You have 50 hours remaining.*
>
> *Maxfield (for MM)*

"At least we won't get bored," pronounced Alexis, scooping out a handful of Styrofoam peanuts, revealing DVD boxes containing the 43 Montgomery Grant movies that Carlton had asked Maxfield to obtain.

"God bless him," exclaimed Carlton, discovering a box of Romeo y Julieta Bully cigars at the bottom of the package, tearing it open and clipping one of the stogies with delight before pulling out a Glock 23 and box of ammunition. He had been forced to discard his own in a trash can outside LAX - empty and minus the firing pin for safety.

"Before we become couch potatoes, I'm going to shower," said Alexis. "This whole thing is a nightmare," she whispered, staring up into his eyes, "but I'm glad that we're living it together."

They paused, gazing at each other. Carlton could no longer resist. He wrapped his arms around her and kissed her. After a jolt of surprise, Alexis responded in kind, molding her body to his as they expressed emotions each had kept bottled during the past week.

"I've wanted to do that for a long time," said Carlton.

"Me too," she replied, her eyes smiling.

"I didn't know if you felt-"

She placed her head on his chest. "You're the first man in a long time who I can look up to."

"That's the best compliment I've gotten in a long time," Carlton grinned, unwrapping his arms from around her waist. "I'll let you take that shower now."

She took his hand, flashed a mischievous smile from behind her fall of blond hair. "I think you could use one too."

* * *

Late that night, Savitch sat in the front seat of a Ford Expedition SUV with deeply tinted windows, beyond frustration, deep in anger. He mentally kicked himself, now oh-for-four. Why had he not thought about stationing one of his people at the hospital helipad?

Outside the box, Savitch. Think outside the box.

By the time his operatives had tracked the Medevac helicopter's flight plan to LAX, Carlton was nowhere to be found in the West Coast's busiest airport. From there, the pair could have gone to any of a thousand destinations, then more. With McLean's Citation jet still sitting in its LAX hangar, Savitch had fallen back on the only other way he could think of to discover Carlton's location.

The security at *Castel* McLean was far too tight to infiltrate, even for Savitch's trained STT members. Even its telephone wires were protected, making them impossible for Savitch to tap without setting off an alarm. Luckily, the STT possessed high-tech equipment of its own.

Perched on a steep slope off Loma Vista Drive in the pricey mid-century Trousdale area of Beverly Hills, Savitch and his team had a clear view of *Castel* McLean's sprawling main house below, including several plate glass windows.

They had waited a long time, with no success. His legs had grown numb.

"Getting something else now, sir," announced one of his men, seated behind what looked like a cross between a rifle and a telescope. Provided by the U.S. government to Saudi Arabia, then made available to Farnsworth Tate by Ambassador Qhibli, the instrument was pointed straight at one of McLean's vast windows, linked by wires to a black box and printer on the floor. Its laser could pick up the slightest vibrations from windows and translate them into speech with a high probability of success.

Savitch shifted impatiently in his seat as a sheet of paper slid out of the printer.

> *Mr. Carl-- it's Max--- did -- receive the -- excellent mrs*
> *Mclane -- coma thank --- how -- deser I'm -- sir yes*

Savitch stared hard at the bits of incomplete text for a long time, then bent down, dug a sheaf of papers out of his attaché case. He scanned the list of McLean's numerous properties and smiled.

"Let's move," he ordered the driver.

"Where are we going?"

"Palm Springs."

27 MOVIES

Summerwind Hotel and Spa
Palm Springs, California
4:03 AM

Carlton and Alexis yawned on the white leather and chrome Barcelona couch, rubbing exhaustion from their bloodshot eyes. He had not been kidding when he told Wallace that he was going to a Montgomery Grant retrospective. They had watched the star's movies throughout the day and deep into the night. There were worse ways to spend time, reflected Carlton, except that this was not entertainment. And they had found no clues.

"We may be looking too hard," said Alexis, stretching like a cat, unable to suppress another yawn. "Grant's clue isn't about Nazis or the government, or even about energy or boxing. Those were personal links to Grant. The clue he wrote on the movie program was an address."

They had gone through this before. "None of the movie titles contain addresses," replied Carlton, sipping a mug of coffee. He grimaced. Its content had gone cold.

Alexis fished through the stacks of DVD cases, grabbed one they had not yet viewed.

"*Dream Home*?" Asked Carlton, reading the title. "How is that related to our clue?"

"Every home has an address, right?"

Carlton sat up, cocked his head. "That's not a bad idea."

Alexis loaded the disc into the DVD player.

They watched intently, scrutinizing every detail. *Dream Home* was about a big city couple who falls in love with a charming old country farmhouse, purchase it on a whim, only to have the crumbling relic threaten to break up their marriage and push them into bankruptcy with one construction disaster after another.

A half hour into the movie, Carlton leaped up from the sofa, knocking over his coffee mug.

"There!" He exclaimed, pointing.

Alexis fumbled with the touch-screen remote, replayed the scene. It showed an architect presenting Grant's character and his wife with remodeling plans.

"Reverse it. Now advance. Slowly." Carlton watched as the frames advanced. "Stop."

The giant flat screen's borders framed an address written on architectural plans.

"2232 Watt Heights Road," Alexis read out loud, stunned.

"You were right." Carlton touched the screen, as if making sure that the image was not a desert mirage. "'BR' is probably the bedroom where Grant hid the documents."

"Bruins one, Trojans one," announced Alexis, grinning.

"Now we need the actual address of the farmhouse in the movie," said Carlton somberly. "There have to be hundreds of places like that."

"The movie's production records would list the address. The studio should have them," Alexis replied. She peered at the back of the DVD case. "Paramount Pictures."

"I wonder how we could get them," Carlton queried, thinking about posing the challenge to Monet.

Alexis shot him a surprised look. "You're a federal prosecutor. Can't you just demand them from the studio?"

Carlton smiled. "If only it were that simple."

Alexis remained unconvinced.

"It works that way in the movies and in most countries, but not in the U.S. The Fourth Amendment to the Constitution prohibits unlawful searches and seizures. Even under the Patriot Act, the government cannot search private records without a warrant, a subpoena, permission, or special court approval." Or a special letter from the head of DOJ's National Security Division, which ruled that mechanism out, he did not add. Not only would Edison fire him for even requesting such a letter on forced leave, but the NSD could only deliver such a letter in terrorist cases, and this was not even an official case. No jurisdiction, no letter. "You'd be amazed at how many cases the government loses in court through improperly obtained evidence, even against defendants as guilty as sin."

"Wait a second," Alexis blurted out. "My friend Jen works at Paramount. Maybe she can find out. Or is that illegal too?"

Carlton held up an index finger. "Not if she gives us the information voluntarily. If you don't ask, you don't get."

* * *

Fifteen minutes later, Alexis hung up the telephone handset and flashed a brilliant white smile, waving a piece of paper, all signs of exhaustion gone from her face. "Jen wasn't happy about being woken up so early, but she logged on to the studio computer from home. She gave me the address of the only location where the studio shot *Dream Home*. 556 Pine Grove, Big Bear Lake. Bruins one, Trojans two." Alexis beamed. "When do we leave?"

Carlton had often gone skiing in Big Bear, a lakeside community 100 miles East of Los Angeles, 7,000 feet up in the San Bernardino Mountains commonly known as the 'Alps of Southern California'.

"Again, it's not that simple," he sighed, scratching the overnight stubble on his chin. "We have to get into the house and search it. Unless the people occupying the house give us permission, we can't go in without a warrant."

"Fourth amendment again?"

Carlton nodded.

Alexis grimaced. "After 9-11, I thought the government could do whatever it wanted. I didn't realize how many restrictions there still were."

The shoe always felt different on the other foot. "Welcome to my world."

"How are we going to get a warrant?"

He shook his head. "I don't want to get a warrant. It's complicated, it takes time, and a judge may refuse to grant one. A scribbled address on a 1942 movie premiere program matching an address in an old movie might make sense to us, but it may be too far out for a judge. Maybe we can convince the owners to let us search the house. First we have to find out who owns it."

Carlton called his friend Marie Owan, a sharp title company rep in Virginia who had resolved a nasty issue during his home purchase. Three time zones ahead, she was already in the office.

"Could you get the owner's name for a property in California? Big Bear Lake. Not sure what county that's in."

"San Bernardino," Owan replied, without missing a beat.

He gave her the address.

"Are you sure?" She asked a few moments later.

Carlton frowned. "Yes. Why?"

"There is no such address listed. The last house with that street address was demo'd in 1939," she said, using the industry expression for demolition.

"Demo'd or reconstructed?"

"Demo'd. Nothing has been built on that lot since. Looks like it's now part of a park."

"Thanks, Marie," Carlton replied, deflated. "I owe you one."

Carlton relayed the information to Alexis, paced the air-conditioned hotel room, torching a Bully with his DOJ Zippo, nervously clicking it open and shut.

"It doesn't make sense. Why would Grant hide documents in a cabin that was about to be demolished?" He asked.

Alexis wrinkled her nose, opened the motorized sliding glass door with the touch of a button. The desert air sucked the smoke clean out of the room. "Maybe Grant thought someone would figure out the clue quickly and get the documents before the cabin was demolished."

Carlton stopped, turned. "Wait." He walked to the DVD case, read the back cover. "*Dream Home* was released in 1940."

"So?"

"Marie said the cabin was demo'd in 1939. If *Dream Home* came out in 1940, the cabin was probably demolished while the movie was being shot."

"The scene where part of the house falls apart," said Alexis, recalling the movie.

"The entire cabin must have come down when they shot that scene. Grant's address could not refer to the Big Bear cabin because it had already been destroyed." Carlton plopped down on the couch, ran a hand through his hair. "We're back to square one."

Alexis refilled their mugs with fresh coffee and handed one to Carlton. "Not necessarily."

Carlton took a sip, looked up.

"I think I know where Grant hid the formula."

He put down his mug, stared at her.

"We were right all along," she explained. "Grant *did* hide the formula in the bedroom used in *Dream Home.* The clue fits too perfectly to mean anything else."

"The house was probably already destroyed when Grant wrote his note. How can-"

"But which bedroom was Grant referring to?" Asked Alexis, flashing a sly smile. "The finished bedroom or the old bedroom?"

Carlton shook his head. "You lost me."

"Think of the movie. Grant's character buys a broken down house in the country, which in the movie is 2232 Watt Heights Road. We know that the studio used the Big Bear cabin to shoot that. In one of the scenes, the house nearly falls apart, which we think may have led to the entire cabin being demolished. Then Grant's character renovates the house. At the end of the movie, there is a scene with Grant and his wife in the renovated bedroom, remember? The studio had to film that scene somewhere. They could not have filmed it in the Big Bear cabin because it was already destroyed. Even if they had shot the scene before demolishing the cabin, I doubt that the studio would have spent the money to renovate a bedroom that they were going to tear down. They reused sets all the time back then."

Carlton rose slowly. "The studio must have used another house to shoot the renovated bedroom scene."

"Exactly."

"Then why do the studio archives list the Big Bear cabin as the only location for the film?" Carlton asked, gulping the rest of his coffee.

"The only *location.* What about the shots that were not filmed on location?"

Carlton's eyes opened wide. "The studio."

"It's the only logical explanation," replied Alexis. "Grant hid the formula before he was killed. At the time, he was finishing or had just finished *Infamous,* which was also a Paramount movie. He could easily have hidden the formula in the *Dream Home* bedroom set on the

Paramount lot. The cabin on location was destroyed, but the bedroom set remained."

Carlton took her head in his hands, kissed her on the lips. "You're brilliant. I think the tables are about to turn."

She blushed. "You bet they are. Bruins one, Trojans three. I'll call Jen when we're on our way to see if she can get us into the studio."

"Lucky for me, I have my own Hollywood tour guide."

If we don't get killed along the way, he did not add.

28 TAIL

Sobieski stepped out of his nineteenth century chiseled limestone apartment building, refreshed after a catnap, shower, and change of clothes following his embassy all-nighter. Paris's muggy summer air immediately made his clothes stick to his skin. He observed the street carefully before walking to his prized communist-era possession: a go cart-sized Polski Fiat 126p popularly nicknamed *Maluch* - Small. Contorting his tall frame into the pint-sized interior, he started its 652 cc engine, slipped a Marlboro from the crumpled pack in his shirt pocket. As he lit it, he watched a sleek navy Renault Laguna sedan drive past him on the narrow one way street, slow, then stop and double-park two spaces ahead.

It immediately piqued his curiosity. The car itself was identical to many other Renaults on the roads of the French capital. But why was it double-parked, he wondered, with a suspicion now so second nature that he did not even realize its presence.

Sobieski's first thought was that the Renault's driver sought to take his parking space, but the Lilliputian Fiat was far too small for the larger French automobile to fit in its place. Besides, there was an available space directly across the street that the Renault could easily back into.

He gazed at the car, smoking, observing. There were two men inside, both wearing crew cuts and dark suits, one shorter than the other. Neither moved. Sobieski noticed the driver looking back at him through the Renault's side view mirror.

He committed the car's license plate to memory and pulled out of his spot. Slowly. As soon as he passed the Renault, it followed. Putting aside his training and his desire to lose the car amid the warren of narrow streets in his neighborhood, Sobieski drove to the Polish embassy as though he was not being followed.

As he suspected, the Renault followed him the entire way. Sobieski drove through the embassy gates, waited for them to close, parked in the courtyard, stepped out. The Renault stopped near the gates and once again double-parked. He noticed its occupants staring at him with undisguised interest as he stepped into the embassy building.

Sobieski strode up the staircase to the third floor, popped his bald head in Zuza's office.

"I need you to run a license plate."

She immediately went to work.

Sobieski sat at his office desk, listened to his newest voicemails. Still no authorization to take action from Warsaw. Damned useless politicians. What is taking them so long?

Several minutes later, while waiting for the latest round of transcripts from the microflies hovering above Prince Qhibli and de Ville, Zuza knocked on his door, stepped inside, closed it behind her.

"I traced the license plate, *panie majorze*." Major sir. "Dark blue Renault Laguna sedan."

"*Tak*. That's it," replied Sobieski, amazed that whoever followed him had not bothered to hide or fake their license plate. Maybe they were amateurs.

"It's registered to the French government. More precisely, to the DGSE."

The hairs on Sobieski's long neck pricked up. DGSE. The *Agencja*'s French counterpart. Definitely not amateurs.

He lit another cigarette, reclined in his chair, running a hand over his hairless pate.

If they had followed him so brazenly, without blacking out or faking their license plate, they wanted him to know it. Somehow, the DGSE had figured out that he knew about Euroil and the Saudis. Or they suspected it, which was essentially the same. He had couriered the transcripts to Peszka, called him on an encrypted telephone, and the colonel was far too experienced and clean to leak any information. But it did not take a genius for the DGSE to figure out - or at least suspect - that Sobieski was the resident *Agencja* officer in the Paris embassy and thus the likely source or conduit of information to Poland about a French corporation.

Sobieski shook his head. He was getting off track. The DGSE's method of discovery was of no moment. The problem was that they would continue following him wherever he went. They certainly would not allow him to leave the country before the Euroil deal with Saudi was concluded.

He was trapped.

29 NANO

Carlton and Alexis strode into the citrus-scented hotel lobby. At this early hour, it was empty save for a caffeinated night manager behind the reception desk. He looked at them, eyes wide open from the effects of the Red Bull in his hand.

"Mr. Carlton. A package arrived for you late last night. I was waiting for a more decent time to bring it to your room." He ducked into the back office and returned carrying a large manila envelope.

"Thanks." Carlton tore it open, slid out a note.

> *This arrived for you.*
> *CM condition unchanged.*
>
> *Maxfield (for MM)*

He dug inside, removed a slender FedEx pouch, read the sender's address.

And froze.

It was from Eche. But how? He repressed the urge to tear it open. This was not the time or the place. They had to get to Paramount Studios before anyone else figured out Grant's clue.

"Do you have a car we can use?" Asked Alexis.

"Certainly. You can use one of the hotel cars." He typed a quick message on his Blackberry. "One will pull up shortly."

"Preferably one that isn't orange," precised Carlton, cringing at the thought of the orange Roller. He exhaled with relief when a white Cadillac Escalade SUV drove up to the lobby entrance sporting shiny chrome rims and windows tinted deep black. Its exhaust vibrated with a throaty growl despite the massive vehicle's hybrid designation.

"You drive," he told Alexis, eyeing the FedEx package with mounting curiosity. He pulled himself into the tall cabin that smelled of leather and plastic. Alexis stomped on the accelerator, pinning him to his seat.

"Holy- Hey, Danica Patrick, I'd like to get there in one piece if you don't mind," he exclaimed, referring to the IndyCar and NASCAR champion, holding on for dear life.

She turned to him, flashed him a wicked grin. "Now you know how it feels."

"*Touché.* Just keep this tank steady while I open the package." Carlton ripped open the pouch, removed a diminutive white Apple Nano audio player. A Post-It note was taped to the screen.

Enter right thumbprint

How had Eche obtained a copy of his thumbprint, he wondered, before remembering that the FBI had the fingerprints of all DOJ employees on file. He carefully pressed his right thumb against the screen and kept it there until the backlight flashed on. He screwed the earbuds into his ears, pressed 'play'.

"Carlton, this is Eche." The murdered agent's voice felt morbid. "I am recording this after our meeting at the hospital. If you are hearing it, it means that I am dead. It also means that I was unable to obtain Tesla's formula. This information is classified UMBRA. After you listen, try to listen to it again without entering your thumbprint. It will erase the data.

"Enough preliminaries. Since the government could not find Tesla's formula, it tried to make his energy application work without it in a project called HEERP, which stands for High Earth Energy Research Project. They never succeeded.

"The Bureau's investigation into Grant's clue didn't follow the Bureau's normal chain of command. Since the last clue was found five years ago, all of the agents in the loop - those on the code-word classified list - have been reassigned or left the Bureau, except me. One died in a car crash just this week. Probably not a coincidence. Since I am now presumably dead, no one at the Bureau knows about the investigation. DOE has clearly been compromised. You must find the formula. When you do, deliver it to a physicist named Asher Ben-David at UCLA. He's the only one who I know for certain is still clean. Even if DOE or the Bureau orders you to deliver it to someone else, deliver it only to Ben-David." Eche paused. "You were wondering why I told you about the code-word classification and warned you about Wallace. It was not just because I needed your help. I knew I could trust you, Carlton. Don't let me down. *Vaya con Dios, amigo.*"

Carlton realized that he had been holding his breath. He exhaled.

Eche died for this. And Ben-David is a scientist waiting for a formula, not a law enforcement officer.

In addition to filling him with sadness and resolve, the message made one thing clear.

Carlton and Alexis were on their own.

30 VISITORS

A dark blue Ford Expedition with tinted windows drove into the Summerwind Hotel driveway and parked. A man dressed in a suit and tie stepped out, strode into the lobby. He eyeballed the room, proceeded to the registration desk.

The young receptionist clutching a Red Bull jumped up from behind the counter. "May I help you, sir?" He asked, curiously observing the newcomer's attire. Business suits were out of sorts in Palm Springs. In summer, they were anathema.

"I'd like to speak with the general manager, please. I know it's early, but it's urgent."

"I'm sorry, sir, but Mr. Bernhardt is not on duty at the moment."

The man leaned forward, lowered his voice. It's for Mr. McLean."

"Oh," the receptionist exclaimed. "Luckily, Mr. Bernhardt has a suite at the hotel. One moment. I'll get him for you."

He returned a few moments later with Richard Bernhardt in tow, dressed in a robe, toupee perfectly arranged, the gold chain around his neck jangling. "I'm the general manager," he announced, groggy with sleep.

"I just drove in from Beverly Hills. Mr. McLean sent me. He asked me to deliver something to you. It's in the car," he jabbed his thumb toward the parking lot with an apologetic grimace. "Do you mind?"

"Of course not," Bernhardt replied, now fully awake, brimming with curiosity.

The man led the way to the Expedition. As Bernhardt approached the SUV, its rear door swung open. A sinewy arm shot out, grabbed him by the collar, yanked him inside. Without breaking his stride, Savitch closed the door, continued to the driver's door, got behind the wheel, engaged the door locks. He pulled out of the driveway at low speed, careful not to attract the caffeinated receptionist's attention.

"Who are you? Where are you taking me?" Bernhardt demanded, squirming in vain against his captor's immobilizing neck lock. He stopped resisting as soon as he felt the point of a blade tear through his silk robe, prick the small of his back.

"It depends. If you tell us what we want to know, we'll drive right back to the hotel and pay you ten thousand dollars for your trouble." Savitch threw two bundles of hundred dollar bills onto the rear seat next to Bernhardt. "If you don't...well, I'm sure you've heard of the severed heads that turn up in the desert near the outlet stores in Cabazon. If you don't tell us what we want to know, we're going to take you outlet shopping."

"I'll tell you," Bernhardt replied, trembling, eyes wide with fear. Everyone in the desert communities had heard the grisly rumors about Cabazon. Bernhardt did not want his life to end as a Palm Springs murder tale.

Savitch smiled. "Good answer. First question. Where are Carlton and Hamilton?"

The receptionist had told him when waking him. "They checked out earlier this morning."

A wider smile. "So far, so good. Second question. Where did they go?"

"I don't know."

Savitch frowned. "Bad answer." He glanced into his rearview mirror at the man who held Bernhardt immobile. "We can take the 111 straight to Cabazon, right?"

Bernhardt's sweat grew cold. "I swear I don't know," he shouted, struggling against his captor's tight grip before feeling another jab of the knife against his back, nearly breaking skin.

"Let's say I believe you," replied Savitch in a casual tone. "Your life depends on whether you can find out where they went."

The receptionist had told him that too. "They took one of the hotel's guest Escalades. They're all white."

Savitch smiled. "Much better. Surely you have a Lojack system on such an expensive loaner," he coaxed, referring to the system that transmitted GPS coordinates of the car's location to the police when activated.

Bernhardt hesitated, earning him another prick in the back with the knife. Deeper, this time, piercing his skin. For once, he was thankful for McLean's obsessive reliance on electronics at the hotel. "Each of the cars has a GPS that can track it for us."

The smile widened anew. "Even better. How do you access it?"

Bernhardt tried to concentrate amid his growing terror. "My Blackberry," he stuttered, through clenched teeth. "In my robe."

His captor removed the electronic device, handed it to him. "Do it."

Less than a minute later, the Blackberry's color screen showed the Escalade's location on a map.

"They're on the 10, heading West," the man informed Savitch.

Savitch grinned. "Fantastic. That wasn't so bad, was it?" He turned around. "So what are you going to do with ten thousand dollars?"

Bernhardt stared back at him, his face slick with sweat. "Go on a vacation," he replied, nearly hyperventilating.

"You'll need some new clothes, then. I think we'll take you outlet shopping after all."

Without even slowing down, Savitch turned and fired a bullet into Bernhardt's head.

31 STUDIO

Main Gate
Paramount Pictures Lot
Hollywood, California
8:33 AM

Carlton and Alexis pulled up to the entrance gate of Paramount Studios, immortalized in Gloria Swanson's *Sunset Boulevard*.

"We're lucky," said Alexis. "Paramount is the only major studio lot remaining in Hollywood. If Grant had hidden the formula in another studio, it would be long gone by now."

They parked the Escalade in the visitor's lot, walked to the security building, its air conditioning a welcome respite from the hot, dusty air outside. A guard seated behind a computer monitor verified their IDs, confirmed their names over the phone with Alexis's friend Jen, printed two passes.

Carlton had left the replacement Glock in the Escalade. Armed only with their passes and wits, the two walked through a metal detector and into the fabled lot. A veritable city unto itself, the manicured Paramount lot was divided into grids of perpendicular streets bearing letters and numbers. Other than the numbered soundstages and the administration offices, each building was named after one of the studio's famous directors or actors.

"I feel like I'm back on the Hollywood tour with you," said Carlton, letting Alexis take the lead. "Tell me about your friend," he added, soaking in the lot's Golden Age feel.

"Her full name is Jennyfer Volta - with a 'y' not an 'i.'"

Carlton rolled his eyes. *Only in LA.*

"She's a consummate Hollywood player in training. Started as an assistant in a small production company that landed a deal with the studio, then plotted her way up the studio ladder through shrewd office politics until she became executive assistant to the VP of production.

The buzz is that the production VP is going to be promoted to a top position. Jen might get a management spot out of it."

Carlton respected talent and hard work, distrusted those who relied on office politics to get ahead. It reminded him of Faraday at the FBI and Edison at DOJ.

"I didn't tell her who you were. She's...well, she's got all sorts of weird government conspiracy theories. Thinks that 9-11 was really caused by-"

Carlton silenced her with a raised palm. "I've heard them all. For some, believing that an all-powerful, evil government in league with secret societies is tracking your every move and lying to you is less frightening than thousands of suicidal terrorists trying to slaughter you." He paused. "You don't buy into that stuff, do you?"

She grimaced. "I don't like the government, Carlton, but I'm not crazy."

They found Jen pacing in the sparse shade in front of the Admin Building.

Alexis hugged her, introduced Carlton.

"Thank you for arranging the passes," he said, observing her appraise him as if to determine his position in the Hollywood or Westside pecking order, coming up blank.

Short, highly exercised, with professionally sculpted nose, lips, and chest, she wore a severe black pantsuit and white blouse with Prada flats, the saccharine perfume of the season, and a well-practiced smile too contrived for Carlton's taste. Other than the Hollywood connection, he could not fathom how two such different women could be friends.

"Alexis told me you wanted to see the Grant set," she replied, squinting, still trying to read Carlton.

His anticipation grew. "You still have it?"

"We do and we don't."

She and Monet would make a good fit, thought Carlton. Both spoke in riddles.

"The *Dream Home* set was already a big attraction when Grant was alive. It became even bigger after his murder. The studio planned to strip it and use it for another movie, but realized it would face riots from angry fans if it did. It decided to keep the set and make it part of the tour, which we cancelled for security reasons after 9-11."

Carlton nodded. As a member of DOJ's National Security Division, he regularly read reports of planned terror attacks against the movie studios and their amusement parks, which Islamist terrorists considered purveyors of decadent Western culture. Except for the regularly briefed top studio executives, the rank and file knew precious little of the danger they faced, for good reason. Had they known how many plots the FBI had foiled, many would refuse to come to work.

"Tony Fontina, the set director, is a big Grant fan," Jen explained. "He seized the opportunity and converted the *Dream Home* set into his private office. I contacted his assistant after Alex called me. Unfortunately, he's in meetings all day in his office and does not want to be disturbed for a tour."

"I understand," said Carlton. "But I really need to see the set," he said, handing her his business card.

Jen's face grew pale as she scanned the card, then sent daggers flying at Alexis for not alerting her to Carlton's identity. "Department of Justice, National Security Division, Washington, DC." She grimaced, as if the words caused her physical pain. "How do I know this is you?" She demanded.

Carlton was momentarily caught off balance. People in DC did not ask such questions. But it was a wise one, he admitted. He answered by flashing his badge and ID.

Jen scrutinized both. "What are you going to do to the studio?" She inquired anxiously, an expression of fear marring her face. Or was it loathing, Carlton wondered.

He shook his head. "It's the other way around. I was hoping the studio could do something for me."

Jen remained unconvinced. "Are we in some sort of trouble?"

"Not at all." Carlton purposely did not elaborate. He might as well let Jen's wild conspiracy theories work for him instead of against him. He could practically hear the gears grinding away behind her suspicious gaze.

"I don't understand."

"Justice believes that Grant hid something on the *Dream Home* set before he died. It's highly classified with urgent national security implications. We want to keep it quiet."

"Everything can be called national security these days," she replied, leaning forward. "What exactly is it the government looking for?" She spoke the word as though it tasted foul.

"I'm afraid I am not at liberty to divulge that," he replied, stoking the fires of her paranoia, "but Alexis tells me that you're the rising star at the studio and can do no wrong. If anyone can get us in, you can." He winked.

Jen could not keep herself from blushing. "I wouldn't go that far. But as I said, it's not up to me. I already asked. If Fontina won't let you in, there is nothing I can do." Her folded arms made it clear that she was not about to go the extra mile, either for her friend or for what she considered a conspiratorial government.

"Now that you know how important it is, could you ask him again?"

Jen shook her head. "Fontina hates the government," she hissed with an intensity that belied her own feelings. "If I tell him that the Justice Department wants to snoop around his office, he'll refuse unless you have a warrant."

Carlton's frustration grew, but he repressed a tirade. He was shocked, but not surprised. He was sworn to protect all Americans, not just those who appreciated government agents who daily put their lives on the line to protect them. That included Jen and Fontina.

"In that case, I'll have to obtain a warrant." Technically, it was not a lie. Carlton lifted Alexis's cell phone. "You spell your last name V-O-L-T-A, correct?"

She paused. "Yes. And Jennyfer with a 'y.'" She cocked her head in suspicion. "Why do you ask?"

"Because to get a warrant, Jennifer with a 'y', I have to list all the people who I spoke to in my investigation for the record." A small fib, he reasoned. "Just a formality. You're not under any official suspicion."

"But still under suspicion."

"I never said that," he replied noncommittally, dangling the insinuation while dialing.

She grabbed his arm tight, attempting to mask her anxiety with a painted smile. "Before you call, Mr. Carlton, maybe I can try something else."

"Please call me Patrick." He was laying it on thick, but this was no time for subtlety. Alexis had done all she could. Carlton had to play both good cop and bad cop. He saw Alexis squint and twist her lips into a jealous smirk.

"Patrick." Jen smiled anew, checking her Bulgari wristwatch. "People here go home at around six. Maybe we can wait until Fontina leaves, then peek in his office. It would be like a tour, but without him present. Would that work?"

"Aces." Carlton did not want to sit around the scalding lot all afternoon, but it was a better place to wait than outside the security gate. He flashed her his best smile. "You may be an assistant, but you're a star in my book."

Jen beamed so bright that Carlton thought he might be able to light a cigar off of her face. Whether from relief or the compliment, he had no clue. Nor did he care. They were in.

"Won't his office be locked?" Alexis snapped.

"I'll call his assistant," replied Jen. "She owes me a favor."

A minute later, she hung up and straightened triumphantly.

"Fontina will leave around six-thirty. His assistant will stay to let us in after he leaves."

Carlton grinned. "I knew you had the juice."

"I'll meet you in front of the Grant Building at six thirty. Until then, enjoy the lot," Jen replied before disappearing inside the building.

"Bruins two, Trojans three," said Carlton, turning to Alexis.

She stood before him, arms folded in front of her chest, scowling.

"What?" Asked Carlton with a look of utter innocence.

Her face turned an angry scarlet. "You can do no wrong? You're a star in my book? I knew you had the juice?" Each statement was louder than the last.

Carlton could not help but smile. "I never pictured you as the jealous type."

She rolled her eyes. "Please. I'm not jealous. I just-"

"That was show business, Alexis. Hollywood. You were spot on. Jen hates the government. I had to schmooze her. You're the one I want."

He wrapped his arms around her squirming body and kissed her before Googling Asher Ben-David's number. He left the UCLA physicist a message to call him back urgently.

At six thirty, a glowing smogset washed the sky above the dream factory in orange hues as they walked up to a two-story brick townhouse. A brass plaque bolted on the façade read 'Grant Building'.

Jen led them into the frosty air-conditioned edifice, up the stairs, into a narrow corridor. Like most first time visitors to studio lot office buildings, Carlton was shocked by the shabby interior. The walls and carpet showed signs of advanced age and wear, accompanied by a matching musty smell. The dusty furniture looked as though it had already been dented and scratched in Grant's time. It gave him a renewed sense of optimism. If the place was so poorly updated, maybe Grant's hidden document was still there.

They followed Jen through an open doorway. A towering blonde darted up from her seat, greeted Jen with obvious relief.

"Thank God you're here. My date is already waiting for me at the guard gate." She leaned toward Jen. "He's an agent at ICM. Just lock up when you leave and please, please, *please* don't touch anything on Tony's desk. He'd kill me."

"Thanks. We won't. I owe you one," she replied to the blonde rushing out into the hallway, all legs and heels. Jen closed the outer office door and locked it. She turned to face Carlton, pointed to Fontina's office door.

"Here you are, G-man," she announced proudly. "Open Sesame."

32 CONDUIT

Polish Embassy
Paris, France
6:03 AM

With no reason or desire to play cat and mouse with the DGSE agents visibly stationed outside the embassy's front gates - and in the Rue Talleyrand in back, he confirmed by looking out a rear window - Sobieski stayed inside all night, a prisoner in his own embassy. Exhausted, he had fallen asleep contorted in his office chair, waiting for the call.

The telephone buzzer sent him bolting upright. He lifted the handset, waiting for the encryption light to turn green.

"It's Peszka. I just got word from the foreign ministry."

"*Tak?*" Asked Sobieski, now fully awake, eyes blinking painfully against the harsh angled sunshine streaming into his stuffy office that reeked of stale cigarettes.

"It's not good. De Ville finally called our foreign minister. He admitted that discussions between the E.U. and the Saudi Kingdom are ongoing but said they occur on a regular basis and refused to disclose their subject matter, pleading confidentiality. He scoffed at the notion that the E.U. would ever agree to the types of demands we suggested."

"Lying politician. *Do djabla.*" *Do dee-abla.* To the devil with him.

"De Ville's reply concerning Euroil was even more interesting. He said that any contract between Euroil and Saudi Arabia would constitute a private contract that the E.U. government could not interfere with."

"*Kurwa twoja mac,*" Sobieski nearly shouted, referring to de Ville. *Koor-vah tv-oya mah-tch.* Your whore mother. He forced himself to lower his voice, feeling his face become hot. "Permission to speak freely, sir."

"Haven't you been doing that already?" Peszka grumbled. "Granted."

"Sir, a contract between Euroil and Saudi Arabia isn't the problem, it's the terms of the contract. As for not being able to do anything about it, the E.U. could kill the Euroil contract if it wanted to. The E.U. squeezes companies it fears all the time. Just ask Intel and Apple.

It just doesn't want to pressure their darling Euroil." Sobieski's blood boiled. He disliked the French and German-controlled E.U. apparatus that treated Eastern European members states like small children and particularly loathed the pompous, arrogant de Ville. "What did our foreign minister suggest?"

"His French counterpart agreed to meet him next week. If he does not receive a satisfactory answer, he will take up the matter at the Council of the European Union meeting next month."

Next week? Next month? The glacial pace of the E.U. made the dithering UN Security Council appear swift in comparison. He wanted to shout, reined himself in. "Sir, we only have a few days. Hours. Many of the E.U. foreign ministers have probably already taken the Saudi bribes the lawyer referred to with that so-called investment fund."

"I understand, but we must go through channels first, major. You know that. Our foreign minister's hands are tied."

Sobieski could not believe Peszka would stand for such inaction. Had Euroil gotten to him too? He quickly dismissed the thought. He knew the man. Peszka was simply playing the political game by its rules. At his level, he had no alternative. "This is madness, colonel. We can't just sit here and wait for results that will never occur by having diplomats lie to each other."

If Sobieski had any hair, he would have torn it out. He had obeyed the rules. He had pushed the intelligence up to Peszka, who had pushed it up to the head of the *Agencja*, who had given it up to the Polish prime minister, who had communicated it to the Polish foreign minister. All the foreign minister had obtained from de Ville was a pack of diplomatic lies, legalistic platitudes, and political posturing intended to obfuscate and delay.

They needed action, not politics. He could not abide this situation. He *would not* abide this situation.

"Colonel, with the greatest respect, we cannot leave this to the diplomats. By the time they're finished, the road signs in Europe will be written in Arabic. Poland's most important ally and military protector will be bankrupt." With Russia's brutal invasion of Georgia, its extortionate winter shutoffs of gas supplies to Europe, and its open threats of war against Poland for agreeing to host U.S. missile defenses still fresh, his country could not afford such a result to befall the United States.

Yet shouts would get him nowhere, he knew. Sobieski calmed himself by taking a deep breath. "We did what we had to do. We went through the appropriate channels, but it has not produced any results. We must now tell the Americans, the Vatican, and Israel."

He moved the telephone receiver away from his ear, expecting another strident tirade about proper channels. The response Peszka delivered in a low voice stunned him.

"That has not been approved, major."

"I know that, sir, but-"

"If you did what you suggest, it would violate my direct orders and *Agencja* policy," continued Peszka, dead calm at similar low volume. "You would be terminated."

Instead of feeling frustrated by the reprimand, he felt a wave of relief wash over him. "I realize that, colonel," he replied.

Sobieski understood exactly what Peszka was telling him without actually saying it. *I agree with you, but I cannot be involved.* Peszka had come to the same conclusion as he. How could he ever have doubted his superior? Peszka had exhausted the proper channels like a good soldier and failed. Yet the colonel was too high up in the *Agencja* to do the dirty work or agree to it. To paraphrase the famous American saying: the zloty stops here.

"A rogue agent who would risk his career by carrying out such an unapproved activity would be especially unwise to go through regular intelligence channels or to more than one individual."

Sobieski understood that message too. If he went through regular intelligence channels - the CIA, the Vatican Secretariat of State, and the Mossad - and the information got leaked to the politicians or, worse, to the press, then the director of the *Agencja*, the Polish prime minister, and the Polish foreign minister would look like fools for not having given the information to the heads of those governments. Or worse, like collaborators.

Yet the high officials could not give the information to those heads of government directly because it would circumvent the E.U. diplomatic process that the Polish foreign minister was bound to follow ever since Poland had become a member of the E.U. So much for national sovereignty under the E.U. regime. To prevent leaks, Sobieski would have to restrict the intelligence's disclosure not only to one country, but to a single person who was not a member of its intelligence service.

"Now that our foreign minister has confronted de Ville, he knows that Poland knows," added Peszka. "Our people in France will be watched and listened very carefully."

The DGSE agents encircling him had already delivered that message loud and clear.

"Yes, sir. *Dziekuje, panie pulkowniku.*" Thank you, colonel sir. Sobieski hung up, still stunned by Colonel Peszka's tacit approval.

Sobieski was now on his own, at greater risk than ever before, quite possibly forfeiting his career and perhaps even his life if the Saudis, the DGSE, or E.U. officials discovered what he was about to do. Despite this, he smiled for the first time in days, knowing that he would do what was right rather than what was politically acceptable, often a luxury for intelligence agents. Today, he did not need any expensive wine.

And he had the perfect recipient for his urgent warning.

But would Carlton believe him?

33 SET

Montgomery Grant Building
Paramount Pictures Lot
6:33 PM

Carlton's heart pounded as he gazed at the door, emblazoned with a plaque that read 'Tony Fontina - Set Director' in curved gold letters.

This is it.

"I appreciate you getting us in, Jen, but Alexis and I have to do this alone."

"If Alexis goes in, I want to go in," Jen demanded, like a jealous child.

It was his fault for feeding her curiosity, he reflected, but he had to protect her. Jen would be in mortal danger if she learned what Grant had hidden.

He looked into her eyes, all smiles gone. "Contrary to what you may want to believe, Jen, this is not some weird government conspiracy. Montgomery Grant was murdered for what may be inside that room," he informed her, purposely avoiding any mention of Tesla. "That was over 65 years ago. In the past few days, several people have been killed for it, including an FBI agent. Alexis and I have been targeted three times. I don't want to add you to the list."

Jen remained adamant. "Either I go in or no one goes in. Take it or leave it." She locked her arms in front of her.

Carlton had no time to argue. He had warned her. It was her decision. "If you insist."

"I do," said Jen gleefully, turning the doorknob, pushing the door. It creaked open and stopped just before hitting the doorstop.

Carlton's jaw dropped. "Oh boy."

Alexis laughed out loud. "What a cathouse!"

Fontina's fandom for Grant was as obsessive as his taste was gaudy. The bedroom layout from *Dream Home* appeared exactly as it had in the movie, but Fontina had transformed the decor into a cross between a shrine to Montgomery Grant and a Las Vegas casting couch.

The room smelled of melted wax from votive candles arranged before a bust of Grant's head at the far end. Red velvet drapes covered the windows. A massive gilded Louis XVI desk sat in the center of the room. Fontina had draped the double beds *de rigeur* in 1940s bedroom scenes with rococo Versace bedspreads.

Jen switched on the lights. A glittering chandelier hanging from the ceiling and golden candelabra topped with *faux* electric candles sprouting from the walls illuminated the room.

"If I didn't know better, I'd think your set director was a Saudi prince," Carlton commented.

"Fontina is definitely, ah, colorful," Jen admitted.

Carlton recovered from his surprise and tried to recall how the room had appeared in *Dream Home*. Grant's bust gave him a chill. It seemed to look directly at him, as if the late star was pleading from beyond the grave for Carlton to complete his wartime mission.

He nodded to the bust before entering.

Help us out, Monty.

"Is this where the set was originally located or was it moved?" He asked Jen.

"Fontina insisted the set remain as it was. This is where it was built."

In that case, Fontina had probably kept the original walls and floors, reflected Carlton. The walls bore the same chintz coverings as in the bedroom scene, although in the 1940s movie they had appeared in black and white. The floors were covered in polished hardwood slats, lovingly buffed to a brilliant shine. Carlton opened the drawers of a dresser next to the bed. All empty. He removed the drawers, bent down, looked under them, ran a hand under their slots. Nothing.

Alexis climbed atop of one of the visitor's chairs and examined the chandelier up close. "Nothing up here."

"Do you mind telling me what we're looking for?" Asked Jen.

It was a good question, Carlton admitted. He had never thought of Tesla's formula in physical terms. "Honestly, I don't know. Papers, probably. Could be a few, could be a lot. Maybe in a folder or box. Could be microfilm," he replied, uncertain whether microfilm had even existed back in 1942. He pulled on a doorknob next to the bed. The door remained glued to the wall. Fake.

He kneeled on the wood floor, crawled around the sides of the room, knocked on the baseboard with his knuckles to detect hollow spaces behind. Nothing. He circumnavigated the room, spiraling to the center, rapping on the floor. Like the baseboard, each knock evidenced only solid ground.

Alexis imitated Carlton and knocked on one of the walls. Jen joined her. The reverberations all sounded the same.

Carlton lifted the framed photos of Montgomery Grant from the walls, peered behind them, half expecting to find a safe like in the movies. He was disappointed to find only brighter, unfaded wall coverings.

He walked back to the office entrance and observed the entire room again, beginning to feel the cold, clammy sensation of failure. According to Jen, after *Dream Home* the set had been scheduled for stripping, to be used in another movie. Maybe Grant had placed the formula where only those tearing it apart would find it. Maybe he had hidden it in an object that was later removed from the set. Heck, maybe Grant had never hidden anything here at all.

"Nothing here," repeated Alexis, screwing a fake light fixture back into the wall.

Carlton watched Jen do the same with a light fixture on the other side of the bed, an idea forming in his mind. He froze.

"Electricity!" He exclaimed, so loud that the two women stopped and stared at him. "That's what this is all about. Grant was not just a conduit," he said, still trying to maintain a modicum of secrecy from Jen, kicking himself mentally for mentioning electricty. "He was the scientist's admirer. Grant knew all about his electric inventions."

"What?" Asked Jen, perplexed.

"Of course," Alexis agreed.

Carlton walked to the light switch on the entrance wall and examined the face plate. "Does either of you have a screwdriver?"

Both women looked at him as though he fallen on his head. The only screwdrivers they were used to carrying were the kind you poured into a cocktail glass.

Carlton plucked a letter opener in the shape of a miniature curved Arabian scimitar from Fontina's ornate desk.

"Don't move anything," Jen reproached.

"I promise to put it back," said Carlton, walking back to the light switch, unscrewing it from the wall using the little sword's blade. Wires behind the switch snaked into the wall. Carlton peered inside the opening, tugged on the wires. "It's real," he announced, crestfallen. He screwed it back into place. "Check all the electrical outlets."

While Alexis and Jen located makeshift screwdrivers and got to work, Carlton kneeled down and unscrewed a nearby outlet. Fake. He unscrewed another two. Same artifice.

"Mine are either fake or contained only wires," announced Jen.

"Ditto," echoed Alexis.

Carlton stood, wiped the beading sweat from his forehead. "Maybe it was too simple after all. There's got to-"

"We missed one," Jen interrupted, pointing to an outlet three feet above the floor, camouflaged by the chintz wall covering.

Carlton walked to it, bent down, unfastened the old screws. He detached the plate from the wall and examined the cavity behind it. Old cloth-insulated electrical wires spiraled into the dusty opening, but there was nothing inside. "Real."

He tugged at the wires in frustration. Instead of encountering resistance, they came away in his hand, causing him to fall backwards on the floor. He stared at the severed wires in his hand for a moment, then scrambled back to the hole in the wall. His heart raced.

He plunged his hand deep into the narrow cavity, felt something cold and hard. "There is something in here," he grunted, grasping an object. "It's heavy," he said, pulling out a metal tube.

Alexis crouched next to Carlton, placed her hand on his shoulder. "You were right," she whispered, bending to look at the foot-long rusted cylinder caked with plaster dust.

"So you were telling the truth," pronounced Jen, staring at the object.

"You thought I made all this up just to see Grant's old set?" Asked Carlton, dumbfounded, before turning to Alexis. "Bruins three, Trojans three," he said, hefting the tube. He estimated its weight at close to seven pounds. Its ends were sealed with round metal caps. He tried to unscrew them, without avail. They were soldered shut. Carlton rotated the cylinder in his hands.

"It has something written on it," he said, blowing dust, plaster, and flaking rust from the container. The words were crooked and of unequal sizes, as though etched by hand in a great hurry.

PROPERTY OF U.S. GOVT. DO NOT OPEN ON PENALTY OF TREASON. IF FOUND DELIVER TO DR. DALIBARD, FEDERAL POWER COMMISSION.

Carlton recalled the name of the scientist Eche had mentioned. Blood throbbed in his temples.

They had found Tesla's formula.

Grant was murdered for this. Like Eche.

"How would Grant have soldered this thing?" He wondered out loud.

"Probably the studio mill where they built the sets," Jen explained.

Carlton shook the heavy tube. He could neither hear nor feel anything move inside.

He screwed the fateful electrical plate back into the wall while Alexis and Jen tidied the office, then rose and stopped before exiting Fontina's office. Carrying a foot-long metal tube through the security hut would be sure to arouse suspicion. He didn't have a jacket to hide it under and Alexis's purse was too small. He thought for a moment, then lifted a leg of his jeans, placed the tube inside his right boot, dropped the denim back into place.

"You would make a great thief," said Alexis.

Carlton turned to Jen as she drove them to the entrance gate in her electric studio golf cart. "Thank you for your help, Jen. I know you took a big risk, especially given your feelings about the government. But not a word about this to anyone," he admonished.

Jen shook her head.

Carlton placed a hand on her shoulder, his eyes boring into her. "I mean it, Jen. If word of this leaks, you'll face far worse than federal prosecution for revealing national security secrets. You'll end up as dead as Grant. Whether you believe it or not, it won't be government agents doing the shooting. And unlike in the movies, there won't be anyone to save you." He paused, unblinking, leaned in close. "Do you understand?"

She nodded. "I promise." Her look of fear convinced Carlton that she did. Alexis thanked her and gave her a hug.

They parted ways. Carlton and Alexis ambled toward the parking lot.

"Now the hard part begins," he announced.

"What do you mean?" Asked Alexis. "We have Tesla's formula."

"Precisely. The Saudis and Farnsworth Tate have been trying to kill us just because we knew the *clue*. Imagine what they will do now that we have the actual *formula*," he explained, hesitating whether to vocalize the thought that had been bothering him for the past few hours.

"There is something else," he finally added, in a tone that caused Alexis to stop and face him. He held up her cell phone. "Ben-David hasn't called back."

She shrugged at the lines of worry creasing his face. "Maybe he didn't get your message yet," she proposed weakly.

Carlton slowly shook his head. "If Ben-David is the only one besides Eche on our side who knows about the formula, he wouldn't ignore his voicemails for hours." He paused. "And if Eche knew about Ben-David, Farnsworth Tate probably does too."

Alexis's eyebrows arched as the implication sank in. "They killed him."

Their next thought did not have to be spoken aloud.

Once again, they were on their own.

PART TWO - LIGHTNING

"There are some areas of the world, such as the Middle-East, that are particular hot spots and where it is important to have the support of your government for a contract....The French government is perfectly aware - and we agree - that it is not for private companies to take it upon themselves to get governments to change their policies."

> Thierry Desmarest
> Former President Directeur General
> (president and CEO)
> Total, SA
> World's sixth largest oil company

"There is no subtler, no surer means of overturning the existing basis of society than to debauch the currency. The process engages all the hidden forces of economic law on the side of destruction, and does it in a manner which not one man in a million is able to diagnose."

> Baron John Maynard Keynes
> Economist

34 PINCER

Savitch sat behind the wheel of the Ford Expedition across from the Paramount main gate on Windsor Avenue, waiting.

He forced himself to remain patient despite the seething cauldron of fury boiling inside him. Unable to afford a repeat of Carlton's disappearance act, he had called in reinforcements, surveyed the studio perimeter personally. The only way out of the lot was through one of three gates, each now covered by a car and two armed STT members.

Savitch had more men, more guns, more cars, and - most importantly - the element of surprise.

Carlton and Hamilton were his.

He spotted them stepping out of the Paramount security office. His heart raced as he watched them walk toward the Escalade. Savitch started his engine, clicked on his three-way.

"All teams proceed to the main gate. Wait for my signal."

Each team confirmed his instructions with double clicks.

Savitch felt his heart pump faster as the pair hoisted themselves into the Escalade. Carlton took the wheel. Seconds later, he backed out of the parking slot, drove forward over a speed bump, then waited for the security guard to raise the gate arm before pulling out onto Melrose Avenue.

"Go! Go! Go!" Savitch shouted, sending the other teams into action. He floored the Expedition's accelerator, roared across Melrose, stood on the brake pedal, screeching to a halt directly in front of Carlton just as a second SUV cut off his retreat. The SUV's passenger jumped out, shot the two security guards running out of the security shed. Hit at near point blank range, they crumpled to the ground, writhing. A third SUV rammed Carlton's door, triggering the Escalade's air bags, automatically shutting down the engine and unlocking the doors. The bags' explosive deployment pinned Carlton and Alexis to their seats, prevented them from escaping, squeezing Carlton's arm so hard that he lost his grip on the Glock. It fell to the floor.

Savitch's passenger jumped out of the Expedition, ran to Carlton's mangled door. Another of his men leaped out of the SUV blocking the Escalade's retreat, positioned himself next to Alexis's door on the opposite side. Each pointed a Beretta handgun at his respective target.

Savitch knew it would take a minimum of two minutes for the police to arrive. Victory was his. He grinned wildly, savoring it.

He prepared to step out of the Expedition when a white Ford delivery van tore across Melrose Avenue, slammed into his front end, knocking him back hard, unleashed his airbag. He struggled to free himself from the safety device squeezing him, peered around the balloon. In a slow motion stupor, he watched six black figures leap out of the Ford van's side door and level giant Pancor Jackhammer shotguns at his men standing on either side of Carlton's Escalade. Their black masks, black body armor, black unitards, black boots, and black gloves displayed neither rank nor affiliation, yet together with their well-practiced movements colored the team with a distinct military aura.

Savitch knew the Saudis faced fierce competition for Tesla's formula, none more ruthless than the Russians. They must have followed him the entire time, waiting until now to sweep in for the kill. He cursed himself for overfocusing on Carlton and not watching his own back.

"Drop your weapons! Face down on the ground!" Ordered one of the Men in Black. His heavy accent confirmed Savitch's suspicion: Russians.

Savitch's men knew their handguns were no match for the Men in Black's 12-gauge automatic shotguns or body armor. They threw their Berettas aside, lay face down on the ground. They had barely reached the asphalt pavement when the Men in Black unleashed explosion after explosion from their shotguns at key points of the vehicles boxing in Carlton's Escalade. Metal fragments tore through tires and engines with deafening fury, yet none of the blasts harmed the three drivers remaining inside, incuding Savitch - until one was stupid enough to return fire. In unison, two Men in Black turned, trained their Jackhammers on the gunman and fired, shredding him in half.

The roar of the blasts was still echoing across Melrose when a second Ford van arced across the boulevard, braked to a halt near the first. Two more Men in Black leaped out its side door, bodily extricated Carlton and Alexis from the Escalade, herded them to the van and pushed them in. The van accelerated East on Melrose while its side door slid shut. The van that had crumpled Savitch's front end backed up with a hideous screech of twisting metal, then followed its twin carrying the attack team away.

The entire operation had lasted less than a minute.

Hyperventilating behind his deflated airbag, Savitch could not believe that he had survived the lightning-quick assault and even less that he was still in one piece. Turning his aching head toward the vans speeding up Melrose Avenue, he noticed that they bore no license plates.

Police sirens wailed in the distance.

His instinct took over. He stumbled out of the mangled Expedition, peered into the abandoned Escalade. The key was still in the ignition. He twisted it. Miraculously, the engine growled to life. He shouted for his surviving men to pile in, hoisted himself up behind the wheel. As soon as his men were inside, Savitch put the SUV in gear, pushed the carcass of his dead vehicle away, and roared off.

* * *

Carlton squirmed against the Men in Black's paralyzing grip in the Ford van's darkened rear compartment. He recalled Eche's revelation that the Soviets - not the Nazis - had murdered Grant for Tesla's formula. The Soviets were gone but it was clear that Russia's interest in Tesla's formula had remained. *Spetsnaz*, he reasoned, from their military efficiency. *Spetsialnogo naznacheniya* - Russian special purpose troops, typically assigned to the Interior Ministry or Military Intelligence. But what- He felt a prick on his arm.

"What are-" He started. His mouth felt stuffed with cotton. His vision became fuzzy. His will to fight back dissolved. A warm sense of serenity overcame him. He held Alexis's hand, wondering where the men in the strange uniforms were taking them.

Then everything went black.

35 ISOLATION

Polish Embassy
Paris, France
4:13 PM

Sobieski reflected on his decision again and again as he typed the decrypted transcripts of Prince Qhibli and François de Ville into a computer file by himself. Career suicide or not, he had to do this. He could see no other way.

Once finished, he drained his coffee cup, lit a new cigarette with butt of his old one. He lifted the telephone receiver to his ear, dialed the number for DOJ headquarters in DC.

Silence.

He hung up, dialed again.

Silence.

"*Skurwysyn*," he muttered. Son of a bitch. He hit the intercom, summoned his assistant. "Danuta. Find out what is happening with-"

"All outside lines are dead, sir."

Sobieski leaned forward. "All?"

"*Tak*. Landlines. Internet. Cell phone and satellite phone lines are out of order too," Danuta replied as Zuza rushed into his office, closed the door behind her.

"We've been cut off, *panie majorze*," Zuza announced. "Cut off and jammed. It just happened just a few minutes ago."

It was not difficult for Sobieski to figure out who possessed the capability and motive. "DGSE," he concluded, reclining, motioning for her to sit.

"They have been following me too," she revealed. "Started this morning. Quite openly. Since the transcripts from Washington and Brussels are arriving via diplomatic courier, at least our intel stream will not be affected."

He was not so sure. "I need to contact someone urgently," Sobieski stated, without further explanation.

"For now, the only communications technology that will work is a carrier pigeon," she replied, without a smile. "I could go outside the embassy far enough to use my cell phone or a regular landline."

Sobieski shook his head. "*Nie.*" No. "Too dangerous. If the DGSE has been following us so openly and gone to such extreme lengths as to cut off our communications, I have no doubt that you or I would be taken into custody as soon as we stepped outside the embassy."

"We have diplomatic immunity."

"They would release us, of course, but only after this Euroil disaster is irrevocably set into motion."

"What are colonel Peszka's orders?"

Sobieski slowly reached forward, retrieved his cigarette from the ashtray, took a drag, exhaled a long trail of smoke, all to give him time to think.

Zuza had demonstrated her loyalty and patriotism so often and to such lengths that he trusted her implicitly, relying on her more than he cared to admit. She knew the potential risks of serving in the *Agencja*. But the course upon which he was about to embark was not official *Agencja* business, but an unsanctioned personal mission. In addition to the standard risks to life and limb that *Agencja* personnel assumed upon joining the elite group, his mission carried the risk of quick career termination, ending not only in a summary dishonorable dismissal, but blackballing by the government, which was likely to follow him to the private sector as well. Sobieski was willing to sacrifice his career, not hers.

Zuza was still young, had a law degree, was interested in politics. She would not remain in the *Agencja* forever, he knew. Like Israel's Tzipi Livni who had started in the Mossad, Zuza would go far in Polish politics. Sobieski also knew that she had a serious boyfriend, a pianist and Chopin music scholar. She had kept the fact even from him, probably in an attempt to protect the man from the ugliness of their intelligence world. He had respected her privacy and never mentioned it. Sobieski knew she would jump at the opportunity to help her boss on such a mission, but he could not allow her to take the risk. This, he had to do alone.

"For the moment, colonel Peszka's orders are classified," he finally replied.

Zuza nodded, clearly disappointed, but she knew better than to insist. "I understand, *panie majorze*. What can I do to help?"

Sobieski took another deep drag, held the smoke in for a long time before exhaling. His response was not what she would expect.

"You can get me the embassy event calendar."

36 AGENCY

Carlton awoke in bed with a splitting headache. He opened his eyes, squinted at the bright fluorescent lights shining down on him. His vision was blurred. His mouth still felt as though filled with cotton. His throat was parched.

"How do you feel?" A voice asked, startling him. He could not see who was speaking to him.

"Like I got run over by a Mack truck," he croaked, confused and disoriented, moving in and out of the haze of drug-induced sleep, his speech slurred. He tried to prop himself up, but his arms were too weak. "Who are you and where am I?"

"We're on the same team," the voice responded, its owner sidestepping the question. "You'll be out of the fog soon. So will Ms. Hamilton."

"Where is she?" Asked Carlton, suddenly alert.

"Safe. Asleep in the room next door."

The man did not have a Russian accent, but that did not mean he was not working with them. "You haven't answered my questions. Where am I and who are you?" He repeated. His vision and speech were starting to clear. He managed to push himself up into a sitting position with his legs. The room smelled more like a mountain cabin than a hospital room. The fuzzy outline of a man handing him a glass gradually came into focus. Carlton eyed its contents with suspicion.

"It's just water," the man reassured him.

Carlton accepted the glass, sniffed its contents, gulped them down. The cold water felt good, even managed to calm the pain in his head. He eyed the white-walled room, which looked like one of the suites at St. John's hospital. Could he be back there with- No. He shook his head to clear the cobwebs, turned to the man.

Carlton was expecting one of the fearsome Russian *spetsnaz*, but was far from the mark. The man wore baggy Abercrombie cargo pants,

LL Bean boots, and a white T-shirt that read 'Actually, *I AM* A Rocket Scientist'. A *yarmulke* skullcap was affixed atop his curly black hair. Combined with his cherubic face and black-rimmed rectangular eyeglasses, his casual attire gave him a youthful, almost collegiate appearance, yet Joe College he certainly was not. His manner, pronounced crow's feet at the edges of his eyes, and slight paunch informed Carlton that he was probably in his mid forties. His bright brown eyes took in every detail.

"I'm Asher Ben-David," the man announced, pronouncing it *Ben-Dahveed*. His easy smile revealed a gap between his two front teeth.

Carlton blinked, remembering what Eche had told him of the physicist. "I'm at UCLA?"

"Not quite. You're in Alaska."

It explained the mountain cabin smell, but little else. "Alaska?" He muttered, confused.

"A classified DARPA facility in Akona, Alaska," précised Ben-David.

Carlton was familiar with the Defense Advanced Research Projects Agency. Created in 1958 by DOD directive 5105.15 in the wake of the Soviet Union's launch of *Sputnik*, DARPA ensured that the U.S. maintained a strong lead in the military application of state-of-the-art technology to prevent technological surprise from her adversaries. DARPA pursued inventions that conventional research organizations considered too risky to finance or simply too far out. Some were. Others found their way into the U.S. military, such as stealth aircraft technology, then later into the marketplace, such as the Internet, the Global Positioning System, and high-definition television.

"You're with DARPA?" Carlton asked, perplexed, staring at the ID that Ben-David proffered. "I thought you were a UCLA physicist."

Ben-David shrugged. "Sometimes I am. It's a good cover," he replied, sitting in a visitor's chair a few feet from Carlton's bed.

"The Men in Black who kidnapped us?"

"DARPA S-I-D. Security and Intelligence Directorate."

He was still confused. "But they had Russian accents."

"Intended to throw Savitch's people off. And credible, considering the Soviets' deadly interest in Tesla and his formula."

Carlton felt a vast sensation of relief. Just as Eche had asserted, Ben-David was on their side. And he was still alive. "Did you get the tube?" He asked anxiously.

Ben-David smiled. "Oh yes. Thank you."

"Aces," exclaimed Carlton, his head falling back on against the pillow.

As his mind cleared, he began to make sense of what Ben-David had just told him. He cross-referenced it to what Eche had stated about the High Earth Energy Research Project. "So HEERP was a DARPA project," he deduced.

"You recover fast, Mr. Carlton. Or should I address you as lieutenant commander?"

"My friends call me Carlton."

Ben-David flashed a friendly smile. "Mine call me Ash. You're correct, Carlton. Originally, HEERP was a joint War Department and Federal Power Commission project. DARPA took it over in 1962. When JFK said 'we choose to go to the Moon *and do the other things*', the 'other things' referred to HEERP, among others. He was sending a coded message to the Soviets, who were trying to piece together what they had stolen from Tesla through one of their Yugoslav agents. Unfortunately, unlike the Moon missions, HEERP failed to produce results and was shut down."

Carlton had long wondered what JFK had cryptically referred to in his famous speech, but this was not the time for historical trivia. "If HEERP was shut down, why are we here?" He asked, without dulling his tone's edge.

"It's long and complicated."

Carlton frowned. "Luckily, I don't have any urgent appointments." He and Alexis had risked their lives finding and delivering Grant's tube. Eche was dead. Claire was in a coma. He wanted answers.

Ben-David scrutinized him, nodded.

"I'll have to start at the beginning." He paused, shifting his stance, choosing his words. "The U.S. imports two thirds of its oil. Politicians have vowed to end our dependence on foreign oil for a long time, but until 9-11, it made little sense other than getting votes. Oil consumers needed to buy as badly as oil producers needed to sell. There was no more reason to end our dependence on foreign oil than on foreign mineral water.

"9-11 changed that. With most Islamist terrorists coming from or funded by oil producing countries, oil transformed from an issue of supply, demand, price, and environmental concerns into one of national security. A secret government study was conducted, with startling predictions: increasing global economic activity and standards of living, especially in China and India, would increase oil demand far beyond the flat supply. Combined with the dollar's steady devaluation by the Federal Reserve's free money spigot and government's runaway spending, it would cause a huge oil price spike by the middle of the first decade. The jump in price would increase other commodity prices and erode consumer spending, severely weakening the U.S. economy to the point of possibly triggering a crisis of confidence, bursting the economic bubble, devastating banks, throwing the world into a depression. Along the way, it would transfer trillions of dollars to oil producers openly hostile to the U.S. and our allies, such as Iran, Russia, and Venezuela, and to others who support terror although their governments do not, such as the Saudis."

All of which happened.

Carlton pushed himself up, dumbfounded. "The government knew this *ten years ago*? Why didn't it do anything?"

"It did. In secret. The crash project was classified UMBRA."

Carlton leaned forward. "Considering that I risked-"

"You've earned the right to know," agreed Ben-David. "The project targeted the oil problem from both sides of the political spectrum: decrease oil consumption to please the left, increase oil production to please the right. Like a bipartisan Manhattan Project for energy national security."

Carlton snorted. "Leave it to the government to spend billions without any results."

Ben-David gave him a hard stare. "There *were* results. Many. But none were announced. Not as such, anyhow." He observed the look of confusion on Carlton's face. "To maintain secrecy, the program was decentralized, conducted within existing government, university, and private industry programs."

Carlton digested the information, appreciating its clandestine brilliance. "So some of the current energy discoveries are the result of the government's program, but U.S. rivals and the public will never know which ones. But *you* know."

Ben-David dismissed this with a shake of his head. "I was only in charge of HEERP at DARPA. But here is what I do know," he announced, touching off fingers on his left hand. "One, to decrease our dependence on unsavory oil producing nations, we must consume less oil. And increase domestic oil production, but we'll leave that for later. Two, the most cost-efficient way to reduce oil consumption is to shift automobiles from gasoline to alternative fuels, which would also help the environment. Three, for it to work in practice - government incentive boondoggles aside - the alternative fuels must truly be cheaper than gasoline.

"Let's examine those alternatives. Hydrogen uses too much energy to produce as a viable alternative fuel. Ethanol sources use massive water and raise food prices. Natural gas is cheap and domestically plentiful, but it would require the installation of a costly infrastructure to deliver it to gas stations and individuals. Electricity is the only viable alternative, produced mostly by natural gas and clean coal plants - nuclear plants are cleanest and most efficient but politically difficult, particularly after the Japanese plant meltdown following the tsunami."

"But?"

"But batteries pose a major impediment. Electric cars predate the Model T Ford, but their batteries have been dangerous, inefficient, bulky, and needed long recharging periods after only a few miles. Yet two days ago, you escaped from the Hollywood Hills in an electric sports car with a range of 220 miles, although those batteries are still too expensive for most consumers."

Carlton leaned forward. "DARPA invented long-range electric car batteries?"

"I was only in charge of HEERP," Ben-David replied, once again sidestepping the question.

Carlton knew he would not get a straight answer, shifted gears. "What about the part of the project tasked with increasing domestic oil production?"

Ben-David arched his eyebrows. "Staggering. Vast new oil fields were discovered in the Gulf of Mexico, off California, and in Alaska. Studies of known fields in the Alaskan National Wildlife Refuge were updated for the first time in decades, revealing much larger deposits than previously believed. By exploiting them, the U.S. could slash its reliance on foreign oil by half within ten years, generate hundreds of billions of dollars of revenue, and create tens of thousands of new jobs."

Carlton stared at him, dazed. "When will drilling begin?"

Ben-David's face darkened. "It won't. Future *exploration* was loudly announced, but there won't be any drilling. A handful of groups have stopped virtually all new oil production, using everything from ads, campaign donations, voter turnout, agency regs, lawsuits, blackmail, and flat-out physical intimidation on every politician even remotely connected to oil. The BP oil rig disaster in the Gulf played directly into their hands - some suspect they were the ones who installed the faulty shutoff valve that caused the spill. The groups have environmental names and have banded with legitimate environmental groups concerned about oil spills and global warming, but they are really shell groups financed by-"

"Let me guess. The Saudis?"

Ben-David shrugged. "We don't know. The money trail ends in Venezuela."

"Like Abu Hassan's," noted Carlton, filing the fact away for later rumination.

"Given Hugo Chavez's obsessive anti-Americanism, the Venezuelan banking authorities refuse to reveal the owner of the accounts or the provenance of the funds. Even with the new car batteries, without a major increase in domestic oil production, we will not be able to reduce our dependence on foreign oil to the point where we can cut out terror-sponsoring oil producers."

Carlton pushed himself off the edge of the bed, stood uneasily. Dizzy at first, he remained immobile while he regained his balance - and his train of thought. "This is all fascinating, but it does not explain what happened to Alexis and me."

"How much did Echeverria tell you?"

Carlton outlined the information.

Ben-David stood. "The last thing Saudi wants is for the U.S. to replace its vehicle fleet with electric cars or exploit new U.S. oil fields, especially now that it has ballooned welfare payments to maintain popular stability after the Arab Spring uprisings. Through its DOE moles, the Saudis learned that HEERP would provide an unlimited source of nearly free electricity, but that DARPA could not make it work without Tesla's missing formula. They have closely monitored the FBI's investigation into Grant's tube for years. When you found Grant's movie program, Saudi found out about it through DOE, used its moles to convince DOE to shut down the FBI's investigation, then continued its search for Tesla's formula on its own. But they lost. We got it first, thanks to your heroics."

Carlton brushed off the compliment, leaned toward Ben-David. "If you knew the Saudis shut down the investigation, why didn't you jump in and take it over yourself?"

"I did. Even before the Saudis killed it."

Carlton was confused. He paused for a moment, then opened his eyes wide. "You're the one who stole Grant's program from my bungalow!"

Ben-David nodded.

"How did you get past the security systems?"

Ben-David curled his lips into a wry smile. "Sometimes the term 'Men in Black' really does apply to DARPA. With all due respect to Al Gore, *we* invented the Internet. You'd be amazed how much can be discovered, done, and undone through the net. How do you think the Stuxnet virus infected Iran's nuclear program?"

Carlton stared at him, astonished. "You disabled McLean's security system through the Internet?"

"I cannot discuss our methods, of course. But we had to get a copy of Grant's program so we could find Tesla's formula before DOE and Saudi.

"Why not get it from Eche?"

"Until she was killed in a car crash earlier this week, the Saudis had a mole inside the FBI. I could not risk the mole learning that DARPA had a copy of the program, so I did not ask Eche for it." He paused. "Unfortunately, like the FBI, we were not able to solve Grant's handwritten clue. It took you and Ms. Hamilton to do that. Thank you."

Carlton recalled Eche mentioning the recent car crash death of a FBI agent involved in Grant's investigation. He reflected about what Ben-David had just told him, took a step toward the scientist. "You bastard!" He roared. "You knew all along that Savitch was chasing us. You could have prevented him from killing Eche and putting Claire McLean in a coma, not to mention nearly killing Alexis and me."

Ben-David stook a step back, hung his head low. "I am deeply sorry about Special Agent Echeverria. And the others in the Bureau who were killed over the years. But DARPA has limited resources. We could not follow everyone. Eche was an armed federal agent with full knowledge of the situation. We focused on protecting those who were still in the dark."

This cut absolutely no ice with Carlton, who thought of Claire's blood soaked body. "Like heck you did."

"We protected you."

"Protected me?" Carlton shouted, incensed, ready to throttle Ben-David. "I can't even count how many times I almost got killed."

Ben-David retained his calm, nodded. "You *almost* got killed, but you did not *get* killed. You know that DARPA SID rescued you at the studio - you're welcome, by the way."

"Thank you. But-"

"*But* did you ever stop to think how serendipitous it was for a car to hit the Chevy Suburban chasing you in the Hollywood Hills? Not to mention other interventions you never even knew about, like preventing Savitch from attacking you and Alexis in the parking lot behind El Compadre in LA." He paused. "Unfortunately, you lost your cell phone in the Hollywood Hills, so we could no longer track you. We only reacquired you after you called me from the studio, which is why we could not prevent the attack in Malibu."

Carlton stared at Ben-David, speechless, his head spinning.

"I knew that DOE and the FBI were compromised," Ben-David continued. "So I gambled and focused on you. You were the only one making any headway with Grant's clue, you were a veteran DOJ prosecutor with a high security clearance and a decorated Navy Reserve officer to boot.

"We followed you the entire way, protecting you as much as we could. I'm generally a loser in Vegas, but this time, my gamble paid off. Not only did you decipher Grant's clue, but you hit the jackpot by finding his tube." He gave a curt bow. "Again, thank you."

Carlton felt duped, used. What he wanted to do was knock Ben-David out cold. He took a deep breath, forced himself to calm down.

"Was Tesla's formula inside?" He asked.

"It was."

Relief. Then curiosity. "What does it do?"

Ben-David grinned. "Let me show you."

37 LUNCHEON

Polish Embassy
Paris, France
11:53 AM

A few minutes shy of noon, the U.S. ambassador's Cadillac DTS limousine and its boxy Chrysler 300C escort drove through the open gates of the Polish embassy under the fluttering white and red bands of the host nation's flag. The gilt-tipped forged iron gates folded closed as soon as the vehicles were safely inside the compound.

The polished black cars with tinted windows had barely stopped in the graveled courtyard when a liveried valet emerged from the arched front doorway dressed in the formal regalia of white tie, tails and white gloves, followed by the Polish ambassador. The valet opened the rear door of the Cadillac, stepped aside.

As the U.S. ambassador emerged, his white-maned Polish colleague greeted him with a hearty handshake and a friendly smile. Diplomatic grins and pats on the back were exchanged for the benefit of the embassy photographer before the two men walked out of the beating sun into the cool confines of the rococo Hotel de Monaco.

Once his charge had disappeared inside, the Chrysler's driver repositioned the beefed-up sedan against a wall, its black snout and wide rakish grille pointed toward the gate. He stepped out, walked to the Cadillac. The ambassador's driver had packed a lunch for both of them.

* * *

Surveying the scene from an upper window, Sobieski decided a better opportunity would be long in coming - if ever. After a quick conversation with Zuza, he strapped on his shoulder holster and loaded it with his SIG-Sauer P-226 handgun - with the DGSE lurking about the compound, he could not be too careful. He descended the staircase to the basement kitchen, strode past cooks stirring oversized pots bubbling on a cast iron stovetop. The pungent smell of *bigos* hunter's stew made his stomach groan with hunger, but there was no time to satisfy his appetite. He ignored both the kitchen personnel and his hunger pangs, walked to the rear of the kitchen, entered the walk-in pantry, closed the door behind him.

He quickly located the dumbwaiter. Used to ferry food supplies from ground level down to the pantry, the pre-World War I mechanism was not meant to carry passengers, certainly not one of Sobieski's height. He stretched against the wall like a runner before a run, then tried to squeeze into the narrow space. Despite his svelte physique and generally limber musculature, not a single contortion seemed to allow the tall Pole to fit.

He sighed, wiped the sweat from his forehead. He was running out of time. Not knowing what else to do, he stretched anew. After several more unsuccessful attempts, he finally found a position that worked by tucking his long legs under him. What it would be called in yoga was beyond him, but besides immediately cutting off the circulation to his legs, it seemed to hold. He wasted no time punching the button labeled '*do gory*' - up.

The motor whined to life, raising the platform. Pulling his arm in at the last moment, he was cast into utter darkness as the creaking pallet ascended through a cold, bare cement shaft. He took deep breaths to ward off a growing sense of claustrophobia. The walls appeared to be closing in. He knew it was merely an illusion, but it was an alarmingly believable one. He could feel them squeeze his chest. Being buried alive was the one thing Sobieski feared above all else, yet he had to do this. And the next thing. He tried not to think of that one, but this ascent would be a cake walk in comparison.

He was sweating profusely, unable to feel his cramped legs, wondering how much longer he could withstand the ridiculously confined space when the platform lurched to a stop. A moment later, the whining motor fell silent.

Sobieski fought the urge to unfold his contorted body and escape the walls closing in. He first had to verify that the contraption was in the right position. He pushed open the door to the exterior with one hand, catching it with the other as it threatened to gape open. Bright sunlight stabbed through the slit, making him blink from inside the stygian darkness. He peered through the narrow opening, saw the Chrysler's driver's side door less than a meter away.

There was no way for him to see whether the driver had returned. He remained silent, holding his breath, pricking up his ears. The only sounds he heard were of traffic on the Rue Saint Dominique beyond the embassy gate.

He took a deep breath and eased the door open, laying flat on his stomach against the driveway gravel. Pushing against the back of the dumbwaiter platform with his feet, he crawled under the automobile, trying to make as little sound as possible as the sharp rocks dug into his shirt and pants. Once completely underneath the car, he nudged the door to the dumbwaiter platform closed with his foot. Craning his head toward the ambassador's Cadillac at the end of the courtyard while twisting his body to avoid the hot transmission fluid dripping from the Chrysler's driveshaft, he noticed that the two drivers were busy eating their lunch. Bantering back and forth, they seemed at ease within the safety of the embassy compound, but they were in his line of sight. Which meant that he was in theirs.

He needed a distraction.

He did not have to wait long. A minute later, a stunning blonde woman in a micromini and platform pumps called out from the other side of the embassy gate.

"Are you open?" She asked in Polish, waving a passport. "I need to renew my passport. Can you let me in?" She repeated the question in heavily accented French, then English before an embassy guard ran over to direct her to the public entrance, without recognizing her.

Sobieski allowed himself a small smile. *Right on cue.*

Hoping that the two drivers were still busy ogling Zuza, Sobieski crawled to the rear of the Chrysler, blindly reached up with his right hand, felt for the trunk release, pushed it. The trunk lid snicked open. He hoisted himself inside, folded his long legs to fit into the carpeted space, gazed at the drivers as he pulled the trunk lid closed.

"*Skurwysyn*," he muttered under his ragged breath. Son of a bitch.

One of them had turned just before the trunk lid shut.

38 HEERP

Carlton checked in on Alexis, still asleep and under guard. He did not wake her, gently touching her hair as if to reassure himself that she was really there. Satisfied, he showered and demolished a plate of steak and eggs before joining Ben-David for a tour of the facility.

"Fewer people know about HEERP than Area 52. It was dormant for years before we reactivated it this week," announced Ben-David.

Carlton cocked his head. "You mean Area 51?" He asked, referring to the ultra-secret government facility in Nevada that for decades had not even officially existed until the very real devastating health effects of toxic substances on its personnel had caused a court to force its disclosure. "Not Area 52, right?"

Ben-David merely smiled in reponse as he led Carlton down a utilitarian hallway illuminated by overhead fluorescent lights. The mountain cabin scent intensified, for the obvious reason that the floors, walls, and ceiling were constructed of wood and had seen no human activity for a long time. He craved a cigar, but his box of Romeos was in the ill-fated Escalade back in LA.

Despite the *gravitas* that surrounded Ben-David like an invisible aura, the physicist's relaxed attire and sociable manner were a far cry from Carlton's experience with his own UCLA science professors. They had preferred shrinking anonymity, polyester short-sleeved shirts, and the company of cold formulae over that of fellow human beings. If Ben-David ever did teach, his students must love him, Carlton reflected.

"As we were discussing, since massive new domestic oil production is off the table, switching to electric cars is the easiest way to decrease our oil consumption. Long-range batteries are still expensive, but the real problem with electric cars remains electricity," explained Ben-David.

"The U.S. generates electricity mostly by burning coal and natural gas. Both are plentiful and cheap, but produce too much atmospheric carbon for environmentalists even though natural gas is far less carbon intensive than coal or oil. As we discussed, nuclear electric generation on the average is safe, but expensive and politically controversial. Hydroelectric, solar, wind, and geothermal are the Holy Grails, but prohibitively expensive and plagued with a raft of environmental problems of their own. Plus wind and solar produce electricity only when there is wind and sun and their electricity cannot be stored."

None of this was new Carlton, who was tiring of Ben-David's lectures. "How does HEERP solve all of that?" He pressed.

"I know you were once an astronomy major, but I'll spare you the advanced physics."

Carlton had to hand it to DARPA - they certainly did their research. He had only been an astro major for a year, until the math requirements kicked in.

"In a nutshell, Tesla's formula explains how to channel negatively-charged solar particles from the Earth's upper atmosphere down to the positively-charged ground in the form of lightning."

Carlton stopped in his tracks, stared at the physicist. "What Tesla sought his entire life. A way to transmit electricity through the air. He found it?"

Ben-David nodded. "On an unimaginable scale. Unlike atmospheric lightning, which lasts less than a millisecond, Tesla's charged particle lightning would be continuous, allowing it to be captured on the ground and fed directly into the electrical grid. The only cost would be the capture array on the ground, which makes it virtually free."

Carlton whistled. No wonder the Saudis wanted to prevent the government from obtaining Tesla's formula. Still, it sounded too much like a free lunch to be true. "Many considered Tesla's later ideas...well, wacky. Does it actually work?"

"That's why we are in Alaska and not at DARPA headquarters in Virginia. I take it you are familiar with the Aurora Borealis and Aurora Australis?"

Carlton nodded. He had seen countless photographs of the ethereal sheets of red, green, and yellow lights that danced in the night sky. "The Northern and Southern lights."

"Correct. They are composed of charged particles flowing from the Sun in what is called the 'solar wind', although I prefer the term 'sun shower' like in the REO Speedwagon song. The Earth's magnetic field channels the particles to the Northern and Southern poles, so to test Tesla's formula, we need to be in the Arctic or Antarctic. We also need to trigger an initial lightning stroke at high altitude to spark the process. Tesla hoped to do it from atop a tall tower. We opted for a satellite. We're making the last changes to the ground equipment now. Come, I'll show you."

They entered a wooden locker room. Ben-David handed Carlton a heavy winter parka before slipping one on himself.

"In summer above the Arctic Circle, the sun never sets, but global warming or not, the temperature is rarely above freezing," he explained.

Looking more like Nanook of the North than a physicist and federal agent, they stepped through two sets of doors into the glacial air outside. They wasted no time packing into the rear of a muddy olive green military Humvee resting on fat tires. Carlton was thankful that its heater was running.

The wide vehicle roared past heavily guarded gates into a pine forest, speeding along a hard-packed dirt road, splashing through mud accumulated in a myriad potholes from recent rains. Its rock-hard suspension sent Carlton and Ben-David flying out of their seats, crashing down in bone-jarring impacts.

Carlton observed the pine trees through the Humvee's side window. Many imagined Alaska as a barren land of ice and snow. In fact, much of the nation's largest state was a lush wilderness of dense forests, green meadows, and grassy tundra. At some other time, the thick pine forest would have filled Carlton with a sense of adventure. All he felt now was a foreboding of violent threats lurking among the coniferous shadows. Despite the hot air blowing through the vents, he could not suppress a shiver.

Suddenly, the Humvee shot out of the forest into the open along a tall triple fence. Signs warned the curious against the folly of trespassing with messages about electrified fences, armed security guards, and the high voltage nature of the facility. Circular razor wire atop the fences and plaques painted with skulls and crossbones underscored the warnings.

Carlton had expected the HEERP array to appear bright, lively, futuristic. Instead, it was cold and desolate. Beyond the triple fence lay a vast flat concrete pad. Instead of pine trees stood a forest of towering metal poles that cast eerie shadows in the pale nighttime Arctic sun. Metal boxes the size of oil barrels were spaced at regular intervals amid the poles. Parka-clad technicians leaned over one of them with tools. Carlton remembered Tesla's fixation on certain numbers. On a hunch, he began to count.

"You're correct," announced Ben-David before he had finished. "Eighteen poles. Just as Tesla said he saw in his dream," he said, explaining how the devices worked while the Humvee's tires slammed in and out of potholes, sending waves of mud splashing on the windows.

Carlton listened attentively as the Humvee plunged back into the forest, squealed to a stop at the chainlink entry gate. A Man in Black in cold weather gear with a submachine gun slung across his chest peered inside the Humvee suspiciously. Spotting Ben-David, he flashed a quick salute, signaled to his partner. A row of cylindrical concrete road barriers as thick as tree trunks disappeared into the ground.

Carlton read a large placard affixed to the gate as it slid open.

U.S. DEPARTMENT OF ENERGY

TOP SECRET FACILITY

WARNING

RESTRICTED AREA

USE OF DEADLY FORCE AUTHORIZED

After Savitch's relentless chase, Carlton found the fearsome guards and the threatening notice oddly reassuring. Yet something about the sign troubled him.

"I thought HEERP was a DARPA facility," he said.

"It's a DARPA project with DARPA staff. The real estate belongs to DOE."

Carlton tensed up. "Did you tell DOE that you obtained Tesla's formula?"

Ben-David frowned. "Are you crazy? DOE has more leaks than a BP oil rig. That's how Saudi got the information in the first place."

Carlton exhaled a sigh of relief, yet a tinge of anxiety remained. He knew better than to ignore it. "Does DOE know that the facility is back on line?"

Ben-David shrugged. "I had to tell them. It's their facility. But it's been operated on and off for years. DOE knows that it's operative, not that we have Tesla's formula."

Carlton was not convinced. "Who did you speak with at DOE?"

"The only DOE official who knows about the facility other than the Secretary. Their Chief of New Technology. Guy named Wallace."

Carlton felt the ball of ice form in his gut. He leaned forward, touched Ben-David's forearm. "Ash. Brendan Wallace is the Saudi mole inside DOE. He used to be at Farnsworth Tate. If he knows about the facility, so do the Saudis."

Ben-David stared back at him, aghast.

"Wallace is the one who pulled the plug on the FBI's investigation, offered me a job to stop investigating, sent Savitch and his goons to kill Alexis and me. He will have no problem connecting the dots between your counter-ambush at the studio and HEERP's grand reopening. You're lucky he didn't have you killed like he did Eche."

Ben-David regained his composure. "I'm too well protected, too hard to find. And you can relax. The Saudis are no longer a threat. They lost. We have the formula."

Ben-David was at DARPA, Carlton reflected, but still a physicist at heart. He dealt with the scientific method more than with people's motivations. He shook his head. "They don't want the formula, Ash. They want to prevent anyone from using it." Despite the cold, he wiped beads of sweat from his forehead.

Ben-David remained immobile while his mind ran through different scenarios. "Wallace could order DARPA to vacate the facility. If we refused, he could send in an armed DOE squad or Savitch and his goons. Neither of those would be able to get past the contingent of DARPA SID guards on base. All are ex-military, trained and armed to the teeth. And the facility is in the middle of nowhere, its airspace restricted, surrounded by a triple electric fence and video cameras."

Carlton squinted out visions of the attack in Iraq. "You're focusing on Wallace, Ash, not the Saudis. I don't mean the Saudi *government*, I mean Saudi *terrorists*. Like on 9-11. Like Abu Hassan. He had over a hundred sleeper agents waiting for his command to attack the U.S. electrical grid. Who knows how many more he could have? These people will stop at nothing to-"

Ben-David held up a hand. "You don't have to lecture me about them," he shot back angrily. "I lost my ten year old niece in a Hamas bus bombing in Tel Aviv."

Carlton winced. "I'm sorry."

"If you're right, we need reinforcements."

Carlton relaxed. "Good."

"No." Ben-David shook his head. "Bad."

Carlton looked at him quizzically.

"I can't just order up troops like a Domino's pizza, Carlton. DARPA is stretched as thin as the rest of the military."

"There are several military bases in Alaska," proposed Carlton.

"And even if they have troops to spare, the military won't send them into a domestic DOE facility without official DOE approval, which, if what you are saying is true, Wallace will refuse." He took a deep breath, exhaled slowly. "I'll make the necessary requests, but we're on our own. In any case, you know what they say: the best defense is a good offense."

Carlton cocked his head.

"We have to get HEERP operational before Wallace sends anyone to shut us down."

Possibly, reflected Carlton. But after what he had been through, he knew they could not rely merely on an operational facility to ward off Saudi terrorists desperate to prevent the U.S. from obtaining a free source of unlimited electricty.

The Humvee lurched to a halt in front of the wood headquarters building that resembled a large mountain cabin far more than a top secret research facility. The two stepped into the biting cold, up a short flight of wooden stairs, and through the double doors before parting ways.

Carlton located a telephone, mulled over who to call.

As much as he hated the idea, he thought about calling Edison. Yet even if his boss listened, there was little he could do. Justice was composed of lawyers. An army of lawyers might scare off corporate CEOs, but could do little to protect a remote research facility from terrorists. They needed armed personnel. The FBI came to mind, but Eche had been the last person in the Bureau who knew about HEERP. Faraday was a nemisis, not an option. The Bureau was out.

He could attempt to navigate Navy channels, but his request would take too long to swim up the chain of command. He would have to explain his urgent request, convince the brass that a law firm representing the Saudi Kingdom was about to send terrorists into the Alaskan wild against a facility no one knew about. That idea would go nowhere fast.

He would have to go outside regular channels, call on personal contacts. But this was no mere personal favor.

McLean was superbly well-connected, but other than Davos's associates and a few rabid guard dogs, he could not summon teams of armed men. At least not without calling in the *mafia*, which Carlton wanted to avoid at all costs. His friend Tom Pink at CIA had been unreachable on extended vacation for some time, Company-speak for 'on covert assignment'. Carlton was acquainted with a prominent member of the CIA aristocracy, but the two had a difficult relationship: Carlton considered him an uncaring robot; he considered Carlton rash and insubordinate. Not a winning bet for military support.

He had one more contact, an Air Force colonel and CIA liaison. But what he needed were boots on the ground, not fighter jets. Plus Colonel Saunders would likely have to obey two chains of command: CIA *and* Air Force. It would take less time to pay off the national debt than to get both to agree on a *domestic* operation far outside their jurisdictions.

Carlton sighed. It was hopeless. Still, he had to do something.

He made the call.

His spirits sank even lower.

All he got was voicemail.

39 TRUNK

Polish Embassy
Paris, France
12:13 PM

Sobieski waited inside the Chrysler's trunk, silent and immobile. His heart raced as he felt the pitch black compartment close in on him. The thick carpet and lining muffled the sounds outside, disorienting him. The trunk's safety vent provided air, but the car was directly under the beating summer sun, making the heat unbearable. Already his clothes were drenched with perspiration. The circulation to his legs was cut off again, making them tingle painfully as though they were being devoured by an angry army of ants. He dared not move them, fearing it would cause the car to sway, giving away his position. To make things worse, something with a sickly smell had recently been spilled on the carpet, making him feel nauseous.

A handle glowed in the darkness - the emergency trunk release. He resisted his swelling urge to open it, feeling an even greater fear than his raging claustrophobia: he had taken too long to enter the trunk. The driver who had glanced over at the last second would find him.

So he waited, paralyzed, heart jackhammering, sweating in the trapped heat, gazing at the glowing hands of his watch.

One minute. Five. Ten.

No one materialized.

Sobieski accepted it as good luck, yet his mission was hardly over. He remained immobile for the next two hours, fighting against passing out from the heat. The swarm of ants he felt in his legs disappeared, leaving his extremeties fully numb. Each claustrophobic breath made him believe it would exhaust the remaining air in the trunk. He itched for a cigarette.

Suddenly, he heard a muffled sound. It sounded like crunching gravel. It was getting louder. Someone was walking toward the car.

His heart sank. The driver had discovered him. But why had he waited so long?

The car rocked. The next thing he heard was not the trunk latch click open, but a low rumble.

He smiled wide in the darkness. The driver had started the engine.

The car lurched forward. Breathing a sigh of relief, he glanced at the dim glow of the hands on his watch. He knew from experience that it would take approximately ten minutes to get to the American embassy - if that was where the driver was going.

Now that they were under way, he contorted his twisted body inside the pitch darkness, trying to regain feeling in his legs and arm. The ants returned. He positioned his face near the weak stream of the car's air conditioning to clear his head.

The car swayed to and fro, stopping every so often before accelerating anew. He had to grab onto the trunk release latch to prevent himself from slamming into the tight compartment's walls, giving away his position. After a few more stops and starts, the floor pitched steeply, then the car stopped. The engine was turned off, returning him to the cocoon of carpeted silence. He heard the car door close, then muffled voices. He glanced at his watch. Twenty three minutes. Where was he?

It no longer mattered. He had no choice. He grabbed the trunk release handle, turned it, pushed up. Nothing. Again, harder. Same. His fear exploded into alarm. He pounded on the trunk lid. "Let me out!" He shouted.

He soon heard a click. The trunk lid yawned open. Sobieski gulped mouthfuls of air, bending his legs painfully, blinking several times before gazing up.

At the barrel of a gun pointed squarely at his forehead.

40 RUSSIANS

Carlton joined Ben-David in the HEERP control room. As a civilian in a classified government facility, Alexis remained restricted to her quarters. She was hopping mad about it, but neither she nor Carlton had any say in the matter. At least she was safe, he reflected.

Carlton's vision of a futuristic high-tech control room dissolved as soon as he walked inside. It was clear that the facility had just been reactivated after a long period of suspended animation. The 800 square foot room was cramped, its equipment antiquated, more *Apollo 13* than *Star Trek*. Illuminated only by electronic readouts and dimmed desk lamps, its lack of windows gave the room a claustrophobic feel, complete with a faint smell of sweat and electronic ozone despite the cold air blowing through the vents. Bulky cathode ray tube monitors rather than flat screen panels were crowded together, displaying images of the boxy metal structures and tall metal poles Carlton had seen during his tour. A screen marked in white with orbital sine curves flowing across a Mercator-projection map showed the position of the HEERP satellite in orbit. A flurry of scientists in white lab coats milled around the equipment.

Carlton spotted Ben-David and an assistant huddling behind a computer screen.

"When is the Moon landing?" He asked jokingly, pouring himself a cup of coffee from a side table.

Ben-David had not heard him enter. He looked up in surprise, exposing a T-shirt that read '*Free the Hybrids!*'

"Carlton! We're just about to start. I understand your surprise. HEERP predates the Apollo program. If Tesla's formula works, we'll replace all the equipment. For now, other than a few upgrades, we have to make do with what is available. Allow me to introduce Dr. Franklin."

Carlton shook the African-American scientist's hand, his grip taking her by surprise before she squeezed back in kind. Shy and pretty in a nerdy sort of way, she seemed far too young to have a PhD. Then again, reflected Carlton, DARPA was in the genius business and geniuses started young.

Ben-David bristled with nervous excitement. "We've almost finished setting up the outside equipment." He carefully removed a sheaf of yellowed pages from the table, handed them to Carlton.

Carlton glanced at the mathematical equations neatly handwritten on the five pages. He had fallen passionately in love with science in high school, only to suffer heartbreak in college upon discovering that he was deaf mute to its language of mathematics. He recalled the exact day, when he had witnessed Russian students younger than him solve complex differential equations orally over lunch at UCLA's Bomb Shelter cafeteria. His path lay elsewhere.

"What am I looking at?" He inquired, confused, still peering at the math hieroglyphics.

"Those are the pages that Grant hid in the tube." He paused. "Tesla's formula."

Carlton now gazed with reverence at the equations that Grant had recopied from Tesla's originals. So many had been killed to discover what Tesla had created to make the world a better place. Hopefully no more would suffer that fate, yet Carlton's instinct screamed otherwise.

Although he could not understand the cryptic symbols, he discerned a logic to them. An orderly, natural flow. "It looks almost..." His voice trailed off.

"Simple? Great scientific formulae often are."

Carlton handed the pages back. "Tesla would be glad to know it is being used to help the world, as he intended with all his inventions."

Ben-David nodded. "*Tikkun olam.*" Noticing Carlton's quizzical expression, he added: "Hebrew for 'heal the world'. According to the Jewish tradition, God did not put us on Earth to curse the darkness but to heal the world, to perfect it."

Carlton recalled the story that had allowed him to reengage with his faith. He smiled. "I could not agree more."

"Tesla was not a Jew, but he lived that belief. He was-"

A loudspeaker crackled, interrupting Ben-David. "Command, this is Team One. We're almost ready. Attaching the wires to the last resonator now," a woman's voice announced.

Ben-David pushed a button on a flexible microphone stalk. "Copy that, Team One." He turned to Carlton. "I need to check something outside before we begin. I'll be right back." He strode out of the control room.

Carlton turned to Franklin, who was busy checking items off on a clipboard. "Can I give you a hand, doctor?"

She smiled shyly. "We're pretty informal out here. Please call me Joanne. Thank you, but there is not much to do until Ash returns."

Carlton sat in a nearby folding chair, watched the aged black and white monitors.

The loudspeaker crackled. "Command, this is Team One. Can you give me a reading on resonator-" The woman's voice abruptly cut off.

Franklin pressed the button on the microphone stalk. "Team One, this is Command. Your transmission cut out. Please repeat." Franklin let go, waited.

Nothing.

She hit the button again. "Team One, this is Command. Please repeat."

The familiar ball of ice reappeared in Carlton's gut. Something was wrong. He glanced at the nearby monitor. Froze.

"My God," he whispered, turned to Franklin. "You'd better take a look at this."

The screen showed a woman's body slumped forward against a metal box, immobile. A dark liquid flowed down her face, her eyes open, unblinking.

Blood.

Two shadows dashed in front of the camera before the monitor went black, confirming Carlton's worst suspicions.

"We're under attack," he announced. "You have to get Ben-David back in here right now."

"Under attack?" Franklin looked at him in terror as a faraway explosion shook the room. She gripped the edge of the computer console. "What was that?"

"Someone is setting off charges."

She trembled. "Who would attack-"

"The Saudis," Carlton cut her off. He wanted to rush into Alexis's room, but a guard was watching over her and Carlton could not leave Franklin and the other scientists here all alone. "You have to get hold of Ash."

She gazed at him, mute, paralyzed with fear.

Carlton leaned toward her, grabbed her shoulders, looked into her eyes. "Joanne. You have to get hold of Ash."

She seemed to overcome her terror for an instant. "I...I don't think he took a radio with him. Team One isn't responding. What are we going to do?" She stuttered. Carlton could see that she was losing her grip fast. He did not blame her. She was a scientist, not a soldier.

"Is there anyone we can call for reinforcements?" He asked, already knowing the answer.

Franklin shook her head nervously. "The nearest help is over a hundred miles away in Fairbanks."

Leaving immediately, flying at 200 miles per hour, it would take them thirty minutes to arrive. Too late. "How do we communicate with the guards?"

Franklin snapped out of her shock, changed radio frequencies, pushed the microphone stalk toward Carlton. "Their callsign is 'Security', led by lieutenant Davenport."

A second explosion rocked the room hard. Closer this time. Franklin and some of the other scientists screamed. The wood beams overhead flexed and creaked, then quieted, reminding Carlton of the library from which he had rescued little Spencer; except he could run out of the library to safety. Outside the control building were killers waiting - and freezing cold. The lights blinked off, then switched back on a moment later.

Carlton punched the mike button. "Security, this is Command. Come in. We're missing Ben-David. Have you seen him? Over."

He scanned the few monitors still in operation while awaiting a response. They showed a group of attackers firing at DARPA guards. Two guards lay immobile on the concrete HEERP array pad. Several attackers branched off, placed something near the base of a tall metal pole, then scurried to the next. Their uniforms seemed oddly familiar to Carlton, but he could not quite place them.

"They're setting more charges," he told Franklin, as a third, then a fourth explosion detonated. A fifth shook the room violently, knocking Franklin sideways to the floor. Carlton nearly fell on top of her, managed to grab the edge of the console at the last moment. He regained his balance, helped Franklin to her feet. Lights swung overhead. Carlton studied the last operational monitor, squinting through the dust raining down in sheets from the ceiling. The explosions had bent two of the array poles.

Carlton prayed that Alexis was safe when the loudspeaker finally crackled to life.

"This is Security. Negative. We haven't seen Dr. Ben-David." The man paused. "Who is this?"

Ben-David was MIA. Franklin was not trained to manage the situation. The other scientists were in a panic. Carlton had to act, but he was merely a visitor. He took a deep breath.

"Lieutenant Commander Patrick Carlton, U.S. Navy Reserve," he announced, unable to resist identifying himself as a military man to a brother in the Armed Services. "Who am I speaking with?"

"Lieutenant Davenport, Security Leader. With Team One gone and Ben-David MIA, it looks like you're second in command, sir. What are your orders?"

Carlton froze. "Second in command? Surely there must be-"

"Once attacked, we fall back to military rank. That makes you second in command. What are your orders, sir?" He repeated. "We're getting chewed up out here."

Carlton remained immobile. *Second in command*? He wanted to lend a hand, not take command.

He still had not recovered from his last command. He shuddered as he pictured his men's bodies sprawled in pools of blood on the decks of his patrol boats and in the murky green water of the Persian Gulf. Some dead, others dying. Most missing limbs, some on fire, screaming. Carlton gripped the edge of the table hard, squinted. A repeat of what happened in Iraq was what he feared most.

But this was worse than in Iraq. He did not know the men who were placing themselves under his command or their capabilities. He was unfamiliar with the facility's layout and defenses. He lowered his head, the explosions relegated to a faraway place, some not even registering in his mind. Taking command now would not only lead to more people dying. This time, he doubted that he could even protect the facility itself.

Carlton shut his eyes, prayed hard and fast, his thoughts racing. People liked to repeat the mantra that failure was not an option, but here and now, failure looked like a foregone conclusion. Yet Carlton could not give failure a free pass. To prevent the Saudis from achieving their goal. To protect Alexis and the others at the facility. To honor the memory of his fallen men. Of Eche. Within his roiling thoughts, he was surprised to find that the thing that motivated him the most was one that had been second nature to him since joining the Navy even before DOJ: duty. Whatever the consequences, he would perform his duty. He felt himself fall back into military mode.

In doing so, Carlton realized that the situation was different from Iraq in one important respect. The present attackers could not stop with killing HEERP personnel as blood sport. They had to destroy the HEERP facility itself. Which meant that Carlton had one small advantage: he knew where the attackers had to go.

But he didn't know the path the attackers would take. Lack of field intelligence was a sure fire way to lose any conflict, he knew. That had to change. Right now.

He stood straight, punched the microphone button. "Acknowledged. I am taking command until Ben-David is located. Give me force strength estimates, positions, objectives, and casualties." He turned to Franklin. "Can you get me a map of the facility?"

She gave a nervous nod.

"Yes, sir," Davenport replied. "Ten dead, three wounded. That leaves twelve of us. Estimate between forty and fifty bandits. Came out of nowhere, sir. Looks like they're trying to destroy the array with plastic explosives. Forward positions report they're wearing *Spetsnaz* uniforms."

That's why the uniforms looked so familiar, Carlton realized. He had originally thought that Ben-David's Men in Black had been Russian special forces soldiers. Confusion struck him. He had expected Saudis, not Russians. What were Russian special forces doing attacking a U.S.

energy research facility on U.S. soil? He recalled that the Soviets had killed Grant. That one of Tesla's intimates had been a Soviet agent, stealing some of the inventor's research. That the Soviets had tried unsuccessfully to make Tesla's invention work. Maybe the NKGB of the time had followed Grant's clue after killing him and its successors at the MGB, MVD, KGB, and its current iteration, the SVR, had continued in their footsteps.

It did not add up. For Russia to launch a military attack against an American government facility on U.S. soil smacked Carlton as implausible. Russia's KGB-alumni, mafia-oligarch government was doing everything to return the anemic country to Holy Mother Russia and its days of imperium, proclaiming its KGB agent leader as de facto czar, abolishing civil liberties for the long-suffering Russian people, assassinating opponents at home and abroad, holding Europe ransom for high gas prices, violating the sovereignty of former Soviet-bloc states, and doing everything in its power to thwart American foreign policy at every turn, but its leaders were neither stupid nor suicidal. Attacking Georgia was one thing. Attacking United States soil was quite another.

Franklin handed him a detailed diagram of the facility, snapping him out of his mental meanderings. Carlton nodded his thanks, scanned the sheet delineating buildings, roads, and perimeter fences. He spotted a small airfield a few miles away.

"Can we airlift the scientists out?"

"Negative," replied Davenport. "Even if we could evac everyone to the airfield, we only have a single ten person aircraft."

"Can you encircle the array and squeeze them?"

"Negative, sir. Not enough of us. But if we leave the array, they'll blow it to bits."

Twelve against fifty. Carlton somehow had to even the odds. He could visualize only a single tactic. "We have to force them out of the array. It will give your men a chance to regroup."

"How do we do that, sir?"

Recalling what Ben-David had told him about the array poles, Carlton let go of the mike, swiveled to Franklin. "Can you lower the poles from here?"

She nodded quickly.

"Get ready to do it, but wait for my signal," Carlton ordered. He pressed down on the mike. "Lieutenant, you're going to evacuate the array and fall back to protect the perimeter of the HQ building. We're going to lower the array poles."

"Sir, if the poles are in the ground, the bandits will have to go to the control room to destroy the array. They'll come directly to you."

"I'm counting on it," Carlton responded. "You'll be able to pick them off on the access road as they move to the HQ building. You've got two minutes. Get moving and keep a lookout for Ben-David."

"Yes, sir." Davenport did not sound convinced.

Carlton checked his watch, then left Franklin and strode to the control room door just as the guard who had been keeping watch over Alexis ran in, saluted him. As he did so, Carlton saw a Marine tattoo on his forearm.

"Corporal Marko Zivonovic, sir. DARPA SID. I was about to join the others at the array."

Carlton returned the young Marine's salute, wondering why the man was saluting someone dressed as a civilian and addressing him as 'sir' before noticing the comm link in his right ear. *He must have heard my conversation with Davenport.*

"Negative." Carlton spotted Alexis running down the hallway toward him. "Thank God you're OK."

"What the heck is going on?" She demanded, panting, frantic.

"We're under attack." He turned to the corporal. "Do you have a protected storage facility?"

The man thought about it for a second. "Walk-in food freezer is the closest thing."

"Good. Get her and the scientists into it before-"

"Cut the male chauvinism, Carlton," Alexis shot back angrily, shrugging his hand off her shoulder. "I can handle a gun. And I don't do meat lockers."

He wasn't being a male chauvinist, thought Carlton. He was simply trying to protect her. Isn't that what she had asked him to do? But Alexis was right. He had seen her in action under fire. And it was clear that rage at being attacked yet again had supplanted her fear. For now.

"Corporal Zi..." His voice trailed off accompanied by an expression of embarrassment, realizing that he had forgotten the soldier's name.

"Zivonovic, sir." The Serbian-American corporal flashed a smile of straight white teeth. "But everyone calls me Zivo."

Carlton nodded. "OK, Zivo. While Davenport and his teams fall back on the HQ building, you two round up all noncombatant personnel and get them into the freezer. Are there any weapons in the headquarters building?"

"Some handguns. Davenport's team took almost all the rest."

Carlton grinned. "It just gets better and better," he said, his grim expression returning. He checked his watch. "Collect whatever you can find and get her a weapon. In the meantime, give me your sidearm."

Zivo handed Carlton his SIG Sauer, butt first.

"Stay safe," he told Alexis.

Perhaps things would have been different had he been able to speak with Colonel Saunders. He shook off the thought. He had to deal with reality.

"Any weapons in here?" He asked Franklin.

"Ash put his sidearm in here," she replied, opening a drawer in the console.

At least Ben-David had good taste in handguns, he thought, removing the Glock 23, chambering a round before slipping extra clips of .40 caliber Smith & Wesson ammunition into his pockets.

The sole active monitor showed DARPA guards retreating to the headquarters building. Some took cover in the woods between the HEERP array and the HQ building, picking off attackers, thinning the enemy's ranks as it moved up the main access road. Carlton handed Zivo's SIG Sauer to Franklin.

She shook her head, pushed the gun back. "I'm a scientist."

"You're going to be a *dead* scientist if you don't defend yourself. The first word in DARPA is 'Defense'. Take it." It was not a request.

Franklin reluctantly took the gun. Carlton gave her a brief lesson on its workings, knowing that the weapon would increase her confidence, real or imagined. He glanced at his watch, waited for the minute hand to reach the two minute mark.

"Lower the poles."

Franklin flipped the switches.

Carlton positioned the remaining monitor's remote controlled camera toward the exterior of their HQ building. Sporadic flashes from automatic weapon bursts lit up the forest on the access road between the array and the HQ building.

He hit the mike. "Command to Davenport. Report, over."

"We're establishing a perimeter around the HQ building and fortifying the front gate facing the access road. Bandits are moving toward headquarters like you predicted. Still no sign of Ben-David."

Carlton followed Davenport's maneuvers on the map.

"Pull back all but two of your men from the access road, lieutenant. Concentrate on the headquarters perimeter."

Where the blazes was Ben-David? Could he be in league with the Saudis or the Russians? Carlton shook off the thought. If he had been, he would not have reactivated the facility and there would have been no need for an assault. There was a much more simple, unpleasant explanation: Ben-David could have been killed in action. Yet until Carlton had actual evidence of it, he refused to consider him dead.

"And keep looking for Ben-David."

"Yes, sir."

Two more explosions rocked the building. Very close. Very loud. The walls, even the floor buckled. Carlton and Franklin fell as the lights extinguished. This time they did not switch back on. Backup lights replaced them with dim lighting. They got back on their feet.

"That was right outside," muttered Franklin, voice cracking, eyes filled with fear. Carlton was not faring any better, but with Ben-David MIA, Franklin, Davenport, Zivo, and the others were relying on him as second in command. They needed to feel confident that he was in charge. This was no time to waver.

A staccato of machinegun fire sounded in the distance. The shots were coming from the access road, some in three round bursts, some spraying in full automatic mode. A few of their attackers had fallen for Davenport's ambush. Their odds were getting better, thought Carlton, but they still stank on ice.

The loudspeaker crackled. "Davenport to Command. All bandits have vacated the array. We've picked off a few on the access road before they figured out our strategy. The rest are headed toward you using alternate paths."

"Casualties?"

"We only have eight people left, sir. We've set a few mines around the building."

So much for the odds getting better.

Machinegun fire erupted all around the headquarters building. Loud. Close.

Zivo burst into the control room brandishing a Belgian Fabrique Nationale P90 submachine gun. Carlton suppressed a pang of jealousy at the corporal's firepower, but with no other heavy weapons available, Ben-David's Glock would have to suffice.

The dim backup lights illuminated Zivo's hard expression with an eerie glow. A sheen of sweat covered his face. His breathing was ragged. "Four of the scientists volunteered to protect the facility. They're arming themselves as best they can, but we're running way low on ammo. We've barricaded all three doors. The rest of the staff is hiding in the locker."

Carlton grimaced, hit the mike. "How many bandits now, Davenport?"

"Best estimate is about forty, sir."

Five to one. Carlton reflected on their options as the firefight outside the wood walls intensified. The attackers had evacuated the HEERP array to converge on the headquarters building. At least his initial plan had worked. The array was safe - for the moment. The true test would be how long Davenport's team could hold back the vastly superior force before it breached the headquarters building. The structure had no windows, but its wood walls would provide as much protection from bullets and explosives as cardboard. He consulted the facility diagram, studied the layout of the headquarters building.

"Does the control room have a self destruct mechanism?" He asked Franklin.

She shook her head.

So much for that idea. He turned to Zivo. "Do you have any mines or grenades?"

"Four Claymores and a few standard grenades. You want to blow up the control room, sir?"

"No. Rig Claymores at each door and have the volunteers pull back to the hallway outside the control room, then set up a barricade on both sides."

Zivo did not move. Instead, he gave Carlton a confused look. "Sir?"

Officers do not take kindly to subordinates who question their orders, but Carlton was not Zivo's regular commanding officer and had not yet earned the soldier's trust. He knew that his plan would only be effective if the corporal trusted Carlton's strategy.

"Davenport won't be able to keep the attackers at bay for long," explained Carlton. "That leaves us, Alexis, and the four volunteers. With the poles lowered, they need to get into the control room to raise them before they can destroy the array. To do that, they need to come down the main hallway." He pointed to the indoor diagram. "If we split up to protect each of the three outer doors, here, here, and here, we'll spread ourselves too thin. But if we rig Claymores at each door, we'll get rid of some of the attackers and face them with two stronger groups in the main hallway, where we can concentrate our firepower, including grenades. We'll use the explosives at the doors to neutralize as many attackers as possible. We have to protect the control room and the array at all costs."

Zivo nodded, now on board with the plan. "Yes, sir." He ran off to execute his orders.

Carlton led Franklin out of the control room, then remembered Tesla's formula. He walked back into the control room, located the five sheets of yellowed paper in the dim light, stuffed them unceremoniously in his pocket. Exiting the doorway, he looked right, then left. The control room entrance was in the middle of the main hallway. There was an exit to the outside around the end of each side of the hallway, a third on the other side of the building. Regardless of where the attackers entered the building, they would have to travel down sixty feet of hallway in either direction to gain access to the control room.

"We'll set up barricades in the middle of each side of the hallway to slow them down," Carlton announced to Franklin. He pointed to the left hallway. "You go that way. Take whatever furniture you can find, pile it on the floor."

As they marched off in separate directions down the corridor through wood and dust raining from the creaking ceiling, the firefight raging outside grew to a fever pitch. Another explosion rocked the building. The backup lights switched off, then glowed back to life, even dimmer than before. The staccato of machine gun fire intensified from three round bursts to full automatic.

It was only a matter of minutes before the attackers poured in.

Death was approaching.

41 PRISONER

U.S. Embassy
Paris, France
2:43 PM

Sobieski stared up at the M-9 pistol, held rock steady in a Marine corporal's hand. He heard a growl, glanced down without moving, shivered. A muscular black and tan German Shepherd strained at the end of a leash, fangs bared. Sobieski's heartbeat accelerated, his mind flashing back to a Rottweiler attack he had suffered as a child. So brutal that the scars were still on his leg. Different breed, same terror.

He forced the thoughts aside. "I am Major Sobieski, Polish Intelligence."

The Marine squinted at him. "And you just decided to stop by unannounced by stowing away in an embassy car's trunk? I don't think so." He kept the handgun trained squarely on Sobieski. "Arms behind your head."

The German Shepherd barked louder. Despite his best efforts, Sobieski flinched.

"I realize this looks suspect, but-"

"Oh, it looks way worse than suspect. Arms behind your head. *Now.*"

Sobieski complied. "I need to see Thundercloud. It's urgent," he pressed, referring to the resident *legat* - onc of 48 FBI legal attachés stationed globally to provide an outer line of defense against terror and crime targeting U.S. shores.

The Marine scrutinized him. "You could have gotten that name from the embassy website. And you could have avoided all this trouble by simply calling him," he concluded skeptically.

"He knows me. Please call him. He'll clarify-"

"If he was here, maybe. But he isn't."

"When is he re-"

"Enough! Now exit the trunk. Slowly." The corporal and a nearby private covering him each took a step back, preparing to avoid a potential booby trap.

Keeping his hands behind his head, Sobieski managed to swing his barely functioning legs out of the trunk, contorted himself out and onto the cement floor, teetered, then straightened. He shuddered as the barking German Shepherd yanked its handler closer, feeling the icy hand of panic grip his throat.

"Search him," the corporal ordered, without taking his eyes or handgun off of Sobieski. The guard dog's barking increased to a fury, jaws slavering.

The handler had detected the dog's effect on the intruder. He smiled. "She won't bite - unless you do something stupid."

Another bolt of terror shot through Sobieski. His claustrophobia had caused him to forget to remove his weapon. "I have a-"

Too late. The private saw Sobieski's holstered Sig Sauer the second he opened the front flap of his jacket. "He's armed!"

The corporal launched himself into Sobieski, tackling him to the ground with the private's help, rolled him head-down against the cold cement floor. He removed the Sig Sauer, tossed it aside, patted him down for more weapons while the private pressed his weapon hard against Sobieski's back.

The German Shepherd sensed the heightened tension, jumped toward them, dragging its handler across the floor, its lips curled back, revealing sharp yellowed fangs, jaws gnashing inches from Sobieski's face.

He tried to calm himself, telling himself that the dog was on a leash, that if he did not resist its handler would not let the dog tear him to shreds, but logic held little sway over his childhood terror. He could not see the dog's maw, but felt its spit splatter warm on his neck, smelled its stinking breath.

"Clean," announced the corporal.

The private bound Sobieski's arms and legs tight with plastic cuff strips, spun him face-forward.

"I have identification in my jacket," offered Sobieski, wincing as the binds dug into his wrists behind his back. He saw the dog's eyes fixed on him, broke out in another cold sweat, feeling little relief in the fact that the handler had managed to move the dog a couple of feet away.

The corporal removed the ID, examined it. "Says who you say you are," he commented, motioning for the private to lift Sobieski to his feet. "But fake IDs are a dime a dozen. And I don't know what this one is even *supposed* to look like." He sighed. "We'll verify your identity through your embassy."

Sobieski sighed. "You can't. All the lines are down." And they don't know I'm here, he did not add.

"Convenient." The corporal shot him an uneasy look. "We'll try anyway. Until we can ID you, you will be placed in confinement."

"I understand the need for security, corporal, but this is urgent," he replied, twisting against his binds, shouting to make himself heard above the German Shepherd's furious din. "We're on the same side. I must see -"

"We can't take any risks."

Sobieski slumped forward.

He had made it all this way. For nothing.

42 BARRICADES

The machinegun fire outside the headquarters building ceased.

Carlton knew what that meant: Davenport and his men were dead or disabled.

They were on their own. Again.

He and Alexis crouched behind the hastily erected barrier of tables, chairs, and filing cabinets providing the only line of defense against the enemy commandos about to pour in. A pair of scientists who had volunteered lay at their side, grasping SIG Sauer handguns with both hands to stop them from shaking. Zivo, Franklin, and two other scientists were in position behind a similar barricade past the control room doorway at the opposite end of the hallway.

Two explosions rocked the building as Zivo's Claymores detonated, their trip wires rigged several feet inside the hallway from the entrance doors. Screams filled the air as the twin hails of directed shrapnel shredded a handful of attackers, followed by a cloud of dust and splinters rushing out toward Carlton and his tiny band.

The rest of the horde came through, emerging from the dust with machineguns ablaze.

So many.

Carlton began firing through a small opening in the barricade. An enemy round hit the scientist next to him in the head. He slumped forward, dead before collapsing against the overturned desk. Alexis stopped firing, recoiled in horror. Enraged at her colleague's fate, the second scientist raised her arm above the desk and fired blindly.

The horde continued its advance.

Carlton grabbed one of Zivo's grenades, pulled its pin. While Alexis and the scientist continued to fire, he ducked to the right, rolled the two pound pineapple-shaped explosive down the hall like a miniature bowling ball.

The exploding shrapnel managed to neutralize only a single attacker, but sent the horde running back behind the corner of the hallway for cover. Instead of exposing themselves, the attackers now exposed only their machineguns. Carlton was familiar with their weapons: Kalashnikov AK-74 automatic machineguns, the 5.45 millimeter version of the AK-47 known the world over. Their steel-cored, hollow tip rounds made short shrift of the flimsy barricade, chewing through the wood furniture like so much wet tissue paper.

Only a steel cabinet crammed thick with documents protected Carlton, Alexis, and the surviving scientist from being turned into human sieves. Splinters dug painfully into Carlton's skin as he prayed that bureaucracy would prove stronger than terrorism. Alexis and the scientist aimed through small spaces in the barricade, felling a second attacker as he poked his head and torso around the corner.

As the scientist shifted her position for a better angle, a round tore through her right leg, shattering bone, ripping flesh and muscle. She crumpled to the floor, remaining silent for a handful of seconds, in shock, staring at the blood pumping through her fingers before the blast of pain hit her. She screamed in agony.

The horde slid out from behind the corner, tentatively, crouching behind fallen comrades.

Carlton shot at the enemy pressing toward them from his position on the right edge of the barricade. He hit one commando in the chest, sent the others retreating. He knew it would not last long.

While Alexis laid down covering fire, he turned back and peered through the heavy smoke and dust to Zivo, Franklin, and the two other scientists at the opposite end of the corridor. The attackers had not yet broken through their barricade, but both teams would soon have to fall back to the control room.

Death was approaching fast.

Carlton faced forward, squeezed off three rounds at an attacker peering around the corner of the hallway, hitting him in the shoulder. The commando fell to the floor, squirming. Explosions and gunfire had numbed Carlton's hearing even to the wailing scientist writhing on the floor, but did not prevent him from feeling a series of deep thumps through his body.

Why would the attackers detonate additional explosives if they were already inside the building? He soon thought of a reason, mentally kicked himself for not visualizing the strategy earlier: the enemy was planning to destroy the entire building, not just the control room.

It just keeps getting better.

One attacker slithered out from behind the hallway corner. Prepared and waiting for such a move, Alexis fired, splintering the wall next to him. He retreated before she could adjust her aim.

Sensing they had culled the small number of defenders, the attackers again appeared from behind the corner. No longer tentative, they now stormed out into the open, tore down the hallway, firing at anything and everything on full automatic.

Alexis dropped two of them. Carlton knew that this time, the horde would not retreat. It would soon close the thirty yard gap.

As she continued firing, he ejected his spent clip, loaded a fresh one, nudged her arm. Knowing she was unable to hear, he pointed to her, then to the injured scientist, then to the control room. She nodded, bent down low, grabbed the writhing scientist under the armpits. While Carlton laid down covering fire, keeping the enemy pinned down behind scattered bits of furniture, Alexis dragged the woman backwards to the control room.

He was about to fire his last shot when an explosion erupted behind the attackers rounding the corner. Two were thrown bodily into the air, then came slamming down hard against the wood floor, one impaling himself on a jagged table leg. Carlton dispatched the other with his last round before the other commando could shake his daze and aim his AK-74. He wondered how any of Davenport's men had managed to survive and lob a grenade from behind the attackers. Maybe the delay had malfunctioned in one of the enemy's grenades. Whatever the cause, it bought him the extra time he needed. He turned, ran to the control room, bent in half.

And came to an abrupt halt.

Alexis lay sprawled on the corridor floor, oozing blood from her chest, half covered by the wounded scientist. He froze, ignoring the danger behind him. Everything around him disappeared as he stared at Alexis's bloody body, feeling desperation before rage pushed the emotion aside. She had been hit while carrying the scientist to safety. He had ordered her to do it. It was his fault.

Carlton dropped to the floor on his knees, checked her pulse. She opened her mouth to say something, but he could not hear her. She needed help fast, as did the scientist she had been pulling to safety. He glanced at the other end of the hallway. Zivo, Franklin, and the two other scientists were running towards him, beating a hasty retreat to the control room between them as attackers converged on their abandoned barricade.

He motioned in alarm to Zivo, who ran past the control room door while firing at the attackers behind Carlton, slid on the floor next to him. He shouldered his P90, grabbed hold of the scientist as Carlton pulled Alexis. Each dragged their charge back to the control room while two scientists inside it valiantly laid down covering fire. As soon as they reached the entrance, Franklin handed Carlton her SIG Sauer, began to apply first aid as he looked on, still in shock, silently mouthing a prayer.

Zivo snapped Carlton out of his thoughts by shoving another loaded SIG Sauer in his chest, butt-first. Carlton grabbed it, shoved the other in his belt, turned toward the attackers at the end of the right hallway before indicating for Zivo to cover the left side. The corporal promptly opened fire with short bursts from his P90 submachinegun. Carlton crouched behind the control room door, fired at the attackers advancing down the other side.

They were beyond outnumbered. Each time Carlton seemed to pin down the attackers, a new wave bore down on him, barely visible through the choking haze of smoke and dust. It would not take long for the remaining attackers to overrun their position.

Death was speeding toward them.

Carlton scanned his position for any opportunity he could exploit. There was little to use, but if the dense clouds of cordite and debris were hiding the enemy from him, they would hide him from the enemy, he reasoned, turning to Zivo, exposing himself beyond the control room door.

Bad move.

Automatic fire turned the door into a sieve inches above his head. Carlton fell flat against the floor.

Not fast enough.

A round hit him in his left arm. The combination of pain and rage at his stupid mistake made him yell, but he could not hear his own shouts through his ringing ears. He fingered his wound gingerly, gritting his teeth at the pain, brought his hand back up in front of his eyes. Blood dripped from his fingers.

Zivo crawled over to him, examined his wound. Carlton waved him off with his good arm. No time for first aid. He signaled Zivo to keep firing down the left side of the hallway, picked up the SIG Sauer.

Lying on his stomach, he extended his good arm, aimed the gun down the hallway, clenching his teeth as each heartbeat sent agonizing bolts of pain through his wounded arm's nerve endings, clouding his vision with white blotches of light.

The good news was that his prone position allowed him to see under the pall of smoke, down the hallway. He squinted. A few seconds later, he spotted movement as a group of attackers stood. Carlton fired his last three rounds, then reached for the spare SIG Sauer tucked into his waistband as two grenades exploded at the far end of the hallway.

The shock waves rocked the wood building's structure, knocking the SIG Sauer out of Carlton's hand. He looked past more raining debris and blotches of light, groaning in despair as his only weapon slid ten feet down the tilted corridor just as Zivo ran out of ammunition.

Dammit.

He propped himself up on his good arm, pushed himself forward with his boots, inching toward the fallen gun with agonizing slowness. Blood poured down his left arm onto the floor, sucking precious energy with it. His throat felt like sandpaper. The grenade blasts made his ears ring so loud that he could no longer hear any gunshots. The smoke and dust teared up his eyes, made him cough dryly, almost to the point of vomiting.

He was going to die, but he would fight to the end to defend Alexis, the others, and the facility. Repeating a prayer to prevent himself from passing out, he continued his painful crawl, forcing himself to focus on each push and the gun in front of him.

Six feet.

Four feet.

His outstretched hand was a foot away from the gun. A boot emerged from the thick pall of smoke, kicked the gun far into the hallway, stopped an inch away from Carlton's face.

With no options left, Carlton strained his neck, peered up to see the person who would take his life, wondering what ignominies the attackers would visit upon Alexis, Franklin, and the other female scientists.

The man reached down to him with a gloved hand. Carlton attempted to roll away, but was yanked up by his right arm. He gazed at the man's pronounced Arab features and thick black beard.

Despair overcame him.

He had failed to protect the facility and its personnel.

Death had arrived.

43 LEGAT

The Marine private led the way deeper in the underground parking garage. Sobieski followed him, flanked by two other Marines, his wrists cinched painfully tight behind his back, his feet barely able to shuffle in the ankle cuffs. The corporal brought up the rear, M-9 still in hand. The rabid German Shepherd remained close by Sobieski's side, barking, straining hard against its leash.

They marched him toward a heavy-duty utility elevator at the end of the parking area, nudged him into the metal-paneled cage. The thick doors slid closed.

"Stop!" A voice boomed, echoing in the cavernous space.

The corporal wedged his arm between the doors, preventing them from shutting.

What now, wondered Sobieski, craning his neck, peering through the gap between the doors, watched a shadow stride across the parking area.

The soldiers surrounding him tensed, he noticed, probably glad that they were not meeting the approaching newcomer in a dark alley. Tall, wearing a navy suit as though it were battle attire, the barrel-chested man had a thick mane of black hair and matching eyebrows above coal black eyes. He looked like a linebacker on steroids.

He reached the elevator, placed a meaty hand against each door, contorted his features into a grimace, staring hard at Sobieski.

"What on God's green Earth are you doing in here?"

"You know this man, sir?" Asked the corporal in surprise.

"That is major Sobieski, Polish Intelligence," replied Jack Thundercloud. "Release him at once. I'm glad you alerted me. I was on my way out."

One of the privates untied the plastic cuff binds while another freed his feet. Sobieski pumped Thundercloud's oversize hand. "Am I glad to see you."

"I'll write up a report for you later," Thundercloud mentioned to the corporal before turning to Sobieski. "Follow me," he directed, escorting him across the parking area to the main elevator.

Sobieski exhaled a deep sigh of relief, massaging his aching wrists, giving the German Shepherd a wide berth. "I thought that monster was going to tear me to pieces."

"Buffy?" Thundercloud asked, the innocent expression of his Native American features soon morphing into a wicked smile. "Puts the fear of God in people, but she's an overgrown puppy. Might lick you to death."

Sobieski was not convinced.

"Welcome to the Rez, Tad. Sorry for the reception, but you could have simply called, you know."

"Our embassy lines are down. Landlines, internet, cell, sat phones. All dead or jammed. And I know who is -"

Thundercloud raised his hand, cutting him off. "Not in here."

"Understood," replied Sobieski, mentally kicking himself for such a rookie mistake, still shaken by the German Shepherd. Even within the U.S. embassy were areas that might not be safe from eavesdropping. "You guys are mobilized like it's 9-11."

"For us, every day is 9-11, you know that," replied Thundercloud. "The frogs don't like us much, but they just demonstrate. It's the towelheads casing the joint day and night that really piss us off."

He ushered Sobieski into another elevator, this one plushly carpeted and paneled in dark wood, inserted a key, pressed a button. The cabin rose without a sound.

A moment later, the doors opened on a very different scene from the bare cement and concrete of the parking lot, far more in tune with the 18th century neoclassical Hotel de Talleyrand that the U.S. government had purchased from France after World War II for use as its embassy. Gilded wall sconces illuminated a white hallway adorned with framed reproductions of American masters, molded ceilings, and a deep pile navy blue carpet. Thundercloud led him past a member of the Secret Service, whose agency provided internal security for all of

America's embassies and consulates. Halfway down the hall, he ushered him into a windowless conference room whose austerity seemed out of place with the rich décor outside. He closed the three inch thick door behind them.

"It's ugly, but in here, no one can hear you scream. We call it the 'Quiet Room'. It's soundproofed, shielded by lead plating, white noise generators and jammers, swept for bugs. Like yours at Rue St. Dominique. The enemy is always listening, not to mention the DGSE." He raised a thick index finger, watched the electronic bug detector light turn green. "OK, shoot."

"That's who is behind our communications blackout," said Sobieski, sitting in one of the chairs around the utilitarian wood table. "The DGSE." He knew that Thundercloud did not smoke, but offered the Native American a cigarette out of respect before lighting one himself. Thundercloud declined, frowned as he pointed to the 'no smoking' sign.

Sobieski exhaled a cloud of smoke through a toothy grin, his first in many hours. "Diplomatic immunity."

Thundercloud chuckled, hunkered down across the table at a seat too small for his wide carriage. "So what is this all about?"

Sobieski filled him in on the DGSE's tails, culminating in its electronic isolation of the Polish embassy.

The FBI legat arched a bushy eyebrow. "Coming from anyone else, I would say that was crazy."

"So would I - if I did not have the intel I discovered."

"Which is?"

Sobieski shook his head, grimaced apologetically. "I'm sorry, Jack. I can't tell you. Not yet."

Accustomed to the vagaries of intelligence work, Thundercloud remained non-plussed. He had worked with the Polish agent in the past, granted him the latitude. "Then why did you come here the way you did? In case you hadn't noticed, those Marines have itchy trigger fingers. You almost got yourself killed."

"I came to give the intel to your government, but I'm doing this on my own. None of my people know. For now, I can only give it to one person."

Thundercloud nodded, appreciating both the huge risk his colleague was taking and the wisdom of his intended narrow disclosure. "Tell me and I'll bring him in."

"He's not here. The person is Patrick Carlton. At DOJ's National Security Division in DC."

Thundercloud stared at his Polish colleague in shock. "You risked all that just to make a phone call?"

Sobieski expelled a cloud of smoke, nodded. "*Tak.*"

"Then I guess I'd better get you a telephone."

44 TABIB

The gun resting on the floor was too far for Carlton to reach, even if he had not been injured and trapped in the Arab's iron grip.

Giving up on his weapon, Carlton focused his attention on his burly captor. His splotchy vision was playing tricks on him. The Arab appeared to be dressed in a U.S. Army Battle Dress Uniform, with a Heckler & Koch Mark 23 .45 caliber handgun in a side holster and a Colt M6 carbine in his left hand. His chest patch read 'Tabib'.

Carlton finally understood: the Saudis had sent in their people dressed in Russian and U.S. uniforms. Clever.

So be it.

He may have failed, but he would not cower. Despite the pain pulsing from the gunshot in his arm, Carlton stood straight, shook off the man's hold, glowered back at him in open defiance. The gunfire and explosions had ceased. His muffled hearing was beginning to clear.

"The area is secure," he heard the Arab announce in a faraway voice before turning again to Carlton. "Who are you?"

"Lieutenant Commander Patrick Carlton, U.S. Navy Reserve. Who are you?" He shot back, not expecting much of an answer.

"Captain Mohammed Tabib, First Special Forces Group," the man replied before saluting crisply.

Carlton stared at him, astonished. "Colonel Saunders?"

"He sent us."

So Saunders had *received his voicemail.* A wide grin split Carlton's face as a wave of relief nearly caused him to lose his balance. "Thank God." He paused for a moment, letting the revelation sink in. "And thank you, captain."

He returned the salute, stumbled into the control room. A medic was tending to Alexis and the wounded scientist. Her eyes were half shut, barely registering the events around her, but her chest was rising and falling, which meant that she was still alive. Carlton moved toward her.

Tabib held him back.

"He needs to do his job, sir," he admonished, stern and calm, motioning for another medic to examine Carlton's injury. "He's very good at it."

There was nothing Carlton could do for Alexis right now. He reluctantly complied, sat in the splintered hallway outside the control room.

"You're lucky, sir," said the medic, cutting off his sleeve with scissors, inserting a morphine pipette before cleaning his wound. "The slug went clean through your bicep. You'll be fine, but it looks like you lost a lot of blood," he explained, inserting a thick IV needle attached to a plasma baggie into Carlton's right arm.

"Thanks," Carlton muttered, clenching his teeth at the sting, feeling little relief as he looked at Alexis on the floor and the medic at her side, both smeared in her blood.

He could not bear to watch, looked up at Tabib, forced his mind to think of something else.

"Colonel Saunders outdid himself. I had expected MPs, not the Quiet Professionals," he commented, referring to how members of the 10,000-strong U.S. Special Forces called themselves. Most others called them by the headgear they wore: Green Berets. Personally created by President John F. Kennedy, the U.S. Special Forces were inconspicuous, highly educated, multilingual, resourceful, and full of traditions, including one that required one member of each team to carry a video of John Wayne's classic movie *The Green Berets*.

"It took some time for the colonel to convince SOCOM and USASOC to send us on a domestic op," he explained, knowing Carlton would understand the acronyms. He referred to the Special Operations Command at MacDill Air Force Base, Florida and to the U.S. Army Special Operations Command at Fort Bragg, North Carolina. The Special Forces were accustomed to legion unconventional tasks. Fighting inside the United States was not one of them.

"The important thing is that you got here. We were about to become mincemeat."

Tabib peered through the dissipating smoke, arched his eyebrows. "Looks like you did pretty good, sir."

Carlton felt light-headed. "How many people do you have?"

"Just the ODA," replied Tabib, referring to his Operational Detachment Alpha, composed of twelve soldiers, each trained in a different discipline.

Carlton nodded, impressed. Again he resisted the urge to stare at Alexis's bloody body behind him, forced himself to change the topic. "You know, for a moment there, I thought you were a terrorist."

Tabib nodded gravely. "I got that a lot after 9-11 and the shootings at Ford Hood. Being of Arab descent is no small challenge, but being a Muslim in the U.S. military is an honor that fulfills two goals for me. One for America, one for my faith."

Carlton cocked his head in surprise, feeling woozy in the process.

"America's last four wars defended Muslims against their aggressors: in Kuwait, Bosnia, Afghanistan, and Iraq. America and Islam face a common enemy of Islamist fanatics hijacking a faith that commands building a better word to seize power, sow violence, destroy anything different, and impose their control. They have murdered hundreds of thousands of Muslims. It is my duty to fight them both as an American soldier and as a Muslim."

America was fortunate to have such men in its armed forces, reflected Carlton. "If you ever want to transfer to the Navy, let me know," he said, beginning to slur his words.

Tabib grinned. "Not a chance, sir." Seeing that the morphine was kicking in, he pressed on. "What are your orders?"

"I want to know who the attackers are."

"From their uniforms, it looks like they're *Spetsnaz* - Russian Special Forces."

Carlton shook his head, opened his eyes wide to clear the growing haziness. "Not buying it. Have to be Saudis or have a Saudi connection," he said, straining to keep his words intelligible. "I want to know what, when and where the next attack will be."

Tabib's dark eyes opened wide. "You think there will be another?"

Carlton nodded weakly, propping himself up against the wall with his good arm. First the failed attack on the U.S. electrical grid. Now the attack on HEERP. Both with a Saudi connection. Too close for coincidence. He peered at Alexis's bloody body, shut his eyes, but his mind filled with the images of his mutilated men, of Claire, of Eche. What he wanted to do was line up every surviving attacker and drill a bullet into the skull of one of them every minute until the rest started vomiting information.

Fantasy, not an option for a DOJ prosecutor. Based on Tabib's information, the attackers wore the uniform of Russia, a sovereign nation. It was a clever ruse: the terrorists had to be considered uniformed national combatants under the Geneva Convention and U.S. law, protecting them from harsh treatment and any interrogation other than a request for the most basic information.

Carlton took a breath, his head swaying involuntarily as he fought against passing out. "Get names, ranks, and serial numbers, then give them to Saunders for verifi-" The morphine cut him off.

* * *

Sobieski left urgent messages on Carlton's office and cell phone voicemails, then tracked down his assistant while lighting his fifth cigarette.

"Mr. Carlton is on vacation. I can give him a message if you'd like."

"I've already left him messages. It is urgent that I speak with him immediately."

"Unfortunately, sir, I have no way of contacting him outside his cell phone. If it's urgent, you can leave a message for Deputy Assistant Attorney General Edison."

Sobieski did not want to contact anyone other than Carlton, but the clock was ticking. Maybe this Edison could track Carlton down if he knew what this was about. "May I speak with him?"

"Not unless I can verify who you are and what this concerns, sir. The Deputy AAG is a very busy man."

Busy man? Sobieski bit back a curse, settled for a loud grunt. Scaling the U.S. government's bureaucratic fortifications was proving more difficult than sneaking into its embassy. He turned to Thundercloud in utter frustration.

The Navajo needed no goading. He leaned over the speakerphone on the table. "This is Jack Thundercloud, FBI legat at the Paris embassy." He read off his FBI code, which helped speed up recognition. "My colleague and I need to reach Carlton yesterday. Not his voicemail, not Deputy AAG Edison. Who on your staff can do that for us?"

"Just a moment, sir." There was a pause while the assistant verified Thundercloud's code with FBI headquarters across Pennsylvania Avenue. "I'm going to transfer you to someone who may be able to help."

45 COUP

In the searing desert heat high atop the mosque's minaret, the *muezzin* sang the *adhan*, the call to prayer. In a loud, lilting voice, he repeated the words of Bilal Rabah, the Abyssinian slave freed by the Prophet Mohammad who first climbed atop the Kabbah stone in Mecca after the Prophet's army conquered the city in 630 AD.

Allahu akbar! God is most great.

Ash-had anna lah ilaha illallah! I bear witness that there is no other deity but God.

Ash-hadu anna Muhammadar rasulullah! I bear witness that Mohammad is the messenger of God.

Hayya 'ala-salatt! Make haste toward worship.

Hayya 'ala 'l-falah! Come to the true success.

Allahu akbar! God is most great.

La ilaha illallah! There is no deity but God.

During the past week, Prince Hakim had tried repeatedly to obtain a private audience with King Fahim. His efforts had failed, resulting only in a group meeting with the king and his advisors. Moreover, Yassin had heard nothing from their allies concerning Alaska. Hakim had to assume that they had failed. After his initial tantrums, he had pushed his rage deep down inside him, redoubling his focus on the other part of his and al Shayk's plan. Two days ago, with Yassin's help, Hakim had found a way in.

It worked, he reflected with glee as he entered the king's private audience chamber. Its green marble walls were inlaid with Qu'ranic verses in white marble. A domed skylight above illuminated a splashing fountain that cooled the room. Ornate white chairs with bright gold inlays and red velvet cushions surrounded a similarly gilded coffee table groaning under heaping solid gold platters of dates, powdered-sugar cakes, and sticky sweets, cut crystal juice carafes, gold teapots filled with green tea, and tiny cups of strong black coffee sweetened with cardamom.

The king had recently done away with the traditions of kissing the royal hand or referring to him as 'your majesty', yet Hakim's world was that of the past. He could not fully stop adhering to those traditions. "*Salaam aleikum*, your majesty." Peace be with you. It will be on you soon enough, Hakim reflected, straining to prevent his smile from becoming a contemptuous scowl. He and King Fahim shared a father, but little else.

"*Wa aleikum as-salaam*," replied the elderly monarch. And unto you be peace.

Heeding the call to prayer, both men kneeled, prostrated themselves next to the *mihrab* niche indicating the direction of Mecca, and reverently recited their midmorning prayers to Allah.

Once finished, the men rose, with Hakim helping the older and larger king up, something allowed in private only.

The monarch sat heavily in one of the ornate chairs, pointed to another. "Please make yourself comfortable, my brother. Have some juice, some dates."

"Thank you, majesty." Prince Hakim took a date from the gold dish, tore into its soft sugary skin. The king's warm hospitality failed to dissolve the hatred that raged in Hakim's heart. His half brother was a traitor, Hakim reflected, about to trade the revered Wahhabi clerics' protection and guidance for the blasphemers' help, bending to the crusading Americans' heresy of free will and the separation of mosque and state in exchange for a few more weapons and a vague promise of defense against the Shiite Iranian devils.

"Thank you for coming so quickly, Hakim." The king paused, shifted in his seat, stroked his jet black beard, adjusted his eyeglasses.

Hakim could tell by the monarch's taciturn expression that something was worrying him deeply. "What is it, majesty?"

"I'm afraid I have unpleasant news, Hakim."

Hakim sat up, cocked his head. "Majesty?"

"I asked you here to warn you."

He moved closer to the edge of his seat. "Warn me?"

"Al Qaeda has targeted you for assassination," the king stated flatly.

Hakim grunted, waving off the warning dismissively with his hand, taking care to hide his seared, nailless index finger. "I am grateful for your brotherly concern, majesty, but this is nothing new. I have often been targeted by the Al Qaeda devils, just like your majesty and the other members of our family."

The king remained undeterred. He leaned forward. "You are brave, but this is not an idle threat. My staff discovered an actual plan to assassinate you and Prince Taballah," he said, referring to the Saudi Defense Minister who was first in line to the throne. "Al Qaeda has infiltrated even the few remaining places we thought safe." He raised his finger. "Thanks be to Allah, we know this ahead of time. Here is the information," he said, handing Hakim a package. "I passed this on to Prince Taballah also. You must take appropriate precautions."

Hakim accepted the package with a bow, nodding dourly. "Thank you, majesty. I will. And my ministry will root out the infestation immediately, *inshallah*." God willing.

"Good." The king reclined, clearly relieved of the unpleasant burden. "Now let us talk about more pleasant things. A pity your little Mohammad could not join us. I always enjoy his company so. He will be a great leader one day, *inshallah*."

"You do my son honor, majesty. But Mohammad did not forget his favorite uncle," he said, smiling. "He drew a card for you. He has already memorized the first fifty *shura* of the Qu'ran. He wrote some of them for you." Hakim removed a small envelope from his *bisht* and handed it to the king.

The king's face creased into a heartfelt smile as he took the envelope, sliced it open with a miniature gold *scimitar* and removed the card inside and his eyeglasses to read it. He choked up when he saw the Qu'ranic verses painstakingly written with a beginner's scrawl. "Adora-"

The king's tearful eyes opened wide, first in surprise, then horror. His eyeglasses fell to the marble floor. Unable to move or speak, he sat as immobile as a statue, staring at Hakim, whose own face was contorted in shock.

"Majesty?" He leaned forward, slid from his chair to the floor in front of Fahim. "Brother? What is wrong?" He peered into the king's wide eyes, touched his arm. No response. He appeared paralyzed. Hakim stood, turned, shouted. "Guards! Guards!"

Two armed guards sprinted into the audience chamber.

"His majesty is ill. Alert the medical team immediately! Not a word to anyone!"

So shocked were the guards by the sight of their paralyzed monarch that they failed to question how the palace medical team that dashed into the room instants later had learned about the emergency before they had summoned them. They administered oxygen, placed the king on a stretcher and rushed him to a hospital suite in Prince Hakim's *Sharia* palace. The vegetable extract to which the king was acutely allergic had acted even faster than Yassin had predicted, reflected Hakim. Doctors loyal to the Interior Minister injected the king with a serum prepared in advance that would allow him to breathe, but little else. The rooms in and out of the miniature hospital were sealed and protected by Hakim's loyal Interior Ministry troops, regularly purged of suspected reformers and other undesirables in the harshest manner.

As to the information in the package King Fahim had given him, Hakim was unconcerned. There was no assassination plot. Not against him, anyway. He had devised the plot himself, making certain that the plans fell into the hands of the king's personal security staff, though not too easily. It had gained him a private audience and removed him from both the king's and Defense Minister Taballah's suspicions. Exactly as he and Yassin had planned.

Yet not all of the plot was a lie.

There was an assassination plot against Prince Taballah, but not the one that Hakim had fed to the king. Focusing on the captured details of the plot, Taballah had made a tragic mistake, dropping his guard against other possible scenarios.

Minutes later, an explosion tore through the streets of Riyadh as Taballah's driver pulled the cord on the detonation device strapped around his waist, blowing himself and the Defense Minister to smithereens.

With Taballah dead, Hakim was next in line to the throne. With the king incapacitated, Prince Hakim would take over the mantle of Saudi power as Crown Prince and Regent. True, Saudi custom first required a consensus among the upper echelons of the other princes before such an accession to power, but neither Hakim, backed by his Interior Ministry, nor al-Shayk, backed by his powerful retinue of like-minded clerics, would give them much choice. Accept or die.

As Hakim's Interior Ministry-controlled state media began to broadcast his fictionalized version of the king's incapacitation by stroke - not an unconvincing story given the monarch's advanced age - he looked up to the heavens, arms outstretched.

"*Labayk, Allahuma. Labayk.*" Here I am O Lord. Here I am. "Tell me what to do."

Prince Hakim already knew the Almighty's response. Al-Shayk had repeated it to him often enough.

Fulfill your destiny.

Unleash the sandstorm against the infidel.

46 IDENTITY

Carlton awoke nauseous after a brief drug-induced sleep. He vomited up the remaining morphine in his system, then forced down one of the Special Forces' Meals Ready to Eat (MRE) rations to regain his strength. Feeling nearly human again despite the pain in his arm, he pounded down cup after cup of bad coffee while listening to Tabib's and Zivo's debriefing in the hastily cleaned up control room.

Alexis and the two wounded scientists had been airlifted to Fairbanks aboard a Special Forces Black Hawk helicopter. Had the medics lacked an ounce of their battlefield training, all three would be dead. The last report was that one scientist was out of danger, with the other and Alexis tenuously clinging to life in intensive care. Carlton recalled the frightened look in her eyes as she lay bleeding on the dust-caked control room floor. He regretted not accompanying her, felt his guilt over her injury rise. He tried to shake off the emotions, reasoning that she had wanted to remain with him for protection, that he could not have done anything more for her. It did not make his pain and fear for her condition any easier to bear. Some protection he had provided. At least she was still alive.

Sure enough, bad news followed the good.

The attackers had decimated the DARPA security team. Of its twenty five members, only Zivo had survived. Lieutenant Davenport had been shot at point-blank range while valiantly defending the headquarters' entrance. The Team One scientists installing the resonator at the array had all met the same fate. Of the five scientists including Franklin who volunteered to defend the building, three had survived, along with all those who had hidden in the food storage locker. At least Carlton and the others had managed to protect them. And forty of the fifty attackers had been killed.

One of the medics walked up to him to check on his arm wound, now stitched. He stood and bypassed him, stumbling down the hallway and into the bitter cold outside wearing only a sweater he had found. The glacial Arctic air spanked the remaining grogginess clear out of him. He walked around the devastated building, saw the line of closed body bags containing the facility's defenders. He fell to his knees, eyes tearing up, forming icicles on his cheeks.

Carlton had not known these men, but he knew who they were. They were the same people as his men in Iraq and countless others who had perished in remote outposts around the world. The best of America. Volunteer heroes who had sacrificed their lives for duty and honor and country. Protecting liberty from her very real enemies.

Also like in Iraq, they had succeeded in their mission, protecting the HEERP facility, although the splintered and charred wood surrounding him evidenced that it had barely survived the onslaught, despite the Special Forces' restoration of basic functions. He recited a prayer, commending their souls to God.

And vowed to bring their killers to justice.

His anger swelled. It was the only thing that thawed the icy memory of Alexis's bloody, violated body and the tragic line of body bags laid out before him. He swore that this would not end with a classified report about a clandestine attack on a remote government facility, filed away in a restricted file cabinet deep in a Pentagon, CIA, FBI, or DOE basement. He was going to make sure that the animals responsible ended up in a cage. Or dead.

All of them.

Back in the HEERP control room, Carlton fell into a chair, gulped down more bad coffee to ward off the cold seeping in through ragged holes and tilted walls. Cleaned, stitched, and dressed, his aching arm wound was on its way to recovery. He needed to think clearly, refused codeine pills for the throbbing pain. He was itching for a stogie, but the battle had not brought his stash in the mangled Escalade at Paramount Studios any closer.

In addition to the barely standing HEERP HQ, there was one other piece of good news. A member of Tabib's ODA had found Ben-David. He had been driving to the array when the attack erupted. Unarmed and unable to return to the headquarters building faced with the horde of attackers, he had taken refuge in the dense forest, twisting his ankle. Forced to wait until the attack ended before emerging with a severe yet repairable limp, but unable to sit idly by while his men were hunted down, he had obtained a handgun from a fallen DARPA guard, fired at the attackers on the access road, killing two before running out of ammunition. The brutal attack had erased every shred of his once boyish appearance.

Carlton removed Grant's copy of Tesla's formula from his pocket and handed it to Ben-David, who accepted it with a curt nod of thanks.

"You were right," he muttered, his face a mess of scratches under a crudely fashioned *yarmulke* to replace the one he had lost in the forest. He looked down at his taped up ankle, shaking his head. "How could I not see it coming? Thank God you were able to get reinforcements." He looked back up, placed his hand on Carlton's shoulder. "Thank you."

Carlton opened his mouth to reply when Tabib strode into the control room.

He looked up at the Special Forces captain hopefully. "Anything?"

"Yes, sir. For one, we figured out how they got here. My team discovered parachute equipment not far from the HEERP array. Not just parachute equipment, but HALO - high altitude low opening - jump equipment, complete with oxygen masks and fins for directional control. The attackers were highly trained."

"Isn't the HEERP airspace restricted?" Asked Carlton.

"It is," replied Ben-David, gazing at the Special Forces captain.

"I did some digging," continued Tabib. "An Aeroflot cargo flight from Vladivostok to Los Angeles reporting engine trouble was diverted to Fairbanks, placing its flight path less than ten miles from HEERP about a half hour before the attack started."

"High enough for a HALO jump to glide to HEERP," concluded Carlton.

Ben-David nodded. "So we know where they came from and how they got here, but not who they are. You still don't believe they are Russian, do you?"

"Their uniforms, training, and now their point of departure all indicate Russia as the culprit. But I still don't believe it," replied Carlton, shaking his head. Despite all the evidence, he remained convinced the attackers were linked to Saudi. "Anything else?"

"It gets better," replied Tabib.

"Good, because I don't think it can get worse," grumbled Carlton.

"The prisoners gave us names, ranks, and serial numbers. I relayed the data to colonel Saunders as you ordered. He just called back. The data is correct, except for one thing."

Carlton looked at him expectantly.

"All the names, ranks, and serial numbers belong to Russian soldiers killed in Chechnya over a year ago. Which means that the attackers are most likely Chechens who used their Russian victims' identities as cover. Their physical appearance supports that theory." Seeing the disappointment on Carlton's face, Tabib continued. "That proves your Saudi theory, sir."

Carlton flashed him a confused look. "How?"

"Because the Chechen rebels are backed by Saudi Islamists."

He stared back at Tabib in shock.

"Stalin absorbed Chechnya into the Soviet Union by force, killing and displacing tens of thousands," Tabib explained. "After the fall of the Soviet Union, Chechen separatists fought to regain their independence. They were mostly Muslim, but not radical Islamists. In 1996, Saudi jihadists hijacked the Chechen rebel leadership the way the Taliban took over the *mujahedeen* in Afghanistan in the 1980s. Today's Chechen rebels are mostly Saudi-backed Al Qaeda adjuncts. Terrorists, not freedom fighters seeking independence. Remember their hostage-taking of Russian schoolchildren in Beslan? So maybe-"

"Saudi sent their Chechen agents on an errand to Alaska," said Carlton, finishing Tabib's sentence. He did not derive much pleasure from his vindicated theory. They had uncovered the link to Saudi, yet something remained unclear. He frowned. "The Saudi government would have a vested interest in preventing the U.S. from implementing Tesla's formula. But it would not commit political suicide by launching an attack on U.S. soil at a time when Saudi is facing increased aggression from Iran. So who did?"

"I might be able to answer that also," replied Tabib. "Saunders gave me the latest intel out of Saudi. The king has been incapacitated by a stroke. The Saudi defense minister next in line to the throne was killed in a suicide car bomb explosion soon thereafter. Interior Minister Hakim has just been installed as regent. Within an hour, he terminated all oil contracts with U.S. firms, ordered all American workers out of the country, dissolved the consultative assembly, and decreed a host of fundamentalist measures even more radical than their current fare, if you can believe that."

Carlton ran a hand through his disheveled hair. "A coup."

Tabib nodded. "Looks that way, sir."

The three were lost in silent thought when Franklin popped her head into the room. "Mr. Carlton? You have an urgent call from a Henri Monet." She pointed to a telephone half-covered in debris on a nearby tilted desk.

Carlton swiveled, lifted the handset, punched the flashing button.

"*Dieu merci*," exclaimed Monet. Thank God. "I've been trying to get a hold of you for-"

"I've been...indisposed. How did you find me?"

"Colonel Saunders told me. I've got an urgent call for you from the FBI legat in Paris."

Carlton frowned. The FBI? Eche was the only remaining agent at the Bureau who had known about Tesla's formula. And what did Paris have to do with any of this? He sensed that the call was instead related to Faraday's vendetta. The Abu Hassan case seemed very far away now.

"I've got an urgent situation to take care of right now, Henri. Tell him I'm not available."

"*Il insiste*. He insists. He says it's a matter of national security."

Carlton sighed. "Very well. Put him through."

He waited until a voice came on the patched line, distant and tinny. "Mr. Carlton. This is FBI legat Jack Thundercloud in Paris. I have a major Tadeusz Sobieski from Polish foreign intelligence here with me - their CIA."

Paris? Polish foreign intelligence? "What does-"

"He says he has urgent information for you," Thundercloud rolled on. "I've worked with him before. You should listen to him. He came to me at considerable personal risk to give you this information. He refuses to give it to anyone else, including me."

"OK. I'm listening, major."

"I am so glad you are still alive, Mr. Carlton," a new voice announced in heavily accented English. "I know what you have gone through at the hands of Saudi agents under Grover Wolf during the past few days."

Carlton sat up. He had no idea who Wolf was, but the Pole had access to some darn good intel about the his recent situation. "Please continue."

"I cannot reveal anything over the telephone, so I will send you an encrypted email. It involves Euroil, it is urgent, and its implications are devastating. You must review it immediately."

Carlton had sensed there would be another attack. What was Saudi planning? "Henri, you getting this?"

"As soon as I receive the major's email from Paris, I will transmit it to you reencrypted via the Special Forces network."

Carlton repeated it to Tabib, who patted an armored steel laptop on the desk.

"Thank you both. I will await your information, major."

Part of the line cut out. "Henri, you still there?"

"*Oui.*"

"Who the heck is Grover Wolf?"

"The lawyer in charge of Farnsworth Tate's Saudi Arabia practice."

Carlton winced as the ball of ice reappeared in his gut. "In that case, you had better do some quick research on Euroil."

"Already done. Very little of it good. You want it now?"

"My calendar is wide open today, Henri," he replied testily.

"Euroil is the largest French company, Europe's top electricity supplier mostly through nuclear power plants, and the world's fifth largest oil company. Over the past ten years, Euroil has swallowed most of its German, Spanish, and Italian competitors *entiers* - whole. Its CEO is Ludovic Metz. Doesn't care where or with whom the company does business as long as it makes money."

"Sounds like some American CEOs I prosecuted when I was in Antitrust."

"Except that some of Euroil's corporate practices make Enron look like a charity. In the 1960s and 70s, Euroil helped the Soviet Union extract oil and gas in Siberia using slave labor from the *gulags*. Euroil's natural gas contract with Burma has helped the military dictatorship stay in power for years. Same arrangement with the brutal dictatorships of many African oil-producing countries and with the Castro brothers to pump oil off of Cuba. Some allege that Euroil transferred nuclear technology to North Korea in exchange for lucrative rights and might be doing the same with Chavez in Venezuela. They believe that technology transfer allowed North Korea to build the secret Al-Kibar nuclear reactor in Syria that the Israelis destroyed in 2007. The company is near the top of the corporate list of most human rights and business watchdog groups, but has powerful allies in the French and E.U. governments."

"Imagine that. A wretched energy company. Tell me more about its activities in the Middle East."

"Euroil has taken full advantage of the fact that unlike the U.S., France does not have bans against doing business with most terror-sponsoring countries. Until recently, at least, it supplied a large amount of Iran's gasoline that the regime desperately needs to stay in power, allegedly purchases a large amount of Iranian oil by falsifying ship manifests, and is suspected of helping Iran's nuclear weapons program in exchange for cut-rate oil. In the late 1970s, Euroil is believed to have helped Saddam Hussein build the Osirak nuclear reactor in Iraq in exchange for lucrative oil contracts. If the Israelis had not bombed the reactor before it became operational, Euroil might effectively have given Saddam a nuclear weapon. Same for Assad in Syria, with Al-Kibar.

"Euroil was identified as one of the biggest violators of the UN Oil For Food Programme. Euroil gave Saddam and UN officials billions of dollars in exchange for vouchers to buy Iraqi oil at bargain prices, which Saddam used to build palaces, rearm, and pay teenage Palestinian suicide bombers while slaughtering and denying medical supplies to his people. A UN official who had once worked for Euroil conveniently lost the incriminating files during the investigation. The list goes on and on."

"Ties to Saudi?"

"I did not find any, but Euroil has been trying to obtain Saudi oil field development contracts for some time."

Something told Carlton that Euroil may have succeeded.

"I just transmitted Sobieski's email," added Monet.

Carlton gestured to Tabib, who tapped on his laptop, nodded, engaged the decryption program, and brought the device over.

"Great work, Henri. I'll call you back."

Carlton's mouth dropped as soon as he started reading Sobieski's email.

47 PETROTERROR

HEERP Facility
Akona, Alaska
11:23 AM

Carlton read the earliest transcripts first, which revealed the conversations between ambassador Qhibli and Grover Wolf, outlining Wallace's attempted bribe with the job at DOE before Qhibli ordered his and Alexis's assassinations. He seethed as he continued to the transcript of the meeting between Wolf, Metz, and de Ville.

His anger soon morphed into outright terror.

The following are unredacted transcripts of conversations between Grover Wolf of Farnsworth Tate, counsel to Saudi Ambassador to the U.S. Prince Qhibli, E.U. Foreign Minister François de Ville, and Euroil, S.A. CEO Ludovic Metz.

Wolf: As you know, Saudi Arabia sits on the world's largest oil deposits and is the world's largest oil producer. Yet its present oil fields are quickly running dry, including Ghawar and Safaniya. Although they have enjoyed a reprieve due to decreased oil demand during the global economic crisis, it is only temporary.

I can see that the Kingdom's effort to keep this information secret has been successful. Most believe that Ghawar and Safaniya have another 20 years of production. At current reduced production levels, they have at most five years. A long time if there were other Saudi fields to replace it.

Metz: But there are none. Are there?

Wolf: No. To replace them within five years, the Kingdom must immediately develop its known untapped oil fields and discover new ones. Despite a rise in the oil price, it is now below the Kingdom's break-even point due to the massive increase in welfare payments necessary to keep the Kingdom stable after the Arab Spring uprisings. The Kingdom is fast using up the surplus it accumulated during the last oil price spike to make up the difference. It does not have the funds necessary to develop new fields, much less discover new ones.

Money is the first problem. The other is expertise. As you know, Saudi Aramco produces 97 percent of the Kingdom's oil, mostly through American petroleum engineers and oil companies. Before 9-11, and especially since, the presence of American engineers has exacerbated relations between the royal family and the Saudi population, which increasingly opposes their presence. Attacks against the royal family and American workers have increased. Yet without foreign engineers and companies, Saudi oil production and exploration would stop within a matter of weeks and send the Kingdom into ruin.

The Kingdom proposes a simple solution to both problems. By ejecting all American oil workers from Saudi Arabia, terminating all contracts with the American oil companies, and replacing them with a single exclusive oil contract between Saudi Aramco and Euroil.

Metz: Surely it cannot be that simple.

Wolf: It is that simple, Monsieur Metz. There are certain requirements, as you correctly assume. One, Euroil will sell all of its oil - Saudi and other - in euros instead of dollars. Many other oil producing countries have wanted to implement this change for some time, particularly Russia, Iran, and Venezuela - and before the war, Iraq. We have assurances that they and many others will quickly join suit as soon as a contract is announced.

Two, the Kingdom will set the price of oil - Saudi and other - to all of Euroil's buyers. Clearly this will be based on the market price, but the Kingdom will set the price, not Euroil or the traders.

Three, the European Union will provide the Kingdom with an interest free loan of $200 billion repayable if and when new oil fields come on line.

There are two other conditions. These will not be part of the formal agreement, but must be agreed to at the time the agreement is entered into.

First, because of current unemployment in Saudi Arabia, the E.U. will agree to issue work visas for 500,000 Saudis a year, for ten years. It may sound like a lot, but it represents only one tenth of one percent of the E.U.'s population of 500 million, which the E.U. can easily assimilate.

Second, the E.U. will force Italy to terminate the Lateran Treaty with the Vatican that creates the Vatican as a sovereign state and the E.U. will withdraw its recognition of the State of Israel. The continuing recognition of both states is incompatible with the E.U.'s rigorous policy of separation of church and state, now enshrined by law in the E.U. Constitution. Individual E.U. member states will undoubtedly retain their recognition, of course, so the move would be symbolic rather than substantive.

Not that you require it after such a proposal, but as a further incentive, the Kingdom will ensure that there will be no terror attacks by Al Qaeda or its affiliates on any E.U. members or diplomatic missions, or against any Euroil facilities. I am not at liberty to reveal how this can be accomplished, but it will soon become clear to you. The Kindgom will also ensure that the American Tesla electrical system does not come on line.

Metz: Nikola Tesla was rumored to have designed an electrical generation system based on channeling charged solar wind particles down to the ground in the form of lightning. His formula was lost when an American agent perished while carrying it to Roosevelt during the war. No one ever found another copy, but the Hollywood star Montgomery Grant was believed to have worked as a covert courier who hid a copy. It has been searched for since, without result. I did not know that the Tesla system was ready.

Wolf: Not yet, but there has been a major recent discovery. Of course, what has been uncovered can be covered back up. To show my good faith, I would like to share an investment tip. Look into a hedge fund by the name of Zurich Global Energy Development Partnership Fund Series C. It is open by invitation only. I believe its returns will more than please you and your colleagues.

The Kingdom's proposal will remain open for exactly three days. After that, the Kingdom will be forced to look elsewhere. I remind you that Euroil is not the only energy giant in Europe. I am certain that British Petroleum, Royal Dutch Shell, Total, and Statoil would be interested in hearing the proposal, among others. Thank you for your time, gentlemen. I look forward to hearing from you soon. Bonsoir.

"My God," whispered Carlton, stunned into immobility. He stared at the page until the words blurred into one, focusing on their consequences instead.

The transcript answered the 'who' and 'why' of the attack on HEERP once and for all. The order had come from Prince Hakim. Not only to protect Saudi oil sales, as Carlton had originally surmised, but to prevent an operational HEERP system from bankrupting Euroil, which Hakim needed to replace the U.S. oil companies and specialists pumping Saudi oil and developing new fields.

Yet it was the transcript's new threats that caused the lump of ice in Carlton's gut to snowball.

Giving Euroil full authority to explore, pump, and market Saudi oil would place a critical part of the world's oil supply in the hands of a single foreign company, exposing Saudi's oil flow to major risks of disruption. The exclusive contract would pole-vault Euroil to the highest rank in the energy world, able to continue gobbling up its competitors, making it a global monopoly. As a former antitrust prosecutor, Carlton knew its significance: Euroil would hold the world's economies hostage, with Hakim calling the shots.

Carlton also understood the devastating impact of Prince Hakim's demands concerning the Vatican and Israel. Most people did not realize that despite its tiny 110 acre footprint entirely within Rome, ever since the Lateran Treaty with Italy in 1929, the Vatican was a recognized separate sovereign state under international law, freeing the Holy See from national state control. As such, the Vatican enjoyed diplomatic relations with over 172 countries, including the United States as of 1984 and Israel as of 1993. Although largely unseen and unheard, the Vatican's diplomatic relations had culminated with many religious and human rights reforms in repressive states, sometimes after decades of fruitless talks, as in Poland when the Holy See had strengthened the Solidarity movement and triggered the collapse of Soviet communism, and currently in China, Cuba, and the Middle East - although most of those were now backtracking fast on religious and most other freedoms. Forcing Italy to abrogate the Lateran Treaty would place the Holy See under Italian - and thus E.U. - consitutional control, terminating its ability to work with governments unhindered as a diplomatic equal.

The move would effectively render the Holy See diplomatically mute and impotent.

The E.U. revoking its recognition of Israel would cut off the Jewish state's diplomatic relations with the massive European bloc, creating a precedent for other states inclined to follow, making Israel ripe for attack by a soon-to-be-nuclear Iran and Arab states smelling weakness. The move would threaten the key American ally's very existence like never before since its birth in 1948.

Based on the bribes Wolf appeared to be offering E.U. politicians through the so-called 'investment fund' he proposed, it was likely that some, if not many, of the E.U. decisionmakers had already decided how they would vote on these issues. The $200 billion loan Hakim had requested as part of the deal would have seemed outrageous in the past, but after the E.U.'s bailouts of Greece and Portugal, with Spain and others soon to follow, it will simply look like the cost of doing business.

The impact of Hakim's currency shift in oil sales from dollars to euros puzzled Carlton. Economics had never been his strong suit, but read in light of Price Hakim's other threats, it boded far from well. In fact, his gut told him that for the United States, it posed the most severe threat of all. There was no shortage of economists to query, but he knew the old saw about asking one question to two economists and getting three answers. There were plenty of oil experts at DOE, but as Ben-David had warned, DOE leaked like a sieve. Carlton had to ask someone who knew about such matters. One whose opinion he trusted and who would not leak their conversation to the markets.

He dialed the number from memory.

"Carlton," announced McLean. "It's about time. Where have you-"

"You wouldn't believe me if I told you. First things first. How is Claire?"

"She came out of her coma yesterday. She'll be in the hospital for a while, but for now she's out of danger."

Carlton exhaled a long breath. "Thank God."

"Now you. Have you found the people responsible?"

Carlton paused, knowing he could not withhold the information from his friend. "Saudis."

"Saudis?" Repeated McLean, dumbstruck. He did not know all the information Eche had divulged. "What could they possibly want with-"

"I'll explain later." He knew that would not hold water with McLean. "Just know that we're hunting the culprits down. Forty of them as of now," he explained.

"Forty? *Santa Lucia*, how big is-"

"As I said: later. Right now, I need information."

"Shoot."

"What would happen if global oil sales were conducted in euros instead of dollars?"

McLean paused, but not for long. "Iraq, Iran, Russia, and Venezuela have pushed that idea for years." His voice became a whisper laced with fear. "What have you discovered, Carlton?"

"I can't, Max. Not yet. Just tell me."

McLean paused, choosing his words. "Imagine the Great Depression of the 1930s, the inflation of the 1970s, and the current economic crisis rolled into one. What you're proposing would be worse."

Carlton winced. McLean was not one prone to exaggeration, yet the effect seemed disproportionate. "Simply from a shift in oil sales to the euro?"

"Just like the U.S. is not just another country, the U.S. dollar is not just another currency. The dollar is the world's reserve currency. Not just because sixty percent of the world's currency reserves are in dollars or because it's the world's safe haven in times of economic chaos, as during the recent crisis. The dollar is also used to buy and sell commodities, incuding oil, which has been transacted in greenbacks exclusively since after World War II. It's also used by banks as the currency for clearing international payments and by governments for economic intervention. All of this makes the dollar both an instrument and a symbol of American geopolitical power. Most international debt obligations are also denominated in dollars, including our national debt, which the government has been monetizing-"

"Speak English, Max."

McLean stopped, took a breath. "For years, the White House, Congress, the Treasury Department, and the Federal Reserve - under both political parties - have artificially devalued the dollar through zero Fed interest rates, massive government spending, and printing money. They do this to make the snowballing national debt technically cheaper - fifteen trillion dollars is cheaper to repay if each of those dollars is worth less than when the money was borrowed. So the dollar is already very weak. As proof, the price of gold has gone through the roof, its dollar price more than doubling in just a few years. The euro has nearly doubled against the dollar since 2001. It has recently decreased against the dollar due to the European debt crisis but that is because the euro weakened, not because the dollar is strong.

"An oil currency shift to the euro would cause governments, investors, and businesses to dump the dollar *en masse* in favor of the euro, which the E.U. has been hard at work to prop up, rocketing the euro and tanking the dollar to unseen depths. Which means soaring dollar inflation. Remember 1930s Germany when people would have to roll in a wheelbarrow of currency to buy a loaf of bread? In a normal economy, the U.S. government and the Fed could control the damage. But they have already exhausted most of their powers and resources fighting the economic crisis, bloating the national debt to unprecedented size, and dropped the dollar to such lows that they have created a critical mass, or a perfect storm - choose your cliché. The point is that an oil currency shift now would trigger a chain reaction, pushing what is left of the battered U.S. economy off the cliff."

"How, exactly?"

"First, the price of oil would shoot up."

"Couldn't the government release the Strategic Petroleum Reserve?"

"Even if it released the entire 700 million barrel Reserve, sooner or later the U.S. would have to buy oil at the higher price because we produce only a small percentage of our oil consumption. There is plenty of oil in the U.S., but the government has not allowed most of it to be tapped." Carlton remembered Ben-David's long explanation of the matter.

"The oil price spike would spark massive inflation. Oil is far from the only commodity sold in dollars. Global food prices are based on the dollar. As are those of gold, silver, platinum, copper, and other metals. So are sales of commercial aircraft, large ships, and many other manufactured goods. If oil shifts to the euro, all those would likely follow. U.S. Treasury bond yields - what the government pays to borrow money - would shoot up, which means that bank interest rates would do the same, restricting borrowing that is already just a trickle, herding even more businesses and banks into bankruptcy. Unemployment and foreclosures would increase to levels much higher than even now. Tax revenue would plummet. The government would probably default on its debt, triggering a deep cut in its credit rating, creating a vicious cycle by making it even more difficult to borrow money and then to repay it. The dollar denominated national debt might look cheaper, but the government would have to borrow so much more, at such exorbitant rates, to keep the country running that it would make the recent giant bailouts and stimulus programs look like student loans. There may not even be anyone left willing to loan the U.S. money, including China, which has already hinted at moving away from dollar holdings to euros and might cut its losses for enormous geopolitical gain. The defense budget would likely have to be cut to the bone, with devastating consequences to national security and our allies."

It was far worse than Carlton had imagined. "What about-"

"I'm not done yet. Inflation generally pushes up stock prices on Wall Street, but a sudden shift of global oil sales from dollars to the euro would cause a panic. Other than commodities, the stock market would not just tank as in the beginning of the recession. It would crash. Pension funds, corporate portfolios, insurance company reserves, 401Ks, IRAs, and individual investments would not just lose value, they would evaporate."

Carlton squinted. "Wouldn't a strong euro and weak dollar hurt Europe by making its goods too expensive and making U.S. exports far more attractive?"

McLean grunted. "In the long run, yes. In the short term, the euro would become so strong and the dollar so weak that European and oil-producing states and their companies would snap up U.S. businesses, real estate, and banks at bargain basement prices. By the time their lower exports started to squeeze them, they would own most of the U.S. economy. And it would not stop at America's borders. As anemic as it has become because of the recession, the U.S. still drives much of the world economy, so the shift in oil currency would send shock waves through almost all of the other economies, most of which are already in recession."

Carlton opened his mouth to respond, but McLean was on a roll.

"There is another possible result. China, Russia, even France have called for the dollar to be replaced by a new global currency controlled by a multinational institution - policyspeak for the UN. It has not happened, thank God, mostly because the path to such a currency is extremely complex. And because despite the economic crisis and the fact that much of the world demonizes the U.S. regardless of the party in power, most of the world prefers the U.S. to other countries as their final protector, especially to an ill-defined UN body. But this shift in currency may make a new global currency a reality, forever eroding U.S. global power. Without it..."

"Chaos," concluded Carlton, pausing before asking his next question. "What if the U.S. could generate unlimited amounts of free electricity? Would that stop the effect of an oil currency shift?"

Momentary silence. "Carlton, what is-"

"Not now, Max. Please. Would it stop the-"

"I don't know. But it would have to be discovered and announced before the oil currency shift."

"Thanks, Max." Carlton hung up without giving McLean an opening to ask questions. "God in heaven," he announced, running his hand down his face, heart pounding.

Hakim and Euroil were not just planning economic disruption. They were about to unleash global petroeconomic terror.

Carlton turned to Ben-David, who had just finished reading the transcript. His face was deathly pale, his expression grim. "How long before you can get HEERP running?"

Ben-David grimaced. "If we can get replacement equipment and personnel airlifted in and we work around the clock, five days minimum."

Carlton shook his head. "Not fast enough." He pointed to the date of the transcript. "The Euroil contract will be signed in two days, tops."

Both avoided mentioning the obvious: HEERP had not yet been tested. It might be a complete dud from the exhausted mind of a dying genius.

"We have to stop the contract from being signed," asserted Carlton.

"How the heck do you suggest we pull that off?" Asked Ben-David, incredulous.

Carlton looked from Ben-David to Sobieski's transcript to Tabib. He did not have an answer. But he was certain of one thing: he would not be able to stop Euroil and Hakim from a shattered facility isolated in the Alaskan wild.

* * *

Arriving at his office shortly after dawn, Wolf dialed Prince Qhibli's number.

"It's Wolf, excellency."

"Good news, I trust."

"Indeed, excellency. There has been no sign of Carlton or Hamilton since the, ah, incident up North."

Prince Qhibli exhaled a sigh of relief. "Finally."

"More importantly, I just received a call from Metz. The E.U. has agreed to the loan and Euroil has agreed to Prince Hakim's proposal, with a few changes." Wolf ran through a laundry list of figures and dates.

Prince Qhibli was not about to quibble with a few minor legalistic modifications to the proposal, most required to save face. Time was of the essence. Once Euroil was locked into the contract, Hakim could easily extract changes, just as he planned on doing with the E.U. The key was to get the contract signed as soon as possible.

"I approve all of Metz's changes," Qhibli responded, almost before Wolf had finished reading the list. "Draft the agreement. We are running out of time."

PART THREE - THUNDER

"*Donors in Saudi Arabia constitute the most significant source of funding to Sunni terrorist groups worldwide.*"

Secret U.S. State Department Cable
from Hillary Rodham Clinton
U.S. Secretary of State

"*This hatred [of the United States, of religions other than Islam, of other interpretations of Islam, and of freedom] fires and sustains those who make war on us with the intention of destroying our way of life. Their power derives from their oil, and it is time to break their sword.*"

R. James Woolsey
Former Director
Central Intelligence Agency

"*A cloud appears above your head*
A beam of light comes shining down on you Shining down on you.
The cloud is moving nearer still
Aurora Borealis comes in view
Aurora comes in view."

A Flock of Seagulls
I Ran (So Far Away)

48 BEAR

DARPA Gulfstream
En route to Washington, D.C.
1:33 PM

The Gulfstream 500 jet that Ben-David had placed on loan to Carlton pierced through the thick cloud cover, rocketing into the bright Arctic sunshine shortly after takeoff from the HEERP airstrip, unscathed in the attack due to its distance from the headquarters building.

Unlike its plush corporate brethren, the DARPA version of the ultra long range aircraft with twin Rolls Royce engines was a study in austere functionality, the feel more economy rental car than Oscar night limousine. Ben-David had proudly explained that the Gulfstream made up for its lack of creature comforts with a dizzying array of electronics and a skin of experimental active paint that rendered the jet invisible to radar far beyond present military stealth technology. Not a surprise for the agency that had developed the technology in the first place, over 30 years ago.

With his head still spinning from Sobieski's transcript, Carlton walked to the Spartan galley and brewed himself a cup of Navy coffee - with a pinch of salt and so strong that you could float a nail in it. At least DARPA had fixings for a decent cup of joe, he reflected. Cradling the steaming mug in his hands, he called his assistant, whom he shared with five other NSD lawyers at Main Justice. He thought about asking her to patch him through to Edison.

Screw Edison.

"Teresa. I need to get the Bear on an encrypted line ASAP," said Carlton, referring to Attorney General Rodrick Thorne by his DOJ nickname.

"Hold on," she replied, returning on the line a few moments later. "Thorne is in wiretapping hearings on the Hill all week. How badly do you want to talk to him?"

"Let me put it this way: whether he's addressing a joint session of Congress or sitting on the can, yank him out and stick a phone in his ear."

Teresa sighed. "OK. This might take a while."

Carlton hit the speakerphone button, reclined in his seat, nervously clicked his Zippo. He pined for a stogie but had to settle for the jet fuel grade coffee, savoring the black liquid.

In truth, he was more than a little anxious about the impending conversation with DOJ's ruling monarch. Attorney General Rodrick "Rod" Thorne had flourished as an Atlanta corporate lawyer. That career vanished the day his nineteen year old daughter died of a cocaine overdose at a Hollywood party. The corner office, fat partnership profits, his and hers Maseratis, penthouse condo, vacation home, first class travel - Thorne dumped them all, becoming a Georgia state prosecutor, prosecuting criminals with amazing success and without a shred of mercy. That and his gruff manner had earned him his nickname - and shocked Carlton during their first meeting several years ago.

Over a handful of conversations, Carlton had come to understand that Thorne's attitude was not personal, but calculated to uncover flawed arguments, missing evidence, and unwise strategies. He also discovered that the nation's chief law enforcement official made decisions quickly, then never wavered. In contrast to the armies of pusillanimous DC bureaucrats more interested in covering their rear ends than in doing right by the American people, Thorne was a breath of fresh air, even if it often arrived as a tornado.

Carlton saw the encryption light blink on at the same time he heard a grunt. "You just pulled me out of a meeting with the Chairman of the Senate Judiciary Committee, Carlton. What the hell is this about and why aren't you going through proper DOJ channels?" Thorne's deep voice boomed, threatening to shatter the small speakerphone. "Speak fast."

Carlton's heart raced as he leaned forward, grabbed the handset. "I'm sorry, sir. There was no time to go through Edison on this and it involves the National Security Division," he was now honestly able to say. "I just received intel about an impending agreement between Saudi Prince Hakim and the French energy multinational Euroil. If it goes through, it would devastate the U.S. far more than Hassan's attempt on our electrical grid."

"Source?" Demanded Thorne.

"A Polish intelligence agent named Sobieski stationed in France. He called from our embassy in Paris. The FBI legat there knows him, says he's legit."

"Tell me everything," ordered Thorne, now at lower volume.

Carlton recounted recent events culminating with the attack on HEERP, then waited while Thorne retrieved, decrypted, and read the email Monet had sent him per Carlton's instructions. It did not take long for it to elicit a response.

"Holy Mother of God."

"That was my reaction, sir."

"How did Sobieski suspect these people enough to bug them in the first place?"

It was a good question. "I don't know, sir."

Thorne paused. "It took brass ones for you to walk on Edison's scalp in your current DOJ limbo, Carlton. I'm glad you did. If CIA vets the intel, it will go to the Boss." Thorne always referred to the president as the 'Boss' and followed the unwritten government rule that the CIA was referred to as 'CIA' and the FBI as 'the FBI'.

Carlton did not like the sound of it. "If they vet it, sir?"

"I can go straight to the Boss, but he won't take action until CIA vets the intel first. CIA is still reeling from charges that it screwed the pooch before 9-11 and Iraq, failed to alert Homeland Security about the Nigerian Christmas Day bomber, conducted a political insurgency from Langley against the previous administration, and left its agents twist in the wind over charges of illegal interrogation methods despite DOJ opinion letters and the fact that the intel gained helped find bin Laden. It's going to be mighty suspicious of intel as huge as this. Especially coming from DOJ rather than one of our sixteen intelligence agencies."

Carlton was well aware of the ongoing institutional war that had raged between the FBI and CIA for over 60 years. The FBI was technically a part of DOJ, which did little to endear DOJ to CIA, particularly after DOJ began investigating CIA case officers for harsh interrogations that DOJ had approved in the first place.

"Our FBI legat in Paris vouches for Sobieski. He said he's worked with him on counterterror-"

"You already said that," Thorne cut him off. "The conduit may be legit, but not the intel."

Carlton bit back a tirade. He detested politics in general, but particularly loathed bureaucratic politics that delayed vital decisions on imminent national security threats while agencies jockeyed for position to feel secure within their jurisdictional fiefdoms. Just like the politics Faraday and Edison played.

"What about the FBI? Can they act on this while CIA vets the intel?"

"A Euroil contract with Saudi is foreign intel, so it belongs to CIA. The last thing I need is DOJ in the middle of a turf war between the Bureau and Langley."

Carlton winced. "Yes, sir." What he wanted to do was break the telephone into a million pieces. He was forcibly repressing that urge when an idea came to mind. "Sir, what if we could get Sobieski to vet the intel?"

Throne grunted. "You're not making sense, Carlton. How can he objectively vet his own intel?"

"Sir, if Sobieski could show CIA how he obtained it, that might satisfy them that it's legit."

Carlton heard the Bear's husky breathing over the line. "To do that, CIA would have to debrief him. Where are you?"

"En route to Dulles. ETA about 7:30PM."

"Here is what I want you to do."

* * *

Wolf's bony fingers were worn raw. Obsessed with secrecy, Ambassador Qhibli had prohibited anyone from helping him draft the contract. Wolf had done it alone, assembling the document by writing new sections and cutting and pasting others from old agreements. He had not eaten, slept, or showered in almost two days. He and his office stank of sweat. With his office door shut and locked, window blinds drawn tight, the cadaverous lawyer resembled a vampire toiling in darkness save for his dim computer screen. Unable to discern day from night, he had lost track of time, was now having trouble focusing, popped handfuls of uppers like jelly beans, washed them down with antacid. Yet he forced himself to scan the 350-page Euroil agreement on his laptop screen one last time, the paragraphs and sentences melting into one.

Ordinarily, Wolf would have provided the draft agreement to Qhibli for review and comment before sending it to Euroil's lawyer. But this was no ordinary transaction. Time was ticking away fast, as Qhibli took great pains to remind him during his incessant telephone calls. There was no time to wait for Qhibli to read through the document before sending it to the other side. And Wolf could not email the contract to Metz. Now that Poland knew about the impending contract, as Metz had reported, other countries were sure to follow, including the U.S. With the government's post-9-11 national security wiretap laws and Patriot Act, its intelligence branches could tap foreign email as easily as foreign telephone conversations.

Wolf printed two copies of the doorstop-sized agreement, placed each in a brushed aluminum Zero Halliburton attaché case, clicked the cases shut, tumbled their cylindrical locks, then handed them to Savitch before giving him explicit instructions.

"Yes, sir," replied Savitch, hoisting both cases and heading for the door, wrinkling his nose at the rancid odors permeating his master's office.

"Savitch?"

He turned.

"If anyone else gets their hands on what is inside..." Wolf's words trailed off.

Their deadly meaning was perfectly clear. Wolf would have Savitch's head. Literally. Given who they were working for, he knew the threat was not an empty one.

49 NEMESIS

Dulles International Airport (IAD)
Northern Virginia
7:13 PM

The DARPA Gulfstream landed at Dulles airport on a runway slick from a recent midsummer shower. It immediately taxied to a waiting Agusta A139 helicopter, its rotors already whipping the muggy air with anticipation.

A woman in a severe black suit and flats stood beside its white fuselage. The rotor wash tousled her toe-white hair. She waited for the jet's door to open, its folding staircase to deploy before dashing up and into the cabin with quick footsteps and no smiles.

All business.

"Patrick Carlton?" A demand, not a question, delivered in a heavy Boston accent. *Caalton.*

"Who's asking?" He replied, standing, smelling the stench of kerosene wafting in from the tarmac.

"Special Agent in Charge Faraday, FBI," she replied, flashing her badge.

Carlton winced. *Aw hell.* Out of all the FBI agents it could have sent, the Bureau had sent Faraday?

With a partner like her, he didn't need enemies. If she had managed to take him off the *Hassan* case, she would probably find a way to finagle the same result in the present situation. And without Carlton, it would take her too much time to get up to speed to do any good.

His dismay morphed into surprise as she approached with a scowl etched on her angular face. He had pictured Georgana Faraday as a dour careerist, not an attractive blonde. Yet he knew that the slender, pale-faced woman with fierce green eyes had earned the nickname 'Iron Lady' in the Bureau, in reference to former British Prime Minister Margaret Thatcher. And not as a compliment. *Haad and smaat.*

She squinted, still without a trace of a smile. "Follow me," she instructed, turning back to the open doorway, as though their bitter history had never existed - or was simply being placed on hold. Sensing that he remained immobile, she turned back. "Don't worry. Thorne and my chief made it clear you were in charge," she announced through straight white teeth clenched hard. "Satisfied?"

Carlton could scarcely believe his ears. In charge? His sudden elation quickly crashed. He could tell by Faraday's sour lemon expression that her long simmering grudge remained. She might follow orders and acquiesce to his leadership, but mere acquiescence would not accomplish the task at hand. He needed an ally.

"I am not," he replied flatly. He saw her arch her eyebrows in shock and confusion. "You and I need a 'come to Jesus' talk. This investigation is far too important to be derailed by old history."

"You want me to apologize for steering the *Hassan* case away from you?" She shot back, ice cold, managing to look down at Carlton despite her lesser height.

He knew that to gain her as an ally, he had to put their long-standing feud to rest. "I don't want an apology, Faraday. I want you to understand why I recommended against Edison hiring you at the National Security Division." He paused, glimpsing an expression of festering pain on her chiseled face. "You never returned my calls."

"I understand why." Faraday leaned forward, head held high. "You wanted to pack the NSD full of your DOJ cronies. You didn't want anyone outside Main Justice. Certainly not a woman."

Carlton shook his head in disbelief. She really believed her fantasy. "No. I did it because I knew DOJ better than you did. You were more of an asset as a Bureau agent than as an NSD lawyer. As for women, I have recommended more of them than men. You can check. It's not my fault that Edison prefers male prosecutors."

She hesitated for an instant before narrowing her emerald eyes into slits. "I could have done just as good a job at DOJ as you, and you know it. Maybe better." She stabbed a finger toward him in the air. "You were threatened."

"You would have done a *superb* job. But so did the person I chose. I studied your file, saw how you investigated cases at the Bureau. Those talents would have been wasted at DOJ when they could do real good at the Bureau at a critical time. And I was right. You foiled Abu Hassan's attacks. And only the best are promoted to Special Agent in Charge. Congratulations, by the way."

His mix of candor and praise knocked Faraday off balance as she digested his words. Cracks appeared in her hardened demeanor. She walked back toward him with cautious steps. "Thanks. It doesn't matter anymore."

"It does to me. I never intended to harm your career. You can believe it or not, but it's the truth."

"I appreciate that," she replied in a low voice, her glacial expression thawing. "Given your explanation, I apologize for pressuring Edison to take you off the *Hassan* case," she finally announced with no little effort.

"Thank you." He paused. "But it isn't enough."

Her face contorted. "Not enough?" She bellowed. "What do you want me to do, kneel and kiss your ring?"

"I want your help."

Confusion replaced her anger.

He looked down at the jet's dark grey carpeting. "I screwed up. I ignored Echeverria's order to stop investigating Grant's clue. It was none of my business, but I investigated it anyway, mostly as vengeance against the Bureau" - he looked up - "against you, for taking the *Hassan* case away from me. It was selfish and stupid. The people behind the Euroil contract murdered him. They might not have targeted him if I had stopped investigating." Carlton leaned forward, eyes boring into her. "I need more than your simple agreement to have me in charge. I need your full *partnership* to stop the Euroil contract, find those sons of a bitches who killed Eche, and nail them to the wall."

His stare chilled her before sparking a bond. "You have it, Mr. Carlton." Her handshake was as strong as Carlton had ever experienced.

"My friends just call me Carlton," he said, striding down the aisle.

"Mine call me Gana," she replied, following him.

"I thought they called you the-"

She shot him a withering scowl. "Not if they want to remain my friends."

He grinned. "By the way, how *did* you get Edison to kick me off the *Hassan* case?" He asked, stepping into the muggy Virginia air that felt like a sauna, descending the metal stairs leading to the drenched tarmac.

"Some things must remain secret, even between partners," she replied, walking briskly to the waiting helicopter.

"What about where we are going? Is that a secret too?"

"That I can tell you. We're going to Yale."

* * *

The helicopter shot off the wet tarmac as soon as Carlton and Faraday strapped in. They donned headsets to communicate over the din of engine noise and rushing wind. Carlton was pleased to see Henri Monet on board, Red Bull in hand, reeking of Gitanes cigarettes.

If one did not know that Monet was a master computer researcher, one would have mistaken the wiry French-American for a nightclub owner, fashion designer, or runway photographer. Not yet accustomed to his third decade, Monet was dressed in a slim-cut black pinstripe suit, a wide-collared white shirt worn without a tie with French cuffs fastened with American flag links, and black and white spectator shoes. His buzz-cut blond hair was spiked with gel, his baby-faced cheeks sprouting a carefully cultivated stubble. His rectangular black-rimmed eyeglasses had a propensity of sliding down a nose disproportionately large for his face. The only clue to his profession was the Apple laptop on steroids that never left his company.

He gazed at Carlton's haggard appearance through thick lenses, grimaced. "*Putain.* You look like hell," he exclaimed.

Carlton flashed him a toothy grin. "Nice to see you too, Henri."

"I have a message for you," he continued, handing him a folded paper.

Carlton opened it.

> *Alexis Hamilton's surgery was successful, but she remains in critical condition in intensive care.*
>
> *Robert Field, MD, Fairbanks Medical Center*

Carlton exhaled a deep sigh of relief. *Thank God.* The 'critical condition' part troubled him, but Alexis had pulled through, which was more than he could have hoped for after seeing her bloody body in the HEERP control room.

"I also thought you'd want this." Monet handed him the portable leather humidor Carlton kept in his own office.

Carlton grinned. "So far, you earn an A+ in fieldwork," he replied, turning to the bald man seated next to Monet. His legs were so long that his knees nearly reached his chin. "Major Sobieski, I presume," he said, extending his hand.

"*Tak*," Sobieski replied, giving Carlton's hand a bone-crushing tug. "A pleasure to meet you at last, Mr. Carlton."

Carlton's first impression was that Sobieski should have tried out for the Polish Olympic basketball team. He gazed at Carlton through eyes ringed with dark circles. His rumpled navy suit appeared slept in.

"*Dobry wieczor*," Carlton enunciated, mangling the words for 'good evening' that he had memorized earlier. "Kosciuszko, Pulaski, John Paul the Great, your thousands of combat troops in Iraq and Afghanistan, and now you. It seems that the list of America's valiant Polish allies knows no limit."

Sobieski beamed, bowed his shaved head. "*Dziekuje*." Djee-koo-yay. Thank you. "I appreciate that, Mr. Carlton."

"On behalf of the United States government, thank you for providing us with the intel on Saudi, major. I am sorry that CIA is so distrustful of our allies."

Sobieski waved away Carlton's concern. "The *Agencja* is the same. As suspicious of its friends as of its enemies, sometimes even more so. I look forward to proving that my intel is valid and helping you track down this stinking cabal. To show my added good faith, I have some additional information for you," he said, handing Carlton a sheet of paper.

He accepted it, scanned the list of numbers and dates. He looked back up at the Pole. "I'm sorry, major, but what exactly am looking at?"

"You and your superiors are probably curious why I bugged Qhibli and de Ville."

Carlton recalled his conversation with Thorne, nodded.

"It started with a detailed examination of wire transfers between bank accounts linked to the slaughter of Polish soldiers and civilians in

Iraq. I will spare you the details, but our investigation led us to a Saudi named Sayyid Yassin, a close confidant of Prince Hakim who serves as his go-between with Prince Qhibli and others. He is the person at the center of this mess - and more." He pointed to the page. "That list of wire transfers and bank accounts allowed us to identify Yassin."

Carlton looked down. "What are the ones circled in red?"

Sobieski grimaced. "Those are the accounts used to finance the killing of Polish and Iraqi troops and civilians in Iraq, of Israeli civilians in Tel Aviv." Staring hard at Carlton, he paused, lowered his voice. "And of your men at Khawr al-Amaya."

Carlton froze. The blood drained from his face as he stared at the circled accounts and wire transfers on the page, his mind instantly far away, recalling images of the bloodbath in Iraq. His free hand clenched into a fist, knuckles turning white. The slaughter of his men in Iraq, the planned attack against the U.S. electrical grid, the attack on HEERP. All linked to Prince Hakim through Yassin. He was going to make them pay.

After a long time, he glanced back up at Sobieski. The look they exchanged was not between a U.S. Justice Department prosecutor and a Polish intelligence officer, but between brothers in arms. "Thank you."

"I expect you would have done the same for me," replied Sobieski. "The information makes clear how important it is to stop not just Prince Hakim, but Yassin as well. Although the only proof we have of their involvement in funding the attacks other than on the Poles in Iraq is Yassin's link to a Venezuelan account. We have not been able to obtain the identity of its owner or the source of its funds."

Carlton again gazed at the account flows on the page. All the accounts were fed by the master account in Venezuela. He recalled Ben-David's statement about the bogus environmental groups preventing U.S. oil and gas drilling being funded through such an account. And about his niece's murder by Hamas in a Tel Aviv bus bombing.

"The same Venezuelan account is being used to finance the Zurich investment fund Wolf proposed to bribe E.U. officials. And as I mentioned to Agent Faraday," Sobieski continued, acknowledging her with a turn of his head, "the same account was used to fund Abu Hassan's attempted strike against the U.S. electrical grid."

As a member of DOJ's NSD, Carlton knew that under Hugo Chavez, Venezuela had become far worse than a dictatorship, failed economy, and thorn in the U.S.'s side. Thanks to Chavez's open courting of all manner of anti-American leaders, including those of Russia and Iran, Venezuela had become a staging area for violent Columbian FARC terrorists, massive drug shipments through Mexico to the U.S., Russian fighter jets, naval vessels, and possibly missiles, and a source of growing regional anti-Semitism with ties to the Hezbollah and Hamas terrorist organizations.

Carlton turned to Faraday seated next to him. "Any intel on the funding source for the Venezuelan account?"

"Unfortunately, Chavez's stooges in the Venezuelan banking authority refused to tell us who owns the account," she replied.

Sobieski nodded. "Our experience as well."

Carlton paused, brows furrowed in thought. "I think I may have a solution to that logjam," he offered after a moment, handing the page to Monet. "Get it to Ben-David via Tabib ASAP," he directed, noticing that Monet had begun typing in the information before he had finished his sentence.

Carlton massaged his eyelids. The information Sobieski had delivered during the past twenty four hours was nothing less than overwhelming. Yet it sounded almost too big, too neat, causing Carlton to think that perhaps he was being led on.

Sobieski appeared to sense his thoughts. "You will soon determine for yourself that all this information checks out," he said, running a hand over his smooth pate. "But I'm afraid there is a problem."

Carlton did not like the sound of it. He crooked his head. Faraday leaned forward.

"The batteries in the microflies transmitting Qhibli and de Ville's conversations ran out," the Pole explained. "As of last night, we are deaf," he concluded.

Carlton grimaced. "Aw hell."

"The last information we received was that Euroil, the E.U., and Prince Hakim had agreed to a final deal and that they were drafting a contract," said Sobieski.

"Proposals get changed through negotiations," replied Faraday. "We have no idea what their final agreement entails. It may involve economic attacks not discussed in the transcripts. If we are going to mount a defense, we have to know what they have agreed to."

Carlton nodded. "And we have no idea when the contract will be signed."

Sobieski nodded. "*Tak*. It could be in a week, a day, or an hour."

"It just gets better and better," said Carlton, grabbing the in-flight phone. He dialed the Bear, waited for the encryption light to turn green.

"We're on our way, sir. Sobieski is with us," he announced to the Attorney General before relaying the Pole's latest information.

Thorne grunted. "Now that his bugs are inoperative, CIA won't be able to verify his intel."

Carlton's heart sank. Then he thought of the contract. "Sir, if Wolf delivered the proposal to Euroil and the E.U. foreign minister, he must have drafted or at least been involved in negotiating the contract."

"And?"

"He'll have a copy in his files. If we can get it, it will vet all of Sobieski's intel."

Thorne did not hesitate. "Do it."

Carlton made another call, then reclined in his seat. The breathtaking late sunset views of the verdant Virginia countryside below were lost on him as he focused on the problem at hand.

"Getting a copy of the contract is one thing," said Sobieski, snapping him out of his thoughts. "But how do we stop Prince Hakim?"

Carlton paused. He had been devising a plan since taking off from Alaska. "I have an idea, but I need to know more."

The others looked at him with undisguised curiosity.

"Hakim's goal is to destroy the U.S. economy, but his tactic relies on a corporate contract," he explained.

"And?" Pressed Faraday.

"Unlike Saudi Arabia, corporations are not run by absolute monarchs."

*   *   *

Savitch's ego swelled as he rode the elevator to the Saudi embassy's top floor. He rarely traveled to the embassy with Wolf. When he did, he typically stayed in Wolf's Rolls Royce next to the chauffeur. Never had he been invited into Prince Qhibli's ornate office.

Qhibli stared at him from behind his desk through a thick cloud of smoke fed by the nearly log-sized cigar clamped between his teeth.

"Your excellency. I am here to deliver-"

"It's about time," Qhibli cut him off, hoisting his portly frame out of his chair, lumbering to where Savitch stood. His manner had become even more imperious now that Prince Hakim had become Regent after King Fahim's removal, the anticipation of a high ministry post in the new government eroding what little patience he had left. "Well don't just stand there, give me the case."

Savitch chafed. Ambassador or not, he did not like being pushed around. "I was instructed to obtain a password first, your excellency. Wolf insisted on it."

"Cohiba," barked Qhibli, thrusting out his arm.

Savitch set down the case, produced a set of keys, unlocked the handcuff binding the case to his wrist.

Qhibli snatched the case, observed the combination lock. "Are you going to give me the code or do I have to guess?"

"I must obtain it from Wolf, excellency."

Qhibli grumbled, lifted his telephone handset and hit a speed dial button. Savitch waited while Qhibli retrieved the combination from Wolf and unlocked the case. His first mission accomplished, he turned and walked to the door.

"Stop," ordered Qhibli.

Savitch swiveled.

"You are headed to Paris to deliver the second copy of the contract to Metz." It was a statement, not a question, delivered with unmasked rage over Hakim's latest change in plan. Originally tasking Qhibli with signing the contract on behalf of Saudi Arabia, Hakim had cast him aside in a fit of megalomania so he himself could take center stage. Qhibli had warned him that it would constitute a dangerous delay, but Hakim had brushed his advice off as petty jealousy.

"Yes, excellency."

"You will give him this," ordered Qhibli, handing Savicth a thin white envelope. Its back flap was sealed with green wax bearing the Saudi sword.

Savitch took it from him, wondering what it contained. Wolf would want to know. He thought about asking Qhibli, but the look in his smoldering black eyes made him decide against it. No matter. He would tear the envelope open and read it after he left the pompous ambassador's office.

"You are booked on a commercial flight?"

"Yes, excellency," answered Savitch, not sure why he was asking.

Qhibli shook his leonine head. "Too slow, too risky. You will take my plane. My limousine will collect you downstairs. Someone will drive your car back to the firm. I will have my State Department protective detail escort you to Dulles to avoid the traffic. They have to be good for something, after all," he smiled, relishing the irony of the State Department providing safe passage for a contract that would devastate the United States. And it was a perfect way for him to get his government minders out of his way so he could slip free of them. "And you will need diplomatic immunity in case you are somehow detained," he said, shoving a forest green Saudi passport at him.

Savitch placed it beside the letter in his jacket pocket while smiling at the thought of smoking Qhibli's Cuban cigars and drinking his booze in the lavish Boeing Business Jet. He'd even take a few of the stogies with him as payment for the ambassador's insulting treatment. The flight attendant might even double as one of Qhibli's infamous hookers, he fantasized, imagining the aircraft's circular bed that Wolf had described to him. There were worse ways to spend six hours en route to Paris. "Thank you, excellency," he replied, itching to tear open the envelope.

Qhibli puffed on his Cohiba, blew a cloud of smoke at Savitch before turning back to his desk. "And don't bother opening the letter. The message is in Arabic."

50 JUDGE

CIA-FBI Safehouse
Code Name: Yale
Blue Ridge Mountains, Virginia
8:03 PM

The FBI helicopter slowed, descended, then flared over a vast lawn near an imposing colonial mansion. Set on over 100 acres of rolling hills and oak forests deep in the Blue Ridge Mountains of rural Virginia, the stately country estate's use as a stud farm disguised its function as a highly-guarded joint CIA-FBI safehouse. CIA field agents had nicknamed it 'Yale' in honor of Deputy Director of Intelligence (DDI) Randall Forbes' beloved alma mater. Since a Russian double agent had blown its cover in the 1990s, CIA had graciously opened Yale to the FBI and, by extension, to DOJ for secure - yet no longer clandestine - meetings.

Two FBI agents in dark suits converged on the helicopter as soon as its landing gear touched the wet grass. A gust of hot, muggy air gusted into the cabin as the door slid open, blowing in fresh smells of the countryside. Bending low to protect themselves from the gale-force rotor wash, the agents escorted the arrivals into the main foyer, which was thankfully air conditined.

While a CIA agent spirited Sobieski away to a debriefing room and Faraday broke off to confer with her Bureau colleagues, Carlton's FBI escort led him to the rear part of the house, where a man was pacing the polished wood floor below an excellent reproduction of John Trumbull's *Battle of Trenton*. Dressed in a navy suit, white oxford button-down shirt, red striped tie, and black oxford lace-ups, he looked like another of the countless cookie-cutter federal bureaucrats populating the nation's capital.

Short in stature, with graying brown hair and thick handlebar mustache, a ruddy complexion, and a red nose that attested to his love of wine, the man strode with a feral intensity that gave him the appearance of a junkyard dog looking for someone to bite. Even the armed FBI agents seemed to be afraid of him.

"Thank you for coming so quickly, your honor," announced Carlton, approaching him.

U.S. District Court judge Kevin Flynn spun around, shaking his hand with a death grip that made even Carlton wince. He grunted. "You can cut out the 'your honors', Carlton. They're not going to help your case any after making me schlep all the way to the middle of nowhere." Federal judges were accustomed to having prosecutors come to them, not making house calls. "In fact, it'll cost you a box of Padrón Anniversarios," he added, referring to the premium Dominican cigars, unable to stop moving, like a shark.

Carlton smiled, knowing that Flynn's request was merely in jest. The judge was such a straight arrow that he made Abraham Lincoln look crooked. Before his appointment to the federal bench, Flynn had served as a capital crimes judge in Los Angeles County Superior Court, earning the nickname 'the hanging judge'. The two had bonded over their mutual love of cigars years ago at a Bar Association event. Because of their friendly relationship, Carlton had steered clear of appearing before him to avoid even the semblance of impropriety. Today had been no different, except that Flynn was the only federal judge available on such short notice.

The FBI escort led them to a private sitting room, then stood guard outside after closing the door.

"Can I offer you anything?" Carlton inquired, scanning a small wet bar.

Flynn sighed. "A glass of Romanée-Conti, but I'll settle for government lava," he replied, sitting on a chintz couch. Carlton poured each of them a mug of coffee from a burbling coffee maker, deeply skeptical about its quality but with no time to brew a fresh pot.

Flynn produced a Pete Johnson Tatuaje maduro cigar, ripped off the cap with his teeth. He lit it with a gleaming silver lighter in one hand while accepting the mug with the other.

Carlton sat on a matching couch opposite Flynn, chiding himself for not having shined his black Nocona boots. He gave Flynn a blow-by-blow account of recent events before handing him a hardcopy of Sobieski's transcript.

"Sweet Mary and Joseph," muttered Flynn, blowing a plume of smoke toward the ceiling. He gazed back at Carlton through squinted eyes. "What do you want from me?"

"Arrest warrants for Brendan Wallace, Grover Wolf, and Mitch Savitch. And a search warrant for the Euroil contract in Farnsworth Tate's files."

Flynn puffed on his cigar, rolling the dark tube of full-bodied tobacco between two fingers while the gears turned in his head. He looked back at Carlton, nodded.

"The arrest warrants I can give you. You've shown more than enough probable cause for all three to be arrested. As for the search warrant" - he shook his head - "no dice."

Carlton stared at him, dumbfounded. "What do you mean, no dice?"

The judge stroked his bushy mustache. "You haven't given me any probable cause to believe Farnsworth Tate is involved in illegal activity."

Carlton stood, his mouth hanging open in shock. "You can't be serious. The contract is-"

"Dead serious," replied Flynn, leaning forward into a cloud of smoke. "The contract between Saudi and Euroil isn't illegal, Carlton."

Carlton could not believe what he was hearing. "It will devastate the American economy. How much more criminal can it possibly get?" He nearly shouted, feeling blood rush into his head, pound against his temples. He knew Flynn was tough, but had not expected him to be hostile.

"Calm down, Carlton," Flynn shot back, scowling until Carlton stood still.

"Just because a contract will have dire economic consequences for other parties does not make it illegal. That's what many contracts are designed to do. I'm on your side here. I want to stop these bastards as much as you do. But I can't authorize a fishing expedition simply because you hope to uncover something illegal in a dusty file cabinet. Unless you can show me probable cause of an illegal act, Farnsworth Tate will have the D.C. Circuit Court toss out the warrant in a heartbeat. You can try obtaining a Section 218 warrant from FISA, but I don't think you'll get that either, for the same reasons," he explained, referring to a section of the USA Patriot Act and to the Foreign Intelligence Surveillance Court. "It won't help you stop Prince Hakim and it will harm DOJ's reputation, not to mention yours," he added.

Carlton frowned. His reputation was the last thing on his mind. "The contract amounts to a terrorist attack, your honor," he argued, as calmly as he could manage.

"No it doesn't," retorted Flynn, twirling an end of his mustache. "The attack in Alaska was a terrorist act, not the contract. The contract isn't with Al-Qaeda. It's between a legal corporation and the Kingdom of Saudi Arabia, a sovereign nation with full diplomatic relations with the United States."

Carlton was at his wit's end. He wanted to tear his hair out in clumps and yell in frustration. He settled for pacing the small room with brisk strides. An impending petroeconomic attack on the United States economy and he could not think of a way to give a friendly judge probable cause to issue a search warrant to prevent it. What kind of lawyer was he? Had Eche and Davenport's men in Alaska died in vain?

Carlton continued creating a furrow along the wood floor while he ruminated Flynn's words. *A sovereign nation.* He continued for a few more steps then stopped as an idea formed in his mind. He swiveled, stared at Flynn. "I'll tell you why it's illegal. The contract is an act of war."

Flynn let out an exasperated sigh. "Now you're grasping at straws, Carlton. An act of war involves the use of offensive military force, not a legal contract."

"No, your honor. An act of war involves the use of weapons." Carlton sat across from Flynn, leaned toward him. "Your honor, if Saudi Arabia bombed America's stock exchanges, banks, shopping malls, and factories without killing anyone in the process, would that be considered an act of war?"

"Certainly."

"The contract will have the same effect. Except instead of using bombs as weapons, Hakim will use oil and currency. It won't destroy the exchanges, banks, malls, and factories by blowing them up, but by putting them out of business, which is the same thing. It's petroeconomic war."

Flynn stared at him in silence for a long time, then blew a cloud of smoke into the air, extended his arm. "Give me a pen."

51 WARRANTS

Federal Bureau of Investigation Headquarters
J. Edgar Hoover Building
Washington, D.C.
3:53 PM

It was the largest FBI raid in recent history.

With Faraday in the lead, 50 agents donned black armored assault garb with 'FBI' stenciled in bright yellow letters, retrieved Glock 23 handguns and Colt M4 carbines from the armory, and piled into five armored trucks and two sedans. They roared out of the Bureau's Pennsylvania Avenue headquarters, sirens wailing, dome and grille strobe lights flashing. Slaloming through packed early rush hour traffic, they arrived minutes later at the ten-story glass and steel office building on K Street where Farnsworth Tate occupied the top five floors.

Two of the trucks turned a corner, dove into the building's underground parking garage, stationed themselves next to the only two stairwell exits. One sedan sped on to Wolf's riverfront condominium at Washington Harbour in Georgetown in case he was home, the other to Department of Energy headquarters on Independence Avenue in Southwest DC to arrest Wallace. The three remaining trucks blasted their horns, drove off the wide avenue, jumped the curb, and crashed onto the sidewalk, scattering alarmed pedestrians. They screeched to a halt directly in front of the lobby. Their rear doors banged open.

A similar scene unfolded simultaneously at Farnsworth Tate's nine other U.S. offices.

Faraday and Carlton jumped out of the lead truck, sweating buckets under their Kevlar body armor in the muggy air, yanked the twin glass doors open. Thirty agents followed, storming into the lobby at the same moment that their twenty colleagues in the garage below rushed up the two staircases.

A startled lobby security guard sitting behind a circular desk stared at the horde of agents in full gear in mute astonishment, eyes wide open.

"FBI," announced Faraday, holding up her badge. "We have a search warrant for Farnsworth Tate and arrest warrants for two of their lawyers."

Instead of putting up a fight or attempting to notify Farnsworth Tate, the guard stood, walked to the elevator bay, swiped his electronic card. As soon as the doors rang open, he swiped his key card anew, then ushered the agents inside with a grin and flourish, betraying his true feelings for the lawyers and lobbyists who occupied the top five floors. The agents packed into three elevators, ascended to their assigned floors, thankful for the frosty air conditioning.

Carlton, Monet, and Faraday rode to the fifth floor with her second-in-command, Special Agent Nikko 'Spiro' Spirodopoulos, who seemed made entirely of muscle and thick black hair. FBI lore had it that the fearsome Greek-American had once made a bank robber surrender simply by staring him down.

The elevator and stairwell doors opened in near unison. Lawyers, clients, and office personnel stopped dead in their tracks, agape at the black-clad armed agents streaming into the hushed, padded office.

Carlton scanned the reception area for any sign of danger.

The office's stark design and photocopy paper smell was typical of mega law firms. It reminded him of his old law firm, the Merchants of Pain. Polished black granite floors. Bleached wood walls and cubicles. Conference rooms with varnished wood tables and black leather chairs behind walls of glass. Abstract lithographs on every wall. Loaded to the gills with brains, money, and influence. Devoid of soul.

Potted palms provided the lone breath of fresh air in the pressure cooker.

Faraday walked up to a redheaded receptionist seated at a lobby desk adorned with the firm's name in gleaming chrome letters.

"FBI," she announced, again holding up her badge. "We have arrest warrants for Grover Wolf and Mitch Savitch. Where are they?"

"May I see the warrants?" The receptionist asked calmly, standing her ground.

Carlton noticed her push a button with her elbow as she reached for the documents. He unholstered his Glock just as two beefy men with severe crew cuts came running into the reception area.

"Firm security. Who are you and what you are doing here?" One demanded before spotting the bold yellow letters on the agents' clothes.

Carlton pointed to the revealing bulges under their jackets. "Those are illegal in the District of Columbia."

Spiro drew his service piece. "Turn around. Place your hands on your head. Both of you. *Now.*"

Carlton saw the conflict in their eyes. The men were likely members of Savitch's Special Transactions Team. They were used to giving orders to people outside the firm, not receiving them. After a tense pause, they complied. Spiro frisked them, removed a pair of handguns from shoulder holsters inside their jackets.

"Beretta M9s," he grunted. "Nice. You are both under arrest."

"We have permission to carry weapons," explained the one who had first spoken.

"Probably not *concealed* weapons," Spiro shot back. "But you can explain it to the judge."

While he handcuffed them and read them their Miranda rights, Faraday turned to the receptionist. "One more time. Where are Wolf and Savitch?"

"I'm not answering any questions. I have the right to remain silent."

Carlton leaned over her desk, jabbed his thumb toward the handcuffed security men. "Mutt and Jeff over there have the right to remain silent. You don't. You're not under arrest." He flashed a smile. "But it can be arranged."

Faraday took over, growing irritated. "We can do this easy or hard. *Where?*"

The receptionist relented. "Tenth floor," she spat out. "I'll dial them." She reached for her telephone.

Carlton blocked her hand, scowling. "Don't even think about it."

"She doesn't move. No calls in. No calls out," Faraday ordered, lifting her cuff mike to her lips. "All squads, the firm's security personnel are armed. Arrest them. Squad Five, Wolf and Savitch are officed on the tenth floor. Find them. "

Carlton turned to Monet. "We'll head to Wolf's office. You assist Oersted." He referred to the FBI computer specialist accompanying the squads, with whom Monet shared a not-so-secret inter-agency rivalry.

Carlton and Faraday rode the elevator to the tenth floor, walked down the main corridor.

"They're not here, ma'am," pronounced one of the agents outside Savitch's office. "And neither of their offices has any files in them."

"All squads, sweep your floors for Wolf and Savitch. They aren't in their offices," Faraday ordered into her cuff mike.

Carlton walked into Savitch's office, found his daily agenda. Its pages were blank. Same with the calendar on his computer. "No clues here."

Faraday stopped as she listened to a report over her earpiece. "Wolf isn't at his condo," she told Carlton.

He proceeded to Wolf's luxurious corner office. It looked as though a tornado had whipped through it, taking every file in its wake. He wrinkled his nose. "Gamey." Wolf must have been caged in his office for too long. He examined the lawyer's desk. In contrast to Savitch's blank appointment book, Wolf's day planner was filled with neatly handwritten entries. Carlton peered closer.

"I know where he is," he announced, pointing at today's page.

3:00PM - Qhibli.

Faraday launched an expletive laced with her Boston accent. "The Saudi Embassy is sovereign Saudi soil. There is no way for us to get in there to arrest Wolf."

Carlton's long simmering anger boiled over into rage. He turned to the agents searching Wolf's office. They had been informed of the warrants, but their reason was classified too high even for them.

"The bastards who occupy these two offices killed Special Agent Echeverria, twenty four DARPA guards, and two civilian scientists in cold blood," he explained. "They are about to unleash a devastating economic attack on the United States." The volume of his voice rose as images flooded his mind - Alexis and Claire bleeding, Eche's body covered with a bloody tarp, the frozen body bags in Alaska, his slaughtered men in Iraq.

"I want you to go through every scrap of paper in this firm," he boomed. "I want to read every word of every line of every page even remotely connected to anything that even sounds Saudi with the word 'Euroil' near it. I want these bastards in a cage! I want them nailed to the wall!" He shouted, kicking Wolf's desk so hard with his boot that the polished walnut cracked. "Do you understand me?" He yelled, his face crimson, body shaking, breath ragged.

The others remained immobile in stunned silence until one agent stepped forward. "Eche and I were in the same class at Quantico, sir," he said in a low voice, his expression grim.

He did not have to utter another word. Brotherhood ran thick among members of the Bureau, particularly between class members at the FBI Academy in Quantico, Virginia. Carlton knew the agent would tear the building apart brick by brick with his bare hands to bring his brother agent's assassins to justice.

Faraday walked to Carlton, observed him with concern. "You OK?"

He took a deep breath, wiped the sweat from his face before nodding.

"Where to?" She asked.

"Where law firms keep copies of everything."

52 MESSAGE

Euroil, SA Headquarters
La Défense
Paris, France
10:03 AM

With the attaché case still manacled to his wrist after all his hours of flight, Savitch followed Metz's prematurely aged assistant through the top floor of Euroil's headquarters, noting that its décor was oddly similar to Farnsworth Tate's.

He was still seething over Qhibli's actions. The ambassador clearly considered lawyers like him mere servants. He had not been allowed to partake in any of the fun on the ambassador's jet. No booze, no cigars, no meals, no movies, no internet. Not even a flight attendant - just the pilot and copilot. All the comfortable areas including the lavish bedroom and ornate bathroom had been locked except for the sterile crew rest area and head.

He wondered if his boss realized that Qhibli also considered Wolf a mere servant rather than a colleague. Deeply loyal to his boss, Savitch had warned him of it. But Wolf was so enraptured by the ambassador's fees that he had not allowed himself to see their relationship was nothing more than master and servant. Savitch did give Qhibli credit for one thing: his limousine, State Department escort, and Boeing Business Jet got him to Paris over three hours faster than his car and Air France flight. Commercial airline traffic had grown slower due to high jet fuel prices, something the Saudi ambassador could not have cared less about.

Metz's assistant knocked once on his boss's blond wood door, waited for a annoyed '*oui*' to escape before opening it and standing aside to let Savitch enter.

He did so, in shock. Savitch had expected a luxurious corporate office. Instead, the spacious corner office could have doubled as a warehouse receiving station. Stark and austere did not begin to describe the space. Giant canvas drapes hung over the floor-to-ceiling plate glass windows like limp sails, obstructing both light and what were certain to be breathtaking views to the *Arc de Triomphe* and beyond, probably out of paranoia over secrecy, Savitch reflected. The floor was composed of distressed concrete, as if unfinished, awaiting carpet. The desk consisted of a rough slab of steel supported by two oil drums bearing the Euroil logo. Standard-issue metal file cabinets filled the two walls, except a space for a white board bearing the name of the legion companies Euroil had acquired under Metz's reign scrawled with a black marker by hand, many crossed out. The scene made Metz look like a corporate Napoléon on a war campaign. It was clear that the diminutive occupant who walked over to him without a word of greeting cared more about power than the luxury a CEO's pay could buy.

"Good afternoon, Mr. Metz. I am Mitch-"

"I know who you are, Mr. Savitch," interrupted Metz in a heavy French accent, squinting through bloodshot eyes that belied his lack of sleep. His suit jacket was off, thrown haphazardly over the back of his chair. His white shirt was rumpled, his blue tie loosened, its sleeves rolled up, sweat stains under his armpits. He stretched out his arm. "The case."

Metz clearly also cared more about power than manners. But just like with the pompous Qhibli, Savitch was not about to be pushed around by the little corporate dictator. "The password first, if you please," Savitch replied slowly, taking pleasure in placing an obstacle in the arrogant man's way, if even for formality's sake.

"Oil," he barked. "Now give me the case."

Savitch unlocked the handcuff, pleased to be free of the millstone around his neck, so to speak. As Metz reached for the case, Savitch pulled it back with a smile. "I must first call Wolf to obtain the combination."

"Then do it," snapped Metz, without attempting to hide his impatience.

Savitch dialed Wolf's cell phone. "It's me. I am here with-"

"No names," Wolf cut him off, before reading off the case's combination. Savitch rolled the numbers into place and clicked open the case. He had barely opened it when Metz reached inside and grabbed the agreement.

"Does he have it?"

"Yes, sir."

"Good. Now listen carefully. The FBI is swarming the office."

Savitch's eyes opened wide. "Are you-"

"I am safe."

"And the files? Do you need me to-"

"Done. They will find nothing."

"Should I stay here?"

"No. I need you here. You are on a diplomatic flight with a diplomatic passport and will be met by an embassy car." Savitch finally understood why Qhibli had given him the passport. "When you return, go to...the place where we met the ambassador on the morning of that hunting trip."

"I understand," replied Savitch, reasoning that it was an excellent hiding place. He paused. He did not know what Quibli's letter contained or whether Metz would share it with Wolf. "The ambassador asked me to deliver this envelope to you, Mr. Metz," he said, with the line still active for his boss's benefit.

Metz was already flipping through the thick agreement on his desk, fountain pen in hand hovering, eager to sign. Hearing Savitch, he looked up and stretched out his arm once more.

Savitch was irritated by the little man, but knew better than to voice his displeasure. He tried to think of himself as a lawyer servicing a client. You did the work and took the hours and abuse - and the pay. And he was being paid handsomely. He produced the envelope, handed it to Metz, who unceremoniously mangled it open with his index finger.

Metz stared at the words on the page and shouted for his assistant, who immediately strode into the room. "*Traduisez ça,*" he ordered. Translate this.

The assistant read the letter, leaned over and whispered in his boss's ear.

Metz's face contorted into a grimace, complete with bared teeth. He clenched his fists. His eyes looked as though they would pop out of their sockets as his body shook. He threw his pen to the concrete floor, breaking the nib in the process and splashing black ink across a bank of file folders. "*Merde!*" He yelled, louder than Savitch thought possible given his size.

Savitch concluded that something had gone awry. "Is there anything I should inform Wolf about, sir?" He inquired as diplomatically as he could.

Metz shifted his gaze in Savitch's direction but seemed to look straight through him, as though he was not even present. He shifted his weight from one leg to the other, weighing his decision. "That pompous Arab has changed the plan!" He shouted. "I will call Wolf and inform him myself." He jutted his head toward the door, ordering Savitch out without as much as a thank you.

"And the agreement? I was instructed to-"

"You are forcing me to repeat myself," Metz barked. "I will inform Wolf."

Whatever it was, Savitch sensed that something had just gone very wrong.

53 ARSON

"There must be tens of thousands of files in here," said Faraday, standing beside Carlton in the center aisle of a cavernous file room. Neatly organized file folder buckets known in legal jargon as 'redwells' filled nearly every square inch of space on floor-to-ceiling metal shelves. To maximize storage capacity, the shelves were crammed together, sliding on rails at the push of a button to allow access between them.

She leaned to the side, peered at muliticolored labels stuck on nearby redwells. "They're organized numerically. We need-"

"This way," replied Carlton, walking to a utilitarian Formica table at the end of the aisle. From his days at the Merchants of Pain, he knew that law firms typically kept an updated hardcopy file index in their file rooms. He located the encyclopedic volume, started leafing through it, stopped. He craned his head, sniffed.

"Smoke," said Faraday, wrinkling her nose.

"Must be Monet and his French coffin nails," he concluded, turning around to look down the center aisle. Monet was nowhere in sight.

"It doesn't smell like tobacco. More like- There!" Faraday pointed behind Carlton.

Black smoke billowed up from between two of the sliding file walls before being sucked hard into rows of ceiling vents - far more vents than such a room needed, he realized.

"They're setting the room on fire," she exclaimed.

"I don't think so," he replied, stepping to the controls for the motorized shelves. He had to slide the rows one at a time before finally getting to the one producing the smoke. They ran to it.

Instead of the cardboard redwells populating the rest of the file room, all the files on these two rows of shelves were housed in metal containers reminiscent of bank security deposit boxes. Carlton touched a metal box next to the fifty or more that were spewing acrid black smoke, confirming his suspicion. "Cold. They're only burning selected files. The Saudi files, I would assume. Remotely, since there is no one here. It would explain why the smoke alarms have not gone off. The incineration trigger must disable them automatically and engage the vent fans." He could only begin to imagine what nefarious secrets the other files must contain for such a mechanism to exist, but for now, his only concern was the contract.

"Maybe we can put them out," Faraday proposed, scanning the room for a fire extinguisher.

Carlton pushed the top of one of the burning file boxes with the tip of his boot. Locked. He kicked it hard. Once. Twice. His third kick cracked the lock. He lifted the top with the tip of his boot, releasing a cloud of black smoke. He recoiled. "Too late."

Faraday crouched, peered inside, coughed. "Ash to ash, dust to dust." She rose. "Maybe Monet and Oersted had better luck."

"Hope springs eternal," he replied, as though reciting the words of Alexander Pope would make them come true.

He knew better. If Wolf and Savitch had swept their offices clean of paper and remotely incinerated the Saudi files, there was little hope of finding anything.

Spiro popped his head into the computer room just as Carlton and Faraday arrived. "We arrested Wallace at DOE headquarters. Still haven't found Savitch. We looked everywhere, even the closets. His car is still in the parking garage."

"Could he have left since we came in?" Inquired Faraday.

The hirsute agent shook his head. "A mouse could not have escaped. I contacted the teams at the other Farnsworth Tate offices. All of their physical Saudi files have been burned."

Faraday launched an expletive. "Keep looking."

Carlton turned his attention to Oersted. "Where is Monet?"

The FBI IT expert shrugged. "I don't know. He stepped out a while ago."

"Were you able to locate the computer files?" Asked Faraday.

"Yes."

She grinned.

"All the Saudi files have been deleted."

Carlton's shoulders slumped. "Aw, hell."

"What about backup files?" Asked Faraday.

"Gone."

"Ghost files?" Asked Carlton, referring to the electronic data that often remained on a computer's hard drive after files were deleted and erased.

Oersted shook his head. "Whoever deleted the files did it with a targeted destruction program. It located the files, deleted them, erased them, then defragmented the hard drive over and over. The remaining ghost data is garbage."

Carlton fell into a chair, massaged his aching arm. Armed with Flynn's warrants, Farnsworth Tate had seemed such a simple target. Instead, it had crumbled like a sandcastle in the waves.

He hung his head low, shook it in disbelief. "Completely FUBAR," he announced, using the military acronym. F-d Up Beyond All Recognition. They had gone through all this for nothing. He thought of Alexis. He had left a message for her doctor in Fairbanks, had not heard back. "FUBAR," he repeated.

"*Pas nécessairement.*"

Monet's voice startled Carlton out of his seat. Not necessarily.

"Where have you been?" He snapped. "We were about to start looking for you on milk cartons."

Monet pulled up a chair, turned it around, sat on it backwards.

"I wanted to copy all of the computer files first, then search them one by one to find the one with the contract," he announced.

Oersted leaned toward Carlton. "I told Henri that absent exigent circumstances, indiscriminately copying all of the firm's Saudi files without selecting the ones specified in the search warrant would violate the warrant," he explained, with more than a little competitiveness in his tone.

"You were right." They now had exigent circumstances, since the files were burned and deleted. Of course, now it was too late. Carlton winced, turned. "Henri, tell me that you didn't violate the-"

Monet placed a hand on his chest with a mock expression of shock. "Me, violate regulations? *Jamais.*" Never.

Faraday was losing her patience fast. "So what did you do?" She pressed.

"While *Monsieur* Oersted was searching through the files one by one," he announced proudly, smiling at his inter-agency rival, "I located the computer folders containing the Saudi files. Since copying them all would violate the warrant, I sent them from one branch office to another by email."

Oersted arched his eyebrows, understanding immediately. "Brilliant," he exclaimed, admitting defeat.

Monet beamed, giving a slight bow.

Carlton held up his palms in confusion. "Not getting it."

"When the file destruction program kicked in," explained Monet, "it only destroyed the files in the hard drive, the backup hard drives, and the firm's email library, but not the files being sent from one office to another in an ongoing email."

Carlton stood. "You mean we can search the Saudi files?"

"*Oui.* As soon as I stop the email loop."

54 TAKING

Interstate 66
Washington, D.C.
6:43 PM

The FBI Ford Crown Victoria sedan carrying Carlton, Faraday, and Monet raced along the Theodore Roosevelt Bridge over the muddy Potomac River at close to 100 miles per hour, swerving around rush hour traffic unable to get out of the lead-footed Spiro's way. Its high beams, strobe lights, and shrill staccato siren pierced the dusk as they flew off the Glebe Road exit, hurtled into the exclusive Virginia suburb of McLean between tall rows of leafy oaks and elms.

"This is even worse than I thought," said Carlton, paging through the Euroil contract Monet had printed after saving it from electronic destruction.

Monet's iPhone trilled. He answered it, handed it to Carlton. "It's Ben-David."

"Ash? What have you got?"

"The funding and ownership of the Venezuelan account Monet sent over."

"Who-" Carlton was nearly knocked to the floor as Spiro careened around a corner, saved from a concussion only by grabbing the front headrest at the last second.

"Opened and owned by a person named Adawal."

"One of Yassin's aliases," said Carlton, recalling a conversation he had with Sobieski. "How is it funded?"

"It's complex, but the money flows ultimately lead to Hakim's Saudi Interior Ministry."

Carlton stared at the blurred trunks of trees outside while he absorbed what Ben-David was saying. "Abu Hassan's attempted attack on the U.S. grid, Wolf's attempt to bribe European foreign ministers on the Euroil contract, and the attacks on Polish troops and civilians in Iraq - all funded by Hakim and Yassin," he concluded. As well as the slaughter and mutilation of my men, he did not add, his fist tightening.

"Also the funding of the bogus environmental groups that managed to stop new oil and gas drilling in the U.S." Ben-David paused. "And the Hamas attack that killed my niece in Tel Aviv," he said in a cracking voice filled with sorrow.

"Ash, I'm-"

"I know you will do whatever is necessary to stop these people. I'll help if I can, but I'm up to my eyeballs in reconstruction out here. In the meantime, I placed a tracker on the Venezuelan account. Monet will be alerted whenever there is a transfer to or from the account."

"Aces. We're going to stop them, all right. And it won't end there. We're going to hunt them down and lock them in metal cages for ten lifetimes." Or far worse. The assertions vented part of his rage, but for the moment, they were more pipe dreams than practical plans. "But how did you manage to get the information on the Venezuelan account? Neither the FBI nor Polish intelligence were able to-"

"As I said before, it's amazing what can be accomplished through the internet," replied Ben-David, cutting him off. He hung up before Carlton could reply, his mouth wide open in shock.

Carlton recounted the information to Faraday while Spiro negotiated increasingly narrow streets still at NASCAR speeds. He slowed only upon approaching twin black Chevy Suburbans blocking off access to a stately colonial house at the end of a cul de sac. Their headlights flashed on, their high beams blinding the newcomers. Two FBI agents armed with M4 carbines moved out from behind the SUVs, held their hands out, indicating for them to stop.

Luckily, Faraday had called ahead.

One of the agents walked to Spiro's open window with his partner a few steps behind, ready to provide cover. The man scrutinized their IDs, spoke into his cuff mike. A few seconds later, he pressed his finger against his earpiece, returned their IDs. "Someone will be right out to get you."

They emerged from the frosty interior of the Crown Vic into air as still and muggy as the swamp that Washington had been when constructed and, some maintained, remained to this day. Less than a minute later, a Japanese-American woman dressed in a smart gray pantsuit walked into view.

"Special Agent Funizawa. Follow me," she said, before lowering her voice and leaning toward the new arrivals conspiratorially. "I'm warning you, the Bear is not in a good mood."

"Great," Carlton grumbled, his stomach churning. It was going to be even more difficult to sell the AG on his unconventional plan.

Floodlights bathed the house's red brick façade in pools of light. Tall white columns supported a two-story sloping front eave. A battalion of manicured topiary trees planted in white boxes stood at attention along a raised front porch.

The three followed Funizawa through the imposing black wood door into a sweeping burgundy red entry hall with cherry wood floors, into a mahogany-paneled elevator, then halfway down an upstairs hallway illuminated with brass faux-candles before stopping at a closed door. The agent knocked.

An unintelligible grunt responded from inside.

"Go ahead. I'll be outside," said Funizawa, leaning toward Carlton. "Where it's safe," she whispered, winking as she opened the door.

Despite the air conditioning, Carlton was sweating heavily as he entered, felt his shirt sticking to his back, his pulse quicken.

The Bear was reading in his electric wheelchair, dressed in a navy blue robe emblazoned with the DOJ seal. A wool blanket was draped over his legs. He observed the newcomers from behind lowered reading glasses as he did all persons: as intruders, with great suspicion. DOJ lore had it that the Bear once told a rookie lawyer that 'the only person who you can trust is your mother, and her, watch very carefully'.

The second African-American to be named Attorney General of the United States, Rod Thorne matched his nickname to a tee. His movements were cautious and calculated, yet he could tear into a person when riled. His dark brown eyes watched everything, betrayed nothing. At seventy, he still possessed a thick mane, now graying at the temples. His beefy forearms sprouted tangles of hair and ended in large, powerful hands. Despite his paralysis from the waist down courtesy of a Viet Cong bullet in Vietnam, he maintained his imposing barrel chest and muscular physique with a strict exercise regimen while indulging in his taste for red meat, potatoes, and martinis. His pointed nose, high cheekbones, and angular chin provided a stark contrast to the muscular contours of his bulky frame. Dark bags tugged at his eyelids, a symptom of the Bear's propensity for insomnia rather than hibernation.

His Labrador puppy J. Edgar dropped a slipper from his mouth, leaped off a sofa, and jumped up on Carlton, licking his hand affectionately. He bent down and rubbed the energetic young dog behind his floppy ears.

If only the Bear was as easy to convince as his puppy, he wished, his gaze moving to a credenza, where a silver frame displayed a photograph of Thorne's teenage daughter, taken only a few months before her death. Carlton could not imagine the sorrow the man must have felt - and continued to feel, considering the fact that the frame was still draped in black with a flickering votive candle before it twenty years later.

Thorne shifted in his wheelchair with a groan, squinted.

"I'm in a foul mood, Carlton. This had better be good news."

Carlton swallowed hard. "I apologize for coming to your home, sir," he replied, sidestepping the question by introducing Monet and Faraday.

Thorne acknowledged their presence with a combination nod and grunt. "I just got off the horn with Forbes," he announced, referring to the CIA Deputy Director of Intelligence. "Were you aware that he thinks you're an unstable and insubordinate *prima donna*?"

Not a promising opening, thought Carlton, wincing inwardly, forcing himself to keep his mouth shut.

Thorne did not drop the matter. "I imagine you don't like him much either," he added.

Carlton could not stop himself, took the bait. "I think he's a heartless bastard who has little regard for the lives of his agents." He paused, already mentally kicking himself. "Sir."

That earned a roar of laughter from Thorne, who shifted heavily in his wheelchair. "Balls, guts, and honesty. That's why I didn't let the Bureau take *this* case away from you, Carlton," he replied, giving Faraday a sideways glance that could have cut glass. She seemed to shrink in response, but said nothing. Carlton blushed, uncomfortable yet pleased at the praise. Too bad his immediate superior Edison did not think that way.

"And I don't give a rat's ass what he thinks about my people." Thorne paused. "I do care what he thinks about intel and foreign ops, since he's so damn good at them. And on that point, Forbes is skeptical, but waiting to see what you come up with to vet Sobieski's intel. If he accepts it, he'll meet with the DNI and NSA, so it had better be good," he concluded, referring to the Director of National Intelligence and the president's National Security Advisor. "So what did you find?"

Carlton cleared his throat. "The good news is that we were able to get a copy of the contract between Saudi and Euroil. That should go a long way in vetting Sobieski's intel." He handed Thorne a copy of the 350-page contract. "It confirms his transcripts."

Thorne leafed through the document's table of contents, making deep guttural sounds of disgust. "If this is the good news, I can't wait to hear the bad." He turned to Monet. "Email a copy of the agreement to Forbes at Langley, encrypted."

Monet immediately went to work on his silver laptop.

Carlton continued. "The bad news is that we believe Wolf is in the Saudi embassy with Prince Qhibli, so there is no way we can find out when the contract will be signed. The last transmission Sobieski received indicated that Wolf and Euroil's CEO had reached a deal with Prince Hakim. That gave us hope that we could still derail the contract negotiations. But if you look at the document's footer, you'll notice that as of this morning, the contract appears to be in final form."

Thorne peered down, grunted. "So Saudi and Euroil have reached a final agreement," he concluded.

"According to Sobieski's transcripts of ambassador Qhibli's conversations, Hakim intends to announce the contract as soon as it is signed, which means that it has not been signed yet. But now that the contract is in final form, they can sign it anywhere, at any time. Even by fax or email." Carlton paused. "I'm afraid that there are two more problems."

Thorne growled.

"As Judge Flynn pointed out, the contract is perfectly legal. President Douglass can try pressuring the French president and prime minister to prevent Euroil from signing it or to terminate it after it is signed, but I doubt that they will have the political will to do so because the contract will greatly benefit France."

Thorne shifted in his wheelchair by gripping its frame with his powerful arms. "We could squeeze Euroil by putting pressure on its U.S. business interests."

Carlton shook his head. "Monet checked. Euroil has no U.S. operations out of fear that they would make the company subject to our anti-terror trading laws. As for its contracts with U.S. firms, I'm sure Euroil would gladly give them up in exchange for the untold billions it will reap from an exclusive Saudi oil contract.

"And as for the E.U.'s political will to agree to the loan to Saudi, it appears that ten of the 25 European foreign ministers have already received what amounts to bribes from Prince Hakim through an investment fund tied to the same Venezuelan bank account that funded Abu Hassan's planned attack on the electrical grid." Ben-David had passed that tidbit to Carlton during their latest conversation. "That seems to indicate that the E.U. ministers will likely agree to the loan."

Thorne shook his head slowly. "You bring me problems, Carlton, but no solutions."

Carlton took a deep breath, paused. "I have a solution, sir, but it's a bit, ah, unconventional."

Thorne frowned. "When has that ever stopped you? Spit it out."

"Sir, one coup deserves another. What if DOJ launched a coup of its own?"

"Against Prince Hakim?" Asked Thorne, perplexed.

"Against Ludovic Metz, the CEO of Euroil. DOJ could take over Euroil."

Thorne shifted his position again, so heavily this time that it caused the wheelchair to creak. "Take over Euroil?" He roared. "Have you lost your mind? It's the largest company in France. How can you possibly hope to do that?" Little J. Edgar howled at the volume of his master's voice.

Carlton was prepared for Thorne's reaction, stood his ground. He had based his strategy partly on the fact that Thorne had started out as a corporate lawyer and would understand it better than would most criminal prosecutors. "Sir, if we could obtain a majority of Euroil's shares, we could kick Metz out as CEO before he signs the contract with Hakim. Monet researched Euroil's ownership. The company has issued a total of one billion shares. About 350 million shares are owned by U.S. institutions and investors. Another 250 million are owned by foreign banks."

Thorne shook his head in dismay. "Carlton. Please. I need a real solution, not a fantasy."

"Sir, I-"

"How much is Euroil's stock trading at?"

"About $150 a share."

"So the 500 million-plus shares you need to get a majority would cost what," he quickly did the corporate math, "*$75 billion*? That's three times DOJ's annual budget. How are you going to get that kind of money? The government is already stretched beyond its limit."

Carlton had anticipated that argument as well. "We don't need to buy the shares to control the company, sir."

Thorne grunted, squinting. "Isn't that your plan?"

"To fire Metz and put in our own CEO, we don't need to own a majority of Euroil *shares*. All we need is a majority of *shareholder votes*." Carlton knew that Thorne was well aware of that critical difference. He paused, letting it sink in before going for broke. "Sir, I propose that DOJ take the shareholder votes by eminent domain."

"Eminent domain?" Thorne grabbed his head, swayed, rolled his eyes to the ceiling. "Eminent domain applies to real estate, Carlton. Land, buildings, oil rights, not shareholder votes."

"Sir, just because it has never been done does not mean that it can't *be* done. The Fifth Amendment states that the federal government can take any private property right for a public use if it pays its fair market value." He ticked off the requirements on the fingers of his hand. "A shareholder's voting right is private property. National security constitutes a public use. And as far as fair market value, as you know far better than I do, a shareholder vote is worth much less than a share of stock. DOJ would have to come up with much less than the $75 billion it would cost to buy the shares themselves."

Thorne leaned back, exhaling through puffed cheeks. "Even if I bought your lunatic argument, Carlton, DOJ could only take shareholder votes by eminent domain from American shareholders. According to your numbers, that works out to 350 million shareholder votes. How are you going to get the other 150 million plus one you need to obtain a majority?"

"I'm going to convince the foreign banks to sell us their shares."

"Oh, is that all?" The Bear huffed, nearly apoplectic. "I didn't realize you were so tight with the international banking community."

"I'm not, sir. But I know someone who is."

Thorne's fierce gaze bored through Carlton's brain for a painfully long time.

"Let me get this straight, Carlton. You want the Justice Department to take 350 million shareholder votes from American owners through a wild and untested eminent domain legal theory, convince foreign banks to sell DOJ 150 million shares of Euroil stock, and fire Euroil's CEO, all before he signs the contract with Prince Hakim, which could be in only a handful of hours. Does that about sum it up?"

Carlton had to admit it sounded crazier when the Bear enunciated it out loud. He broke into an anxious sweat. Maybe Thorne's background as a corporate lawyer had been more bane than boon to his strategy. But it was all he had. He leaned forward. "Sir, if we don't -"

Thorne cut him off by raising a beefy hand. "You convinced me, Carlton. It's lunatic, but at this stage, given the political dimensions, it may be our only shot short of invading Saudi. Or France."

Carlton's heart leaped.

"You still have two huge problems," Thorne continued, stabbing a thick index finger at him in the air. "You need to find the money to take the U.S. shareholder votes and buy the shares from the foreign banks. And you have to devise a way to delay Hakim and Metz from signing the contract until then. The only way to do that is to determine when and where the contract is going to be signed. Since we're not receiving any more transmissions from Sobieski's bugs, the only way to obtain that information is to get Wolf, but if he is at the Saudi embassy like you say, we're out of luck. The embassy is sovereign Saudi soil."

He threw up his hands. "More problems without solutions," he exclaimed, when the telephone rang. "Now what?" Thorne moved a toggle on one of the wheelchair's arms, sending the electrical device whirring across the room at breakneck speed. He braked a half foot from a wood banister, grabbed the handset.

"Thorne," he boomed, remaining immobile while listening to the voice on the other end.

Carlton turned to Monet. "Get our people started on those takings orders ASAP," he directed in a low voice. Monet pulled out his iPhone, began texting the NSD team.

Thorne hung up, pivoted the wheelchair back towards Carlton. "Our two problems may have just been solved."

Carlton looked at Thorne quizzically. "Sir?"

"That was Sec State. Prince Hakim just cut off diplomatic relations with the United States."

55 EMBASSIES

Saudi Embassy
Washington, D.C.
8:03 PM

Based on Saudi regent Prince Hakim's virulent anti-American diatribe severing diplomatic relations with the United States and appropriating all U.S. government and private assets in Saudi Arabia, the president wasted no time ordering the immediate repatriation of all Saudi diplomatic personnel to the desert kingdom and freezing billions of dollars of Saudi government assets in the United States.

Within minutes, armed teams of FBI and Homeland Security agents descended on the Saudi embassy in Foggy Bottom, choking off the complex with a tight security cordon. FBI Black Hawk helicopters out of Quantico thumped above, shining spotlights brighter than the noon sun along the white compound's perimeter.

State Department personnel identified, searched, and checked each individual funneling out of the complex and placed them, for their protection, on heavily guarded buses bound for Dulles airport and a government-chartered flight to Riyadh. Those not in the embassy at this hour would be tracked down at their homes.

Carlton and Faraday stood on either side of the line, scanning the dozens of exiting personnel for Wolf and Savitch in the miserably hot and humid air heavily laden with smoke from Carlton's Romeo y Julieta. Over an hour later, a dispirited Spiro walked through the embassy gate. "No sign of Wolf, Savitch, or Prince Qhibli. We looked everywhere."

"If they're not in the embassy, where the heck are they?" Snapped Carlton, impatient and frustrated. "Could they have slipped out undetected?"

Spiro shook his head. "Our cordon is so tight even the air inside could barely get out."

"What about other buildings that the Saudis own?"

"They own plenty of real estate in the DC area," answered Faraday. "Prince Qhibli has a mansion in McLean."

"Wolf is a lawyer," replied Carlton. "He would only hide in a building that has diplomatic immunity. What about a consulate?"

"All their consulates have been cordoned off and evac'ed with no sign of them," replied Faraday, her eyes on Carlton but her mind farther away. "But there is another possibility."

Carlton crooked his head.

"Most countries have only one embassy compound in Washington. The Saudis have two."

The comment took him by surprise. "Two?"

"Few people know about the second one. The Saudis and the State Department have kept its existence heavily under wraps. Its official name is the 'Military Division of the Saudi Embassy'. Minutes after the 9-11 attacks, FBI agents surrounded the building, but most of the time it's nearly vacant."

"We have it surrounded, ma'am, but the interior lights are all off and no one has come out," said Spiro.

"Where is it?" Asked Carlton.

"Between Georgetown and Foggy Bottom," Faraday replied. "A couple of blocks from Wolf's penthouse." Her green eyes opened wide as she made the connection.

"Aces. Let's go."

A mere three minutes later, the Crown Vic braked in a diagonal skid in front of a five-story brick building in a dark side street. Carlton stepped out, scanned the property.

It was enclosed by a brick wall, with landscape and architectural lights illuminating its façade. All the windows were dark, just as Spiro had said. On its left side sat a commercial office building. On its right was a fenced-in flat area covered with gravel that had the disturbing appearance of a minefield. A forest of antennae and satellite dishes sprouted atop the building above its angled metal roofline.

FBI agents were already guarding the front and side entrances. After examining the IDs around their necks, they allowed Carlton, Faraday, and Spiro to proceed to the front gate.

"No signage, no flag. Zip," Faraday added.

Carlton leaned close to a gleaming brass plaque near the closed entry gate. Scrolled black letters recited the building's address, but revealed no ties to the Saudi Kingdom. He tried the gate handle. Locked solid. He peered up at the dark windows. The drapes were all drawn, hiding the interior.

"The windows are all green."

"Bulletproof glass," Faraday explained.

"*Lawrence of Arabia* meets *The Addams Family*," commented Carlton. "Spooky. Entrances?"

She consulted a diagram of the building that one of the FBI guards had handed to her. "Front door, one side exit, no parking garage."

"Rear?"

"Apartment building," she answered, still studying the diagram. "If the windows are bulletproof, the Saudis probably reinforced the rear common wall."

"Not enough time to tunnel in."

"We'll have to go in through the front or side door."

"Anyone thought to ring the doorbell?" Asked Carlton, pointing to a buzzer near the brass plaque. "Trick or treat?"

"Several times, sir," replied one of the FBI agents. "Nothing doing."

Carlton smirked, looked at Faraday. "You'd better call in one of your teams."

Ten minutes later, an armored truck pulled up to the curb and disgorged one of the teams from the Farnsworth Tate raid, once again in full assault gear. Carlton and Faraday pulled on faceplates, plugged in comm links, checked their weapons. She divided the agents into two squads of five before outlining her plan.

Carlton felt his heart pump faster. Sweat beaded on his forehead in the hot, soupy air.

"You and the two agents guard the building," Faraday directed Spiro. "No one goes in or out unless I say so." She turned to the two squads, pointed to the gate. "Let's move."

Squad One leader wrapped a short spiral of detonation cord around the gate lock, igniting the explosive-laced rope with an electronic detonator. The cord burned through the heavy-duty lock at over a thousand feet per second, shearing it clean off the gate. Faraday swung the doors open, led Squad One into the courtyard.

Squad Two ran to the façade, shot crampons onto the roof, started scaling the brick wall without as much as a scrape or whisper.

Carlton recalled Davos's comment about Spiderman at *Castel McLean*, shook his head. Spiderman had nothing on these guys, he concluded, duly impressed.

Two minutes later, a voice crackled through Carlton's headset. "Squad Two here. Roof is secure."

Carlton and Faraday stood with Squad One at the front door, consisting of two large panes of glass.

"Probably armored," Squad One leader announced.

He placed det cord along the front door's inner frame, attached the detonator, stood back, triggered the electronic mechanism with the push of a button. Within a millisecond, the det cord melted the armored glass off the door frame like so much warm butter. The thick glass slab crashed to the marble floor inside the lobby, shaking the entire front entrance of the building, yet remained in one piece.

"Squad Two here. Roof door is open."

"Squads One and Two, go!" Faraday ordered.

M4 carbines at the ready, Squad One turned on the night vision equipment embedded in their faceplates, stepped into the dark entrance hall, fanned out in precise movements.

"Electricity's off," announced the leader. "They must have killed power to the building."

"A benighted kingdom it is," remarked Carlton.

Faraday reached over, turned a switch on the side of his faceplate. The room in front of him glowed to life in a variety of green hues. "Thanks."

He and Faraday followed Squad One as they searched the first floor, resorting to flashlights when the ambient light grew too dim even for their night vision sensors. The air was even hotter than outside and stuffy, like a school after being shuttered all summer. Carlton scanned the walls, located an electric breaker panel, opened it.

"The breakers are all switched off," he said. He pointed to a small digital readout next to each breaker. "Look at this. Timers for delayed electrical shutoff."

"God knows what kind of stuff the Saudis were doing in here," replied Faraday. "Let's leave them off for now. Even with flashlights, night vision gives us an advantage."

They walked through ornate offices, a kitchen, two bathrooms. All deserted.

"Squad One here. No one on floor one, ma'am. Proceeding to floor two."

"Squad Two here. No one on the fifth floor. I think we found the head honcho's office, though. Looks like a cathouse. Nasty white and gold furniture with a huge painting of some sheik dude."

"Skip the interior decoration review," snapped Faraday. "Proceed to the fourth floor."

She and Carlton followed Squad One up a polished wood staircase inlaid with white marble to the second floor while Squad Two descended to the fourth floor.

Thick curtains were drawn over each window. Without ambient light from the street, the second floor was even darker than the first. Most doors were locked. Squad One kicked open the flimsier doors, blew the locks of the heavier ones with det cord. They came up as empty as Squad Two on the fourth floor.

The two squads joined up at the third floor staircase landing. Each took an opposite side of the floor while Carlton and Faraday remained in position, waiting anxiously in the dark, sweating profusely in the trapped heat. Five minutes later, both teams reappeared.

"Nothing, ma'am," Squad Two leader announced.

"Same here," echoed Squad One leader.

"Not very promising," said Carlton.

"Where the heck are they?" Faraday demanded, frustration soaring. "We checked every room, every closet. We have the layout, so I doubt we missed anything." She paused. "Wait. We didn't check the elevators, did we?"

"No ma'am," replied Squad One leader.

"The electricity is off," replied Carlton. "They couldn't get inside the elevators after shutting off the power."

"The breakers have a time delay function, remember?"

Carlton's eyes opened wide. "Right. They could have programmed the breakers to switch off after they entered the elevator."

They strode down the staircase to the lobby, sandwiched between the two squads.

Carlton turned down the hall to the breaker panel, punched in a one minute time delay, engaged his watch chronometer. He switched all of the breakers to the 'on' position, ran back to the twin lobby elevators.

"Fifty seconds," he announced.

Carlton switched off his night vision function, inhaled a series of deep breaths. Luckily, his faceplate had a fog-proof coating, but perspiration stung his eyes. He mouthed a prayer, glanced at the glowing second hand of his watch. "Fifteen seconds."

A series of metallic clicks sounded from the breakers as the electricity switched back on. Overhead fluorescent lights blinked to life. Faraday punched the elevator call button.

The elevator on the right opened first. Two members of Squad One thrust their weapons inside.

Empty.

The second elevator's doors opened thirty seconds later.

Empty.

"Check the maintenance hatches," Faraday ordered.

While Squad One got to work on the elevator to the right, Carlton removed his faceplate, walked into the other elevator.

"Give me a boost."

Carlton stepped up onto Faraday's clasped hands, reached up to the metal elevator hatch. He pushed it open, shined his flashlight into the darkness, revealing only a cement shaft, elevator cables, and fire doors. It smelled of old dust and burned oil.

Placing his flashlight between his teeth, he grabbed the edges of the hatch opening, placed his feet against Faraday's shoulders, pushed, lifted himself up onto the elevator roof. He pointed his flashlight beam upward.

And froze.

56 BANKERS

Castel McLean
Beverly Hills, California
6:43 PM

McLean was keenly aware that far more than his reputation was riding on his impending conference call.

He sat alone in his pale green silk-paneled office, behind an aircraft carrier-sized glass and chrome desk. The sleeves of his baby blue Charvet shirt were uncharacteristically rolled up, top button unfastened. The brushed aluminum window blinds were squeezed shut. The only illumination came from a halogen spotlight above a large Frankenthaler abstract expressionist painting on one of the tall walls.

With Claire now out of her coma and on the mend, McLean should have felt deep relief. Instead, after what Carlton had divulged, all he could feel was a rising tide of anxiety. Despite the meat locker-cold air conditioning pumping into the office, he was perspiring heavily as he waited for all participants to join his international conference call. The dark circles of sweat under his arms matched those ringing his eyes.

McLean personally knew five of the twenty one CEOs on the list of banks Monet had provided. They promptly agreed to the conference call, in the middle of the night for most. His reputation in international business circles ensured that more joined in. The fact that he was acting as an agent for the United States Department of Justice on a 'matter of international economic urgency' as he described it prodded the remaining recalcitrants to action.

"All parties have joined the call," an automated operator's voice finally announced.

"Ladies and gentlemen," began McLean. "Thank you for participating on this conference call."

If he wanted their help, he could not keep the matter secret. And there was no time for confidentiality agreements. His disclosure to the bankers would roil the markets, but a far worse fate awaited them if

Carlton's plan failed. He dove straight in, summarizing Prince Hakim's intended contract with Euroil and the shift in the global oil currency from the dollar to the euro.

The alarmed mutterings on the line informed him that the senior international bankers did not need an explanation of the dire consequences that would ensue. Good. It meant they would act.

Once their shock abated to a dull murmur, McLean set forth Carlton's proposed solution and offered the full market price for the assembled banks' Euroil shares, secure in the knowledge that President Douglass had frozen more than enough Saudi government assets in the U.S. to pay for them. After resting his case, he temporarily took himself off the call so the CEOs could discuss the matter between themselves in private and reach a decision.

Confident that the bankers would trip over each other in a stampede to prevent a global economic meltdown, McLean was utterly unprepared for what happened next.

"We cannot sell you the shares, Mr. McLean," announced Erich Hertz, the CEO of Deutsche Kapital, AG, the German finance powerhouse that owned the greatest number of Euroil shares among the banks.

McLean was astonished. "I beg your pardon?"

"*Ja.* We want to, but we cannot," replied Hertz in perfect English spoken with a pronounced German accent. "Trading the shares at this time would constitute illegal insider trading."

McLean could not believe his ears, but trusted the stench his nose smelled, no doubt the result of terminally risk-averse lawyers lurking in the background. He was accustomed to their twisted reasoning. Many would prevent firemen from saving people inside a burning building because the ladder might present a liability. His love of bankers was not much greater.

"Insider trading?" He repeated, still in shock. "How?"

"*Ja.* We would be selling our Euroil shares based on the knowledge that the company is about to sign a substantial contract with Saudi Arabia. Since the contract has not been made public and knowledge of the contract came from parties to the deal, most likely through, shall we say, unpermitted actions, we would be trading the shares based on inside information."

McLean wanted to scream. Not yet made public? *Santa Lucia!* The entire purpose of buying the shares was to *prevent* the contract from being signed. He bit back a tirade, took a deep breath, knowing that vociferous outrage would get him nowhere fast with this group.

"I understand," he lied. "But I can assure you that the U.S. government will not prosecute your banks for insider trading, especially since you would be selling your shares to the U.S. government at its own request. I can probably have that delivered in writing by the Attorney General personally if you wish."

"*Nein.* Not the U.S. government, *Herr* McLean," corrected Hertz. "Many European governments are undoubtedly in favor of the contract. Certainly France, since Euroil is a French company, other European countries whose energy companies have been purchased by Euroil, the European Union, since I understand it has tentatively agreed to make a substantial loan to Saudi Arabia, and governments who dislike the United States no matter how much they like your president. If we prevent the contract from being signed, those governments would swiftly exact their revenge by prosecuting our banks under their own insider trading laws."

McLean argued with Hertz and his colleagues for nearly an hour. Bankers were conservative by nature. He found out just how much. They would not budge a millimeter.

He thanked them for their time through clenched teeth, hung up and launched an Italian expletive, wiping sweat from his forehead.

A rogue Saudi prince in collusion with one of the world's largest energy companies was about to unleash a massive attack on the U.S. dollar and the global economy and the CEOs of the world's largest banks were arguing about the legality of selling shares to prevent the disaster. His dislike of lawyers and bankers turned into outright loathing as he paced the office in his sockless Gucci moccasins.

McLean had not built a global business empire by taking no for an answer. There had to be another solution, he knew. And he knew what it was.

But could he allow himself to make the call?

57 DEATHBED

Military Division of the Saudi Embassy
Georgetown, Washington, D.C.
9:53 PM

Two startled faces stared back at Carlton from a dozen of feet up in the elevator shaft. One man with a wide girth, a goatee, and glowering eyes was barely hanging on to a metal rung embedded in the concrete wall. The other was as gaunt and terrified as a subject in an Edvard Munch painting. Prince Qhibli and Grover Wolf averted their eyes as he shined the bright beam of his flashlight onto their faces.

Carlton grinned. "Well, well. In a spider hole, just like Saddam. Without wanting to mix metaphors, I think it's time for you to come down from your ivory minaret."

His grin was short lived, quickly became a scowl as he held up his badge.

"Patrick Carlton. U.S. Department of Justice. You are both under arrest. Please step down into the-"

"I think not, Mr. Carlton," Prince Qhibli interrupted in a haughty tone, staring back him defiantly despite the light beam. "Per President Douglass's order, I have full diplomatic immunity until midnight as ambassador of the Kingdom of Saudi Arabia. So does my special assistant, Grover Wolf, who is credentialed as such by the State Department. It is *I* who order *you* to provide us safe passage to Dulles Airport. We are returning to the Kingdom."

The evidence Carlton possessed against both men was incontrovertible. What he wanted to do was shoot both men then and there. Instead, Carlton dammed his rising fury, forced himself to take a deep breath. He nodded. "In time, perhaps. For now, you are under arrest and you will come with me."

"Are you deaf, Carlton? The ambassador and I have diplomatic immunity," the wraith-like lawyer snapped back with supreme confidence.

Carlton felt his face grow hot. He steadied himself. "In a perfect world, yes. But what an imperfect world we live in, don't you agree, counselor? Since you are the ambassador's special assistant and his chief U.S. counsel, perhaps you would be so kind as to explain to his excellency that diplomatic immunity does not extend to murder and acts of war on U.S. soil, with which he is charged." Carlton had no arrest warrant for Qhibli, but reasoned that the exigent circumstances of his intended flight out of the country made one unnecessary. "Or to the murder of a federal agent and treason against the United States, with which you are charged, Mr. Wolf, among many, many other crimes."

"We'll see about that," Wolf spat back.

In contrast to his lawyer, the Saudi ambassador knew the truth when he heard it. Qhibli's jowled face grew pale as his arrogance melted away. He shifted his weight to lower himself down the metal rungs. Carlton reached out to help him.

Gunshots erupted.

Bullets slammed into the elevator roof inches away from his feet with loud metallic pings. He dropped the flashlight, leaped for cover behind a tall, narrow metal utility box.

The explosions reverberated and echoed in the narrow shaft, making it difficult for Carlton to pinpoint their origin, although they could only have come from higher than the two men. To make matters worse, the spinning flashlight cast wild, oscillating shadows on the grimy walls.

Crouching behind the utility box, he scrambled to unholster his Glock with his right hand while retrieving the flashlight with his left. Before he could direct its beam upward, three more shots rang out, ricocheting against the lip of the utility cabinet inches above his head.

He pointed the flashlight into the darkness, above Qhibli and Wolf's positions, peeked out from above the lip. Nothing. He angled his flashlight higher.

There. A man glared down at him from a precarious perch nearly three floors up. His left arm was wrapped around a metal rung. His right arm was outstretched, aiming a handgun at him.

Carlton ducked behind the cabinet an instant before another gunshot exploded, the bullet slamming into the wall of the shaft behind him, spraying him with concrete chips. "You're under arrest, Savitch.

Drop your weapon and come down." He glanced up. Seeing the man shake his head, he added: "There are twelve agents inside the building and more outside. You can't escape."

"Neither can you," replied Savitch, sneering. "It's about time you died."

In his peripheral vision, Carlton caught a head poking through the elevator hatch.

"Down!" He yelled, rolling away from the utility cabinet, shoving the FBI agent back into the cabin just as Savitch fired. It was too late. A shout filled the air as one of the rounds traversed the hatch opening, shattering the agent's shoulder.

Carlton was now a good two feet away from the metal cabinet, out in the open. Savitch fired again. This time, Carlton was not lucky.

Three bullets hit him in the chest with the force of falling bricks, punching him down hard against the metal roof.

Groaning, writhing on his back, gasping for air, Carlton clutched at the pain flaring through his chest, each breath searing his lungs. He tried to push himself off the roof, could not. A metal object clanged on the roof near him.

Grenade.

He rolled toward the open hatch to escape from the coming explosion, hit a sharp protrusion on the elevator roof with his injured bicep. He shouted in agony. Splotches of light danced before his eyes. He forced himself to keep his grip on the Glock but his other hand let go of the flashlight. This time it fell through the hatch opening, clattered on the marble floor below. Light continued to emanate from the elevator cabin, but it was too dim to illuminate the roof. He tried to move into the hatch opening. His shoulder was wedged too tight against an unknown metal object. He peered left and right. Where was the grenade? The seconds ticked away. The FBI teams were sure to eliminate Savitch by entering the shaft from a higher floor, but by the time they did, he would be shredded to bits. He kept looking, feeling. Where was it?

Turning to attempt another roll into the elevator hatch, Carlton saw something inches from his face in the dim glow from below. A handgun magazine.

Savitch had not tossed a grenade. He was reloading. Carlton looked back up. Darkness. He could not see Savitch, but Savitch could see him.

Faraday called out from below, attempted to reach him, but he yelled for her and the others to stay away from the open hatch. Summoning all his strength, he pushed himself with his feet, roaring in pain, rolled himself back behind the protective cabinet, searching for a way to slide down the hatch without anyone exposed below.

By then, Savitch had finished reloading.

Another gunshot exploded, the round slamming into his upper chest, expelling the air from his lungs, pinning him against the roof once again. Already felled by the the first gunshots, he felt his life bleeding away with each heartbeat. His vision was becoming blurry. On the verge of sinking into oblivion, he exercized his only option.

Mustering his remaining strength, he raised the Glock and blindly fired its entire complement of thirteen .40 caliber Smith & Wesson rounds into the shaft above.

Moaning in agony, sucking air in ragged gasps, ears buzzing from the deafening gunshots in the narrow shaft, forcing himself to hang on to consciousness, Carlton strained to hear the result.

Nothing. He had missed.

Refusing to wait for the hail of bullets sure to pelt down in response, shaky and teetering close to shock, he fumbled with the Glock to change magazines when a muffled yell filled his ears, followed by a loud crash as Savitch's body slammed onto the metal cabinet next to Carlton, bounced off, then crashed onto the elevator roof.

He pushed himself toward Savitch's unnaturally twisted body, felt for a pulse. The assassin was already dead.

He felt no remorse.

Shaking the blotches of light from his vision, breathing in quick rasps, he gingerly touched his chest. It was on fire. He removed his hand, examined his fingers in confusion. No blood. Then he remembered.

"Thank God for Kevlar," he croaked, pushing himself to his feet with a loud groan to take the edge off the pain, just as Wolf lunged at him. Amid Savitch's gunshots, he had nearly forgotten about Wolf and Qhibli huddled in the corner of the elevator roof. Although much lighter than Carlton, Wolf caught him by total surprise in a compromising position. His foot struck Carlton's battered chest, sending bolts of agony through his body, knocking him sideways directly into the yawning hatch opening.

He fell.

Carlton shot his arms out, managed to grab a supporting cable with both hands, howling at the pain exploding in his chest and lancing up from his bicep wound. He felt the stitches stretch, pop open. His reflex braked his fall, but caused him to drop the Glock. His only weapon fell to the elevator floor.

Faraday started up through the hatch, but Carlton's position blocked her.

Wolf scurried past Qhibli, began to scramble up the elevator shaft, ascending the same rungs Savitch had used, like a rat fleeing a rising tide. Carlton pushed himself away from the hatch opening, shouting to vent his pain. He looked up at Wolf through blotches of light, unable to see Faraday's proffered Glock nearby. He shook his head to clear his vision, jumped up with his good arm stretched high.

Wolf shrieked as Carlton tugged down hard on his bony leg, repeating the maneuver several times before succeeding in yanking him off the metal rungs. He fell to the elevator roof, crumpled onto his knees, glaring up at Carlton, teeth bared like a trapped animal.

Carlton leaned over him, panting. "You are under-"

Wolf uncoiled, lunged at Carlton, who shifted aside, barely avoiding the feral lawyer. With Carlton no longer in his path, Wolf fell through the open hatch, too surprised to scream. He hit the marble elevator floor with a loud thud. When Wolf managed to open his eyes a few seconds later, he was staring up the barrel of a Glock pistol at Faraday's glowering green eyes.

Members of Squad One placed a step ladder in the elevator, squeezed the portly ambassador through the roof hatch. Carlton followed, still gasping for air, stepped down to Wolf still laying on the elevator floor. He bent over him, looked into the lawyer's crazed eyes.

"If you think that was painful, wait until Justice gets through with you," Carlton announced, voice rasping. "Murderers and traitors are not entitled to lounge at Club Fed," he added, referring to the minimum security federal prisons where white-collar felons served their time watching TV and reading. He leaned closer to Wolf, his gaze boring into the man's brain. "You're going into a cage with the other animals."

"I can pay," Wolf whispered.

Carlton seethed. Radical Saudis concocting an economic attack on America had not surprised him. But an American? A *lawyer* who had taken the oath? And now the bastard was offering him a bribe. His fury exploded.

"You traitor son of a *bitch*," he yelled, kneeling down hard against Wolf's body, shoving the Glock's barrel so hard against the disgraced lawyer's bony skull that his capillaries burst, forming a ring of blood around the muzzle. Carlton felt blood pump in his temples, bleed from his reopened bicep wound, his face burning with rage as bloody images of Alexis and Eche and Claire filled his mind's eye.

"Carlton, don't!" Faraday cried out.

His mind barely registered her plea. His gaze remained locked on Wolf's bloodshot eyes, his index finger tightening against the trigger, teeth clenched and grinding as his conscience fought his thirst for revenge. Scum like this did not deserve to live.

Time slowed. Carlton's internal struggle continued for what seemed like an eternity. Then he noticed something change in Wolf's eyes. Defiance gave way to terror. The man began to cry. Carlton felt something warm under him. Wolf had wet himself.

He jerked the Glock away and stood, holstering the weapon.

"You don't deserve a quick death."

Wolf gasped with relief, nearly hyperventilating, fingering his temple. "I meant I can pay for what I did. With information," he croaked, trembling, pale as a sheet.

"I don't need your information," spat Carlton, peering down at the vile figure. "I already have a copy of your stinking contract."

"But you don't know how and when it will be signed."

Carlton squinted. That was the reason they had searched for Wolf and Qhibli. "How?"

Wolf propped himself up against the floor, massaging his joints. "Metz wanted to sign the contract quickly, at the Saudi embassy in Paris or with Hakim by fax or email, but now that Hakim is regent, he wants to make a big splash by signing it with Metz personally at a live press conference at Riyadh airport. Metz will-"

A gunshot cut him short. Carlton swiveled. Before he could draw his weapon, two agents returned fire, hitting Qhibli in the shoulder and chest. A gold-plated Beretta M9 fell from his thick fingers, skittered on the marble floor. The Saudi ambassador slumped back, gasping, covering his wounds with his hands, muttering curses in Arabic as blood seeped through his thick fingers. Inexplicably, no one had bothered to frisk the high-ranking diplomat for weapons.

While Faraday summoned the paramedics outside tending to the injured FBI agent, Carlton kneeled next to Wolf. The lawyer's own client had shot him in the back, near the heart. Blood soaked the front of his shirt, spurted from his mouth. He moaned, his eyes glazing over.

"What about Metz?" Asked Carlton, holding up the man's head, leaning forward. "What about Metz?"

"Metz-" Wolf coughed up a glob of blood. It splattered on Carlton's face and hands. He ignored it, staring into Wolf's eyes.

"Tell me!"

"Metz is leaving-" he croaked, struggling for words, wincing in pain, gurgling blood. "Leaving for Riyadh tomorrow at nine. To...to sign. Leaving from-" he heaved and coughed up more blood, his words a raspy whisper.

"Stay with me, Wolf! Leaving from where?"

"From-" Wolf's head slumped back in Carlton's hands. He checked his pulse.

Grover Wolf was dead.

58 HUDDLE

His wound hastily restitched, Carlton dashed to the Crown Vic idling outside the eerie building, Faraday in tow.

"Get us to Dulles, Spiro," directed Carlton, his chest and arm still on fire. "As fast as you can."

"Why Dulles? What did Wolf tell you?" Asked Faraday, jumping in behind him. Spiro punched the accelerator, slamming both of them back against their seats as he hurtled around the corner.

"The DARPA jet is hangared there," explained Carlton, dialing Monet. "Henri. What's the ETA on those eminent domain orders?"

"They should be finished within the hour."

"Aces. Have them couriered for delivery tomorrow morning as early as possible. Send them by email and fax also if you can, then meet me at the FBI hangar at Dulles with your passport. You've got one hour."

Carlton hung up, called the pilot to prep the Gulfstream.

"We won't make it to Riyadh in time, Carlton," argued Faraday.

"Not Riyadh. Paris."

"Why Paris?" She asked, perplexed, latching on to Carlton's good arm as Spiro slalomed through traffic on I-66, cursing at other drivers in Greek as the speedometer needle touched the century mark.

"To fire Metz. Wolf said that Metz is flying to Riyadh tomorrow at nine to sign the contract with Hakim. He didn't say where Metz was leaving from or if he was flying out at nine AM or PM. To be safe, we have to assume that he meant nine AM. Euroil's headquarters are in Paris, so we have to assume that Metz will be leaving from Paris." He glanced at his watch, calculated the time difference. "That's less than five hours from now. Riyadh is closer to Paris than Paris is to Washington. If we're going to get to Euroil headquarters and fire Metz before he makes it to Riyadh, we have to leave immediately."

Faraday nodded. "We can take an FBI jet out of Reagan National. It would shave thirty minutes off our drive time."

Carlton shook his head. "By now, the DGSE must have figured out that Thundercloud spirited Sobieski away and that we have his intel. They'll never allow an FBI jet to come within a hundred miles of French airspace until the contract has been signed." He recounted Ben-David's explanation about the Gulfstream's active stealth coating. "The DARPA jet will allow us fly into French airspace undetected. It has no government markings, so we can tell French air traffic control that it's a corporate flight - which is technically true given that we're going to Paris to fire a CEO. By the time the DGSE figures it out, we'll already be in France," Carlton explained, grabbing the front headrest just before Spiro shot across three lanes of traffic.

Spiro glanced back at the two in the rearview mirror. "So where am I going?" He asked. He liked Carlton. The man from Justice had what the Greeks called Θράσος - *thrasos* - audacity, guts. But Faraday was the boss he answered to.

"Dulles," Faraday acquiesced, turning back to Carlton. "Even if we do get into France, how are we going to get into Euroil headquarters to fire Metz?"

Carlton had not thought that far. "Good question. I'm open to suggestions."

Faraday shut her eyes tight in concentration. "If we can delay Metz from leaving Paris, we may buy some time."

"Brilliant." Carlton grinned. "And you wanted to waste your operational talent to be a DOJ prosecutor."

Faraday blushed. "But we'll still be in the air by the time Metz is scheduled to take off," she pointed out. "We need someone who is already on the ground in Paris."

"Sobieski's field operative would be perfect, but the DGSE probably still has her trapped in the Polish embassy, cut off from communication." Or worse, he reflected.

"CIA probably has assets in Paris."

Carlton nodded. "Right idea. Wrong agency. Even if the DDI has vetted Sobieski's intel, CIA isn't up to speed on this operationally. Thundercloud is the FBI legat in Paris. He's been brought into the loop on the Euroil contract by now and he already managed to get Sobieski out of France."

Faraday frowned. "The Bureau doesn't have jurisdiction to conduct ops outside U.S. borders, Carlton. Foreign intelligence ops are reserved to CIA. You know that."

Carlton stared at her, astonished. "Saudi is about to unleash petroeconomic devastation on the U.S. and you're concerned about jurisdiction?" He shot back. He was getting the distinct impression that the FBI, CIA, and DOJ were all on different sides. "There are only two sides in the War on Terror, Gana. Good and evil. Us and the enemy. This is a war, not a law school exam."

"It may not be a law school exam, but it is the law," replied Faraday, indignant.

"And we took an oath to protect the American people. We're bound by that first. We would never have gotten Sobieski's intel if I hadn't violated jurisdiction by investigating Eche's case or if Sobieski hadn't gone rogue."

"It's illegal, Carlton," replied Faraday, standing her ground.

No wonder they called her the Iron Lady, Carlton reflected. "*Technically* illegal. But the reason for that illegality does not apply here. The reason the FBI and CIA have separate jurisdictions is so CIA doesn't spy on Americans. What we're talking about is an FBI agent legally in a foreign country to provide a first line of defense against terrorism aimed at our borders." He paused. "9-11 taught us that we have to share intel between agencies. That means sharing resources in emergencies. I think this qualifies, don't you?"

Faraday stared back at him, unswayed. "You may want to risk your career. Not me."

He clenched his jaw tight. That's what this was about? Her career? Just like when she applied to transfer to DOJ. Just like when she forced Edison to kick him off the *Hassan* case.

Carlton glared at her, dumbfounded. "The U.S. economy is about to be laid to waste and you're worried about your career?" He shouted.

She sidestepped the question. "Of course I want to stop the contract. But I want to do it legally."

"So do I. If you know how it can be done on time, I'm all ears."

She remained silent.

"That's what I thought." Carlton shifted in his seat. He was in charge of the operation, but he couldn't order Faraday to violate jurisdictional rules. And he could not give orders to Thundercloud, an FBI agent. He needed her help. Somehow, he had to convince her. A moment of reflection made him realize that he was using the wrong argument.

"You're right, Gana. It's jurisdictionally illegal," he stated calmly. "Is that what you're going to tell a Special Congressional Investigation Committee? That you failed to prevent a devastating attack on the U.S. economy because the FBI lacked proper jurisdiction? How do you think your career will survive that? Look at what proper jurisdiction accomplished before 9-11, with the FBI and CIA not sharing domestic and foreign intel because of the arbitrary jurisdictional wall. The American people don't care about jurisdiction in a terrorist emergency. They want their government to protect them from terrorists trying to wipe them out and they couldn't care less which government acronym does it."

Faraday paused, staring at him, then slipped out her telephone and dialed the main FBI switchboard. It connected her to the Paris embassy seconds later.

"This is FBI Special Agent in Charge Faraday in DC." She gave the operator her FBI code. "I need to speak with FBI legat Thundercloud. It's an emergency." She strained to hear the voice on the other end over the angry car horns protesting Spiro's aggressive racecar moves. "No, not when he wakes up. Right now. I don't give a damn what time it is!" *Daam.* "Do it or you'll be answering a switchboard in Kabul!" She shouted, murmuring an expletive.

"Thank God you're on our side," said Carlton, smiling wryly while she waited for Thundercloud to get on the line. "So. How *did* you convince Edison to take me off the *Hassan* case?"

Faraday paused, telephone pressed against her ear. "He was having an affair," she replied, handing him the telephone.

"Thundercloud? It's Carlton. Sorry to wake you, but Faraday has an op for you. I'll explain it and she can authorize it. Here is what we need."

59 FALCON

U.S. Government Hangar
Charles de Gaulle Airport (CDG)
Roissy, France
5:03 AM

Thundercloud and his deputy, Special Agent Benjamin Kim, boarded an FBI Cessna Citation X jet in the U.S. government hangar at Charles de Gaulle airport outside Paris. They remained silent as the pilot increased power to the twin turbofan engines and inched the jet out of the hangar onto the tarmac. Once the tail cleared the hangar, the pilot turned the aircraft to starboard, proceeded past the airport's numerous general aviation hangars, each marked with a large number. At this early hour, the Citation was the only aircraft on the general aviation tarmac.

Thundercloud gazed out of his oval port side window. Dawn had not broken, yet a mile away, the commercial sector of the airport was a hive of activity, abuzz with preparations for another busy day, illuminated in the deep yellow glow of sodium lights. Turning to a starboard window, he could see the brightly illuminated façades of the hangars, the narrow spaces in between shrouded in total darkness.

"Five more," announced Kim, counting down the number of hangars. This was his first real covert mission, a fact underscored by his jittery legs.

Not so for Thundercloud, who waited calmly until the Citation reached Hangar Fifteen. "Begin now," he directed the pilot.

The pilot increased power to the engines, then decreased it by half. He repeated the same sequence twice before jerking the aircraft to a halt. He alternated the sequence on each engine with the wheel brakes set tight, prohibiting the plane from moving forward despite the roaring thrust. Finally, he shut off all of the aircraft's running lights, then its interior lights.

"Control, this is U.S. government Citation One-Oh-Three taxiing on the general aviation tarmac," he announced to ground control, patching the communication through the PA in the cabin for Thundercloud and Kim's benefit. "We're experiencing some type of malfunction with our main power unit. I think it can be fixed by shutting down and restarting. Should take about five minutes. Over."

"U.S. Citation One-Oh-Three, this is control. Understood. Keep us updated. Over."

"U.S. Citation One-Oh-Three. Roger that, control. Out." The pilot shut down all power.

Thundercloud opened the exterior hatch, extended the retractable stairs, stepped down to the tarmac with Kim in tow. Even at this pre-dawn hour, the summer air was balmy. Both walked away from the jet toward the space between the nearest two hangars, then turned back toward the aircraft, as though waiting for the pilot to fix whatever problem he was experiencing. The jet's interior and exterior lights blinked on.

As soon as the pilot emerged a few seconds later and opened a small panel on the underside of the aft portion of the fuselage, Thundercloud dissolved into the darkness between the two hangars, leaving Kim on his own.

He did not have much time. After their allotted five minutes, an *Aéroports de Paris* security team would be sent to investigate.

Despite his urge to run, Thundercloud walked down the dark path. Like the U.S. government hangar, Hangar Fifteen should have a utility door on its left side. Before his eyes adjusted to the darkness, his left leg slammed into an oil drum blocking the path. He let out a low grunt, went around it, kept walking.

Still no sight of the side door. Could this hangar be different, he wondered. If so, he would have to walk down the other side of the hangar. By that time, the airport security team would have been dispatched.

Thundercloud continued onward. Five feet. Ten feet. Twenty feet farther, he found the door.

He slipped on a pair of surgical gloves - it would not do to leave fingerprints on this job - then turned the door handle and pulled.

It was padlocked.

Not wanting to risk attracting attention by using his penlight, Thundercloud leaned close to the padlock and examined it with his fingers. It was heavy and crude. He smiled. Crude meant easy to open.

He removed a set of keys from his pocket and slid a lock pick out from what looked like a switchblade car key. He closed his eyes. People too often relied on their eyes to do work better suited to the touch, he knew. Thundercloud carefully inserted the pick into the keyhole, moved the lock pick around, slowly, gently, without forcing, feeling its progress. Sweat beaded on his forehead. Little by little, the metal rod slid into the lock. Once it reached the end, Thundercloud moved it to the left, then to the right.

The lock clicked open.

He unhooked the padlock, moved to open the door, hesitated.

It should not be so simple. He felt the edges of the door, smiling again when his fingers touched the contour of an alarm sensor. He removed his penlight, unscrewed its tiny bulb, exhaled half a breath to minimize his movements. He pressed the exposed battery onto the alarm sensor with one hand while turning the door handle and gently pushing it in with his leg, hoping the change in voltage would not set off the alarm as long as the electric circuit remained unbroken.

No horn. No flashing lights.

The alarm could be silent, of course, but there was no time to worry about that. He would have to chance it.

Thundercloud dragged the penlight along the sensor into the hangar, closed the door, wiped the sweat from his face, turned.

Sitting under dim security lights in the center of the cavernous structure was a sleek Dassault Mystère-Falcon 7X transcontinental business jet. Its tapered fuselage was painted white between bright blue wings. Any doubt that he was in the wrong hangar evaporated as soon as he gazed at the Euroil logo on the jet's white tail: a blue 'E' styled to look like an oil derrick, surrounded by red stars.

* * *

Special Agent Kim stood on the tarmac, facing the supposedly crippled Citation. He felt his heart beating fast, nervously shifted his weight from leg to leg. Sweat trickled down his chest, drenched his underarms. The stench of kerosene added nausea to the mix.

He soon spotted a white Renault van with dome lights ablaze racing down the tarmac.

His sweat turned cold.

It was heading straight toward him.

* * *

Thundercloud walked to the Falcon's front landing gear, examined its wheel assembly. Definitely not as crude as the door padlock, but he was prepared. The trapped heat of the sealed hangar had triggered sauna-like perspiration, reminding him of the sweat lodges of his people. First taking care to wipe his brow, he then removed a cigarette-sized box from his jacket pocket, unspooled a length of det cord, started wrapping it around the thick metal strut above the twin tires.

* * *

Kim retreated into the shadows between the two hangars as the Renault screeched to a halt a dozen yards away. Two uniformed security personnel wearing sidearms stepped out, examined the Citation. They were early, probably had not much else to do at this early hour, thought Kim, feeling his pulse quicken. The pilot had retracted the staircase, shut the door, and restarted the engines, now screaming at a high pitch.

One of the guards walked to the nose of the jet and waved her arms at the pilot, indicating for him to open the door.

A minute later, Kim watched the retractable staircase extend to the tarmac.

This is not good.

* * *

Thundercloud would only get one chance. He verified that the det cord was wrapped tightly around the front landing strut. After wiping the sweat from around his eyes, he moved away from the aircraft's nose, walking backwards in slow steps, paying out a thin line of cord in front of him. He did not want to be anywhere near the jet when he triggered the detonator. He glanced up. The Falcon's nose was still too close. He continued stepping back, half-crouched to avoid breaking the cord tethered to the front landing gear.

* * *

Kim held his breath, felt the nervous sweat plastering his shirt to his back, waited for something to happen. The two guards had climbed into the Citation. They would soon discover that neither of the two passengers that customs had cleared for departure were on board.

The twin engines continued to scream at high pitch, as though the pilot was unable to ratchet down their power.

Suddenly, Kim spotted the guards walking down the jet's staircase. Around the tail. Straight toward him.

This is not good.

Where the heck is Thundercloud?

* * *

Thundercloud triggered the electronic detonator. The explosive-laden det cord combusted too quickly for his eyes to follow the bright flash arcing away from him along the concrete floor toward the jet. It burned so hot and fast that it melted through the landing gear's four-inch thick high-tensile metal like so much warm butter on its first circuit around the pillar, completing its ten circuits a millisecond later.

Destabilized by the molten metal, the top portion of the front landing strut slipped off its severed base. With its only support gone, the entire front end of the majestic Euroil Falcon unceremoniously crashed to the hangar floor with such force that Thundercloud thought that the entire structure would crumble down on him.

* * *

The senior guard stopped less than a foot away from Kim, extended a gloved hand.

"*Passeport*," he demanded, scowling, clearly displeased that two foreigners - American government officials, no less - were running amok on his tarmac.

Kim felt a loud vibration in his feet and legs, as though the tarmac had been hit by an earthquake. The Citation's roaring engines drowned out all other sounds. He swallowed dryly. With any luck, the guards would attribute the tremors to the ailing aircraft.

Kim handed the man his diplomatic passport. Where the heck was Thundercloud?

The junior guard stepped forward, fixed Kim with a suspicious stare, jutted her angular chin forward. "*L'autre passager*. Where is the other passenger?" She demanded in a heavy French accent.

Kim stared back at her. That was the question he had feared. What could he say to buy Thundercloud more time? He had to say *something*. His mouth was dry, his tongue felt like sandpaper. "He's-"

"Right here," said Thundercloud, emerging from the shadows with an embarrassed grin, zipping up his fly. "*Pipi*," he said, gesturing to the next hangar up with his thumb, adding a Gallic shrug for good measure. He handed his passport to the junior guard, who seemed convinced by this very natural explanation.

"I am afraid that I have bad news, gentlemen," announced her senior colleague, grimacing.

Kim's relief evaporated. *This is not good.*

"I cannot allow your pilot to take off. Your aircraft is unsafe."

Ten minutes later, Thundercloud and Kim were speeding back to the U.S. embassy, with Kim behind the wheel. Either no one had yet discovered the vandalized Euroil jet or they had not tied it to the two U.S. embassy personnel.

In the passenger seat, Thundercloud terminated his cell phone call.

"The embassy just finished reserving all available private transcontinental jets for rent in France and all of the remaining seats on today's Saudia Airlines flights to Riyadh - using randomly generated names, passport and telephone numbers, of course. Metz could leave from another country, but it would take time." He allowed himself his first genuine smile since their departure from the embassy less than two hours ago. "Metz isn't going anywhere anytime soon."

* * *

Behind drawn curtains in the plush rear compartment of a black Maybach sedan, Metz ended his cell phone call, stunned. The blood had drained from his face, turning it from merely pallid to deathly white.

Seated beside him, E.U. foreign minister de Ville noticed the expression on the diminutive CEO's face. "*Qu'est ce qu'il y a?*" He asked. What is there?

Metz turned to de Ville, glowering. "The Euroil jet at Charles de Gaulle was sabotaged. Its front landing gear was severed, like a tree trunk." He motioned with his hand sawing his forearm. "Even though the Falcon is manufactured in France, it will take two days to repair. I was also informed that there are no long range jets available for hire in France and that all of the seats on today's flights to Riyadh have been booked."

"It cannot be a coincidence," concluded de Ville, nervously turning his family crest ring. Colonel Hulot of the DGSE had not seen Sobieski or his deputy emerge for two days. He squinted. "The Poles must have alerted the Americans. *Les salauds.*" The bastards. How they could have done it without leaving the Polish embassy during its communications blackout, he had no idea. Nor did he care. The damage was done. "Why can't the Poles just do as they are told?" He hissed. "We let them into the E.U. They should be grateful and stop causing problems."

Despite the dire news, the impish Metz could not suppress a grin. "It does not matter. By the time they figure out we are leaving from Brussels instead of Paris, we will be long gone."

The Maybach drove into Zavantem Airport's general aviation zone, deposited de Ville, Metz, and their two assistants in front of a boxy aircraft hangar. Inside was a Euroil Falcon 7X identical to the one at Charles de Gaulle airport, except that this one's front landing strut was very much intact. Metz stepped up the stairs into the cabin first, toting a boxy attaché case containing two copies of the voluminous contract. De Ville strode up the staircase next, followed by the men's assistants.

Scant minutes after the four passengers strapped into the glove-soft leather seats, the pilot opened up the Falcon's trio of rear-mounted Pratt & Whitney Canada PW307A turbofans, hurtling the sleek white and blue jet down the runway with 19,000 pounds of thrust. The aircraft swept into the overcast sky above the Belgian capital, arced Southeast.

The PA system clicked on.

"*Bonjour messieurs.* The duration of our flight today will be six hours, four minutes. Our ETA in Riyadh is 4:06PM local time, which is two hours ahead of Brussels time. We will be flying at an altitude of 41,000 feet at Mach 0.8. The weather is clear straight to Riyadh except for some scattered thunderclouds over Southern Greece, which we will remain well above. *Bon voyage.*"

60 ALLY

DARPA Gulfstream
55,000 Feet
Over the Atlantic Ocean
6 hours, 21 minutes to Paris arrival

While the DARPA Gulfstream rocketed toward Paris at full throttle, its three passengers sat huddled around the Spartan conference table. After Carlton changed into a clean set of clothes found on board that fit reasonably well, he and Faraday warded off their exhaustion nursing cups of his jet fuel-grade Navy coffee. Monet opted for his customary Red Bull. Many things had to happen before they reached Paris. Sleep was not one of them.

The onboard telephone trilled.

"The Director and I just met with the Boss and the foreign intel acronyms," announced Thorne, referring to the head of the FBI. "It's not going well. The DNI, DDI, and NSA don't think your plan will work, so they refuse to send a covert ops team into France to round up Euroil's board, fearing a diplomatic crisis."

Carlton could not believe what he was hearing. "A diplomatic crisis?" He exclaimed. "The U.S. economy is about to implode and they're worried about-"

"Stow it and listen, Carlton," Thorne boomed, cutting him off. "The DDI and NSA got intel from inside Saudi confirming that Hakim mounted a coup. They are developing a plan with members of the Saudi Defense Forces loyal to King Fahim to put him back on the throne, but the Boss refuses to green-light their op unless a majority of key allies agree. Right now only a handful are on board. The Secretary of State is pushing hard, but it's going to take some time.

"At the same time, the Boss, joined by the Poles, the Israelis, and the Vatican are doing a full court press to persuade the French president and PM to kill the Euroil contract, but the French are stalling. The bottom line is that the contract will go into effect unless you can stop it from being signed. Don't let me down, Carlton," Thorne growled, hanging up before Carlton could get a word in.

He slumped back in his chair. "FUBAR once again." He turned to Monet. "The eminent domain orders went out?"

"*Oui.* The hardcopies should arrive in a few hours. The emails and faxes have already hit, along with the IOUs," he replied, referring to DOJ's promises to pay for the Euroil shareholder votes owned by U.S. persons, backed by frozen Saudi government assets.

He nodded. "At least that's 350 million shareholder votes in the bag. No word yet from McLean about whether the banks will sell us the 150 million Euroil shares we need to make up a voting majority, but it's still early." His glee abated as he thought about Alexis's condition. No recent updates from her doctor.

Faraday leaned forward. "I hate to spoil the party, but even if we get the votes and shares, we still have no plan for getting into Euroil headquarters."

"What about Thundercloud?" Proposed Monet.

Carlton shook his head. "Thundercloud can pick us up at the airport under diplomatic immunity and drive us to Euroil headquarters, but Gana is right. The DGSE will never let us get a mile from Euroil headquarters. This would be so much easier if the French were working with us instead of against us." Carlton exhaled an exasperated sigh. "So much for a change in administration reversing European anti-Americanism."

Unlike the former French president and PM, the current men in the job were committed socialists, blaming the free market system for their country's and the rest of the world's economic ills. That was the popular cover story. The truth was that they, like Gaullists such as de Ville, wanted to put an end to American economic and military supremacy.

"I've been thinking about that," said Monet, lighting a Gitane cigarette, immediately crushing it out under Faraday's withering scowl, making Carlton abandon his hopes of torching a cigar. "Five hundred thousand Saudi immigrants for ten years is five million. It will devastate Europe."

Carlton frowned. Immigration to Europe was the least of their problems. And Monet was sounding like a French xenophobe. "It's just over one percent of the E.U.'s population," he replied, knowing he was using the same argument as Wolf with Metz and de Ville. "I'm a lot more worried about global economic devastation and the neutering of the Vatican and Israel."

Monet shook his head. "Because you are looking at it from an American perspective, not from the European side. America's free market economy and melting pot social philosophy make it easy to assimilate immigrants. Europe by nature is homogeneous and its economy is so congealed with regulations that it can't even grow jobs for Europeans, much less Muslim immigrants. In America, Muslims can become Americans first, Muslims second. Not in Europe."

Carlton listened in silence, deciding to see where Monet was going. It was a long flight, after all.

"After 9-11, the Italian prime minister said that we were in a war of civilizations that Western civilization would win because it was the best. Commentators howled in politically-correct protest. I think he was right. But he did not explain why Western civilization was best: freedom. But why is it free? Because its institutions are based on Judeo-Christian principles rooted in individual free will. Europe does not even try to assimilate Muslim immigrants because any serious attempt would require Europe to fully embrace those Judeo-Christian foundations. This is not theoretical. It was a big debate at the time the E.U. constitution was adopted. Europe even refused merely to acknowledge those foundations in the preamble, so terrified of Judeo-Christianity it has become ever since the French Revolution."

"Since when are you so religious?" Asked Carlton, surprised at the French-American's argument.

"I'm not. I'm an atheist. But even atheists cannot deny that Judeo-Christian thought and values are the basis for European civilization, leading to the Renaissance and then to the Enlightenment, which has been more successful than any in history. Instead of assimilating Muslim immigrants through schooling, employment and community participation stressing those values - not the Jewish or Christian religions but their values - Europe marginalizes them while caving to their radicals' demands. France bans headscarves and reserves its few jobs for the non-Arab, non-Muslim French. England is empowering *sharia* courts to hear disputes among Muslims, outside British courts.

The Dutch even kicked out their Muslim parliamentarian Ayaan Hirsi Ali for pointing out the error of their ways.

"Islamists are the ones assimilating Europeans who do not know who they are anymore, converting them to jihadism. Abu Hassan's sleeper agents in the U.S. were radicalized *Europeans*, not Arabs. The negative European birthrate is accelerating the effect. A flood of radical Saudis combined with the cutoff of diplomatic recognition of Israel and the termination of the Vatican's sovereignty might very well achieve what many in Europe believe the Muslims have sought ever since Sobieski's ancestor kicked the Turks out of Vienna in 1683: the reconquest of Europe and its transformation into Eurabia."

Carlton shifted in his seat, unsettled by Monet's rant, mystified by how it had any bearing on the crisis they faced. "De Ville, the French government and the European foreign ministers taking bribes from Yassin's fund seem more interested in the money and European influence that Euroil will generate than in Saudi immigration, radical or otherwise."

"*Oui*. Because the *grosses têtes* - the big heads - in Washington are using the wrong argument." He opened his mouth, arched his eyebrows, stretched out his palms in Gallic fashion to underscore his point. "Of *course* the French president and *premier ministre* want Euroil to get the contract. It's a French company. By nationalizing Euroil with a simple legislative vote, the French government would become a top oil player. The contract would help win France's power struggle with Germany inside the E.U. And it will transform the euro into the global oil currency. Arguing with France about a Euroil monopoly and the destruction of the dollar is a dead end."

Faraday leaned forward. "What would you suggest?"

Monet turned to her, puzzled by both his interlocutors' lack of comprehension. "Mass radical Islamist immigration will end the French - and European - way of life."

Carlton gazed at Monet, reflecting that his argument might be a more powerful one to the French than one based on economics, even if was a bit extreme. "Even if you are right, the French president and PM are now so entrenched that they probably won't back down even if President Douglass used that argument."

Monet lifted his index finder. "Except that the French president and PM are not the only French politicians with power."

"Who are we missing?" Asked Faraday, eager to move from political and cultural theory to practical facts.

"The French interior minister, Nicolas Fouché." *Foo-shay.* "He is responsible for French domestic security - a cross between the FBI Director and the Secretaries of Homeland Security and Interior. He is a descendant of Napoléon's first Minister of Police in 1799. And from what I hear, he is just as ruthless. Fouché has been cracking down hard on radical Islamist terror cells. He is also a vocal critic of the French president and PM. Many say he will run for president. I think they may have kept him out of the Euroil loop."

"Sounds like a potential ally," said Faraday. "Maybe he can get us into Euroil headquarters."

Carlton sat up. "At this stage, I'd be willing to learn French and smoke Gitanes if I thought it might help."

"We only have six hours," Faraday reminded them, checking her watch. "How do we get in touch with Fouché?" She asked Monet, who turned to Carlton for help.

"The FBI Director and the Bear would be able to get hold of him, but with the political wrangling going on, it would take too much time," said Carlton, running a hand through his hair. "We need someone in France who has access to Fouché."

"The U.S. ambassador would have to get approval from Washington first, so he's out," said Faraday.

They looked at each other for a moment and in unison announced the obvious choice. "Thundercloud."

Faraday picked up the telephone and dialed. She hung up two minutes later.

"Thundercloud says he's been in meetings with Fouché and that he's responsive as heck. He'll deliver our request and Sobieski's transcripts to him personally inside the hour."

"Aces," said Carlton, smiling for the first time in a long while.

It did not last long.

"Uh-oh," Monet muttered behind his silver laptop, his baby face creasing into an acid wince. "*Aie.*" Ouch.

Carlton had seen that look before, knew it did not herald anything positive. "What?"

"I accessed Europe's air traffic control system. I didn't think I'd get through, so I used the jet's DARPA browser. It punched through the firewalls like *papier de toilette.*" Toilet paper. The computer expert looked genuinely perturbed.

Carlton nodded, no longer surprised by DARPA's back-door net access. "And?"

"A Euroil Falcon took off at precisely 9AM this morning, headed for Riyadh."

Carlton straightened. "Thundercloud disabled the jet. He said it was the only one in France. How could Euroil repair it so quickly?"

Monet looked up, grimacing. "They didn't. The jet took off from Brussels. We got the *time* of departure right but the *point* of departure wrong."

"Aw, hell." Carlton stared through a large oval window at the starry night sky, felt the frustration well up inside him with no avenue of release, exacerbated by his inability to learn anything further about Alexis's condition. "What is Metz's ETA in Riyadh?"

Monet glanced at his screen, performed a quick calculation. "One hour after we arrive in Paris. At least it gives us time to get into Euroil."

Carlton leaned forward. "Can you show me his flight trajectory?"

Monet typed in a few commands, swiveled the computer toward his boss. Carlton studied the curved red line linking Brussels to Riyadh, superimposed on a map of Western Europe, the Central Mediterranean, and the Western Middle East. A flashing red dot marked Metz's current position over the heel of Italy, South of Taranto. A box next to it contained the aircraft's tail number and GPS location.

Carlton could not think of a single legal maneuver to delay Metz. He switched to military mode. "What is our closest air base?"

Monet typed in more commands. "Aviano, near Venice."

Carlton moved his finger Northwest to the City of the Doges. "Send Metz's tail number, position, and trajectory to the DDI at Langley and Saunders at Bolling Air Force Base. Along with this," he directed, scribbling on a memo pad before sliding it to Monet.

Faraday peered at the note, glared at Carlton, apoplectic. "Have you lost your mind? We can't shoot down a civilian jet!"

61 DON

Castel McLean
Beverly Hills, California
7:03 PM

McLean's anxiety crested to a flood tide; more debilitating than the gnawing frustration and utter failure he felt after his moribund conference call with the bankers. He had not eaten, slept, or showered in over twenty four hours, surviving on Cuban cigars and espressos that Maxfield brought in every hour on the hour. Even the latest positive update on Claire's condition had not lifted his spirits. He stank of sweat, his stomach churned.

Seated at his glass slab desk in semi-darkness amid a haze of cigar smoke, he had argued with each banker one-on-one throughout the day. Out of earshot from their brethren, a few had agreed to sell their Euroil shares to DOJ, including bankers from Britain, Japan, and most notably China, whose government was terrified at the prospect of a worthless dollar decimating the value of the country's accumulated $1 trillion in U.S. Treasury bonds. But they collectively owned only 35 million of the 150 million shares Carlton needed. For all of his arguments and pleas, the Western bank holders of the remaining 115 million Euroil shares gave McLean the identical reception they had during the ill-fated conference call: total intransigence.

Still stunned and now thoroughly disgusted, McLean shifted from his business banking contacts to his personal banking friendships. These bankers faced more than a simple investment risk in the contract between Prince Hakim and Euroil. One was Cardinal Giovanni Benedetti, the former head of the Institute for Works of Religion in Rome, commonly known as the Vatican Bank, who was now retired. The other was the great nephew of Abraham Cohen, a close family friend whose life McLean's father, then serving as a U.S. Army medic, had saved during the liberation of the Dachau Nazi concentration camp at the end of

World War II. The great nephew was a rising star at the second largest Israeli bank.

The good news was that both were eager to help.

The bad news was that neither had much ability to do so. The Vatican possessed vast moral authority, political influence, real estate holdings, and art treasures, but contrary to common belief, held surprisingly little liquid weath with which to influence global banking decisions. The Israeli bank had a large capital base and Cohen's great nephew had the ear of the Israeli Finance Minister, but neither it nor any other Israeli bank owned any appreciable amount of Euroil stock. Both pledged their help, which McLean knew was not a hollow promise, but doubted they could accomplish much.

He was at an impasse. Of sorts.

McLean did not have to think about his next move. He knew exactly who to call. Neither a business contact nor a personal friend, but a powerful figure who was far more than a simple acquaintance. Yet the churning sensation in his stomach felt nothing like the solution he knew the man could possibly provide. He continued to stare at his desktop telephone, immobile, unblinking.

McLean did not want to make this call. He had promised Carlton, his loyal friend, the man who had saved him and Claire, who had risked his life to prevent him from going down this path, that he would not make such a call. How could he go back on his word, betray Carlton's trust? His personal honor dictated that he could not.

Yet the stakes were too high, more important even than his personal honor. He had *America*'s honor to uphold, not only as a citizen who had reaped so much from her blessings, but as an appointed agent of the Justice Department. After all, Carlton had asked for his help, he reasoned. He could have asked someone else, but Carlton had asked him, not in spite of his connections, but because of them.

All of them.

As hard as he tried, McLean could find no other solution to the task Carlton had entrusted to him. He wiped a sweaty palm on his coffee-stained baby blue Charvet shirt, lifted the handset, dialed, then waited for the electronic signal to wind its way to the Southern European countryside.

"*Pronto*," a man answered, trying to suppress a yawn, unsuccessfully.

"*Don Forza, per favore*."

The person recognized McLean's American accent. "Please, who is calling?"

"Max McLean."

The name registered immediately. "*Si signore. Subito*." Yes, sir. Right away.

Don Forza had officially retired from the *cosa nostra* several years ago. Yet retirement for a mafia *don* was not the same as for a corporate CEO, especially now that the Sicilian mafia had once again begun a springtime bloom after suffering a long winter of government crackdowns in the 1990s. More than ever, the current *dons* and their *uomini di rispetto* - men of respect - sought Forza's esteemed wisdom. They came in pilgrimage with their *soldati* - soldiers - to his *palazzo* high atop Mount Pellegrino in the arid countryside of Palermo, showing the *cosa nostra*'s elder statesman respect by allowing him to wet his beak in their lucrative deals. As a result, although *Don* Forza no longer wielded power, he continued to exercise vast influence in business and politics. Since the reach of the *cosa nostra*'s black hand extended far beyond Sicily's borders, so too did *Don* Forza's influence.

A heavily accented voice came on a few minutes later, elderly but strong. "*Don* Maximilliano. It has been a long time."

McLean shuddered at Forza's use of the honorific, a simple statement signifying a great deal: *Don* Forza considered McLean the heir to his father Giancarlo Innocenti's *cosa nostra* ties even if he had no part in its affairs, including the responsibility to adhere by its severe rules. "*Don* Forza. Please forgive the hour of my call."

"*Per piacere, Don* McLean. Your father was my *padrino*," replied Forza, his elderly voice dripping with eagerness to draw McLean into a favor. My godfather. "For you, I am available at all times. What can I do for you?"

62 INTERCEPTION

31st Fighter Wing
Aviano NATO Air Base
Pordenone, Italy
11:33 AM

Stretched between the towns of Aviano and Pordenone at the base of the Italian Alps, Aviano Air Base served as headquarters for the 16th Air Force and home for its 31st Fighter Wing, including the 555th 'Triple Nickel' Fighter Squadron. Although most of the Triple Nickels had been deployed to the Middle East, several members remained to conduct U.S. and NATO operations in the European Southern Region, most recently in Libya.

Alerted to their mission only ten minutes earlier, USAF Major Milo 'Cigar' Vanovich and Major Sophia 'Dallas' Starr were now fully briefed. They strode out of the ready-room under the 31st Fighter Wing's crest and motto - *Return With Honor* - dressed in flight suits, sporting mirrored sunglasses, carrying helmets under their arms.

The pilots climbed into the cockpits of their flat gray F/A-16/CG-DG Fighting Falcons under the blazing sun. With the help of their ground crews, they strapped into their harnesses, closed their bubble canopies, proceeded through their preflight checklists. Seconds later, they ignited their single Pratt & Whitney F-100-PW-229 engines, taxied into position at the end of the designated runway. After receiving clearance from the tower, Cigar and Dallas lit up their afterburners, roared down the runway under 27,000 pounds of thrust each, rocketed into the skies of Italy.

"Base Control, this is Interceptor. Wheels up. Requesting verified target bearing and range. Over."

"Interceptor, this is Base Control. Target is range 7-1-2 nautical miles, bearing 1-2-6, heading 1-3-5, speed 6-0-3 knots, altitude 41,000 feet. Over."

"Roger, Base Control. Climbing to 50,000. Over and out."

Cigar and Dallas placed the Earth to their backs, shot vertically into the now cobalt blue sky above the Adriatic Sea, then arced Southeast toward the Ionian Sea, accelerating to twice the speed of sound.

Despite its great distance, their target was already on the F-16s' APG radar scopes, moving at less than half their speed.

One hour later, Cigar and Dallas were ten nautical miles due North of their target, well over international waters, as their instructions dictated.

Dallas was the first to spot the Euroil Falcon's silhouette shining below and ahead, on her port side.

"Cigar, I have visual contact, over."

"Roger that, Dallas. Now I've got it too. You take the high road and I'll parallel park. Maintain radio silence with target until in position."

"That's a rog."

Cigar rolled to starboard, pitched his needle nose down to match the white and blue Falcon's altitude. He sidled up to its port side, easing back on his throttle, matching speeds. The corporate jet was unarmed and no match for the F-16's speed and agility.

Just to be safe in case the Euroil pilot tried something stupid, Dallas remained 300 feet above the jet's 'six'.

Cigar switched to the air traffic control frequency while jamming the Euroil jet's long-range communications. "Euroil Falcon, this is the United States Air Force. You are requested to follow us to base, over."

"What the hell are you doing coming up on me like that?" Demanded the Falcon's outraged pilot in a heavy French accent, sprinkling in more than a few curse words for emphasis. "*Vous êtes dingue*?" Dang. "Are you crazy?"

"I repeat. You are requested to follow us back to Aviano Air Base."

"Why would I do that? This is an important corporate flight."

"You are suspected of terrorist activities."

"*What*? Are you crazy? You have the wrong jet."

"You can complain to the base commander once we have landed."

"And if I refuse?"

"You will be shot down," replied Cigar, bluffing uncomfortably. The U.S. Air Force was not in the business of shooting down unarmed corporate jets and he resented even pretending otherwise.

Cigar was sweating heavily under his jumpsuit, feeling the need to itch, far more comfortable engaging multiple armed enemy aircraft than this type of mission. He cursed whatever genius up the military or political food chain had authorized the op, but knew that person had to be very high up to be able to authorize it. Which meant it was extremely important. Unless they were wrong, of course.

He hoped that the combination of his warning, side cannon, serrated load of air-to-air missiles, and the radar image of Dallas's F-16 on the pilot's 'six' would prove sufficiently convincing while he waited for the pilot's reply with growing impatience.

"Very well. I will follow you to Aviano. But I can assure you, there will be hell to pay."

Cigar exhaled a deep breath of relief, banked to port. The Euroil Falcon followed a few seconds later.

The Euroil Falcon touched down on one of the Aviano runways over an hour later. A bright yellow truck fitted with a large sign that read 'Follow Me' met the aircraft, led it to an open area near two parked Military Police Humvees. As soon as the truck stopped, the Euroil pilot did the same, spooled down the Falcon's engines.

The only person dressed in a civilian suit on the entire base hopped out of the lead Humvee under the beating sun. Special Agent Kim jestured for the pilot to open the door, then stepped up the short flight of steps and boarded the aircraft with two heavily armed MPs in tow.

"Who are you and why has this aircraft been diverted?" Demanded the pilot, placing his arms behind his head.

Kim flashed his badge. "Special Agent Kim. FBI. You can put your hands down, sir. You're not under arrest." He turned to the main cabin, looking for the passengers. They were probably hiding in the head, he thought.

The pilot put his arms down as Kim opened the bathroom door. "Why has this aircraft-"

Kim swiveled, cut him off with a raised hand. "Where is Ludovic Metz?"

The pilot squinted. "Who?"

"Ludovic Metz. The CEO of Euroil," replied Kim, feeling the pit of his stomach fall away.

"I told your crazy pilots that they had the wrong plane. I'm not carrying any passengers. I demand an apology and the payment of fuel costs by-"

Kim blocked out the pilot's litany, stared at the empty passenger cabin and bathroom.

They had been had.

* * *

Euroil Falcon 2 hours, 9 minutes to arrival in Riyadh

High above Egypt, Ludovic Metz picked up the Falcon's satellite telephone receiver.

"Please forgive the interruption, *monsieur le directeur*, but I thought that you would want to know," announced the Euroil aviation fleet director. "The Falcon that left Brussels at 9AM as you instructed was intercepted by the U.S. Air Force and forced to land at Aviano Air Base in Italy. They were looking for you."

"*Merci*," said Metz, hanging up. He allowed himself his second smile of the day.

"What now?" Asked de Ville.

Metz explained.

"*Les salauds*," spat de Ville, nervously twisting his family crest ring. The bastards.

Metz was happy with his subterfuge, but far from content with the situation. If that megalomaniac Prince Hakim had listened to him and not insisted on making a grand spectacle of signing the contract with him in Riyadh in front of the Arab press, the contract would have already been signed by now, its signature pages exchanged by simple faxes or emails, originals by overnight couriers. Hakim's monumental ego was putting the entire enterprise at risk, yet Metz had no choice in the matter.

He sighed, glanced at his watch. Two more hours and they would be in Riyadh, the contract signed. Euroil would become the largest energy company in the world, Metz the most powerful player in the private oil business, and France a global oil power.

Only two more hours.

63 APPROACHES

DARPA Gulfstream
2 hours, 3 minutes to arrival in Paris

Carlton chomped down on his unlit Bully, picked up the warbling handset.

"I've got bad news and really bad news," announced Thundercloud. "The Euroil jet was intercepted and forced to land at Aviano."

"That sounds like good news."

"Metz was not on board."

Carlton grimaced as he hit the speakerphone button so all could hear. "How is that possible? It left Brussels at 9AM, exactly the time Wolf told us Metz was supposed to leave."

"He must have used another plane."

Monet turned to his computer, accessed European air traffic control.

Carlton slumped back into his seat, felt the icy tentacles of failure squeeze him. As though the world was dropping away from under his black boots into the 55,000 foot void below.

Monet peered at the screen, winced. "*Merde*. A Euroil Falcon took off from Brussels at 8:02AM. I only searched for Euroil aircraft leaving at 9:00AM and later. I didn't - it never occurred to me to check for earlier flights." He looked down, unable to mask the humiliation spreading across his pallid face. "I screwed up. It's my fault."

Carlton wanted to tear his own hair out, but he was not interested in apportioning blame. What he wanted was to fix the problem. He took a deep breath, clapped a hand on Monet's shoulder.

"Don't beat yourself up, Henri. We're all doing our best with very little. If DDI Forbes had authorized the op to grab Euroil's board, the contract would already be a distant memory." He paused. "Where is Metz's plane now?"

Monet gazed at the new target's trajectory on his screen, his spirits lifted by Carlton's reaction. "If he is aboard the jet that left Brussels at 8:02AM, he's over Egypt, South of Alexandria."

"ETA?"

Monet hit a few keys. "In Riyadh within two hours."

Carlton checked his watch. "About the same time we arrive in Paris." He exhaled loudly. "Forget getting to Euroil headquarters. Metz and Hakim could sign and announce the contract before we even get off the plane."

Faraday stood to refill her coffee mug, then Carlton's. "Maybe Saunders can intercept Metz's plane like he did with the decoy."

Carlton shook his head. "We can't intercept a civilian aircraft in Egypt's airspace without their government's permission, especially now that their political situation is in such turmoil. Even if we obtained it, Metz would be over another country by then. But you do have a point." He turned to Monet. "Send Metz's tail number, trajectory and position to the DDI and Saunders anyway, just in case they think of something."

"I don't want to rub salt in open wounds, Carlton, but there is more," continued Thundercloud, his words coming through the speakerphone in an almost apologetic tone.

Carlton had forgotten that the FBI legat was still on the phone. "Let me guess. Fouché is on vacation in the South of France," he replied with a dark smirk.

"No. I delivered your request and the intel to him, personally. That was two hours ago. He said that he'd get back to me, but I have not heard or been able to get in touch with him."

"Let's hope it's because he's a slow reader." Carlton checked his watch. "We only have two hours left. Keep trying."

Carlton hit the disconnect button, stood, noticed his reflection in a small mirror.

He had seen better looking corpses. His hair was disheveled, skin sallow, chin stubbled, and eyes bloodshot, tugged down by dark bags of exhaustion and worry.

Monet's laptop beeped. Carlton turned, observed worry spread over the man's boyish face as he tapped the keyboard. "What now?"

Monet kept his gaze fixed on the screen. "The tracker that Ben-David placed on the Venezuelan bank account just signaled a transaction."

Carlton felt the ball of ice grow in his gut. "And?"

"*Mon Dieu.* It just received a wire transfer of fifty billion dollars. From the Arabian Monetary Agency - the Saudi central bank."

Carlton stared at him, aghast. "Billion, with a 'b'?"

Monet nodded. Faraday drew near.

"I didn't think regular banks accepted transfers that large," said Carlton.

"They don't normally, but- Wait. It just left the account," exclaimed Monet.

"Where did it go?" Asked Faraday.

"Looks like it got transferred to" - Monet peered at the screen - "fifty different accounts. One billion each."

"Can you track them?"

Monet paused. "*Ordinairement, non.*" Ordinarily, no. "But with this DARPA software on steroids, *qui sait*?" Who knows? He launched himself on the keyboard.

"Fifty billion is a lot of dead presidents," commented Carlton. "I hate to imagine what Hakim is up to."

Monet sucked in air through clenched tobacco-stained teeth, looked up from his screen, face ashen. "I can't believe it. The DARPA software -" He paused, collecting himself. "It sliced through the banking system's firewalls just like the air traffic control system."

Carlton rolled his eyes. Ben-David's use of the secret parts of the internet were now old hat. "I don't care about the software, Henri. What's happening with the accounts?"

Monet nodded, peering at the screen. "The dollars in each account are being converted into euros."

"That fits," concluded Faraday.

Carlton cocked his head. He knew there was something wrong here, but not sure what it was.

"It's not a problem if they are converting only a few billion dollars," explained Faraday. "But Henri said the funds were coming from the Saudi central bank, which Hakim now controls. The Saudis amassed nearly a trillion dollars in reserves during the oil price spike. The global downturn and Saudi's ramped up welfare payments melted that down, but if they convert even half of what's left into euros within the space of a day or two, it would tank the dollar."

Carlton recalled McLean's litany of dire predictions. "And if it's done in conjunction with the Euroil contract's shift in the global oil currency from the dollar to the euro..." His voice trailed off.

"Critical mass. A dollar meltdown," concluded Faraday.

Carlton paused, nervously running a hand through his mat of hair, now greasy. He turned to Monet. "Can you pull up Yassin's other accounts?" He asked, referring to the accounts Sobieski's *Agencja* network had uncovered.

Monet pulled up the accounts. "*Voila*. Let's start with the so-called investment fund that Yassin is using to bribe European foreign ministers," he began, typing commands. "*Mon Dieu*. One hundred billion in that one. Distributed to" - he typed in more commands - "one hundred accounts." He scrolled through the remaining accounts on the list. "All of them are converting dollars into euros. And those are only the accounts we know about."

Faraday massaged her gaunt cheeks. "Too much money in a single block to convert at once. They are spreading out their currency trades to execute them more rapidly."

Carlton turned to Monet. "Can you see all the accounts that the Saudi central bank is transferring funds to?"

"With this DARPA software, I could probably tell you the account holders' favorite colors," said Monet, still stunned by the power at his fingertips, going to work.

It gave Carlton an idea. With more than 500 *million* terrorist pages on the internet, it was time to turn the tables and use the net against the terrorists. As Faraday walked down the aisle to the lavatory, he called Ben-David.

"Tracking account transfers is one thing. What you're asking for is something entirely different, Carlton. I might be able to do it," replied the DARPA physicist. "But it requires authorization from way up in the federal stratosphere. Even with that it's probably illegal."

It was. And Carlton knew it. He paused, remembering Judge Flynn's words back at the Yale safehouse.

The Euroil contract is legal.

So was the conversion of hundreds of billions of Saudi dollars into euros. But like the Euroil contract, it was also an act of economic war against the U.S. and the West, a conclusion with which Flynn had concurred.

What Carlton was asking Ben-David to do went far beyond crossing jurisdictional lines, more akin to pole-vaulting over them into illegal territory. Yet CIA had vetted Sobieski's intel, Flynn had agreed that the Euroil contract constituted an act of war, and Monet had shown him the massive currency conversions in progress. For him, that was enough evidence.

Given sufficient time, Carlton would never have made the request without authorization. It went against everything he stood for as a Justice Department lawyer. But he had started down that murky path when he had decided to investigate Grant's program. And this is where it had led him. He had no time left. Faced with a global economic meltdown, he had no choice but to act, do something - anything. If he made a mistake, he would take the blame, but if he was going to err, he would err on the side of the United States.

He took a deep breath.

"You mean illegal like Yassin's attacks on civilians in Iraq, on the HEERP facility and his impending Pearl Harbor attack on the economy?" He was about to add the attack on Ben-David's niece in Tel Aviv, stopped himself.

"You know what I mean, Carlton."

"And you know why it has to be done now, Ash. I'm not hiding anything. You have the same intel I do. We don't have days for legal opinions and formal court approval. We barely have two hours. And you're the only one with the technical capability. If you want, I will take full responsibility in writing on behalf of the Justice Department."

"I'm not one of those, Carlton," snapped Ben-David, irritated. "I'm just pointing out a major legal issue for both Justice *and* DARPA." He exhaled loudly, paused.

Carlton waited anxiously.

"You put your life on the line getting Tesla's formula to me and saving HEERP. I read Sobieski's intel. And I know what Yassin's accounts have funded. That's all the authorization I need. If we sink, we sink together. Let me see what I can do."

"Aces." Carlton hung up.

"What was that all about?" Asked Faraday, returning from the bathroom.

Carlton recalled her alarm over a simple FBI legat op on French soil. That was a jaywalking ticket compared to the violation he was asking Ben-David to commit with him. "You don't want to know," he replied. He was willing to commit this violation, but would not put her at risk.

Faraday frowned, but his expression made it clear she would be unwise to press further. "So what do we do now?" She asked instead.

"Pray for a miracle."

* * *

DARPA Gulfstream
364 miles Northwest of Paris, France

The PA system clicked on. "We are beginning our final approach into Paris Charles de Gaulle airport. ETA thirty five minutes."

The telephone rang.

"You get it," Carlton told Faraday, clenching his teeth. "One more piece of bad news and I'm going to tear this plane apart."

Faraday picked up, listened. "Yes, of course," she replied, locating and reading off a telephone number. "One moment," she said, handing the handset to Carlton.

"It's McLean. How are things on your end?"

The roller coaster crises since the beginning of the flight had nearly made him forget about McLean. "We're about to finish third in a two-horse race, Max. You?"

The fax line trilled.

"Most of the banks refused to sell us their Euroil shares," McLean replied somberly. "We were only able to get 35 million shares."

Carlton's heart sank. Without the remaining 115 million Euroil shares, there was no way for them to unseat Metz as CEO. Now nothing stood between Euroil and Hakim signing the contract. "Bloodsucking bastards. Why not?"

McLean explained.

"Insider trading?" Carlton had not even considered it. "The world economy is about to-"

"You better read this," interrupted Faraday, handing him the first page of the incoming fax.

Carlton scanned the page, still warm in his hand. "My God," he whispered. "I thought you said they refused to-"

"They refused to *sell* us the remaining 115 million shares, but they agreed to *proxy* their shareholder votes to us," replied McLean, referring to the mechanism shareholders used to transfer their shares' voting rights to others.

"How many?" Carlton asked, immobile, holding his breath.

"All 115 million."

"Aces!" Shouted Carlton, the smile on his haggard face threatening to split his skin. They now had enough Euroil shares and shareholder votes to unseat Metz. "How did you manage that?"

"The banks are all heavily invested in U.S. Treasuries and dollar-denominated loans," explained McLean. "Their value would tank if the global oil currency shifted to the euro."

Carlton frowned. Something did not add up. "That explains why the banks agreed, but not why *all* of them agreed to sell or proxy *all* their shares. Especially if they feared E.U. retaliatory prosecution for insider trading. What are you not telling me, Max?"

A pause. "You don't want to know."

Carlton felt the ball of ice reemerge in his gut. "Now I really do."

A long silence ensued. "I did a favor for my father's former associates," McLean finally replied in a flat monotone.

Aw, hell. Preventing his friend from going to the mafia was the very reason he had agreed to continue this nightmare investigation. "Max, please tell me that you-"

"You didn't hear me, Carlton. I didn't *ask* them for a favor. I *did* them a favor."

Carlton grimaced. "What's the difference? A favor with these people is a debt you can never repay. It-"

McLean cut him off. "The *cosa nostra* doesn't hide its money in jars of olive oil, Carlton. It invests it just like everyone else. Like the banks, much of the *cosa nostra's* fortune is invested in dollar-denominated holdings, costing them untold billions if the global currency shifted to the euro. They would go to great lengths to preserve their investment, something they made clear to the bank CEOs. *Painfully* clear. The CEOs did not need much imagination to figure out what that meant. The Vatican Bank and a major Israeli bank forced the remaining holdouts into compliance."

Carlton thought about it for a moment, confused. "What could the Vatican do other than threaten to excommunicate the bank directors?"

"I don't think a refusal to sell shares is grounds for excommunication. Besides, I doubt these bank CEOs care much about their souls. but they care a great deal about the Vatican's and Israel's influence. The Vatican promised to appeal directly from the pulpit to the one billion Catholics worldwide to withdraw their funds from banks that allowed the Vatican to lose its sovereignty."

In today's economic environment, a run on a bank was no small threat, reflected Carlton. "And the Israeli bank?"

"Its CEO spoke to the Israeli finance minister and prime minister, who promised the recalcitrant banks that they would launch the same appeal with all accounts held by Jews. How is that for inter-religious cooperation?" He paused. "I've done my part, Carlton. Now it's up to you to close the deal. *Buona fortuna.*" Good luck.

Carlton hung up.

The U.S. economy saved by the Vatican and Israel he could accept. But by the mafia? The irony left a foul taste in his mouth, but at least neither McLean nor DOJ owed the mafia anything. If anything, as McLean had described, it was the other way around.

As the Gulfstream began its approach to Charles de Gaulle airport, Carlton took over Monet's laptop and furiously began drafting a shareholder resolution ousting Metz from his position as CEO.

His pleasure over McLean's success was short lived.

They still had not heard from Fouché.

Without the French Interior Minister's help, they had no way to get into Euroil headquarters to deliver the resolution and unseat Metz.

* * *

Euroil Falcon
King Khared International Airport (RUH)
Riyadh, Saudi Arabia
4:03PM local time (2:03PM Paris time)

Metz and de Ville grabbed their armrests as the Euroil Falcon landed at Riyadh International Airport.

Metz glanced out his oval window. The airport shimmered in the burning desert heat. He drummed his fingers, impatiently waiting for the aircraft to taxi across the searing tarmac to the Royal Terminal, where Prince Hakim and his entourage would meet them to sign the contract.

He opened his attaché case, fingered the copies of the contract inside with anticipation.

Only a few more minutes and the world, now his, would change forever.

64 ENDGAME

DARPA Gulfstream
Charles de Gaulle Airport (CDG)
2:13 PM local time (4:13PM Riyadh time)

Carlton peered through one of the jet's windows, anxiously considering the team's next step as the Gulfstream touched down, then taxied under the bright afternoon sun. It would have been much easier if Fouché had agreed to help. Instead, it appeared that the French Interior Minister had joined his government colleagues in mute inaction.

Once again, they were alone. Carlton would have to do what he had done all along: improvise. How, he had no idea.

The aircraft lurched to a halt, shaking Carlton from his thoughts. He did not bother to wait for the pilot to power down the twin turbofans before standing and twisting the hatch open. A gust of hot air blasted him as he extended the folding staircase. Standing on the bright tarmac below, a tall, muscular figure with a thick mat of black hair towered like Paul Bunyan over two French customs agents in front of a navy blue Citroën minibus. Thundercloud, Carlton presumed.

"*Passeports, s'il vous plait,*" demanded one of the agents.

Unable to return to FBI Headquarters to pick up her passport, Faraday had called ahead for Thundercloud to create a new one. He had gone one step further, creating diplomatic passports for all three to grant them a measure of immunity while on French soil.

After a quick inspection of their green-jacketed passports, the customs agents pointed to the minibus with *Contrôle des Frontieres* painted in white on its side - Border Control. They piled in and remained silent while the minibus weaved through parked jets, past rows of private hangars. Gusts of hot air blew in through the open front windows, imbued with the stench of kerosene. Carlton resisted looking for the Euroil hangar in which Thundercloud had disabled the Falcon by asking Faraday a question.

"How did you know Edison was having an affair?"

She looked at him, paused, glanced away. "I was the other woman."

Carlton was still in shock when the minibus squealed to a halt at the base of the general aviation arrivals terminal several sweltering minutes later. He, Monet, Faraday, and Thundercloud followed the two French agents up an escalator into the customs area, collectively sighing with relief at the glacial air-conditioned interior.

Then everything went FUBAR.

* * *

Euroil Falcon
King Khared International Airport (RUH)
4:23PM local time (2:23PM Paris time)
Riyadh, Saudi Arabia

Metz, de Ville, and their two assistants stepped out of the Falcon, walked into the air-conditioned Royal Terminal jetway. Segregated from the other terminals, the Royal Terminal enabled members of the Saudi royal family to escape the indignity of mixing with the plebe under the beating desert sun.

Metz's short stature contained little patience. He was itching to open his attaché case and thrust the contract into Hakim's hands as soon as he caught a glimpse of the new Saudi ruler, decorum be damned. He scanned the group of bearded men in flowing *dishdasha* robes waiting for him at the end of the frosty jetway. They were flanked by a uniformed retinue of Interior Ministry guards, armed with stern expressions and submachine guns held as though Metz and his tiny party were a group of crusading knights.

Metz's stomach churned. Not because of the armed guards, but because Hakim was nowhere in sight.

A man with an intense gaze stepped out of the crowd and extended his hand, looking down at Metz's squat frame. "*Salaam aleikum.* Welcome to Saudi Arabia. I am Sayyid Yassin, chief of staff to his royal highness Regent Crown Prince Hakim."

"Thank you," replied Metz, looking to and fro for Hakim as he shook the man's hand, feeling his chest constrict with anxiety.

"*Wa aleikum as-salaam,*" replied de Ville, better versed in international diplomatic greetings than his impatient compatriot. "*Comte* François de Ville," he continued, extending his hand, hoping his title of nobility would help them gain an advantage with the Saudi royal now in power.

Yassin shook it, adding a curt bow. "Count de Ville. It is an honor to have you present for this important event, minister."

Despite outrage at the suggestion that he might pose a threat, Metz allowed Yassin's minions to search his person and attaché case for weapons and explosives. He was past personal insult. The only thing he cared about was getting the contract signed as soon as possible. He was prepared to crawl through kilometers of burning desert sand if that was what it took to get it done.

"If I may be so bold, Mr. Yassin, where is his highness?" He inquired with grave concern. "I thought he was supposed to meet us here."

"There has been a change of plans. His highness has moved the signing ceremony and press conference to a more secure location. I will take you to him presently."

* * *

General Aviation Arrivals Terminal
Charles de Gaulle Airport (CDG)
2:33PM local time (4:33PM Riyadh time)

Carlton stared at the two men blocking the path to the customs booths. The shorter, stockier man squinted at him, leaning forward in a combative stance, ready to pounce. A second man flanked him, taller yet exuding less authority. Both were dressed in dark suits and wore conservative ties, but Carlton could tell by their body language, hardened faces, severe crew-cuts, and soft rubber-soled shoes that the pair was not interested in whether they had anything to declare.

Forget getting about getting into Euroil headquarters, he reflected. We're not even going to get into France.

"*Colonel* Hulot. DGSE," the man finally announced, flashing his credentials. *Ko-lo-nel Ew-low*. He replaced them in his inside pocket, deliberately giving Carlton a good look at the handgun he carried in a shoulder holster, shiny from years of use. Carlton remembered Sobieski telling him about the DGSE cutting off the Polish embassy's communications. But how had the DGSE managed to pick them out from a thousand other flights? No matter.

Without missing a beat, Carlton smiled, stepped forward, flashed his own credentials.

"Patrick Carlton. U.S. Department of Justice. Thank you for meeting us, colonel. Should we take one car or two?"

Hulot stared back at him without a hint of a smile, unblinking and impassive. He leaned forward on the balls of his feet, hands clasped behind his back.

"I am not amused, *Monsieur* Carlton. U.S. government agents flying into French airspace in a stealth aircraft pretending to be a private corporate flight. Stealing French corporate secrets." He turned to Thundercloud. "Issuing a false passport to aid the escape of a foreign national suspected of espionage." Carlton understood. The DGSE agents had not tracked their flight. They had followed Thundercloud. "These are serious offenses," finished Hulot.

Stealing? Carlton twitched. He wanted to launch himself at the man.

"So is the aiding and abetting of terrorists," he replied instead.

Hulot raised an eyebrow. "What does terrorism have to do with this?"

His question was too much for Carlton.

"Are you a terrorist collaborator, colonel, or are you simply incompetent?"

Hulot was too smart to take the bait. Instead, he pursed his lips in the Gallic fashion indicating severe ennui. "I will tell you what I am not, Mr. Carlton. I am not swayed by insults."

Carlton was trying to get a rise out of Hulot, but he knew that the French Foreign Intelligence Directorate was far from incompetent. After all, the DGSE had managed to discover that Sobieski had obtained and passed on critical intelligence concerning Euroil. Could it be that the DGSE did not know what the intelligence contained, he wondered.

"They are part of a diplomatic mission and bear diplomatic passports," announced Thundercloud.

Hulot answered with a shrug.

At present, Hulot had the advantage, reflected Carlton. He had no reason to lie. The only conclusion he could draw was either that Hulot did not know about Euroil's link to Hakim or that he was moonlighting for Euroil - or for de Ville. In either case, there was no benefit in Carlton hiding what he already knew.

He gave Hulot a summary of the situation.

It fell on deaf ears.

Hulot shook his head in pitying disbelief, as though Carlton had just informed him that the French president was an extraterrestrial. "You Americans and your obsession with terrorism. We were following major Sobieski to prevent him from passing corporate secrets stolen from Euroil to your government. This is about espionage, not terrorism."

If Hulot was lying, he deserved a Cannes Film Festival *Palme d'Or* for Best Actor, reflected Carlton. He had cross-examined hundreds of witnesses at trial. Hulot believed what he was saying.

He thrust out his head, squinting. "Who told you this, colonel?"

"Like you, I have my orders, but I do not reveal from who they come."

Carlton was beginning to suspect who had fed Hulot the lies. "If it is François de Ville, then you have been used, colonel. Used to enable a corrupt company and a twisted E.U. official to attack the world economy and flood France with millions of Saudi fundamentalists. But since you don't believe me, I will give you proof." Carlton turned to Monet, who was already opening his laptop.

"*Arretez!*" Shouted Hulot's partner, unholstering his SIG Sauer. Stop.

"I do not pretend to be a diplomat, Mr. Carlton," said Hulot. "But I am fair. You will have a chance to explain yourself to the appropriate French government official."

"Minister Fouché?"

The colonel grunted. "Most definitely not." His tone and grimace made it clear Hulot possessed little love for the French Interior Minister.

"Then we are under arrest?" Asked Carlton.

Hulot shook his head. "*Non.* You cannot be arrested because you are not technically on French soil and because your passports grant you diplomatic immunity. The French official I was referring to is the DGSE liaison at the French embassy in Washington. You will return to your aircraft and leave French airspace." He squinted. "*Immédiatement.*" Immediately.

Carlton was crestfallen. They had come so far, accomplished so much.

For nothing.

Hulot was correct about one thing. The two customs agents had checked their passports, but had not formally admitted them into the country. They were in a no man's land: outside the U.S. but not yet inside France, whose border technically stood a mere ten feet beyond Hulot and his partner.

What was the old saw? So close and yet so far.

* * *

Interior Ministry Convoy
Riyadh, Saudi Arabia
4:43PM local time (2:43PM Paris time)

Metz and de Ville sat across Sayyid Yassin in the chilled rear compartment of a speeding armored Cadillac DTS limousine. Their two assistants followed close behind in an identical automobile.

While de Ville twisted his family crest ring, Metz gazed through the tinted bulletproof windows as they rushed by the ultramodern Kingdom Centre tower in the heart of Riyadh. With a population of five million, the Saudi capital was choked with traffic, sand, and exhaust, yet the throngs of mostly American sedans and SUVs did not impede the official motorcade.

Escorted fore and aft by Hakim's fearsome Interior Ministry soldiers on motorcycles with sirens blaring and lights flashing, the two black Cadillacs sporting twin green and white Saudi fender flags sped along the boulevards at a rapid clip.

Metz could not stop drumming his fingers on his attaché case. "Please forgive my impatience, Mr. Yassin, but how much longer is it? I am very anxious to get the contract signed."

His undiplomatic tone and query earned him an icy gaze from de Ville. Metz also detected aristocratic disdain in the expression, but could not have cared less. He clutched his case. He only cared about the contract.

Yassin merely smiled. "Soon, *Monsieur* Metz. Soon."

* * *

Customs
Charles de Gaulle Airport (CDG)
2:53PM local time (4:53PM Riyadh time)

"Hulot, Hulot," a voice announced from behind Carlton, lilting as if reprimanding a small child.

Carlton turned to see a short man with droopy eyes and a pronounced aquiline nose walking toward him, smartly dressed in a navy suit, white French-cuffed shirt, and pale blue tie. Two severe crew cut officers flanked him wearing armored black riot gear, pants tucked in spit-shined black boots, wielding deadly FAMAS F2 submachine guns with experienced movements. The large red CRS patches on their chests identified them as part of the *Compagnies Républicaines de Sécurité*, anti-riot forces part of the *Police Nationale*.

What have I gotten us into now?

The newcomer positioned himself between Carlton and Hulot, facing the colonel.

"You know that the DGSE has no jurisdiction inside France," he stated flatly.

"They are not in France, *monsieur le ministre*," replied Hulot with reluctant deference.

"But the Polish embassy is." The man observed the look of shock on the DGSE colonel's face. "Do not look so surprised. I know all about the communications offensive against our fellow E.U. member's embassy," said the man, glancing furtively at Thundercloud.

If forced to rely on his French to order food, Carlton would have starved, yet Hulot's words were easy enough to understand. *Monsieur le ministre.*

His heart leaped. They still had a fighting chance.

The man turned to the customs agents who had earlier accompanied the group. "*Leurs passeports*," he demanded, arm outstretched, motioning impatiently with his hand. "*Vite, vite.*" Quickly.

The agents handed him the three passports without hesitation. He took out a gold pen, scribbled a few words inside each before returning all three to Carlton, tilting his head with a gracious smile. "Welcome to France."

He turned back to Hulot. "Now that they are legally in France under diplomatic immunity and that the DGSE does not have any jurisdiction inside the *territoire*, I am certain that you can find better things to occupy your time than checking passports. They are my responsibility now, *colonel*," he admonished, gesturing to the two nearby CRS officers.

Hulot was visibly furious at the trampling of his jurisdiction by the simple stroke of the ministerial pen, but dared not challenge the man's authority.

"And until the *Procureur de la République* determines whether to press charges in your communications offensive against the Polish embassy, I am placing you under *garde a vue*," the man continued without a trace of excitement, referring to the national prosecutor and the placement of the colonel under custody.

The look of shock on Hulot's and his partner's faces lasted only a second. Seeing the two CRS officers remove handcuffs from their belts, they turned in unison, only to find their escape cut off by two additional CRS officers.

Hulot faced forward, the expression on his face belying not fear but outrage as his and his partner's wrists were shackled. "You cannot-"

"I just have."

"We were following orders," Hulot insisted, his face scarlet with indignation.

"I am certain you were. For your sakes, I hope you have solid proof of them and that they came from the appropriate chain of command." He waited for the CRS officers to march Hulot and his partner away before turning to Carlton and the others. "Nicolas Fouché, Interior Minister," he announced, extending his hand.

"Patrick Carlton, Justice Department," he replied, appreciating the man's iron grip. "Thank you for your assistance, minister."

"Please forgive me for not contacting you sooner," Fouché announced with a genuine smile in perfect, heavily accented English. "Once colonel Hulot discovered that your FBI Legal Attaché Thundercloud had contacted me, passing along not only your information about Euroil but of the DGSE's actions against the Polish Embassy, his people started following both Thundercloud and I, even though their jurisdiction lies outside France. Since you were not yet in France, you were still under his jurisdiction. Luckily, my ministry controls France's borders," he explained, turning to the others as Carlton made the introductions.

To Faraday's blushing embarrassment, he lowered his head to mock-kiss her hand, then did a double take when Monet addressed him in perfect French.

"It is I who am deeply indebted to you for revealing Hakim's plans for an Islamist invasion of France and Europe." He bowed slightly. "*Merci.* As you can tell, our president and prime minister do not share all of their information with all the ministries. Like them, I too want France to regain its position as a superpower. Unlike them, I believe the path to that goal is to work for real results on common security goals with our allies, not simply to oppose America at every turn. Thankfully, you obtained the information about Euroil and Hakim on time."

"We're not done yet, sir," replied Carlton urgently. It might even be too late, but they had come too far not to try. "Unless we oust Metz very soon, French women will soon be wearing *burkhas*."

"We certainly cannot let that happen," said Fouché, flashing a brief smile. "I will take you there personally." He advanced a few steps to Faraday and Thundercloud. "I have deep respect for the Bureau, but I would prefer that you not accompany us. FBI agents storming into a French company would create an...unwelcome political situation."

The displeasure on Faraday's face was evident, but under the circumstances, she did not have a choice. She and Thundercloud nodded their assent.

"I'll contact you at the embassy when this is over," said Carlton, leaning closer. "Keep working with Ben-David. He's our Plan B if we can't get to Euroil on time."

Faraday had no idea what he was talking about, but she agreed to contact the DARPA physicist.

Carlton followed Fouché, who eschewed the customs booths. Turning back to the escalator, he led Carlton and Monet downstairs, the group escorted fore and aft by the two fearsome CRS officers, gazes alert, weapons ready. They packed into the minibus and rushed across the tarmac, dome lights ablaze, to a white Dauphin Eurocopter emblazoned with the round French *tricolore* and the words *Contrôle des Frontieres* on its side panel. Its rotors were already whipping the hot summer air. As soon as they settled into the sleek helicopter's rear compartment, it shot up, retracted its landing gear, and whirred toward the French capital.

Carlton glanced at his watch.

They were nearly out of time.

* * *

Sharia Palace
Outside Riyadh, Saudi Arabia
5:03PM local time (3:03PM Paris time)

A sense of dread fell over Metz as the Cadillac left the congested Saudi capital behind.

How far were they going, he wondered, without asking.

Soon all vestiges of the city disappeared, its office towers, retail shops, and apartment buildings giving way to barren sand dunes.

Silent and intractable, Yassin divulged nothing.

Twenty kilometers farther and a nerve-wracking amount of time later, the convoy slowed, then stopped in front of an ornate forged iron gate set into a high stone wall. Peering through the tinted windows, Metz saw that the gate itself was merely decorative, but concluded that the raised cylindrical metal barriers at its base could probably repel a tank. Interior Ministry guards emerged from a camouflaged pillbox recessed several yards from the gate. They were clad in the same uniforms as their motorcycle escorts, toting machineguns.

The lead guard identified Yassin, shouted an order toward the fortified pillbox. The metal cylinders sank into the ground. The gate crept open.

The convoy proceeded into a vast compound hidden behind soaring crenellated walls. The lush oasis secreted inside was a sharp contrast to the bone-dry desert from which they emerged. Rows of tall palm trees lined a crushed-rock driveway. On either side lay verdant lawns, manicured flower beds, splashing fountains, and ponds topped with lily pads. Metz's gaze remained fixed on the roadway ahead as it wound toward a majestic edifice straight out of the Arabian Nights.

Covered in brilliant white marble, crowned with a green mosaic dome shimmering in the burning sun, the palace was made to resemble a giant tent secured to the desert sand by six minarets, each topped with the fluttering green and white sword flag of the Saudi Kingdom. Unlike de Ville next to him, who craned his neck and nodded with admiration at the breathtaking structure, Metz had no interest in the stunning Arabic architecture. The only thing he cared about was the monarch inside, whose royal hand would sign the contract in his attaché case.

The tempo of his heartbeat increased as the motorcade stopped before a wide staircase of gleaming white and green marble. The Interior Ministry troops hopped off their motorcycles, leaned them against their kickstands, and encircled Metz's Cadillac, gazes and machineguns pointed outward toward potential threats.

The searing heat sucked the air from Metz's lungs as soon as he stepped out of the air-conditioned limousine. Squinting against the brilliant sun, he and de Ville followed Yassin up the staircase. Their two assistants followed close behind. All looked painfully out of place in their dark business suits amid Prince Hakim's assistants dressed in flowing white *dishdashas*. A shining gold door opened soundlessly as soon as they crested the top of the stairs. More men in white robes were stationed inside, amid the cool air and shadows of the palace entrance hall.

"Welcome to the *Sharia* palace, gentlemen," announced Yassin. "*Sharia* is the pure form of Islamic law. It means 'the path to the watering hole'. I am certain you agree that the palace is far more pleasant and secure than the airport," he explained, politely ushering his guests inside. "Would either of you care to refresh yourselves before your audience with his highness?"

Seeing that de Ville was about to accept the invitation out of diplomatic propriety, Metz shook his head briskly. "No," he replied tersely. Did Yassin and de Ville truly comprehend the rush he was in, he wondered, before realizing that one had to tread lightly here, particularly when one was a Christian, even if in name only. "Forgive me, Mr. Yassin. I mean no offense. I am grateful for your kind and gracious hospitality, but I cannot overstate the urgency of our meeting."

Yassin sneered. "Westerners. Money, always money. Very well." He turned and led the way down an interminable marble hallway inlaid with dark green, blue and white mosaics. Armed Interior Ministry troops in crisp starched uniforms outnumbered the many potted palms and gurgling fountains lining the cool stone walls. Other than the new Saudi ruler's hatred of America and his paranoia about security, Metz did not understand why everyone was so upset about Prince Hakim. Despite his agonizing impatience, from everything that he had seen so far, the new monarch seemed perfectly civilized.

After what seemed like a kilometer of hallways, they stopped in front of another golden door, this one so large that it seemed to belong in the palace of a fairy tale giant. Yassin reached up and banged a heavy ball-shaped knocker against the glittering surface. Metz felt the loud, vibrating impact in his molars, certain the oversize door was constructed of solid gold.

How perfectly gaudy, he reflected, taking no pleasure from the knowledge that he would soon be able to afford a similar palace in the South of France. In fact, he could already afford more than he could reasonably spend. What Metz cared about was expanding his corporate empire. Power, not money. He wiped his sweaty palms on his trousers, licked his lips. That corporate victory was only moments away.

An Interior Ministry soldier opened the door from inside and stepped aside.

"His highness's audience chamber," whispered Yassin with reverence, ushering them in.

* * *

French Border Control Eurocopter
Above Paris, France
3:13PM local time (5:13 PM Riyadh time)

Carlton directed his attention away from their increasingly short window of opportunity. He admired the blurred view below as the Border Control Eurocopter rocketed across the French capital, soaring above the *Avenue des Champs-Elysées* and the *Arc de Triomphe* at the center of the *Etoile* - Star - with its twelve giant avenues that shot out from Napoléon's triumphal arch like the rays of just such a celestial being.

They soon closed in on the *Grande Arche de la Défense*, a gigantic hollowed-out white cube that served as a portal to the capital's only group of skyscrapers known as La Défense, Paris's corporate district. *Day-fahnce.*

Carlton reflected on Sobieski and Fouché - and on McLean's contacts, both good and evil. America still had plenty of allies, he concluded. It was simply a matter of looking in the right places.

The pilot reduced the helicopter's speed as they approached a forty-story glass and steel office tower in the sterile corporate zone. Any doubt that they were in the right place dissolved upon seeing the Euroil logo atop the building. The helo circled once, extended its landing gear, set down gently on the rooftop helipad.

Fouché turned to Carlton. "Welcome to Euroil headquarters."

One of the CRS officers jumped out of the front passenger seat, slid the helicopter's side door open. The three joined a waiting CRS officer in armored gear like the others, who saluted Fouché and led them to an alcove on the far side of the roof.

Carlton leaned close to Monet as they walked, hunched over to avoid the powerful rotor wash. "See if you can find out about Hakim's press conference in Riyadh," he shouted, barely audible amid the wind and engine noise.

Monet nodded, patting his computer case.

They stepped into a luxurious elevator cabin. Carlton remained silent as the doors slid shut, reflecting that one interior minister was helping him defeat another. He caught himself. They had not defeated Hakim yet. The burning issue now was to whom he should deliver the shareholder resolution ousting Metz. In a perfect world, he would deliver it to Euroil's *conseil d'administration*, its board of directors. But Fouché had not enjoyed the time necessary to convene the board on such short notice, its members undoubtedly scattered among far-flung vacation homes during the sacrosanct French summer vacation. Once again, he would have to improvise.

Fouché seemed to read his mind. "Thundercloud did not give us much time to act before your arrival, but we did our best."

A chime announced their arrival on the 40th floor. The doors opened onto a brightly lit, airy reception area of black marble floors, blond wood millwork, and crisp white walls adorned with abstract tapestries. It immediately reminded Carlton of Farnsworth Tate and the Merchants of Pain. They even smelled the same; of paper, pressure, and power, as if corporate wickedness possessed its own smell.

Not a single employee was in sight. The only occupants were more of the uniformed CRS officers guarding the reception area and office doors.

Carlton was impressed. Fouché had accomplished a great deal in a short amount of time. He wondered how much more his people could have done given greater notice.

Fouché stopped in front of one of the guards, jutted his chin.

"*Où sont-ils?*" He asked. Where are they?

"*Suivez-moi, monsieur le ministre.*" Follow me.

He led the group down a hallway, pointed to a tall set of bleached wood double doors. Gleaming chrome letters spelled out '*Chambre du Conseil*'. Fouché grasped the matching door handles. "We were only able to assemble eight board members."

Carlton swiveled toward him, his spirits soaring. The Euroil board was composed of twelve members. Eight constituted more than a quorum; the number of board members required for their vote to bind Euroil. He was about to thank Fouché when the minister cut him off.

"I did all I could. The rest is up to you. *Bonne chance.*" Good luck.

* * *

Sharia Palace
5:23PM (3:23PM Paris time)

Metz was no stranger to displays of power and luxury. Yet it took him a moment to recover from his shock upon entering the resplendent audience chamber.

The cathedral-sized hall seemed as though carved from a giant block of white marble. Four arched walls held up the palace's massive dome overhead, tapering to the floor in tall columns linked by filigreed arches so finely carved that they resembled Belgian lace. The green mosaic on the dome's exterior was reproduced inside, inlaid with white ceramic to form stylized verses selected from the 114 *shura* of the Qu'ran. A single massive chandelier of gold and crystal hung down from the center of the cupola, illuminating the chamber with shards of brilliant white light. In the air hung the sweet smell of almonds.

And of sweat: on both sides of the cavernous room stood a thronging retinue of bearded men wearing white *dishdasha* robes and red and white checkered *keffiyeh* headpieces secured by black *agal* rings. In the rear center of the hall, elevated atop marble steps, stood a man with a neatly trimmed jet black beard, wearing a dazzling white *dishdasha* and matching *keffiyeh* headpiece. He gazed down at the newcomers with an expression merging indifference, condescension, and impatience. His handsome features, regal bearing, and air of moral superiority left little doubt as to his identity.

"You may come forward," Prince Hakim proclaimed in a loud voice without a trace of a smile.

Metz chafed. Who does he think he is speaking to? We are his business associates, not his subjects.

As he and de Ville approached the marble steps, the crowd of men on either side closed in on them, encircling them in a tightening ring of white robes, far too close for Metz's comfort. They prevented their two assistants from ascending the stairs. Metz soon noticed that behind the tightening cordon sat battalions of television cameras, boom microphones, klieg lights, reporters and cameramen. Metz could make out some of the names scrawled on the cameras. *Al-Jazeera. Al-Arabiya. Dubai TV.* Metz was surprised to see the four main French television stations also present: the private *TF1* and the state-owned *France 2, 3,* and *5.* They must have come at de Ville's request, he concluded, knowing that the diplomat craved recognition as the deal's broker to catapult his career to the presidential *Palais de l'Elysée* in Paris.

This was obviously where Hakim intended to hold his press conference, Metz reflected, climbing the steps alone with de Ville. The man was far more handsome, younger, and svelte than he had imagined, towering well over two feet above him. Metz extended his hand in greeting. Hakim stood still, keeping his hands clasped behind him, as though touching Metz would render him unclean. Embarrassment flushed Metz's face red as his unshaken hand hung limply in front of him, to the laughter of the bearded assembly.

De Ville gave a slight bow before the Saudi monarch. "Your majesty."

"*Comte* de Ville," he replied, allowing himself a curt nod and the faintest of smiles, which disappeared as quickly as it had come. "Let us conclude our business," Hakim continued, motioning to a vast gilded table of polished wood behind him. Metz's embarrassment swelled as he made to sit before Hakim, catching himself at the last moment as de Ville held him back with a firm hand and a scornful gaze. Relief finally descended as Hakim sat and Metz and de Ville took their assigned places at the opposite end of the table.

"The agreement," demanded Hakim, snapping his fingers before extending his arm toward Metz. An order, not a request.

Metz shuddered as he noticed that one of Hakim's index fingers was little more than a gnarled stump, its fingernail missing. Trying hard to ignore his host's imperious manner and mangled digit, Metz lifted the attaché case onto the table, clicked it open, and removed both copies of the thick document.

* * *

Euroil, SA International Headquarters
3:33PM (5:33PM Riyadh time)

Carlton shivered as he stepped through the doorway into a frosty boardroom. The severe chamber would likely have felt cold even if a heater had been running full blast, he reflected.

The room looked and felt like a temple to the god of corporate power. Circular, forty feet in diameter, twenty feet tall, with curved walls dwarfing a round glass table at the center like a sacrificial altar, the room was devoid of windows and decoration, down to the unpainted industrial concrete walls and brushed aluminum floor. In contrast, the ceiling was painted white, with a dark blue Euroil logo at the center encircled by halogen lights. Their tight beams shot down onto the conference table.

Carlton almost expected to hear Darth Vader breathing.

Eight of the twelve high-backed black leather seats around the table were occupied, each by a white man in his sixties or seventies.

The board members must have skipped the diversity training, he reflected.

Each of the occupants stared at Carlton's grizzled features, rumpled clothes, and scuffed boots with undisguised contempt. They remained silent, deferring to their corporate master, who occupied a slightly elevated center seat directly across from Carlton.

The man rose. In his mid-seventies, his dark gray hair matched the color of his bespoke pinstripe suit, his pallid complexion that of his starched white shirt. Tall and rail thin, his arrogant bearing and condescending expression gave Carlton the impression of a feudal lord who beat impoverished farmers for being hungry. He reminded him of Wolf.

The man pointed a bony finger at him. "*Qui êtes-vous?*" He demanded in a surprisingly strong voice.

Carlton ignored him, stepping deeper into the room, observing its every detail. He soon realized that he had been mistaken. There was one decoration.

Off to his right, an aquarium roughly ten feet long hugged the curved wall. Carlton loved aquariums, but this one did not contain any living thing. It encased a miniature oil pumping station sitting on little sand dunes, linked by a pipeline to an oil derrick and a supertanker floating on water, all built to scale down to the tiniest detail and proudly emblazoned with the Euroil logo.

He stepped to it, peered down. The intricate machinery even worked, complete with flashing lights, spinning wheels, a flame atop the oil pumping station, and oil traveling through the clear pipeline. The elaborate monument to Euroil's global energy empire must have taken painstaking weeks to construct, Carlton reflected.

"Impressive," he remarked sincerely, standing straight.

"*Qui êtes-vous?*" Repeated the imperious man, now squinting.

Carlton observed the beautiful model for a moment longer before turning to face him. "I'm sorry, but I've exhausted all of my French," he replied calmly, allowing himself a faint smile.

"Who are you and why were we brought here by force?" The man demanded, this time in perfect English laced with a heavy French accent. His tone suggested that he was accustomed to being obeyed without question.

He was in for a surprise, thought Carlton, feeling the familiar heat of anger flash on his face as pent up rage welled up inside him.

The dour Euroil board members before him oversaw a corporation that was about to launch a devastating attack not on a competitor, but on the United States and world economies. Metz was CEO, but he could not have negotiated the contract with Prince Hakim without the knowledge and consent of the people in this room. The corporate vampires arrayed before him could feign insult, but could not plead innocence. To Carlton, they were not mere white-collar criminals, but full-fledged petroeconomic terrorists just like those who had cut down Davenport's men in Alaska. And Alexis.

His simmering anger boiled over. He wanted to launch himself across the table and throttle each of the smug bastards with his bare hands, so much that they started to tremble. Instead, he forced himself to remain still, hands clasped tight, staring impassively at each of the board members in total silence until he could see them grow visibly uncomfortable.

He then flashed his badge.

"Patrick Carlton, United States Department of Justice," he announced, emphasizing the last word before casually jutting his chin toward his interlocutor. "Who are you?"

The man recoiled, eyes glaring with affront. Whether it was a reaction to his impertinent manner, nationality, or government affiliation, Carlton did not know.

Nor did he care.

"I am Georges La Tour, *Directeur Général* of Euroil. Chairman. I demand an explanation," he replied, slamming his bony palm against the glass tabletop.

Without uttering a word, Carlton placed Monet's case on the table, removed the shareholder resolution together with its many exhibits. There had been no time to make copies. He turned the resolution so that it faced La Tour, slid the thick document across the glass table.

Without being invited to do so, he pulled out the nearest empty chair and sat facing the semicircle of board members, his casual manner deliberate.

La Tour sat and read the one page resolution, riffled through its attachments, shot Carlton a disdainful look.

"*Ridicule*," he scoffed. "Ridic-"

"The game is over, gentlemen," interrupted Carlton in a voice far louder than necessary to be heard. "There will be no exclusive oil contract between Euroil and Saudi Arabia and no shift in the global currency from the dollar to the euro. We won. You lost."

La Tour glowered back at Carlton, smirked. "How *American*, forcing your way in here dressed in cowboy boots, ordering us in our own company and country." He wagged a wizened finger. "It will not work. You have no jurisdiction here." He shoved the document back at Carlton. "The board will not endorse this ridiculous resolution," he replied flatly, folding his arms to underscore the finality of his point.

* * *

Sharia Palace
5:43PM local time (3:43PM Paris time)

Despite the palace's cool interior, Metz felt drops of sweat bead on his forehead. He looked over at de Ville. In contrast, the diplomat seemed calm and collected, twisting his family crest ring.

He can afford it, thought Metz. He does not have as much at stake as I do.

Metz removed his pocket square, wiped his brow, waiting impatiently for Regent Crown Prince Hakim's paranoid legal assistants to pore through the 350-page agreement that sat on the table before them.

Metz had learned long ago that people often suspected others of doing what they would do in the same situation. If Hakim's legal assistants were scrutinizing the contract, which bore the date, time, and number of the document version they had agreed to at the bottom of each page to avoid confusion with prior drafts, they must have had a habit of modifying agreements and slipping something in at the last minute, without changing the version at the bottom. Barbarians.

They could examine it all they wanted, but Metz could wait no longer. The agreement on the table was the one they had agreed to through Wolf. To the devil with formalities. He removed a gold fountain pen from his jacket pocket. De Ville touched his arm, glared at him, shaking his head at the attempted *lèse majesté* - lax behavior before the king. He had warned Metz that the Saudi code forbade anyone from acting first in the monarch's presence.

Metz snarled back, shook off de Ville's hand, unscrewed the cap of his pen. Leafing to the signature page of the contract, he thought about asking de Ville to witness his signature before realizing that the formality-obsessed diplomat would never do it unless Hakim first invited him to. Metz snapped his fingers at his assistant. A gasp rose from the men in white robes crowding the base of the stairs as they watched Metz act without the Regent Crown Prince's consent.

Hakim remained engrossed in the contract with his assistants. He either had not noticed Metz's act or did not care.

As soon as his dutiful assistant stood beside him, Metz signed the contract in dark green ink - de Ville had informed him that the color of the Saudi flag was the only ink color the monarch tolerated. He heard an audible groan rise from the cameramen behind their switched-off cameras. They pined for a shot of the historic signatures, but knew better than to proceed without Hakim's invitation.

Metz handed the pen to his heavily perspiring assistant. Despite the visual daggers launched by de Ville, he signed on the witness line, then shakily printed his name.

Metz smiled. *Now for Hakim and we will be done.*

* * *

Euroil, SA International Headquarters
3:53PM local time (5:53PM Riyadh time)

"The U.S. government may not have jurisdiction, *Monsieur* La Tour. But your shareholders certainly do. And they have spoken quite audibly," said Carlton, placing his hand on the shareholder resolution, straining to keep his alarming sense of urgency at bay. "I'm afraid that you don't have a choice."

La Tour flashed a wicked smile. "Oh, but we do. We choose not to endorse your resolution."

Carlton stood and paced the room in silence, stopping to examine the intricate Euroil diorama in the glass case. The miniature model was beautifully handcrafted, he reflected, but it was also the symbol of the perfidious global energy giant.

"I don't think you understand what a choice consists of," he replied through clenched teeth, no longer able to hold back his pent up rage. "Allow me to demonstrate."

In a swift, fluid motion, he shot his foot out to the side, shattering the glass edge with the heel of his boot, stepped back. A wail of outrage wound its way from the assembled board members as water and sand poured out of a jagged hole in the aquarium, carrying away bits of glass that sparkled as they bobbed on crude oil collecting in dark pools on the brushed aluminum floor. The model Euroil supertanker began to sink, stern first, gushing oil. The offshore drilling platform tilted wildly, its flame setting the structure on fire. It quickly spread along the pipeline that split in two, engulfing the miniature onshore refinery before a jet of frozen carbon dioxide gas shot down from above, asphyxiating the conflagration.

He felt a tinge of remorse over destroying such handiwork, but none over eliminating Euroil's symbol of power.

His rage partially vented, Carlton walked back to the table, calmly placed his palms flat against the glass, leaned forward, scowling at the men seated across from him. "*That* was a choice. You don't have one. Your bosses, the Euroil shareholders, have already made the choice for you. A *fait accompli*, I believe you call it."

La Tour sneered. "Your brutish American show of force does not impress me, Mr. Carlton. And you are the one who is mistaken. Under French law, the board must certify your resolution as valid before it can come into force, and then only at a duly-noticed board meeting. You can sue us, as American shareholders are so fond of doing, but for now, we choose not to certify the resolution." He crossed his arms before him.

Carlton felt his temples throb as time sped away, forced himself to calm down, keeping his palms flat against the table. He knew precious little about French corporate law, so he improvised on the fly based on his knowledge of its American counterpart.

"Duly noticed or not, a quorum of the board *is* present during an emergency, for which notice can be waived. And you cannot refuse to certify the resolution simply because you do not feel like it. You need legally valid grounds to refuse." Carlton sat. "On the other hand,

I can choose to exercise the legal right granted to me by a majority of the Euroil shareholders," he touched the resolution, "and draft a new resolution that replaces a majority of your board with directors chosen by my government, as the majority vote holder.

"If I did, I would make sure the resolution also stripped you of all stock options, legal defense funds, and bloated golden parachutes for reason of criminal misconduct. You could sue, as would be your right, but I would remind you that the Justice Department is the largest law firm in the world. Its 9,000 lawyers are just itching to descend on you like a Biblical swarm of locusts, exposing to government prosecutors and to the bright light of public opinion the material support your wretched company provides to terrorists who kill women and children and to despicable regimes that use your euros to keep their people in bondage. Not to mention all the government officials you are bribing. *Allegedly*, of course." Carlton reclined. "*That* is your choice. It is the only one you have."

Cracks began to appear in La Tour's armor as he shifted in his seat. Yet he continued to stand his ground, refusing to give a *centimetre*. "We have no way of determining the authenticity of your resolution. How can we possibly ensure that those signatures are true and correct?"

Carlton nodded. "Perhaps you should have started with that argument and spared your quaint little corporate monument from my brutish American show of force, as you call it. Verification of the signatures can be arranged, but asking for it is not a wise decision."

La Tour threw Carlton an indignant scowl. "*Pourquoi?*" Why?

"Because it is unnecessary. *Monsieur* Metz's actions with the illegitimate coup government of Regent Crown Prince Hakim - with this board's approval - are so criminal that failure to oust him immediately will lead to a full investigation by your government, resolution or no resolution. This is not a threat, but a statement of fact."

La Tour smirked, gave a pitying shake of his head. "Unlike your idealistic, naïve country, France's government does not penalize its companies for making a profit in countries simply because they have unpopular regimes. Our president and prime minister are great allies of French industry. No such investigation would ever take place. The government would reverse your resolution as an illegal act of intervention by a hostile foreign government." His smug grin persisted.

Carlton nodded. "I am well aware of your government's obsolete protectionism masquerading as *patriotisme économique*. And yes, the French president and PM are great allies of Euroil as a national strategic asset. However, your interior minister is a staunch supporter of the free market and a strong opponent both of France's terrorist enemies and of your president and PM. I can assure you that Minister Fouché will investigate this case with such public scrutiny that the French people's reaction to his revelations will make union demonstrations on the Champs-Elysées look like a picnic. He may not even allow you and your fellow board members to call your families before throwing you in jail with all the other criminals. Unlike our idealistic, naïve American system, as you call it, I will remind you that French law will consider you guilty until proven innocent," explained Carlton, watching La Tour's smile disappear as fear reshaped his aristocratic features.

Fouché stepped into the room. He did not say a word. He did not have to.

La Tour slumped back in his chair, defeated.

"I see that you have wisely decided to certify the resolution," said Carlton. If you'd be so kind as to formalize that decision, I will leave you to your business of collaborating with other dictatorships." Carlton cupped his hand over his ear. "Did I hear a motion?"

Led by a less than enthusiastic La Tour, the eight board members grudgingly voted to ratify the resolution. All of a sudden, the chamber seemed to warm, as though exorcized.

"*Merci*," said Carlton, not allowing himself the luxury of a smile. Simply certifying the resolution was not enough. If Metz entered into the contract with Hakim while both believed that Metz was CEO, the contract could still be enforced if later ratified by Euroil's board.

"Now if you would be so good as to call *Monsieur* Metz."

* * *

Sharia Palace
6:03PM local time (4:03PM Paris time)

Prince Hakim's assistants whispered something in their master's ear, causing him to look up from the contract at Metz.

"It seems to be in order."

Metz leaned forward, handed Hakim his pen. The monarch ignored it, accepting one from his minions instead.

Metz's cell phone trilled, resulting in a grimace from Hakim and an even more acute glare from de Ville. Metz reached into his pocket. Only his personal secretary and a few top people at Euroil had his cell phone number. It had to be important, he knew, but nothing could possibly be more important than the contract. He shut it off.

Hakim was about to sign when Metz's assistant's cell phone trilled, earning him a withering scowl from the taciturn monarch.

Metz thrust his finger at his assistant. "*Eteignez-le!*" He shouted. Shut it off.

The trembling assistant fumbled with the device to shut it off before his boss's glare burned a hole straight through him.

"I detest technology," hissed Hakim, lifting his pen anew.

A third phone trilled. This one belonged to de Ville, who flushed red with embarassment as he reached for the device.

Hakim sensed that something was afoot. He snapped his fingers and gestured for de Ville to bring him the telephone.

Metz cringed. His heart raced. He could feel sweat plastering his shirt to his skin. What could Hakim care about de Ville's cell phone? Why is he not signing? He wanted to stand and shout, but fear paralyzed him. Something was very wrong.

Beside him, de Ville obeyed, handing his phone to one one of Hakim's bearded assistants.

Seconds after answering the telephone, Hakim's assistant's face went pale. He leaned over, whispered something in his master's ear, careful not to touch any part of the royal physical person.

Hakim's eyes shifted from de Ville to Metz, narrowed into slits. He slammed the pen on the contract's signature page, splattering dark green ink on the pristine white paper. His hand shot out, his gnarled, nailless index finger pointing at Metz.

Metz's breath quickened. He accepted the telephone with a shaky hand, lifted it to his ear. "Metz," he said, voice cracking, his parched throat squeezed tight with anxiety.

"This is La Tour. The United States government has obtained over fifty percent of Euroil shareholder voting rights. Their representative just handed me a signed resolution, which the board has certified."

* * *

Carlton listened on a second telephone handset. Thank goodness Monet had possessed the foresight to obtain de Ville's private cell phone number, undoubtedly with Ben-David's help.

"Mr. Metz," he announced, once La Tour had finished. "This is Patrick Carlton of the United States Department of Justice. The United States government has exercised its majority Euroil shareholder voting rights." He paused, savoring the moment. "You're fired."

"What?"

"Any contracts that you sign or negotiate are null and void," he added. "Regardless of who signs on behalf of Euroil. And I warn you not to backdate the contract. It will be annulled by the board and charges will be pressed if you do."

* * *

Metz's mouth hung open, his mind too shocked to reply. The world around him started to disappear as his vision filled with blotches of light. His arms fell limp by his sides, the cell phone clattering to the marble floor. He stared forward, immobile, seeing little. His gamble had failed, and with it, his dream of being at the helm of the largest and most powerful energy company in the world.

It did not end there. Charges would be pressed. Even if he managed to avoid prison, he would never again be allowed to serve as a corporate leader to build another corporate empire.

Blaming himself was not in his nature. He blamed Hakim. If the megalomaniacal barbarian had allowed Ambassador Qhibli to sign on the Kingdom's behalf, the contract would have been concluded long ago. He felt like slitting the bearded savage's throat.

It was also the incompetent weasel de Ville's fault, with his inability to get the DGSE to protect the interests of France's most important company. What good was paying off government ministers if they did not deliver? He felt like plunging his fountain pen into the haughty diplomat's neck.

Hakim glared at Metz, again thrusting his gnarled index finger at him. "Your miserable failure will not stop us. The Kingdom does not need Euroil or the E.U. to wage economic *jihad*."

De Ville's diplomatic instinct came alive, seeking to remedy an irremediable solution. He rose. "Your majesty."

He was too late. Hakim had already turned his back on the Europeans. Metz watched the monarch stride down the steps toward the television cameras, parting the sea of fundamentalist sycophants in white robes with a wave of his hand.

"I will now make my announcement. Start your cameras!" He ordered, illuminated in the brilliant white light of the klieg lamps. "I am Prince Hakim ibn Khaled Suleiman al Najd, Crown Prince of the Kingdom of Saudi Arabia, Regent..."

Metz understood the economic suicide Hakim was about to peform. Unable to shift the global oil currency to the euro, he would shut off the Saudi oil taps, de facto imposing a global oil embargo. It would devastate the oil-dependent Saudi and world economies, but the fanatic did not care as long as the United States was plunged into chaos far beyond economics. War would erupt as major economies sent their militaries to seize the Saudi oil fields located in the same country as Islam's two holiest sites in Mecca and Medina. The ensuing Muslim cry for global *jihad* would make the same call over the Iraq War seem muted in comparison. The Shiite Iranians would gladly join their hated Sunni brethren, possibly armed with nuclear weapons.

Yet Metz was beyond caring what the Saudi monarch did to the world. It was no longer his world. His world had already come crashing down.

* * *

Euroil, SA International Headquarters
4:13PM (6:13PM Riyadh time)

"I hacked into Al-Jazeera's feed!" Exclaimed Monet. "It's broadcasting Hakim's conference live." He swiveled his laptop toward Carlton, punched up the volume. The bottom of the screen identified the Qatar-based station, which many had described as 'all Al Qaeda, all the time' for often transmitting terrorist beheadings, *fatwas*, and hate-spewing Islamist diatribes nearly unchallenged.

Carlton and Monet stared at the live audio-visual stream in terror, impotent to stop the madman on screen.

They were not prepared for what happened next.

The audience chamber's massive golden door exploded clear off of its hinges, slammed onto the marble floor with a deafening crash.

Soldiers stormed into the cavernous hall. Dressed in the black uniforms of the Saudi Defense Forces (SDF), wearing black face paint, they fired staccatos of M-16A2 machinegun bursts into the dome above, splintering tiles, shouting orders in Arabic. Hakim's Interior Ministry troops appeared, immediately opened fire on the SDF troops.

All semblance of fundamentalist discipline evaporated as soon as the gun battle erupted. Herds of robed men scampered in terror to different corners as each tried to save his skin. The fast and young trampled the slow and elderly. People hid under furniture, behind potted palms and marble columns. Some jumped into fountains.

Cameramen and reporters remained at their posts, crouched behind cameras and boom microphones still transmitting live, including Al-Jazeera. The story was too good to lose.

A contingent of Hakim's Interior Ministry troops scrambled out from behind the cameras, encircling their still raving leader in a protective cordon. They pushed him up the steps toward a hidden exit door near the signing table.

And suddenly stopped as the door burst open from the other side.

* * *

Sayyid Yassin scrambled to escape the SDF troops pouring into Hakim's audience chamber. With all the exits blocked, he too jumped into a fountain.

Always planning several steps ahead while others around him lost their heads - some literally - Yassin chose his fountain carefully. He had memorized the *Sharia* Palace's detailed plans long ago for just such an eventuality.

He knew exactly where this fountain led.

He took a deep gulp of air, ducked under the water's surface, removed his *dishdasha* robe, scanned the bottom. Light from the chandelier filtered through the clear water, providing enough illumination for him to locate an underwater tunnel. Not daring to risk being identified by poking his head out for another lungful of air, he angled his body, entered the tunnel, kicking his toned legs hard as the light faded into stygian darkness.

Yassin continued kicking while touching the smooth edges of the tunnel with his hands to follow its twists and turns. He was quickly running out of air. Blotches of light began to flash in his vision. His lungs felt as though they were about to burst.

He thought about turning back. Death might take him in the tunnel, but the SDF troops were sure to take him if he retreated to the audience chamber, he knew. He kicked forward, lungs burning in agony, using every ounce of self-control to prevent his mouth from opening.

Light finally appeared, far brighter than from the chandelier. Was his mind playing tricks on him? No. He was out of the tunnel. Angling upward, he pushed hard against the stone floor, broke through the water's surface, gasping for air.

He allowed only his head to remain above water while he caught his breath, partially hidden under a lily pad in the beating sun outside the palace walls.

He wasted no time reveling in his escape. Instead, he used the confusion roiling all about him to his advantage as cover, crawling through the tall reeds growing at the pond's edge as panicked men shouted and ran amok with nowhere to escape. SDF soldiers had sealed off the palace gates, leaving the high walls of the desert compound as the only possible exit route - an impossible task.

As the searing heat wicked away the moisture from his clothes, Yassin spent the next several minutes searching for a manhole cover among the reeds, ignoring the plants' sharp leaves slicing his skin. He could not find it. Panic overtook him.

If forced to remain here, the SDF troops scouring the palace grounds would soon discover him.

* * *

Carlton and Monet watched the audio-visual feed in rapt attention. They saw Metz and de Ville cowering under a massive wood table, peering hopefully at the nearby open door, unable to understand the soldiers' orders in Arabic for Hakim and his troops to stand down. Seizing the opportunity, they crawled out from under the gilded table, crossing the no-man's land between Hakim's Interior Ministry guards and the SDF troops toward the open door, abandoning their two assistants to fend for themselves.

Rather than lay down their weapons as ordered, the Interior Ministry guards ringing Hakim leveled them at their military brethren.

They were too slow. A sustained hail of bullets cut them down before they could fire, simultaneously tearing through Hakim. Caught in the line of fire, Metz and de Ville were ripped to bloody shreds along with the partially signed contracts lying on the table. Seeing their leader and comrades dead and dying, the remaining Interior Ministry guards threw down their weapons, raised their arms in surrender.

The commander of the SDF strike team raised his gloved hand, spoke a few words into his comm mike. The gunfire ceased as abruptly as it had begun.

Amid the cries of the injured, strips of the contract floated down through the smoky air onto the mangled bodies of Metz, de Ville, Hakim, and his felled guards like snow, turning red on contact with the collective pool of blood. Soon the victims stopped moaning, ceased twitching. Within minutes, the SDF troops had Hakim's surviving cronies and guards firmly bound in plastic zip cuffs.

Metz and de Ville's assistants survived by laying flat on the ground, shaking, arms held up. One had wet himself. The other promptly bent in half and retched at the bloody carnage.

Inches away from Monet's laptop screen, Carlton's eyes opened wide as he recognized one of the bearded men in SDF uniforms despite his black face paint. He grinned.

Captain Mohammed Tabib had fulfilled his double duty to America and his faith, he reflected.

"Colonel Saunders must have used your ID of Metz's jet combined with intel satellite feeds to track him to the meeting in Hakim's palace. Good job," he told Monet before clasping his hands together, bowing his head, and reciting a prayer of thanks.

The Saudi sandstorm had ended.

Monet's iPhone interrupted the moment.

"For you," he told Carlton, handing him the device. "Thundercloud."

Carlton listened, his features and gaze hardening. "On my way now," he replied, already striding to the door. "If Ben-David's information checks out, I'll bet you dollars to donuts that the Bear will give us the green light. Problem is: we're going to a lot need more juice than the Bear and Saunders on this one." He hung up.

A lot more.

* * *

Sharia Palace
6:23PM local time (4:23PM Paris time)

Yassin's methodical search grew increasingly frantic as the minutes passed. Each second brought him closer to the SDF soldiers searching the palace grounds. He moved faster, ignoring the sharp leaves, slashing his hands and forearms, drawing blood as he shoved the reeds aside hard to locate the manhole cover. He knew it was here somewhere. He had seen it before. It had to be-

He froze in terror, eyes wide. Unless someone had filled it or planted over it. A gardener, perhaps, not knowing its true purpose. Yassin grew alarmed, his heart raced. If that was the case, then he would never-

There it was, under a thick mat of dried vegetation debris.

Grinning, he bent down, scraped his fingers to the bone to clear and pry the heavy round metal plate open, squeezed his body into the tight confines of a utility tunnel below, replaced the manhole cover above him, descended along steel rungs implanted into the concrete tube.

As in the underwater tunnel, it was pitch dark. After descending twenty feet, he could not even see his bloody hands. The tunnel's angle changed from vertical to horizontal. Its diameter grew, but not enough for him to stand. He crawled on his raw hands and knees through the stygian darkness.

Luckily, he did not need to see anything. There was only one possible direction. He followed it in silence so complete that his ears buzzed, all sounds from the palace muffled by the thick layer of sand above him. The temperature dropped so much that it became downright cold, particularly in his clothes, still damp. He could feel blood oozing from the deep pulsing cuts in his face, hands, arms, and now his knees. He ignored the pain, pressed forward. The SDF soldiers would be looking for him. Since their perimeter around the palace had not caught him, they would search for a method of escape. Sooner or later, they would find the tunnel.

Nearly an hour later, Yassin poked his head out of another steel manhole cover. The palace was nowhere to be seen, hidden from sight by rolling sand dunes that he knew were over two kilometers from the palace. He pulled himself out of the tunnel, remaining on all fours to avoid attracting attention. He found a group of boulders, advanced toward it. Although the sun was now setting, his hands and knees burned on the still blistering sand, slightly blinded after the inky darkness. He turned one of the smaller smooth rocks over, then a second, then a third. His panic returned. Where was it?

He turned over five more rocks before finding and removing the cell phone he had hidden long ago.

Would it still work?

Yassin powered it up, punched in a number, hit 'send'.

He grinned. It still worked.

He recited an innocuous phrase, promptly hung up. He disconnected the battery, removed the chip, dismantled the phone, buried its parts, then patiently waited inside the tunnel opening to protect himself from prying eyes and the brilliant sun. His wounds ached. He fought against the rising urge to pass out.

Precisely three hours later, he emerged into the cool desert night at the sound of an approaching vehicle. He scurried to a nearby dirt road, guided by the arc of stars shimmering in the clear vault of night above. He ran along it, spotted a ramshackle van driving slowly, headlights off. He followed the vehicle, gained speed, grabbed hold of the open rear door. Then slipped and fell hard on the ground. The van continued driving.

Supressing a roar of anger, he scrambled back to his feet, bolted to the van. The cloud of dust in its wake made his eyes sting, his lungs protest in violent coughs. He pushed himself hard, leaped into the back, shut the door.

Four hours later, Yassin arrived at a small regional airfield outside Riyadh. He stepped out of the van freshly shaved, beard shorn, hair dyed gray, wearing thick black rimmed eyeglasses, a wedding band, and a Western suit and tie several years out of fashion. His jacket pocket contained a passport and credit cards bearing one of his many identities. He boarded a short flight to Dubai, another to Damascus, then a third, longer flight to his final destination across both the Mediterranean Sea and the Atlantic Ocean.

65 SAFEHOUSE

Safehouse
8:03 AM Local Time

Money could not buy happiness, but for Yassin, it bought safety.

In this case, safety came in the form of a secret, blast-proof, underground compound deep below a dense tropical jungle, invisible from air and land, inaccessible from both the Sierra de Perija mountain range in the West and Perija National Park in the East, North, and South, surrounded by armed guards and electronic detection systems, and granted the full protection of both the State of Zulia and the Venezuelan government.

No one could touch him here.

His host, Fernando 'El Matador' Ochoa profited handsomely from providing Yassin and his terrorist colleagues a safe haven, but drugs were the true source of his prodigious income. A network of underground tunnels allowed Ochoa to transport cocaine and methamphetamines produced in Colombia right through the Sierra de Perija mountains to the West down and through his compound, to his fleet of boats on the shores of the Palmar River, down to Lake Maracaibo, North through the Gulf of Venezuela and the Caribbean Sea to Mexico, to violent distribution gangs and then end users in the United States, with deadly consequences.

The huge sums that the Venezuelan government demanded both as personal bribes and to fund the Marxist-Leninist Revolutionary Armed Forces of Colombia (FARC) terrorists seeking to topple the democratically elected neighboring Colombian government, Ochoa considered a minor cost of doing business. They hardly made a dent in his massive profits or had the slightest impact upon his lavish lifestyle.

Ochoa's living space in the underground compound consisted of fifty rooms, complete with a 100-seat movie theatre, a swimming complex shaped like a grotto, an immense dining hall resembling that of a medieval castle, a 10,000 bottle wine cellar, a gilded throne room, and its centerpiece: a vault reminiscent of a pirate's treasure cave, larger than most banks, piled high with mounds of gold and silver bars and coins, precious jewels, bearer bonds, and bricks of cash in multiple hard currencies. Ochoa used ten of the rooms to house a harem of men, women, boys, and girls purchased from human traffickers to slake his and his men's lust for rape - and worse. The drug lord had not earned his nickname of 'El Matador' - The Killer - by killing bulls: after a recent orgy and ensuing bloodbath, the rooms were empty, cleared of the victims and washed down, awaiting the next wave of slaves.

Yassin preferred an austere desert tent to creature comforts and felt only contempt for those like Ochoa who gave in to the pleasures of the flesh. Yet he gladly accepted these in exchange for the only place in the world where he felt truly safe.

Of course, nothing was ever perfect. Spies from the Colombian foreign intelligence service, the *Servicio de Inteligencia Nacional* (SIN), had infiltrated Ochoa's underground jungle fortress in the past. Yet none of them had known a thing about Yassin or his Hamas, Hezbollah, Al Qaeda, and Taliban colleagues in the compound. As a further precaution, Yassin maintained a villa in the tiny hamlet village of Alegre a few kilometers away, easily accessible from the compound by tunnel in case of emergency. And Ochoa had found the SIN moles, tortured and executed them personally. He particularly enjoyed torturing the women, recording their screams to replay on his iPod, something Yassin considered strange but gave no further thought to.

Yassin slumped back into a chair in the hot, stuffy, pitch black room, allowing himself only a short moment of rest. There was much work to be done.

He did not mourn Prince Hakim's death. Al Shayk had always been his true master. Hakim had been no more than an instrument, a means to an end. His passions and ego had long been a problem. Al Shayk had managed to redirect them from debauchery to *jihadi* Wahhabism for years, but had not foreseen the megalomania that emerged upon Hakim's illegitimate accession to the Saudi throne. It had consumed not only him, but Al Shayk's otherwise well-laid plan.

With their instrument destroyed, Yassin and al Shayk would have to find another weak leader to nurture, elevate, and fund to do their dirty work. The United States and its allies were slowly restricting the number of viable candidates, their funding, and their safe havens, but finding one would not be difficult given Yassin's contacts, track record and, most importantly, the vast funds he had stolen for years from under Hakim's upturned nose.

Even those would not be necessary.

Hakim had directed the Saudi Arabian Monetary Agency - the Saudi central bank - to transfer the nearly one trillion dollars of the kingdom's reserves for conversion into euros, in transfers of $50 billion each, using up all of the kingdom's cash despite the vast sums needed for welfare payments to the simmering unemployed population. The order had been given by Hakim. Yet as soon as the funds left Riyadh, they entered a complex system of accounts entirely within Yassin's control. Hakim's death had not altered that fact. It was now time to put those euros to work.

Yassin's first order of business was to make certain the funds did not return to the Saudi central bank.

He wiped the sweat from his brow, removed his address book from the floor safe in complete darkness as always, found the chair, clicked on the desk lamp. He immediately began using the coded information to access the master account in the Venezuelan capital of Caracas on his heavily firewalled laptop. He set a three-minute timer to ensure that the session lasted less than the four minutes needed for ECHELON to pinpoint any communication's exact origin.

His jaw dropped well before the timer ran out.

Empty. The account was empty.

He cursed.

This was not possible. The FBI knew only a fraction of what the account had funded, such as Abu Hassan's failed attack against the American electrical grid. Even if the FBI had learned more, it would have to obtain many lengthy authorizations before acting, including special court orders, possibly even presidential authorization. Even then, the Venezuelan banking authorities would never comply with a request to freeze the funds. If they ever did, he would have moved them first. And this account was not frozen, but empty. Bone dry. Not a cent.

There had to be an explanation, thought Yassin, forcing himself to remain calm despite his rising anxiety. Perhaps the Venezuelan government had simply taken the money. No. As corrupt as the Chavez government could be and as badly as its failed Bolivarian socialist model needed funds, news that such a huge amount of money had been stolen by the Venezuelan government would travel fast. Flows of dirty hard currency would stop making their way to Venezuela. The government would be unable to take a cut. It would be bad for business. So what else could have happened?

Exhausted as he was after his arduous escape, it took Yassin a while to piece things together. The funds must still be in the legion sub-accounts where the dollar-to-euro trades were made, he reasoned. Located in secrecy-worshipping tax havens like the Cayman Islands, Cyprus, and some jurisdictions far less above-board, it would take a long time for U.S. authorities to locate the accounts, let alone freeze them. He disconnected, reset the timer, accessed the accounts.

All empty.

He launched another curse, then stared at the dusty floor, head spinning and hands shaking in the heat and semi-darkness. Even if a few of his bankers had tipped off the Americans - doubtful, given the deadly risk they knew it entailed - each of the accounts they controlled were separate from the rest. They would not *all* be empty. He thought of another explanation. The funds had probably been repatriated to the Saudi central bank, he concluded. Problematic, but not fatal. He verified the account histories.

This time, he was too shocked to curse.

The funds had not been repatriated to Riyadh.

But they *had* been transferred.

The owner and location made his blood boil.

United States Department of Justice. Federal Reserve Bank, Washington, DC.

The timer rang, shaking him from his nightmare.

He stabbed the keyboard, terminating the connection.

Yassin stood and paced the Spartan room in shock, inhaling deep breaths to calm himself, taking stock of his situation.

Al Shayk had long ago taught him to design plans within plans, backups to backups. This operation had been no different.

The hundreds of billions of dollars Hakim had transferred from the Saudi central bank to the Venezuelan master account, that Yassin had arranged to be converted to euros to sink the dollar, were now in the possession of the U.S. government. Permanently out of his control. There was nothing he could do about it. The U.S. government had foreclosed his last remaining strategy tied to Hakim.

But he would never have been able to use the funds themselves, Yassin reasoned. Hundreds of millions could be hidden, perhaps even a few billion. Not hundreds of billions. They would stick out within the banking community like antlers on a camel. No matter where they were located, sooner or later the Americans and other Western powers would have isolated them.

Sooner, as it turned out. Although the speed with which it had occurred troubled him deeply.

The only other funds Yassin could actually use were those Hakim had embezzled from the Interior Ministry over the years and given to Yassin to safeguard in various accounts under different names around the world, most of which Yassin had stolen by placing it in separate accounts under his sole control, ostensibly to give Hakim plausible deniability. Having located and appropriated the giant Saudi reserves Hakim had sent out of Riyadh, the Americans would have no reason to believe there were any other funds, Yassin reasoned.

His calm and confidence returned. He reset the timer, reconnected to the net.

His mouth hung agape.

Empty.

Despite the trapped heat, his sweat ran cold. He verified the account histories, already knowing where the funds had gone, just like those of the Saudi central bank: the U.S. Federal Reserve Bank.

He was wrong.

The funds were not at the Federal Reserve Bank in Washington. Nor were they in any other account owned by the Justice Department. Instead, they were located in various banks across the Middle East and

North Africa, in the name of organizations that whipped his fear and frustration into a froth of white hot anger.

Campaign for Egyptian Democracy.
Coalition for Tunisian Freedom.
Libyan Democratic Alliance.
Fund for a Free Algeria.
Yemen Human Rights Fund.
Syrian Democratic Secular Alliance.

He read on, the names of the next organizations turning him from angry to hopping mad.

Arab Action Committee for Women's Civil Rights.
Institute for Islamic-Christian-Jewish Dialogue and Tolerance.
Arab Coalition for a Free Press.

He stared at the stone wall, eyes welling with tears. His enemies had short-circuited everything he had worked for. They had laid all his meticulous planning, patient waiting, and bold execution to waste. They had turned the tables on him in the most unimaginable way: instead of funding *jihad* against his enemies, he was funding his enemies.

Yassin's rage erupted. In a single motion, he terminated the connection, launched out of his chair, sent the laptop crashing onto the wood floor. He shouted, screamed, wailed as he kicked the machine, disintegrating it into smithereens. Searching for another target, he made the chair his next victim, smashing, splitting, cracking it into unrecognizable matchsticks. With nothing left to destroy, he pounded the blast-proof reinforced concrete wall until his fists bled. His shouts exhausted themselves into whimpers.

His fury spent, spirit crushed, he fell to the floor on his knees. He slumped his back against the wall, contemplated his fate.

Yassin's fanatical hatred of everything other than Wahhabi Islam motivated his actions, but his vast funds had always been the true source of his power. Without them, he was no longer the master of his fate. Having failed so miserably, he was unable to return to - or even contact - Al Shayk. Mercy and forgiveness were not the cleric's strong suits. His tolerance for failure lasted only as long as it took to order a public stoning or beheading. Without funds or support from Al

Shayk, Yassin would sink from master planner to mere peg in whatever organization he joined.

No longer a master, but a slave.

To make matters worse, his notoriety in jihadist circles would only multiply the difficulty in finding an organization that would take him in. He did not even have enough money to pay Ochoa's bloated rent.

His face hot, streaked with tears, he shuddered at the thought of having to work for Ochoa, an infidel whose life motive was the accumulation of lucre. A weakness. He stopped and smiled. A weakness that he could exploit.

As he lay against the cool concrete wall, Yassin began to formulate a plan to take over Ochoa's business. Strangely for a jihadist, Yassin was nothing if not optimistic. He would begin by using his Taliban contacts in poppy-growing Afghanistan and those harbored in Ochoa's compound to add heroin to Ochoa's deadly mix of meth and coke. He would use Ochoa's Mexican contacts smuggling drugs into the U.S. as a conduit for the heroin. Needing little himself, he would be far more generous than Ochoa, both with his men and with the Venezuelans, building greater support. Once he had taken over, he would kill his host and use his massive cash flow to build another organization to wage *jihad* against the West, this one based in Venezuela only a short distance from U.S. shores.

He would begin tomorrow. Right now, he needed sleep. He stretched out on the dust caked wood floor, closed his eyes.

The Americans may have learned of one or more of his identities upon discovering his accounts, but they neither knew his location nor could they get to him if they did.

His eroding adrenaline was no match for his exhaustion. He quickly fell asleep.

66 SPIRIT

509th Bomber Wing
Whiteman Air Force Base
Montana
12:53 AM

To preserve secrecy, both the hangar and the mission were pitch black. United States Air Force pilot Captain Thomas 'Jefe' Gonzalez and mission commander Major Tamara 'China Doll' Chen sat in the *Spirit of America's* cockpit, running through their preflight checks. The secret ordnance was so large and heavy that only two bombs could fit into the bomb bay. On this mission, one would suffice.

Commonly known as the Stealth Bomber, its deep-black origins at Area 51 dating back nearly six decades to Eisenhower's U-2 CIA spyplane, everything about the Delta-shaped B-2 *Spirit* was staggering. With a wingspan of 172 feet, it was nearly as wide as a Boeing 747 jumbo jet. At a total program cost of over $2 billion per aircraft, Northrop Grumman had built only 21, the complement now down to 20 after a takeoff crash in 2008. The B-2 required a cavernous air-conditioned hangar to prevent its stealth coatings from degrading and 119 hours of maintenance after each hour of flight - twice as long as its B-52 and B-1B predecessors. Yet the taxpayers had gotten their money's worth. Capable of reaching any target on the globe without landing by refueling in mid-air, the B-2's flying wing design, buried jet engine intakes and exhausts, revolutionary materials, and absorbent coatings so reduced its infrared, radar, and acoustic signatures that the giant aircraft was nearly indistinguishable from a bird to even the most sophisticated anti-aircraft defenses.

With all systems nominal, Jefe taxiied the *Spirit of America* from the darkened hangar onto the tarmac under cover of night. Only then did the runway lights blink on. Less than a minute later, he reached the edge of the runway, turned the aircraft into position.

Static crackled in his headset. "Strike, this is Control. You are clear for takeoff."

"Roger Control."

Jefe pushed the thrust controls forward in their grooves, pouring kerosene into the bomber's four General Electric F118-GE-100 turbofans, sending the 340,000 pound behemoth rolling, then hurtling down the runway. The flying wing tilted up into the starry night sky. The runway lights winked off.

"Control, this is Strike. Wheels up. Proceeding to 470 knots and 50,000 feet. Initiating radio silence."

"Roger, Strike. Good hunting."

67 TERRORIST

The massive detonation shook the floor and walls, awaking Yassin by throwing him into the air. He struck the floor and twisted into a crouch in the total darkness, remaining still, eyes wide open, ears pricked up. The tremor abated, leaving the deep rumble echoing through the halls of the underground compound. A wailing klaxon indicating a security breach soon replaced it.

Yassin wasted no time pondering whether the attackers were coming for him, his fellow jihadists, Ochoa's drugs and treasure, or Ochoa himself. Relying on instinct and training, he hoisted himself up into a ceiling trap door in the inky darkness, using the movements he had rehearsed so many times before.

He emerged into a cramped upper space just as dark as the room below. When illuminated, to all appearances it served as a storage area. Crawling to the far end of the space, Yassin felt the floor with his hands, located a dusty trunk. He shoved it aside, touched the rim of the circular opening beneath it. He slid into it feet first, felt the purchase of metal rungs, descended a few, reached back up. He heaved the trunk back into position overhead, concealing the narrow opening and triggering dim lights embedded in the reinforced concrete walls.

Yassin proceeded down the tight, soundproofed shaft with calm, methodical movements. A hundred feet down, the slender tube enlarged into a wider cavity carved directly into bedrock. He descended another fifty feet, leaped off the last rung. Landing on his feet, he grabbed a flashlight from a wall charger, switched off the tunnel lights by punching a numeric code into a keypad, then ran down the damp tunnel, not stopping once to listen for the sound of pursuers.

Even if Ochoa's guards squealed or if the enemy stumbled upon this tunnel among the dozens of others in the compound, Yassin enjoyed substantial advantages. First, he had a head start. Second, the tunnel's lights could be turned back on only by entering the exact code he had just used. Third, the tunnel branched off into multiple secondary and even tertiary tunnels to throw off pursuers. Fourth, he had convinced - and paid - Ochoa to install tear gas containers along the tunnel walls, which he could explode from either end.

Only his flashlight beam illuminated the dark, chiseled tunnel, yet Yassin found no difficulty jogging down the hot, humid passageway. He had practiced running through its tortuous path so many times that every wall, every turn, every step was indelibly etched into his brain.

After the first kilometer, he stopped to catch his breath in the soupy air trapped among the slick stone walls. He shut off his flashlight, pricked up his ears. The only thing he could hear was his heavy breathing. He held his breath, listened again.

A rush of footsteps. Distant, but growing louder. Far behind him, the tunnel seemed to glow faintly, probably from flashlights. Someone must have talked, he concluded. He would take his revenge on them, but for now, he had to complete his escape. He switched his flashlight back on.

Yassin bolted down the single correct underground route, zigzagging to bypass the clever decoy tunnels, continuing even after repeatedly smashing his head on thick roots of jungle vegetation sinewing down from the ceiling. He stopped at the second kilometer marker, massaging his aching skull. Despite his pounding heart and loud panting, with sweat streaming down his face in rivulets, Yassin could still hear the sound of footsteps approaching, as though his pursuers had not tired a whit.

Yet there were fewer of them, he detected. He grinned. Some of his pursuers must have entered the decoy tunnels. He continued onward, energized by the thought of the enemy stumbling down passageways leading nowhere and having to retrace their steps inside the chiseled stone labyrinth. Many would never find their way out.

Three more kilometers to go. The tunnel became trickier now, winding backwards, water seeping in from the jungle high above, dripping down and collecting into pools on the rock floor, causing him to slip and fall more frequently, tearing clothes and skin. By the time Yassin broached the final kilometer, a sharp pain lanced his chest.

He ignored it, kept running, his flashlight switched off to avoid giving away his position, the fear of yet another failure nipping at his heels. Now in complete darkness, he had to feel his way along the walls with his grime and blood coated hands. His nervous and physical exhaustion increased his slips and crashes onto the sharp slick rock floor. His gashes, cuts and contusions ached, but he forced, willed himself onward.

Until he slammed into a slab of cold metal.

Fumbling for his keys, his entire body throbbing, chest constricted and erupting with pain, Yassin heard footsteps racing toward him, noticed a brightening glow in the tunnel behind him. He grimaced. Not all of his pursuers had fallen for the decoy tunnels. How the devil had they managed to figure them out, he wondered, blinking back stinging beads of sweat.

No matter. They would soon be in for a surprise. He clicked on his flashlight long enough to slide the trembling key into the lock, pulled the door open, stepped inside a narrow passage, shut and bolted the armored door behind him. He took a deep breath of cool air in the basement of his villa in Alegre.

In the dim light of a dust-caked low-wattage bulb, he found the rear section of a wine rack weighed down with dusty bottles. An artifice, since he did not consume alcohol. He ran his hand over the wood panel, located a recessed handle on the left. He grabbed it, heaved the panel to the right. It slid with ease on well-oiled rails, revealing the confines of his *cava* - his cave. Walking into the small room, he shoved the heavy wine rack back into position, lifted one of the bottles, pressed a button underneath.

Laughter croaked out from Yassin's parched throat at the sound of tear gas canisters exploding along the entire length of the tunnel. How he wished he could witness his pursuers' agony as thousands of pounds of compressed tear gas were released into the tunnels. Those who did not choke to death on the potent chemical would have no choice but to turn and run back the way they had come, like rats - that is, if they could find their way.

The thought lifted his spirits, but he dared not waste time relishing it. He was not free yet. He had to dress in a Venezuelan military uniform and hop behind the wheel of the military Jeep parked outside his unassuming villa kilometers away from Ochoa's compound. At that point, no one would dare stop him. He would make Caracas within eight hours. There he would speak to his contacts to determine the nature and outcome of the attack on Ochoa's compound. If need be, the Venezuelan cargo aircraft that had brought him from Damascus would take him back. He would be in Pakistan within twenty four hours. The resurgent Taliban controlling a large swath of its mountainous territory would likely welcome him when presented with the letter of introduction he had obtained from one of its most wanted chiefs, a fellow guest at Ochoa's compound. He would bide his time and engineer the takeover of Ochoa's drug empire from there.

Yassin ran upstairs to the ground floor, negotiating each step expertly in the dawn light that managed to sneak past the drawn shutters. He snatched the keys to the Jeep from a plate on a credenza, walked to the floor safe where he kept his account passcodes, the letter of introduction, and his multiple passports.

And gasped.

* * *

If anyone could have silenced the shrieks of the jungle's nocturnal inhabitants and glimpsed a patch of open sky through the canopy of lush vegetation, they would not have managed to see or hear anything. Not even condensation trails, which Ophir-manufactured electronics prevented by warning the pilot to alter altitude when the telltale sign of high altitude jet engines might form. Yet even if someone could have spotted the *Spirit of America*, they would have had no cause for concern, as the bomber flew above the airspace of neighboring Colombia, the staunch U.S. ally that had authorized the overflight.

"Coming into position," Jefe announced into his headset mike.

China Doll leaned forward, scanned the navigational screen indicating their exact location, compared it to the position in their orders, nodded. "Confirmed. No signal to abort or modify coordinates. Opening bomb bay doors." She hit a switch.

A vibration rumbled through their seats as air roared into the bomb bay at nearly 500 miles per hour, tugging hard at the aircraft's belly. The bomb bay door indicator light switched from green to red.

"Bomb bay open." China Doll placed her finger on the weapons release switch, shifted her attention back to the navigational screen, waited. "Now." She hit the switch, checked the ordnance indicator. "Bomb away. Closing bomb bay doors."

The turbulence abated, the indicator light turned green.

"Heading back to the ranch," announced Jefe, placing the *Spirit of America* into a wide 180-degree turn back toward Montana.

China Doll barely heard him as she focused on the weapon's systems display, verifying its flight controls and internal electronics. "Weapon is active. Systems nominal." She reclined into her seat, exhaled a deep breath. "I'm sure glad we're up here and not down there."

* * *

Yassin stared at the man standing before him. He wore cowboy boots and a hard gaze. The Glock 23 in his hand was aimed squarely at Yassin's head.

"If you wait long enough, the rat will emerge from the tunnel. Hands in the air," the man ordered calmly.

Yassin's first instinct was to jump sideways into the adjoining hallway and fire the Beretta M9 handgun tucked in his waistband at the small of his back. That option evaporated when someone rammed the barrel of a gun into his back, relieved him of the weapon.

Yassin spun around, grimaced in humiliation as a blonde woman squinted at him with green eyes, aiming another Glock 23 at his groin. His only remaining option was to duck and roll sideways into the hallway.

That option too was foreclosed, this one by a bald giant with a withering scowl clutching a SIG-Sauer P229 handgun, its barrel pointed at his chest.

Yassin reluctantly raised his arms, turned back to the man with the Glock, who now held up a silver badge.

"Patrick Carlton. U.S. Department of Justice."

The two others held up their identification.

"Special Agent in Charge Faraday. FBI."

"Major Tadeusz Sobieski. *Polska Agencja Wywiadu*," said the Pole, torching a crooked Marlboro with a red plastic Bic lighter, blowing the smoke into Yassin's face.

"Sayyid Yassin," anounced Carlton. "Or whatever your name happens to be today. You are under arrest for planning, funding, and ordering terrorist attacks."

"Including a planned attack against the U.S. electrical grid, currency, and economy," continued Faraday.

"And for the murder of over fifty Polish Special Forces and Polish and Iraqi civilians in Iraq," Sobieski added through clenched teeth, slapping handcuffs on Yassin's wrists, tightening them until he winced.

"And for the murder of countless others in Iraq, Afghanistan, Spain, Great Britain, Israel, Indonesia, India, Russia, and Saudi Arabia," announced Carlton, stepping toward Yassin until his face was inches away, his gaze boring into the man's brain. "Including the murder of civilian men, women, and children in a bus in Tel Aviv."

Yassin shrugged nonchalantly. "Jews. Not human beings."

Carlton was barely able to restrain his fury. His arms trembled. "And the murder and mutilation of ten U.S. Navy sailors at Khawr al-Amaya."

A look of confusion crept over Yassin's face.

"Those were my men," said Carlton, his voice nearly cracking.

Yassin broke into a pleased smile, paused, spat in Carlton's face.

The spittle had barely hit his nose when Carlton unleashed his pent up rage, driving head first into Yassin, slamming him so violently against the wall that chunks of plaster fell away. He pressed his Glock against the man's left temple while squeezing and pushing his neck up so hard that the stitches of his bicep wound split open once more.

"Carlton, no!" Shouted Faraday.

Carlton ignored her and the pain shooting up his arm and shoulder, pressed harder, squeezed tighter.

"An empty threat," croaked Yassin, winded, sneering despite his subjugated position. "You will not kill me. You are American. You have to play by the rules," he taunted, his voice lilting. "You cannot even waterboard people plotting to kill you." With his windpipe in a vise, his laugh came out as a cackle. "Your ACLU would put you in jail instead of me. That's why you will never vanquish us," he announced triumphantly, infuriating Carlton with another grin. "Your freedom makes you weak."

He had played Carlton perfectly, he concluded. Making him explode in anger yet leaving him impotent, unable to do anything about it.

Yassin's self-satisfied grin continued until he suddenly doubled in two, caught by complete surprise, nearly passing out in agony as Carlton removed his knee from his groin. Stars flashed in his vision while he held his private parts, gasping for air. Carlton had been as prepared as he, Yassin reflected through his searing pain, orchestrating his response to make his own point.

"You are right. We cannot shoot you. Not without a trial. Which is why we will win. For now, you are under arrest." His statement fell on deaf ears, Carlton knew, but hearing himself say it made him feel better. He turned to Faraday. "Shackle the swine."

Yassin scrambled back, apoplectic with humiliation as Faraday cuffed his ankles. He clawed at her arms, kicked her hands, receiving only a condescending scowl in return.

And the muzzle of Sobieski's SIG Sauer against his skull.

"You cannot arrest me," he exclaimed, groaning in pain, looking up defiantly from the floor, still trying to catch his breath. "I have diplomatic immunity. The United States and Poland have no jurisdiction over me here. You must get permission from the Venezuelan government. Where is your warrant?" He demanded.

Carlton nodded. "Ah, yes. Jurisdiction," he replied calmly, sucking on a tooth, betraying none of the rage still bottled inside him. Although he had steeled himself against Yassin's pathetic arguments and reactions, it still took every ounce of his self-control to keep from drilling multiple bullets into the death merchant's skull.

"Tell me, Mr. Yassin. Were you legally inside Iraq when you organized the murder of Iraqi civilians, Coalition troops, and Polish aid workers? Or legally inside the other countries when you organized suicide bombings there?"

"You obviously have the wrong person. Everywhere I went, I traveled under a diplomatic passport issued by the Saudi Kingdom."

"And we have American and Polish diplomatic passports," Carlton shot back. "Which means that we have as much right to be here as you had in the countries whose citizens you murdered."

Yassin remained unfazed. "That does not make it legal for you to arrest me on Venezuelan soil. And Venezuela has no extradition treaty with the United States or Poland."

"As legal as it was for Venezuelan authorities to deny us access to your account despite international banking treaties," Faraday shot back, "not to mention harboring a terrorist."

Carlton shrugged. "The Venezuelan authorities have their jurisdiction, we have ours. They will rant and rave, but I doubt they will fight for your return once the world hears that they kept such an active terror account secret. And that they gave you safe haven in the compound of a drug lord responsible for the deaths of thousands of Americans and others." He leaned forward. "You can appeal to the Attorney General, who follows the law to the letter, but I doubt you'll get far. His daughter was killed by a drug overdose."

Yassin knew there was no immediate way out, but engaging in communication might distract his captors and buy him time to create one.

"How were you able to redirect the accounts?" He asked, as a deep thumps reverberated in the dawn air, approaching steadily.

Carlton glanced at the shuttered window, then back at Yassin. "Let's just say that it's amazing what can be accomplished through the internet," he replied, using Ben-David's explanation. Thank goodness the DARPA physicist had possessed the *chutzpah* to go along with his plan, he did not add. The government might reprimand Ben-David for moving the funds and repatriate them to Saudi Arabia, but the action had served its purpose.

An astonished expression traced itself on Yassin's face as the thumps outside grew to such volume that the shuttered windows threatened to shatter. He kept talking. "But my internet lines were not local. How did you know I was here?"

"Prince Qhibli."

"You tortured him."

The irony of a terrorist alleging such a thing shocked Carlton, but did not surprise him. Now the walls were shaking.

"We did not even need to interrogate Qhibli. He was desperate to avoid being returned to Saudi Arabia to face King Fahim's wrath." He watched as more surprise - and fear - revealed itself on Yassin's face. "Yes, King Fahim has been freed. The Justice Department agreed to try Qhibli in the U.S. on the condition that his information lead to your capture," Carlton explained in a loud voice to make himself heard above the din of the approaching helicopters. He walked to the nearest window, glanced at his watch, peered at the sky through slits in the shutters. "FARC helicopters."

"We need to go," said Faraday.

Carlton turned to the others, shook his head anxiously. "We have to give the others more time."

Yassin's hope surged. FARC helicopters were heavily armed, he knew, its soldiers ruthless. And allied with the Venezuelan government that funded them. If he could give them more time, they would save him. "Qhibli knew about Ochoa, but not about my villa," he said, trying to keep his enemy talking.

Faraday took that one. "But the SIN did," she replied in a loud voice over the deafening helicopter rotors, referring to the Colombian foreign intelligence service. She let the new shock course through his system. "That's right. The spies Ochoa tortured and murdered knew not only about his compound and tunnels, but about your presence and villa as well."

Carlton swiveled as ten heavily armed men crested the top of the basement staircase, wearing FARC camouflage fatigues and black face paint.

Yassin noticed gas masks hanging from their frontal body armor. Those were the people who had followed him through the tunnel, not Americans and Poles, he realized, relieved.

He grinned at his saviors.

The tables were now turned.

* * *

Developed by Northrop Grumman and Lockheed Martin, the GBU-57A/B bomb far surpassed its predecessor, the GBU-28. Nicknamed the

Massive Ordnance Penetrator or 'MOP', it weighed a staggering 30,000 pounds, 5,300 pounds of which constituted a high explosive warhead. Other than its gargantuan size, the MOP was unique in that it could penetrate 200 feet of 5,000 pound-per-square inch reinforced concrete while capable of precision-guided flight to exact GPS coordinates through the use of nimble computerized winglets.

Within seconds upon its release from the *Spirit of America*'s cavernous bomb bay nearly ten miles above the Earth's surface, the MOP's winglets shot out from its sleek metal body, guiding it to the preprogrammed coordinates sharply to the East of the bomber's flight path.

* * *

"I see you have captured your *rata*," announced the commander in heavily accented English, using the Spanish word for 'rat', increasing the volume of his voice to make himself heard over the helicopters outside.

"Possible only because of your men's bravery, colonel Sanchez," replied Carlton, massaging his aching wound. The bleeding had already soaked his shirt. "We are in your debt."

Sanchez gave a curt nod, checked his watch. "We have very little time left, *Señor* Carlton. We must leave immediately. We sealed all the exits and booby-trapped the tunnels, but many of Ochoa's men will surely make it through."

Yassin listened to the conversation in shock, unable to accept that the enemy had outmaneuvered him. This colonel Sanchez and his men were not FARC insurgents but Colombian military, probably SIN. "But how did-"

"*Kurwa twoja mac*," cursed Sobieski, tossing his cigarette to the floor, stomping down on it - and Yassin's foot, causing him to yelp in pain. Your whore mother. "Stop talking, start walking," he ordered in his heavy Polish accent, roughly shoving Yassin out of the villa.

Two aged Huey helicopters sat hovering inches from the hard-packed dirt road outside, side doors open. Their hurricane rotor wash sent dust flying into the air, forcing all to cover their eyes. Painted olive green, they bore the FARC terrorist logo of crossed machineguns over the outline of Colombia superimposed over the nation's yellow, blue, and red flag.

Yassin observed the aircraft, stunned. It was now obvious what had happened. The Colombian *Agrupacion de Fuerzas Especiales Antiterroristas Urbanas* - Urban Counterterrorism Special Forces Group - had used captured FARC uniforms and helicopters to camouflage their raid from Ochoa's men and the Venezuelan government. He had little time to reflect on it as Sobieski unceremoniously manhandled him into the first helicopter's cargo bay.

Just as machinegun fire erupted from inside the villa.

Faraday and two Colombian special forces troops were instantly hit, including colonel Sanchez. They crumpled to the ground. The eight other soldiers immediately returned fire with their M-16s in full automatic mode, providing enough covering fire for Carlton and Sobieski to grab Faraday and Sanchez with Carlton howling in pain, heave them into the first helicopter, and jump in after them.

As the helicopter began to ascend, the M-197 General Dynamics electric Gatling guns that the Colombian special forces had newly fitted to the two helicopters lit up. Their three spinning barrels rocketed deadly streams of 20 millimeter rounds into every exposed area of Yassin's villa at 735 rounds per minute, one from the ground, the other rising into the air, shattering windows, tearing through masonry, shredding plaster, exploding roof tiles. The onslaught of bullets allowed the soldiers to retrieve their remaining comrade and pile into the second helicopter.

As the last soldier jumped inside, the engines strained to claw the heavily-laden aircraft into the air while the Gatling guns continued to rain their deadly hail of bullets.

None noticed a grenade launcher poke through a jagged gash in the villa's façade until it fired. The first Gatling gun operator immediately swiveled the weapon and ripped the shooter in half, but he was too late. The grenade landed precisely in the middle of the helicopter cargo bay, exploding a millisecond later.

Carlton witnessed the fuselage blow apart before shielding his eyes from the erupting ball of fire that engulfed the Colombian special forces soldiers inside. Burning fragments of the destroyed helicopter struck the one he was in, one flying in through the open bay door before Carlton let go of his handhold and kicked it back out. The helicopter suddenly lurched down then swung to the side as the pilot fought the massive turbulence, sending Carlton flying out the open door. Sobieski grabbed him by the collar, yanking him back inside.

"Thanks." He turned to Faraday and Sanchez lying on the floor in a rapidly expanding pool of blood. She was hit in the leg, he in the stomach. He kneeled, grasped Faraday's hand, peered at her face. She was breathing but unconscious. Next to her, Sanchez writhed, grimaced, shouted words that could not be heard over the thumping rotors beating the air above. The copilot crept in from the cockpit, grabbed a medical bag, assessed their wounds. He started administering crude first aid, gave Carlton a thumbs-up. Survivable.

Carlton peered down at the receding villa, now aflame from the exploded helicopter's burning kerosene. The Colombian special forces had managed to infiltrate one of the world's most insidious drug dealers' compound, drive Yassin directly into their shackling embrace, and save their lives. Heroes. Like Davenport and his men in Alaska and those Carlton had lost in Iraq. All directly or indirectly killed by Yassin. He mouthed a prayer for their souls, shuddering at the notion that Yassin had survived when the heroes below had lost their lives. His anger welled up, masking the pain in his arm. This time, he could not control it.

He turned to Yassin, who clutched a safety harness with both hands, eyes open wide, face pale as a ghost, clearly terrified of the vertiginous height. So much the better. He glanced at Sanchez laying on the slick metal floor, saw his field knife in the scabbard attached to his calf. It would take only a quick slash to slice through Yassin's harness.

Accidents occurred frequently on combat missions.

He reached for the blade.

Sanchez leaned forward and grasped Carlton's forearm, squeezing it while shaking his head.

Their gazes locked. Sanchez's words were lost amid the deafening noise, but Carlton understood the message in his eyes. His men had given their lives for something far greater. He could not sully their honor with personal revenge.

He nodded. Then crawled through the blood to Yassin anyway.

The man turned to him, eyes wide as saucers, clamped his hands around the harness, knuckles turning white. "I demand to know where you are taking me," he shrieked in terror, barely audible over the deafening rotors and howling wind.

Carlton ignored his question, glanced at his watch. "I want you to see something," he shouted into his ear instead, grasping him from behind in a full Nelson before pointing to the area of the jungle where Ochoa's fortified compound lay buried.

* * *

Locked on the GPS coordinates that the Colombian SIN had provided at the cost of its agents' lives, the MOP finished adjusting its lateral course, miles away and now across the border from where the *Spirit of America* had released it. Shrieking straight down from the dawn sky, it plowed through the soft jungle ground cover as easily as through the air above, drilled through 100 feet of 2,000 psi reinforced concrete like so much butter, coming to a halt in the working area of Ochoa's facility less than one tenth of a second after impact.

The 5,300 pounds of high explosives detonated, instantly vaporizing occupants, weapons, drugs, and building structures within a 500 foot radius from the impact.

The MOP's effects did not end there. Its blast unleashed a deadly shock wave. The fortified enclosed space concentrated it. It drove outward through every room and tunnel in the facility with such speed and heat that the air itself became compressed into a weapon, pressing, searing, destroying everything in its path. Nothing alive or usable remained in Ochoa's once vaunted fortified compound, including El Matador himself, who was drowned, cooked, and sealed in the molten gold and silver of his treasure vault. When the shock wave finally dissipated, it had destabilized the compound's structure to such a degree that the entire facility collapsed on itself under thousands of tons of jungle rock, dirt, and vegetation above.

Seconds after the initial explosion, which appeared minor and localized from their distance and height, Carlton and Yassin watched the jungle canopy drop 100 feet in the blink of an eye, sending dark clouds of dirt and ash billowing high into the air, obscuring the dawn sun, giving the scene an otherwordly effect, as though they were witnessing a Biblical cataclysm rather than a man-made event.

Carlton felt Yassin shudder under his grip. He placed his mouth against the man's ear.

"Like bin Laden, wherever you murderers flee, we will find you. And we will destroy you."

* * *

Carlton had promised Yassin a trial, but he had not mentioned where. The new administration had continued rendering terrorists to foreign governments for interrogation, a practice initially begun in the Clinton administration, but promising that they would not be tortured. National security implications had made closing the Bush administration terrorist holding facility at Guantanamo Bay, Cuba - Gitmo - too dangerous, but Attorney General Thorne was not convinced about the wisdom of conducting a trial by military tribunal at Gitmo of a terrorist like Yassin. That left only one place the U.S. government could legally send Yassin for trial other than the United States, where a criminal trial and appeals would last decades and force the release of critical intelligence that would severely damage U.S. and global counterterror efforts: Yassin's homeland.

The fate awaiting Yassin in Saudi Arabia was considerably less pleasant than the *halal* menu, clean cells, full medical and dental care, copies of the *Qu'ran*, Red Cross visits, and *mihrabs* on the floor pointing to Mecca for prayers provided at Gitmo.

The proceedings against him under *sharia* law - the last before King Fahim adopted a constitution and a new criminal code - had none of the due process or evidentiary rights provided even by U.S. military tribunals.

The trial was swift, the sentence immediate, its execution brutal.

Beheading in a public square.

68 LIGHTNING

Bone-tired despite sleeping the entire way from Colombia without bothering to change, Carlton wished that DARPA offered a frequent flyer program as the agency's Gulfstream touched down at the HEERP airstrip in Akona, Alaska. The tarmac was already choked with military and government agency aircraft.

After popping a couple of Advil to numb the throbbing pain in his left bicep, stitched up for the third time, Carlton stepped down the aircraft's staircase, squinting in the bright Arctic sun, shivering in the glacial wind. He flashed his ID at a harried Marine private who waved him through while warily regarding his disheveled appearance, pointed to a waiting mud-splattered Humvee.

The government could work fast and well when properly motivated, he reflected. The pothole-riddled access road had been groomed and freshly asphalted. Apart from stops at three newly-erected security pillboxes guarding entrances through three new perimeter walls, the ride was smooth as silk all the way to the new, unrecognizable headquarters building.

One hour later, he was seated behind Ben-David in a state of the art control room, from where he watched the final preparations for what the DARPA physicist called 'Solar Lightning'. He listened to Ben-David, Joanne Franklin, and six other scientists in lab coats through noise-cancelling headphones that doubled as communication devices. The ventilation system pumped in cold air from the Alaskan wilderness outside, yet the air inside the crowded room remained unpleasantly warm and stuffy. And despite the facility's reconstruction, the scent of cordite seemed to linger in the air as a memory of the attack only a few days ago. Perspiration beaded on his brow.

Ben-David worked in an unshaven frenzy of manic activity, *yarmulke* tilted wildly atop his mussed hair, eyes bloodshot and surrounded by dark circles from his around-the-clock work to get HEERP repaired and functional. Carlton smiled at his T-shirt, which bore a design by LA artist Greg Gould depicting a person pointing a gasoline dispenser to his head like a gun above the caption 'Self Serve'.

"All systems nominal," announced Franklin, seated at the control console. She too appeared exhausted. But there was something more. Carlton noticed that the attack had erased the innocence from her young face, replaced it with a gritty confidence.

Ben-David mouthed a silent prayer, took a deep breath. "Initiate ground array charge."

Franklin turned a knob. "Ground transmission initiated."

Ben-David glanced at a gauge to confirm that the system was functioning. "Initiate satellite leader stroke."

Franklin tapped the command on her keyboard and waited for the orbiting satellite to respond. "Satellite leader stroke initiated."

"Ten percent power."

Despite her obvious excitement, Franklin forced herself to conduct the procedure with mechanical calm. "Ten percent."

"Fifteen percent power," ordered Ben-David.

"Fifteen percent."

Ben-David and Franklin continued their incremental dance.

Twenty percent.

Twenty five percent.

Thirty percent.

"Come on, Nicky Tesla, help us out," Ben-David muttered, taking another deep breath. "Thirty three point three percent power," he ordered.

Carlton recalled Tesla's numeric fixation, just like with the eighteen array poles outside.

Franklin turned the control knob to the designated power level.

And lightning struck.

Not an ordinary lightning bolt. One so bright that its light glowed through the joints of the walls and under the doors, reminiscent of a horror movie. A microsecond later, a thunderclap louder than any jet engine roared through the Alaskan wilderness. The headphones immediately cancelled out the noise, but Carlton could feel its immense power rumble through his body. The HEERP headquarters structure shook and groaned ominously once again, but the new materials held firm.

Any belief that the lightning and thunder were natural quickly evaporated.

Both were continuous.

Ben-David allowed himself a cautious smile, but the test was far from over.

He and Franklin continued ratcheting up the resonators until they reached full power. He sucked in a deep lungful of air before turning to the scientist monitoring the flow of electricity.

"How much juice?" He asked through his headset.

The scientist swiveled, eyes wide. "You're not going to believe it."

"Try me."

"Nearly 25,000 megawatts. And we're grounding out seventy five percent of the juice."

Ben-David stared back at the scientist, mouth agape, stunned into immobility and mute disbelief, hands on his head. The creases and pallor of exhaustion on his face vanished.

"That's 100,000 megawatts at full power." Slowly, he allowed himself a smile. Then a grin. Soon he could no longer contain himself. "Yes!" He shouted, hugging Franklin, herself in tears, then Carlton.

"I take it that's a lot of power?" Asked Carlton after recovering from Ben-David's bear hug.

"A city of 40,000 uses about ten megawatts," explained Ben-David, unable to remain still. "U.S. consumption is about 800,000 megawatts. At full power, eight of these arrays could power the entire U.S. electrical grid. This is bigger than all energy discoveries since nuclear fission. It could bury the economic crisis."

Carlton gazed at him, dumbfounded. Ben-David had informed him how Tesla's system worked, but not its potential yield.

"Of course, we could not use it continuously," added Ben-David.

"Why not?"

"Heat."

"I thought the lightning was only striking the rods."

Ben-David nodded. "It is. But a lightning bolt superheats the ambient air to about 18,000 degrees. The roar of that air is what we hear as thunder. If we kept the lightning continuous, it would create a giant atmospheric heater, disrupting weather patterns and possibly the global climate."

"The environmentalists are going to love you."

Ben-David shrugged. "Maybe the radicals will put up a fight. But Tesla's system will eliminate coal-fired electrical plants and a large portion of gasoline use, curbing carbon emissions below any level thought possible. We will have to limit the length and frequency of lightning strikes, but the system generates so much energy that it will not make much of a difference. Luckily, work has already begun on upgrading our outdated electrical grid so it can handle the extra juice."

"Congratulations, Ash," said Carlton, clapping him on the back.

"And to you," replied Ben-David. "This would never have been possible without you. Or Alexis. I'm sorry that she could not be here."

"Me too." Now out of danger, Alexis was still recovering from her injury. Even if she could have traveled to Alaska, Carlton and Ben-David combined could not have pulled the strings necessary to get her into the control room, packed as it was with an alphabet soup of government agencies, at least one of which did not officially exist.

"I haven't had a chance to thank you for locating and transferring the funds from the Saudi central bank and Yassin's accounts before they could tank the dollar. And nice touch donating Yassin's stolen funds to democratic and women's organizations throughout the Middle East."

"And thank you for avenging my niece and all of Yassin's other victims," replied Ben-David, on the verge of tears, quickly changing the subject. "Where will the Saudi billions go?"

"From what I've been told, the funds will be repatriated to Saudi as soon as King Fahim completes his reforms, minus costs."

Personnel from every corner of the facility converged on the control room wearing protective headphones, all formality abandoned, replaced by high-fives amid hoots and grins. The place looked like JPL Mission Control after a Mars landing.

Ben-David squeezed past the throng, directed Franklin to terminate the lightning stroke to avoid overloading the grid.

A portly man in a dark suit who had quietly watched the test with an apprising eye stepped toward Ben-David. "Congratulations," he said. "As far as DOE is concerned, Solar Lightning is now officially operational."

"Thank you," replied Ben-David, turning to Carlton. "This is Dr. Harlan Maxwell. He replaced Brendan Wallace as Director of New Technology at DOE." Carlton found the man's handshake pleasantly firm.

"It's an honor to meet you, Mr. Carlton. I heard you were awarded-"

Carlton raised his hand. "I'm afraid I can't comment on that." His presidential commendation would forever remain classified deep black, as would the actions and events that had earned it. The American people would soon learn of Tesla's energy source, but as on several previous occasions, it would never know how close the country had come to devastation and ruin.

"The important thing is that the country is safe and has a new, clean, low-cost energy source," he said instead.

Ben-David nodded. "Solar Lightning will make electricity so cheap that it will shift electrical production away from most other energy sources. It will create huge market pressure to shift non-electric energy uses to electric, especially cars," he explained, pacing with nervous agitation. "It will boost research and production of long-term electrical car batteries."

"Once those batteries come on line, I estimate that it will slash our oil consumption by one third," added Maxwell. "We will still need oil for air travel, synthetics, and pharmaceuticals, so it won't free us from foreign oil, but it will make one heck of a dent."

Carlton knew enough about basic economics to realize that market changes never occurred in a vacuum, particularly not one so vast. "It will bankrupt Euroil," he replied, noting that the company was not only a major oil producer but derived a great deal of its income from gasoline refining and nuclear electrical production. The notion did not displease him, but raised an alarming concern. "It will also bankrupt the oil-producing countries that rely heavily on their oil for revenue, including the Gulf States, Russia, Iran, Venezuela, and Mexico, to name a few. It will cause economic hardship on their people and make Islamist terrorists even stronger in the Middle East."

"That's where Solar Lightning comes in," interjected Maxwell.

Carlton gazed at him, sensing what he was about to say. Eche had told him that the U.S. government had originally pursued HEERP for its military applications. "You're going to make it into a weapon," he concluded. "Tesla wanted his inventions to be used for peace for all mankind."

"A weapon, yes, but not a military one," replied Maxwell.

Carlton remained unconvinced.

"Until now, the U.S. has focused on defeating Islamist terrorism by helping monarchs and dictators fend off radicals, as in Saudi and Egypt until Fahim's reforms and Mubarak's fall," explained Maxwell. "Or attempting to replace them with democracies, as in Iraq and Afghanistan. But the resentment and hopelessness that breed fundamentalism cannot be eliminated by political and religious reform alone. People must also have economic opportunity to direct their efforts to the good of society instead of terror."

"Democratic reforms will bring about economic reform," said Carlton, thinking of Sobieki's homeland. "As in Eastern Europe after the fall of communism."

Maxwell nodded. "Yes, but we want to speed it along. After World War II, the U.S. helped transform Germany and Japan into peaceful democracies by rebuilding not only their political systems, but their economies through the Marshall Plan and postwar aid to Japan. The E.U. obtained democratic and economic reforms in communist Eastern European countries by offering them lucrative E.U. membership as an incentive. The president intends to do the same with Middle Eastern and African dictatorships."

"How will Solar Lightning accomplish that?"

"Israel turned bone-dry sand and rock into fertile agricultural ground in 30 years," said Maxwell. "Now that Solar Lightning is operational, President Douglass will announce what he calls the 'Strategic Electric Partnership'. Any country that implements democratic and market reforms and ends support of terrorism will be able to use low cost electricity from Solar Lightning. Depending on the country, its resources, and labor force, they will be able to use it for everything from creating manufacturing centers to desalinating water and pump it into the desert to create vast fertile regions. At the risk of sounding too Biblical, it will transform swords into plowshares."

Carlton was at a loss for words. Countries did not change their ways easily, particularly not in the Middle East. The plan still sounded a touch idealistic, much like Tesla himself, but at least there was a plan. He had known that finding Tesla's formula was important, just not how much.

"Solar Lightning should supply Tesla's native Serbia and Croatia with free electricity," he announced. "It's the least we can do to repay him after the way he was treated."

"I will see what I can do about your request," said Maxwell with a sincere look. "After all, you and Ms. Hamilton are the ones responsible for making Solar Lightning possible."

Carlton shook his head. "Ash, Franklin, and the rest of their team made it work. I just dodged bullets. One of them unsuccessfully," he replied, moving his left arm stiffly. "Many heroes gave their lives to make it possible." He paused, thinking of Davenport and his men. "I'm just glad that Solar Lightning will be put to good use." He turned to Ben-David. "What will you name the facility?"

Ben-David and Maxwell exchanged a silent glance, faced Carlton.

"We would like to give you the honor of naming it," replied Ben-David.

Carlton was overcome with emotion, but did not have to think long. Only one man deserved the recognition - a recognition that had been stolen, maligned, denied, and lost since his death in 1943 despite his legion achievements for mankind.

"Call it the Nikola Tesla Station."

"I knew it had to happen - felt the tables turning,
Got me through my darkest hour.
I heard the thunder clapping - felt the desert burning,
Until you poured on me like a sweet sun shower."

REO Speedwagon
Roll With The Changes

EPILOGUE

U.S. Department of Justice Headquarters
Robert F. Kennedy Main Justice Building
Washington, D.C.
10:03 AM

Haggard, disheveled, unshaven, with his restitched left arm heavily bandaged and his blood-encrusted clothes stinking of sweat, Carlton looked like a wild mountain man as he strode straight past Edison's protesting assistant into his boss's office, where the Deputy Assistant Attorney General was in the middle of a conference call.

Carlton walked to his desk, pressed down on the telephone receiver, terminating the call. Silencing the DOJ aristocrat's outrage with a raised index finger and bone-chilling glare, Carlton clasped one side of the desk, leaned over it, and bored into Edison's eyes, causing the head of the National Security Division to lean back, his face ashen.

"I forgive you for kicking me off the *Hassan* case, sir."

Edison swallowed hard, rose. "Carlton, I-"

"I'm not finished," he interrupted, causing Edison to sit back down. "I am not in the habit of revealing my superiors' personal sins. But if you *ever* lie to me or place personal or any other politics above the mission of this Division again, as sure as God made little green apples, I will confess those sins for you."

Without waiting for an answer, Carlton strode out of the office. For good measure, he stopped at the doorway, turned back toward Edison. "Special Agent in Charge Faraday sends her regards."

* * *

One month later, after pulling yet another all-nighter with his National Security Division team on Abu Hassan's prosecution—now his again— Carlton drove home to his modest brick house in the leafy Northern Virginia suburb of Westover, quietly tucked away across the Potomac River from the nation's capital. Sinatra singing about occult practices gushed through the speakers of the topless 'Shark', Carlton's white tailfinned 1958 Cadillac Eldorado Biarritz.

He slammed on the brakes as soon as he edged into the driveway, stared ahead in disbelief.

McLean's 1942 Series 62 Cadillac convertible gleamed in the afternoon sun.

Carlton staggered to the vintage automobile, circled it in shock. A little over four weeks ago, he had abandoned the car a pierced, shattered, burning hulk in downtown Los Angeles. Since then, the wartime Caddy had been resurrected like a Phoenix, its curved body and glasswork flawlessly restored. The gray leather seats and varnished wood dashboard smelled new. The multiple coats of lavender on black lacquer were so glossy that he had to touch the paint to make sure it was not wet. Not a trace of damage remained.

He removed a thick note card from under one of the windshield wipers.

> *A Star to keep your Shark company.*
> *Possunt quia posse videntur.*
>
> *MM*

Carlton translated the Latin out loud. "They can who believe they can."

He walked inside his house, telephoned his friend.

"I can't accept the car," he told McLean. "Not after what I did to it." He cringed. "And to the Tesla. And after what happened to the Rothko."

"My insurance company may never insure me again, but it replaced the Tesla, paid for the Rothko and the Cadillac's restoration. The painting was irreplaceable, but as beautiful as it was, it was only an object. Honor and friendship are more beautiful than any object."

"I agree, Max, but I can't accept-"

"*Per piacere*. You saved my life. You brought the animals who shot Claire to justice, just as you promised. You prevented me from dishonoring my name with my father's former associates. And you allowed me to obtain satisfaction by asking me to make the government's deal with the banks. Nothing I can buy will ever be capable of showing my true gratitude." McLean paused. "As for the Cadillac's value, it's a drop in the bucket compared to what I made shorting Euroil stock." He laughed. "I'm plowing the profits into a venture to manufacture efficient batteries for electric cars. Like all beautiful ideas, I am confident it will be profitable one day."

McLean had no idea how true his words were, although Carlton could not divulge anything about Solar Lightning.

"Thank you, Max."

"*Grazie a te, mio fratello.*" Thank you to you, my brother.

"How is Claire?"

"As good as new, thinking about entering the LA Marathon. She sends her love."

* * *

Early the next morning, Carlton put the gleaming Caddy's top down, set out of for the Blue Ridge Mountains. McLean had restored the car to its original condition, except for one thing: its engine had not been rebuilt, but replaced with an electric engine - silent and fast.

Two hours later, he flashed his ID at a hidden camera, waited for the gate to open. He drove up the long driveway to the Yale safehouse, listening to the gravel crunch under the Caddy's fat tires, walked up the front stairs of the stately colonial manor.

Alexis was waiting inside the doorway.

With her fall of blonde hair covering her left eye, wearing a vintage red dress and black heels, Alexis once again looked as though she had stepped straight out of a 1940s fashion magazine. She would not be jogging in the Hollywood Hills anytime soon, but except for stiff movements, nothing indicated the nearly fatal gunshot she had suffered.

Carlton wrapped her in his arms and kissed her, held her close. The two melted into one. He imbibed her presence, not wanting ever to let go. Her citrus scent inebriated him with a vision of sunny lemon groves and a feeling of renewed optimism.

"Nice car. Where are you kidnapping me to this time?" She asked with a sly grin a few moments later.

"Home to Hollywood," he replied, grimacing in feigned shock. "Don't tell me you forgot about our dinner date at Musso & Frank?"

Carlton zapped the electric engine to life. Alexis snuggled next to him on the front bench. Her hair fluttered in the breeze as they wound along country roads dappled in the Indian summer sunlight. They soaked in the autumn foliage afire in yellows, oranges, and reds, trailing wisps of smoke from Carlton's Bully.

"I think we should pay homage to Montgomery Grant," she said, shutting off Sinatra crooning about love being a trap, laughing at the look of shock on Carlton's face. She slipped a CD into the hidden stereo system. Glenn Miller's *Sunrise Serenade* wafted from the dashboard speaker, sending visions of Old Hollywood dancing in Carlton's head. "That was Grant's favorite tune. And my father's."

Carlton smiled, feeling the vindicated ghosts of Montgomery Grant, Nikola Tesla, P.E. Foxworth, Eche, Davenport and his team, Sanchez's and Carlton's own fallen men, and Alexis's father riding with them. It felt good.

In turn, he handed her an envelope.

Alexis tore it open, pulled out Grant's original *Infamous* movie premiere program, complete with the fateful words '2232 Watt Heights Road BR' that the star had handwritten in the upper corner.

"Ash gave it to me in Alaska. I can't imagine a better person to give it to. You can place it in your father's diary."

"Thank you." She leaned over, teary-eyed, and kissed him. "I can't imagine how infuriated the Saudi jihadists must have been when they realized that a Hollywood movie star destroyed their terrorist ambitions." She paused. "Speaking of which, where will you be staying in LA? With Max and Claire?"

"Unless you have a better place to recommend."

"I know this great big house in the Old Hollywood Hills. Free room if you cook."

"I like the sound of that. Maybe it's time we stopped living in the past and started living in the present."

She nestled against him, closed her eyes. "In a while."

Carlton grinned. "In the words of Bogie in *Casablanca*, that sounds like the beginning of a beautiful relationship."

THE DIAMOND CONSPIRACY

PROLOGUE
Arkansas, 1920

The United States Geological Survey team set out in August. Unrelenting heat, suffocating humidity, and deafening choruses of crickets ruled the Arkansas countryside. They traveled in a convoy of Model T Fords weighed down by camping equipment, delicate surveying tools, crates of canned food, pickaxes, shovels, and dynamite. Despite their hardy construction, the Model Ts became bogged in mosquito-infested swamps created by the torrential summer downpours. Veteran geological surveyors, they had experienced conditions far worse. Besides, they had been sent by Washington on an official mission, and Washington paid well. They pressed on.

Their efforts yielded utter disappointment. Explode and dig and sift through mounds of dirt as they might, the geologists could not locate their quarry. Hours stretched into days, days into weeks. After a month's toil under the beating summer sun, supplies dwindled to a few meager boxes. The hired hands were exhausted, covered with chigger bites, on the verge of walking off the job. The rickety cars could barely move. Morale was at a low point, the contract nearly expired. Exhausted and dejected, team leader Samuel Osage called off the expedition.

On the swampy road back to Murfreesboro, one of the Model Ts again overheated in a deep pool of mud. The team decided to let the engine cool off and broke out the last few cans of beans and chipped beef for lunch. As Osage negotiated his way through the sticky substance around the car, he misjudged the depth of the mud and lost his balance. He thrust an arm out to break his fall, but it plunged deep into the ooze. Osage fell face forward into the muck. He fought to prop himself up amid the roaring laughter of the men. After several failed attempts, he managed to stand. He shook dollops of heavy mud from his body, scooped handfuls of dark slime from his face and arms. The clay stuck to his arms and hands. But it wasn't smooth. He could feel rocks embedded in the mud scrape his fingers. He cleaned himself as best he could and looked at his filthy hands.

Suddenly, Osage went rigid.

A rough pebble was stuck between two fingers of his left hand. Still partially caked with mud, it stood out to Osage's trained eye. He picked it from his fingers, carefully wiped it on the only remaining clean part of his shirt, and lifted it to the burning sun between two grimy fingers. The translucent pebble glowed in the sun. Osage's dirty face creased into a wide grin. In his fingers was the object of their quest.

A diamond.

Washington wasted no time. Within two months of the team's report, the USGS constructed a mine. It immediately produced a large number of carats. Washington directed Osage and his fellow geologists to determine the exact extent of the diamondiferous deposits. Their findings surpassed Osage's wildest expectations. What originally had been thought a remote deposit was an underground ocean of diamonds.

Despite the fact Washington kept the operation heavily under wraps, news of the surprising discovery managed to find its way to South Africa, where the domestic discovery of vast diamond deposits had been big news for forty years. News of the Arkansas deposits sounded an ominous tone to South Africa's Waterboer Mines Limited.

Since the discovery of diamonds at Kimberley in South Africa's Orange Free State in 1871, South African diamond miners had used every conceivable strategy to consolidate the legion ad hoc diamond mines into a single efficient operation. After years of cutthroat tactics, shady deals, and backroom politics, Waterboer Mines Limited had emerged the victor. Waterboer controlled diamond production in South Africa, then on a global scale. The Arkansas discovery spelled disaster for the Waterboer monopoly. An immense diamond deposit outside its control would send prices plummeting. Waterboer had to act. Fast.

Head of the world's largest monopoly, Cecil R. Slythe was a force. The diamond monopoly brought wealth. Wealth brought influence. Influence brought power. In South Africa and Europe. In America as well. Particularly in Arkansas.

Cecil R. Slythe arrived in Washington in the autumn of 1920. Within one hour of his meeting with his clique of financial and political power brokers in the nation's capital, Osage and his team were split up and sent on urgent expeditions in faraway lands. The Murfreesboro diamond mine was fenced in, boarded up, and shut down. The Arkansas diamond miners were transferred to high-paying jobs in different parts of the country. Journalists and politicians were silenced. The USGS report was sealed in a vault in the basement of a nameless edifice in Washington, never again to see the light of day.

Upon his return to his native Arkansas in 1932 from an unusually perilous emerald expedition in Colombia, Osage decided to pay a visit to what he still thought of as his Arkansas mine. Not because of financial interest– he had received no stake in the government mine– but out of professional, nearly paternal interest.

Where hundreds of carats of diamonds had been excavated daily at the time of his departure now stood creaking wooden boards and rusting machinery. Why? He himself had plotted the vast diamond deposits, millions of carats. The mine could not possibly have exhausted the deposits. So why was it closed?

He decided to investigate.

He started in the most logical place, the Washington headquarters of the USGS. The official response astounded him. They were sorry, but they had no records of any diamond deposits in Arkansas. They vaguely remembered a diamond mine in Arkansas, but it had been shut down twelve years ago. He knew it had been shut down, but why? No one would give him a straight answer. Befuddled, Osage traveled to Arkansas and contacted state and local authorities. They, too, evaded his questions and pleaded ignorance. Back in Washington he tried to meet with the members of Congress who oversaw the USGS. None had time to speak with him. Finally, he decided to speak with members of his original geology team, the men who had struggled through the mud with him. He had lost track of them over the years, while each went from dig to dig in often remote locations. They would know.

Not one was alive. Each had perished under mysterious circumstances during faraway expeditions.

Anguished, Osage tried to convince himself his colleagues had died accidentally. He could not. He tried to believe the mine had depleted the diamond deposits, but could not. He tried to forget about the mine altogether, but the diamonds haunted him. There had to be an explanation.

Finally, Osage resigned himself to the only option that remained. He contacted the press. In the midst of the greatest depression the country had ever experienced, news of diamond deposits in Arkansas was bound to constitute front page material. One by one, large, then medium, then small newspapers brushed him off as a senile lunatic. But Osage was a tenacious old bird. His resolve strengthened, he made it his personal mission to contact each newspaper in the country. After several weeks, when it appeared no journalist would speak with him, a young rookie reporter from a low circulation Little Rock rag agreed to listen to his story the very same day. Osage set course for Little Rock, a hundred miles away, in his battered black Model A Ford.

Roads in 1932 Arkansas were far from safe. Potholes, mud, and rocks conspired to destroy automobiles unfortunate enough to attempt the dirt paths that masqueraded as roads. At thirty miles per hour on the rough path, the Model A's rattling frame shook Osage to near numbness. He began to think the car might fall apart.

The sun had begun its dip below the horizon, and Little Rock was still over forty miles away. If he didn't make it before dark, he'd have to cut his speed by half and risk losing his opportunity—his only opportunity, he reminded himself—to tell his story to someone who would actually listen.

Between his concentration on the road and the flurry of thoughts in his mind, Osage had little attention left for the world around him, or behind him. Muted by the roar from Osage's shorn muffler and hidden from view by a missing rearview mirror, a car approached. Also a Model A, it was very different from Osage's. Although the two cars shared body style, even color, the car behind hid a massive Duesenberg eight-cylinder engine that drove its wheels far faster than Osage's Ford engine. So fast, in fact, it was not until the car was twenty or thirty feet from Osage's rear bumper that he noticed its square radiator and round headlights in his side mirror.

Where had this maniac come from? The driver wanted to pass. Disadvantaged in the horsepower department, Osage eased back on the accelerator. As the Model A slowed, he edged toward the right side of the dirt road to let the crazed driver pass.

Instead of unleashing the "Duesie" engine, the driver inched forward, matched speeds with Osage. Thinking the driver lacked sufficient width to pass, yet careful not to fall into the ditch that paralleled the road, Osage stared ahead, gestured for the driver to pass.

The driver continued matching speeds with Osage, inches from his door. Concluding the driver lacked the power to pass, Osage slowed further. Still, the car did not pass.

Genuinely angered, Osage turned to glare at the driver. Before he could discern the man's face, he felt a sharp pain in his head. And everything went black.

Because of the execrable conditions of the country roads, it did not strike local residents or police as strange when Osage's Model A was found burned to the ground on the side of the road, its front end wrapped around a large tree trunk. Sad, perhaps. Certainly not strange. Without even a glance at the body, the local coroner assumed the driver had perished as a result of the accident and so avoided the hassle of an autopsy. Had he performed his duty, the coroner would have discovered that Samuel Osage had been killed by a bullet fired at close range. Further inquiry would have revealed the bullet was manufactured exclusively for the Federal Bureau of Investigation. Even further inquiry would have revealed that a rookie reporter had met an identical fate on his way to Little Rock. Assiduous inquiry would have revealed that not all of Osage's Arkansas diamond surveys were locked away in a vault in Washington.

1 ASSIGNMENT

2003
United States Department of Justice (DO])
Robert F. Kennedy Main Justice Building
Washington, D. C.
10:20 A.M.

Patrick Carlton rushed into Justice Department headquarters through the main entrance of the marble-and-granite federal fortress, beneath an immense American flag that waved ponderously in the cold wind. A late night's work and rush-hour gridlock had conspired to make him late for work. Again. He slid his identification card into the electronic turnstile, waved to the guard pulling morning duty, and hurried past the seal of the fabled agency, the largest law firm in the world.

Qui Pro Domina Justitia Sequitur was its motto.

He who seeks to rule follows justice.

Carlton shunned the slow elevators, bolted up the graceful staircase to the third floor. The tap-tap of his cowboy boots reverberated through the marble corridors as he strode past the offices that lined interminable hallways. Despite his exhaustion, a smile tugged at the corners of his eyes as he approached his office. *United States v. Global Steel* was Carlton's first serious assignment after three grueling years of paying dues in the DOJ trenches. It was an important case because of its substance and because it was his case. He was lead counsel. He made the strategic decisions. He called the shots.

One of the new lawyers straight out of law school walked toward him down the hall. He had not formally met her yet. She was very attractive, but to entertain romantic thoughts, far less act upon them, regarding subordinates at DOJ was more than against policy; it was punishable by immediate termination. Carlton was about to wish her a polite good morning when he noticed an expression of anxiety on her face, her green-eyed gaze darting toward his office. He stopped, stared at his office door in confusion as she walked past, trailing a wisp of Calandre perfume.

The reason for her grimace was clear as soon as he opened the door. Harry Jarvik, director of the Antitrust Division's Economic Litigation Section was seated in Carlton's chair, feet propped on the desk.

"Well, well. Good morning, Carlton. Or should I say good afternoon?" He glanced at his pocket watch, nodded theatrically. "How good of you to join us. Is this what they taught you in that white-shoe law firm of yours?"

Jarvik was short in stature and temper, a man who made himself appear taller by cutting others down. The staff of the Antitrust Division referred to him as Stalin. A corpulent man, his thick mustache and piercing gaze gave him a sinister look. He looked over Carlton head to toe with beady eyes, his gaze lingering on Carlton's trademark spit-shined cowboy boots.

"Good morning, sir," Carlton said. "There is a reason. I worked very late on *Global Steel* last ni—"

"Of course, of course. Tomorrow another excuse." He stood, all five-feet-four bristling. "Do I really look that stupid?"

Carlton decided sincerity would only aggravate matters. "I'm sorry, sir."

Jarvik grunted, he pointed a thick finger at the visitor's chair next to Carlton's desk. "Sit down."

Carlton peeled off his overcoat and scarf, hung them on a battered hat rack. He removed a pile of legal publications from the cracked leather chair and sat. He awaited his sentence, a visitor in his own office.

"Now," Jarvik sat and reclined, "tell me what you know about diamonds."

"Diamonds?" Carlton wondered if the question was designed to lead to further humiliation, then decided Jarvik was serious. "I don't know anything about diamonds, sir. Except that they're very expensive."

"Just as I thought. Most people don't, but Rothenberg loves them." He referred to the Deputy Assistant Attorney General in charge of DOJ's Antitrust Section. Jarvik's boss. "She's nuts about them, and for some reason, she got it into her mind to prosecute a local mom-and-pop diamond mining outfit in Arkansas for antitrust violations."

Diamonds in Arkansas? I though diamonds came from Afri—"

"It's a miniature deposit. A freak of nature, from what the geologists say. Strictly mom and pop. Raymond Mines, the outfit is called. Nuts, if you want my opinion. There's hardly any evidence, but Rothenberg's got this crazy idea the Raymonds accepted money to shut down operations, asked me to make sure it gets followed up. You're the lucky one. I'm taking you off of *Global* and putting you on *Raymond Mines*."

Carlton's jaw dropped. "What?" The word cracked in his throat. "You heard me."

Had he been standing, the blow would have knocked him to the ground. "Off *Global*? Sir, I've been working on *Global* for six months. I've done all the trial prep. The witnesses. The strategy. The questions on direct and cross. Everything." He stood, fought to retain his composure. "The trial is in a week. One week, sir. And *Global* is a corporate maze. Dozens of witnesses. It'll take another attorney weeks to figure out what's going on." He stood. "I'm going to–"

"Sit down! The case is closed, Carlton. Literally. You're off *Global*. On *Raymond Mines*." He stood, indicating the finality of his ruling. "I'll send down the *Raymond Mines* file." He walked to the door, turned. "One more thing. I want you to wrap this up quickly. I know Rothenberg wants it prosecuted, and she's the boss, but Justice has never won a diamond case. Ever. *Raymond Mines* won't be different. The last thing this Section needs is another embarrassment in the press. Rothenberg or no Rothenberg, you are not to risk Section credibility by taking this to trial. Get a little settlement for show. Move on."

"Sir, I—"

"Settle!" He shouted, then lowered his voice to a whisper. "Then move on. Do I make myself clear?"

Carlton paused, still in shock. "As a diamond, sir."

"Good." Jarvik walked out and slammed the door.

Carlton sat for a long moment, trying hard to contain his anger, then walked to the window across the room. The thick glass was stained with the deposits of countless rains. Outside, dark clouds loosed freezing rain onto the red tile roof.

Global Steel. Carlton had come too close to being able to win the case so many others thought unwinnable. With a victory, Carlton would shine, brightly enough to raise the level of cases assigned to him after three years in the trenches, brightly enough to outshine Jarvik. Something Jarvik's pride could not, would not, tolerate. By giving *Global* to another lawyer right before trial, Jarvik could simultaneously prevent Carlton from shining and blame his unlucky replacement for the loss. Tidy. No matter to Jarvik the real losers would be those harmed by Global Steel Inc.: the American public.

Raised by parents slightly south of middle class and graduating from parochial high school with a perfect GPA and attendance record, Carlton moved from his parents' home in El Centro, California, to attend UCLA. He worked his way through college doing odd jobs on boats in the marina. He worked hard. He had a goal, and he stuck to it. His goal was money. The 1980s, Carlton's formative years, was the Decade of Greed. For him, like so many others, a big salary, a German sports car, and a condo in a coveted zip code were all that mattered. His hard work paid off. He earned a full scholarship to George Washington University law school in D.C. Three grueling years later, he attained his goal: a six-figure job in a top-ten Washington law firm.

But private practice in a D.C. megafirm did not live up to his image. Neither the status of the firm nor the bloated salary made up for its shortcomings. It took only two months for him to christen the firm the 'Merchants of Pain' and begin to question his choices. The firm name and money were great, the work unspeakably stressful, tedious, and repetitious. His questioning coincided with a spiritual quest for the faith he'd considered an obstacle to success and abandoned ten years before.

Was this all there was? Had he endured the repeated mental beatings of law school for such meaningless work? Day after dreary day, meaningless memos to faceless clients. Dilatory depositions. Endless research. Scant hours of sleep punctuated by anxiety attacks. The rumors in law school had been true. As clichéd as it sounded, he had traded his life, his health, his soul, for a salary. After three years, Carlton gave up the fat paycheck and made the lateral hop to Justice, hoping law practice there would be different. But at Justice nothing changed except the salary, which was now a pittance.

A soft knock at his door shook him out of his sullen introspection. He turned. "Yeah."

The rookie lawyer with green eyes peeked through the half-open door. "You okay?"

He tried hard to smile, failed. "No, actually. But thanks for the warning." He stood and offered his hand. "We've never met. I'm—"

"Patrick Carlton." Her eyes were smiling now. "I'm Erika Wassenaar." Carlton was surprised by her strong grip. And by the thumping in his chest.

At five-feet-eight, the young redhead in her mid-twenties was slim but not starved. A first year lawyer, her demeanor suggested a confidence rarely attained without a few years of practice. Her lively eyes shone with curiosity. Professionally dressed in a smart navy blue suit and white blouse, she exuded freshness. She smiled with bright white teeth, slightly crooked, that added a girlish quality to her impish, mischievous charm.

Carlton forced his thoughts to professional matters. "You're new in the department, right?"

"Two weeks. The ink is still wet on my Bar certificate." She laughed genuinely, like a child.

"Congratulations. That's impressive." DOJ hired only the elite of law students directly out of school.

"Thanks, Mr. Carlton."

"Mr. Carlton sounds like my dad's in the room. We're a bit more informal around here. Pat'll do just fine," he paused. "Wassenaar. Dutch?"

"That's pretty good. Most people can't pin it down."

"Beginner's luck." He motioned to a chair. "Grab a seat."

Erika's gaze wandered over the framed photographs, diplomas, and awards on the office wall. Bar of the Supreme Court of the United States. Federal District Court here, Federal District Court there. Court of Appeals for this and that Circuit. California Bar. District of Columbia Bar. George Washington University National Law Center. University of California at Los Angeles.

"I went to UCLA undergrad," she said.

"Aces. I could use another Bruin in this Ivy League prison. Where did you go to law school?"

"Pepperdine."

"We've got a couple good lawyers from there."

The phone rang. "Excuse me," Carlton said as he reached for the receiver.

Erika assessed the man facing her. He seemed genuinely friendly, a bit nervous around her, which she found refreshing. Despite black hair worn in a crew cut, his strong nose, intense blue eyes, and angular jaw, Carlton was not exactly handsome. Nor was he particularly fit, brilliant, or wealthy, from what she'd heard. The word at DOJ was he smoked cigars with a vengeance, but never Cubans, because they were illegal. He had a temper, but lost it rarely. He wore conservative navy blue suits with white shirts to work, always with spit-shined cowboy boots. But the buzz didn't quite get it, didn't point to the intensity she sensed in him.

When he hung up, she pointed to a grainy discolored photograph on the wall, an elderly man and a teenager smiling next to a dusty biplane. "Who's that in the picture?"

"My grandfather and I. He was a crop duster in El Centro back in California. He taught me to fly when I was a kid."

"You still fly?"

"Not since he passed away. I've moved on to boats," he announced, picking up a small wooden model of a gray boat with white lettering on its side from the edge of his desk.

She cocked her head. "You're in the Navy?

"Lieutenant Carlton, Navy Reserve. I skipper this little guy on the Chesapeake two weekends a month. After this morning, I may be doing it full time real soon."

They chuckled. After a moment of silence, she stood. "I have to go. Please let me know if you need any research. I hope we can work together sometime."

So did Carlton, and that rang alarm bells. He stood, nearly knocking a pile of documents off the desk in the process. "Thanks again for the warning."

AUTHOR'S NOTE

The Tesla Formula is a work of fiction. All of the characters, companies, government actors, locations, and events in *The Tesla Formula* are fictional or used fictitiously. Yet, to be believable, a novel must be based in reality. This is why I selected the elements involved.

I used Saudi Arabia because the country is not only the world's largest oil producer but the only major oil producer with a "swing capacity" to produce more oil on demand when supply disruptions occur in other oil-producing countries. This gives Saudi Arabia immense influence in much the same way as the U.S. dollar's global reserve currency status bestows influence on the U.S. Despite its government's severe crackdown on terrorism and cooperation with the United States on many security issues since 9-11, Saudi Arabia remains an absolute monarchy symbiotically tied with Wahhabism, the most fundamental version of Sunni Islam, and the largest funder of Sunni terrorism, as Secretary of State Clinton recently stated. Most of the 9-11 plotters, including Osama bin Laden, were Saudi. As the locus of two of Islam's holiest sites of Mecca and Medina, Saudi Arabia is the principal leader of the Sunni Arab world - far more numerous in followers (about 85%) than Shiite Islam (about 15%) - and thus holds great sway among other Sunni countries and populations. Again, I stress that *The Tesla Formula* is a work of fiction. Many of the plot elements used, including those in connection with Saudi Arabia, are fictitious, such as the concept that the country faces a near-term depletion in available supply from its active oil wells, or that the Saudi ambassador to the U.S. or the Saudi Interior Minster are involved in nefarious or terror activities.

Before I get hit with email barrages accusing me of being anti-French (I am half French), I selected France because it is a leading member of the European Union, a member of the euro currency, was for nearly two centuries a superpower (at one time ruling almost all of Europe and beyond under Napoléon), possesses one of the largest oil companies in the world and its foreign policy since Charles de Gaulle after World War II (until President Nicolas Sarkozy) has mostly been characterized by an almost pathological obsession to deride and derail U.S. supremacy while dueling with Germany to become the leader of the European Union. As much as Americans often feel targeted by France's anti-Americanism and in reverse point to France's sometimes weak and sometimes reprehensible actions during World War II, we also should remember that were it not for France's support during the American Revolution at the very moment of its fledgling founding, America likely would not have survived the conflict. No other European country combines all of these elements.

I chose the European Union because despite its present existential, structural, debt and currency issues, its common currency - the euro - constitutes the only present closest candidate for replacing the U.S. dollar as the global reserve currency and the European bloc regularly aspires to match the U.S. as a global superpower.

Poland presented an interesting opportunity (not just because I am half Polish) because of its attempt to reestablish its domestic and international positions after over five decades of oppression, first by the Nazis, then by the Soviets, its intense pro-U.S. foreign policy and domestic sentiment, its active combat participation in the Iraq and Afghanistan wars, its current non-participation in the euro currency, and because Poland often chafes at French criticism of not following its foreign policy, most recently on Iraq.

Venezuela's geographic proximity to the U.S. (less than 1,200 miles, roughly equal to the distance between Los Angeles and Dallas or Washington, D.C. and Dallas) and its intent-on-being-president-for-life leader Hugo Chavez's rabid anti-Americanism and support of drug-trafficking terror organizations such as the FARC in neighboring Columbia made the country an easy choice. Since I finished the book, this situation has gone from bad to worse: journalists from several countries have reported that Venezuela plans to host Iranian terror-training groups and allow Iran to station missiles in the country, if they have not already done so. Combined with Iran's fundamentalist theocratic Shiite leadership's virulent anti-Americanism and attempt to build a nuclear weapon, such acts could push the world to the brink of nuclear war once again in a repeat of the Cuban Missile Crisis of 1962.

The pool of inventors, engineers, and physicists who have contributed to the field of electricity is wide and deep, yet I chose Nikola Tesla because no other inventor possesses the combination of genius, foresight, tragedy, mystery and near mysticism as he. Questions (and conspiracies) about inventions he may have developed and the deep classification of his documents continue unabated to this day, nearly 70 years after his death. The events in the prologue about the FBI's review of Tesla's papers immediately upon his death and FBI Special Agent P.E. Foxworth's subsequent death in mid-air on his way to the Casablanca Conference are true. As is the fact that Tesla worked on the wireless transmission of electricity and energy beams for years. And that the U.S. electric grid is woefully obsolete, sadly not benefitting from any substantive portion of the recent $800 billion-plus government stimulus program.

Although fictional, Montgomery Grant is based loosely on Cary Grant, the great Hollywood actor born in England who rose from poverty to international fame and fortune before passing away in 1986 at age 82. Few may know that Grant is suspected of having worked clandestinely for the British Intelligence Services during World War II (King George VI privately awarded Grant the King's Medal for Service in the Cause of Freedom in 1947) and that Grant turned down the role of James Bond in *Dr. No*, the first film in the Bond franchise. Montgomery Grant's movie *Dream Home* in the book is based on the 1948 movie *Mr. Blandings Builds His Dream House* starring Cary Grant, Myrna Loy, and Melvyn Douglas, which was remade in 1986 as *The Money Pit* starring Tom Hanks, Shelley Long, and Alexander Gudunov.

I opted for the U.S. Defense Advanced Projects Research Agency (DARPA) among the many secret U.S. military-intelligence agencies for several reasons. Although far better known today than when I began to write the book, DARPA remains far more intriguing and mysterious than other secret U.S. agencies due to its amazing, unique mission to travel down possible research dead ends in the quest for the most advanced technology in the world to keep the United States safe. Since I began writing the book, I was amazed but not surprised to discover that DARPA and other groups have been developing robot bugs not that different from the microflies used in *The Tesla Formula*.

And yes, DARPA did invent the internet and stealth technology. What it is inventing now and will develop in the future provides an instant trip from non-fiction to science fiction.

I based the High Earth Energy Research Project (HEERP) facility loosely upon the U.S. Air Force's existing High Altitude Auroral Research Project (HAARP) array in Alaska. Although HAARP was originally constructed to communicate with submarines using the Earth's ionosphere, it is rumored to be able to disrupt global communications - and more. Conspiracy theories abound about HAARP's origins and purposes. Combined with my astronomy studies in college (which, like Carlton, I reluctantly abandoned upon realizing that I would never master mathematics to the requisite proficiency for an employed future in astrophysics), I found HAARP a congruent match to Tesla's wild predictions and genius wireless electrical inventions to come up with my theory in the book about channeling electricity from the charged solar electric particles that flow around the Earth's magnetic field down to the ground in controlled lightning.

A (short) word about oil and the U.S. dollar, about which I shall skip long and boring statistics. The U.S. remains a net oil importer. Since 9-11 and the continued attempts to attack America, its interests and allies, national security has been added to economics and environmental concerns as a necessary factor in America's oil consumption, production, and importation strategy. Despite the laudable national security and environmental desires for alternative energy sources to replace oil, such as solar, wind, geothermal, wave, ethanol, and other non-fossil fuel sources, the fact remains that these sources are insufficient and prohibitively expensive to replace oil, even with massive government subsidies that attempt to dictate energy winners and losers - for now. Research and development will one day change this. As a case in point, the recent development of hydraulic fracturing (aka "fracking") in the U.S. has enabled such a large increase in the production of natural gas and a concomitant decrease in its price that despite its status as a net *oil* importer, the U.S. has become a net *energy* exporter. Far cleaner and less carbon-intensive than oil or coal, natural gas will soon replace coal in many electrical generation plants, decrease the cost of electricity, and increase the attractiveness of both natural gas and electric vehicles. The final point that I will make about oil and energy in general is that despite popular belief or desire, there is no perfect energy source. Every energy source, no matter how seemingly perfect - even the Tesla solar-particle-to-harnessed-lightning source I came up with in the book - involves costs: economic, environmental, societal, political, national security, and otherwise. Therefore every selected energy source entails trade-offs. Only by exhaustively listing and examining these costs objectively can intelligent energy strategy be developed.

As concerns the U.S. dollar, despite the intense economic crisis suffered in the United States and worldwide and the rating cut in the grade of U.S. debt, the U.S. dollar remains the global reserve currency. The U.S. dollar's global reserve currency status bestows an influence on the United States far greater than the simple collective value of all the U.S. dollars in existence, as Max McLean explains in the book. During the depths of the economic crisis, countries and institutions worldwide fled other assets to the safety of the U.S. dollar and the U.S. economy by buying U.S. government debt in the form of U.S. Treasuries, increasing their cost and dramatically decreasing their yields, believing that although the U.S. economy was in terrible shape, it was still in better shape in their crystal balls than the other large economies. At one point, Treasury yields - the percentage of interest paid based on the value of the debt - went negative, which means that countries and investors actually *paid* the U.S. to hold U.S. debt (although massive Federal Reserve intervention by purchasing U.S. bonds helped create these inverse yields). A confidence made possible in part by the U.S. dollar's global reserve currency status.

The question is: how long will the U.S. dollar remain the global currency? The gargantuan, unnecessary, and unsustainable U.S. national debt and Washington's incapability to decrease its pantagruelian borrowing and stimulate growth have placed the U.S. economy - and thus the U.S. dollar - in great peril. Both teeter on the precipice and will continue to face dire consequences from one or more sharp economic jolts unless Washington gets its act together, finds common ground between left and right, restrains borrowing, and spurs growth by freeing the immense capacity of the American people for innovation and its deep reserves of entrepreneurship and hard work. Realism among

America's leaders is necessary, yet woe, doom, and gloom are both unnecessary and unproductive. America is an exceptional country founded on exceptional principles and populated by an exceptional people. Its brightest days still lie ahead.

I wish to extend a special note of deep gratitude to the men and women of the U.S. Armed Forces, American government intelligence and law enforcement agencies, and in the governments of America's allies for keeping America and its allies safe. Heroes one and all.

The Tesla Formula would not have been possible without the contributions of many people, too numerous to list here. Among them, I would be remiss if I did not single out the editorial support of Ed Stackler, Alex Lubertozzi, Natasha Kern, Peter Riebling, Gerhard Heusch, Tadeusz Kublicki, and William D. Gould, as well as the wizardry and hard work of my agent Jenée Arthur, cover and map designer Jae Macallam at Yoyostring Creative, and typsetting/interior designer Stephanie Martindale. I would like to make a special mention of my friend and fellow scribe Vanina Marsot for encouraging me when the chips were down. I had a great deal of research assistance from persons who, because of the sensitivity of the subject matters and plots involved, I do not wish to mention by name, so I will acknowledge them simply as a former DOJ official, a former State Department official, a former National Security Advisor, and a former FBI Special Agent in Charge. You know who you are. Thank you. Any and all mistakes are mine alone.

Finally, I would like to thank Divine Providence, my family and friends for their inestimable support while I was writing the book, especially my loving wife Molly. I am blessed to have you in my life. Most of all, I would like to thank you, the reader, for whom I wrote this book. I hope you enjoyed it and will continue to follow Patrick Carlton's adventures. If so, please consider writing a review and telling fellow readers about the series. I would enjoy hearing from you and invite you to visit me at www.nicolaskublicki.com.

Nicolas Kublicki
Los Angeles, California

ABOUT THE AUTHOR

Nicolas Kublicki worked on national security issues on Capitol Hill and on administrative and environmental issues at the U.S. Department of Justice in Washington, D.C. before going into private law practice, then the real estate business in his native Los Angeles. He teaches law as an adjunct professor at Pepperdine University and is involved in several civic and charitable activities. Nick is married and has two daughters. Like his protagonist Patrick Carlton, he is a vintage automobile enthusiast, cigar aficionado, and fan of Frank Sinatra (who was once his neighbor). He invites you to visit him at www.nicolaskublicki.com.